River of Souls

Chronicles of Aurderia

The Balance

River of Souls

Queen of Shadow

Chronicles of Aurderia
River of Souls

J. Steven Young

ISBN 13 : 978-1-943924-21-9 (Paperback LSI)
ISBN 13: 978-1-943924-22-6 (Hardcover LSI)

This is a work of fiction, any similarities to any persons or places, is purely coincidental.

To my Great Nephew:
Landyn's Prayer

My time was not long to this life,
Precious few moments I shared.
The love that was freely given to me,
Will guide me to my final peace.
I shall wait, protected by that love,
Until the time we all meet again.

Landyn Parker Gniadek
2/26/2013 - 05/08/2013

<u>**Chapter One**</u>

Shuran found himself surrounded by such darkness, he felt himself melting into a shadowy nothingness. He was cut off from the Zidu'Si, not completely, but enough so that he was utterly alone. Shuran felt relief in being alone with his thoughts. All else was shut off, and he let out a sigh that allowed the weight of his responsibilities to fall from his young shoulders. His solitude would not last as he remembered where he was, the previously unknown chamber hidden within the Vault.

Shuran created an orb and closed his eyes in response to the flood of light that pulsed forth from his open palm. The darkness swallowed the light, leaving a soft glow when Shuran finally opened his eyes. The room was circular and smaller than he expected. Arms extended at his sides Shuran sized the room up as approximately four arm spans across. He could see no ceiling in the darkness so he let the sphere of light lift from his palm into the space above him.

The ceiling was half his height above his head. The walls were covered in carvings unlike anything he had ever seen or read about. As he traced his fingers across the intricately worked stone walls, he took in scenes of beings performing what must have been rituals of varying kinds. What these acts were meant to accomplish, Shuran could not begin to understand.

The human-like people were dressed in ornate robes and hats. They carried odd tools or weapons and communed with creatures unknown to him. As he continued to gingerly stroke his fingers across the works, he came to find a series of indentations in the wall. There were ten holes that if connected would resemble two half moons facing one another. Inside were two stars on the same plane. Without hesitation, Shuran reached out with his hands and found that his fingers all fit in the holes. With a slight pull, he lifted the section of wall away.

A small compartment behind the section contained a cloth wrapped bundle. Shuran set the rock panel down to investigate the contents of the wrapping. As soon as he lifted the heavy bundle, the cloth disintegrated into a pile of musty grit and powder. In his hands, he held a book that was beautifully crafted of pure gold.

As Shuran stepped back with the book, a pillar rose from the floor just below the compartment. The top of the pillar was carved to hold the book so Shuran set it down. A new light shone down from the ceiling upon the book, casting golden rays of reflecting light all over the chamber. What Shuran saw upon page after page was more of the same scenes from the walls. He turned to open the door and realized it would not budge.

***

"What is keepin' that boy?" Moona complained.

"Don' suppose that room is some privy for the Shin'Ar? Or perhaps a bottomless trap?" Codger began to wonder aloud.

"Clap your trap Codge! Ol' fool!" Moona said as she whacked him in the back of the head.

"I am certain Shuran is fine, I can sense him on the edge of my consciousness," Moltar reassured Moona from his limited space on the other side of the Vault. "If he needed our assistance, I would be able to feel his need."

"Well, that makes me feel better," Moona mumbled. "Shouldn' someone take them beasts out for a walk or somethin'!"

Moona walked over to the hidden door and reached out toward it as if to knock.

"I wouldn' do that Moony!" Codger warned.

Not to be told what to do, Moona reached further and made contact with the door. The resulting jolt sent her flailing back several paces to land between Moltar's feet. Her stringy thin hair standing straight on end, she looked dazed and confused. Her eyes focused to see Moltar staring down at her ready to give her a good lick.

Reaching up with a fist Moona stopped him as his tongue began to slither out. "If you value that particular part o' your body, you best keep it ta ya' self!"

***

Shuran struggled to pull the lever to release the door. No matter how he tried it would not move and Essence was less effective than brute force. Shuran stopped short when he saw a pattern to the reflections on the wall. Symbols formed upon particular sections of the wall. This was the ancient language of the Telukukal but in a form he had never seen.

Somehow Shuran was able to sense that it was the First Ones original form of writing, though he was unsure what it meant. There was no pattern to the placement. He reached for the book and turned the golden pages with great care. The reflections changed as did their placement on the walls.

As he studied the glyphs and symbols, he sensed a familiar pattern to them and was mesmerized by them as the reflections danced around the walls. Page after page, he watched as the patterns moved and shifted.

Shuran lost track of time as he watched the patterns change and move around the room. He did not know what to make of any of this and needed help. Shuran thought to use his communication crystal finding that it worked.

"SHURAN!" Moona screeched. "What has kept you? Gonna send me to an early grave, you are!"

"Too late for that!" Codger managed before getting another whack.

"I have found the most amazing golden book," Shuran answered.

"So bring it out. You missed a meal while distracted Shin'Ar," Orian stated.

"I have tried to exit but-" Shuran started.

"A trap! I knew it!" Moona interrupted.

"No Moona, I believe that it is a safety built into the room," Shuran began. "The place was hidden from us for a reason. Perhaps the book is not meant to leave."

Shuran explained his experience in the room and how he came across the book. As he described the scenes he observed, Codger took notes and the others discussed possible meanings. Shuran continued to describe the ways in which the symbols reflected upon the walls, changing form and position as the pages of the book were turned.

"You can continue your tale out here boy! Now put the fancy book back and get your tail out here. This pet o' yours needs walkin'," Moona barked.

"What has gotten into her?" Avrank asked Orian.

"I think she is run out of her frost moss."

Shuran slid the book back in the wall and replaced the panel. The pedestal lowered back into the floor and the strange light dimmed. When the light completely left the room in darkness again, the lever moved in Shuran's hand easily.

The door slid open to reveal a wiry-haired old woman standing ready to yank him from the chamber. Her hand could not pass the threshold. She dared not perform a repeat of the tumbling act that had the others already giggling as she pulled back her hand. Frustrated she stomped off toward her work table.

Shuran exited the room and continued into the night describing all he saw as best he could remember.

More than once Codger would stop him to ask questions or to repeat descriptions.

Mallick and the other Zidu'Si listened quietly to everything Shuran had to tell.

"Something I am certain of is a symbol I saw that represents knowledge. The symbols and their placement upon a picture depicting a treasure, lead me to believe it describes a compendium of some sort," Shuran sighed. His frustration stemmed from the awareness on the edge of his mind that was just out of reach. He did not understand where the knowledge and intuition came from and that confused him further.

"Perhaps it refers to the Vault?" Gregoran asked.

"Doubtful, since it would be redundant to reference a treasure of knowledge from within that very place," Mallick said. "I think that since it is in the language of the Telukukal, perhaps it refers to a Compendium of Telukukal knowledge. The room and book together may be a vast library in code of some sort."

"Code yes, but that room is not the Compendium. There is indication that this treasury of knowledge somehow moves or can be moved. I am still unclear on that bit. I think the room may be a means of locating where and when it will be accessible," Avrank said matter-of-factly.

"Yes, well that may be difficult since we have little reference of how to translate the ancient symbols," Mallick pointed out. "The Vault library contains no mention of the ancient script, only a few drawings with no correlated meaning."

"The images depicted on the walls are also confusing," Shuran added. "They make no sense, unless the meaning is hidden or symbolic as well."

Moona left the boys to their debates and went about working her herbs and mixing potions. She enjoyed having her ability back to sense the potency of plants and other ingredients of her mixtures. During the long years she lived with her Essence wielding abilities hobbled, Moona had to make mixtures for others on memory and experience. She trusted her knowledge, but having the power to reach her mind into a poultice and feel the potency, allowed her to definitively decide the dosage and length of effectiveness. Having her spark to activate charms back was what she was most happy about.

She was working on something that came to mind after hearing Shuran talk about exploding rocks when he was feeling frustrated. The Melammu Nanna and Aknard's fleet of magurmu could use better offensive weapons after the battle in Drakkfoth. Instead of relying on individual power, Moona thought to create ready-made Essence exploders. She was working on her first prototype while the men all talked of Compendiums and symbols.

She had been working through a rather difficult spell on setting a two-part trigger. First, she needed a spell to activate the device. Second, a spell that would cause the device to explode when in range of darkness was required. She was having trouble with the proper wording for the second spell.

"PAD - TEGE - NERI!" Moona spoke to no effect. "Blast! Still not right."

"PAD-TE'GA-NERU," whispered a voice just barely audible to Moona.

"Yes! That's it…" she started before looking to see who had given her the words.

Moona looked around to see the men all still on the opposite side of the Vault. The drakkon were both outside hunting. Moona was alone. She shook her head and fingered her ear clean of wax.

"PAD-TE'GA-NERU," she heard again.

"Who's there?" Moona called.

She looked around and saw nothing but the looming figure of an Ancient carved from gug. It was one of the many statues placed all alone the Vault's perimeter walls. Moona dismissed her unease, until she saw a faint shimmer glide across the surface of the large statue before her. It was not until that moment, Moona took more than passing notice of the statues. She retrieved a stool to gain height enough to examine the figure closer.

The features seen under close inspection were that of a female. Large eyes with a thin nose and lips dominated the narrow face. The statue wore elaborately carved robes with inlaid decorations of stars, leaves, acorns, and other heavenly and earthly objects. Her hands rested across her chest with long thin fingers clasped. Moona's eyes scanned the likeness of this other-worldly looking creature, until she noticed the pendant around its neck.

"DAMKIANNA!" Moona yelled as she lost her footing and fell to the hard ground with a grunt.

Hearing the clatter of instruments followed by a loud thud, the others ended their debate and looked for the source of the commotion. What they found was Moona laying upon the floor and a multitude of her bottles and herbs splayed out around her.

"What on Ersetu has gotten into you ol' woman!" Codger came

rushing over to help her as he saw her fall.

"Damkianna…" was all Moona could mumble as she pointed to the statue.

Shuran and Mallick soon came to assist, lifting Moona to her feet. Mallick simply thought Moona was shaky from too much work and not enough rest. Shuran felt it was more than that.

"Moona, what is wrong?" Shuran asked, concerned. He took her hands in his and felt their tremble. When she did not answer, he finally looked up at the statue. At first he did not notice anything, but he, like the others had never given them much thought. Hanging around the neck, was a golden chain with a pendant. In the center of the pendant was a clear crystal with a symbol etched inside. The face of the statue was familiar.

"Mallick, what do we know about these statues?" Shuran asked.

"Little to nothing is recorded. I just assumed they were representations of the original Zidu'Si and Shin'Ar since there are eight of them," Mallick answered.

"But there should be nine…" Avrank started, "one for each of the seven races, the Shin'Ar, and his Isten."

"There are six statues and five empty alcoves," Orian observed. "It would appear as though there are missing statues. What do you suppose this means Shin'Ar?"

"I am uncertain, but this female idol before me is not likely of the seven races of man or the Zidu'Si of old. I believe it is the Lady Damkianna." Shuran stated pointing to the pendant.

"Damn right it is! And she spoke to me!" Moona added.

"There goes our quiet time boys!" Codger said as he ducked out of Moona's reach. "Have you been hittin' the kegs woman? What would one o' the old gods be havin' to say to you?"

Moona explained, with great animation, how she had trouble with a spell when a voice whispered to her. She spoke of the glimmer of a face that drifted across the statue, and then finding the pendant with Damkianna's sigil appear inside the crystal.

"Perhaps the Shin'Ar of old and his Zidu'Si were more devout in their practice of religion. I see no other reason for the statues' presence,"

Mallick said trying to play down Moona's experience. He did not believe for a moment that one of the ancient Gods was talking to her. "Perhaps it was Tianna who spoke to you?"

Moona grumbled at that possible explanation, but her eyes never left the statue's, until the others led her back to her table.

Shuran was skeptical about Mallick's explanation. Tianna rarely appeared and when she did it was to Shuran or at least in his presence.

"What is it you are doing here?" Gregoran asked, trying to change the subject.

"A WEAPON!" Moona became excited and motioned her boys to come closer. "This here is a darkness triggered exploder. Got the idea from Shuran," she added with a smile to her young foster son. "Two spells work it. First one sets it with a word. The second spell triggers when it comes in close contact to the dark. I thought the Mellamu Nanna and Aknard's vessels could do with something what could be dropped from up high. Not gettin' so close as last time when fightin' might save a ship or more," Moona finished.

"How big of a boom are we talkin' 'bout Moony?" Codger asked.

"Take out all them death walkers within forty paces or so. I could make 'em stronger, but they would get too heavy." Moona showed them her diagrams and continued talking about how to make them.

They all agreed that those who stayed back from the trip to locate the giants would help create as many as they could. Their discussion was interrupted by the sudden appearance of Jade.

<u>**Chapter Two**</u>

"TROLLS! They march this way from the Frozen North," she explained. "Moltar is keeping a distant watch on them."

"How near are they?" Gregoran asked.

"A full cycle at the pace they keep."

"We cannot have an encounter on our doorstep." Shuran began to pace. "If they venture too close, they will notice the Mellamu Nanna as well as the ruins."

"Strike them down now!" Avrank said. His people detested the trolls, but they generally did not openly engage them. "They are likely looking for their kin that attacked us moons ago."

"No, they are too near us, and if they travel under the direction of the Order, they may have weavers guiding them. Better we find a way to change their path if they venture near Durangug," Shuran said.

Mallick and Orian talked amongst themselves before offering an option.

"Perhaps we can create a shielding spell like that we use on the Mellamu Nanna. With my knowledge of influencing the mind, Mallick and I could devise a way to subtly keep them away. The elfin rangers do this when outsiders venture too near Entensiama," Orian offered.

Shuran nodded his approval and saw them off to their task. He and Gregoran went out upon Jade to check on the trolls and keep Moltar from mischief. In spite of his vast size, Moltar was still as much a hatchling as Shuran was technically still a boy. This fact bonded them more than the magic that joined Shuran as Moltar's Lugaldur.

As Jade flew toward Moltar's position from the South, Shuran extended a cloaking spell around them. Finding Moltar was not difficult for him since he could sense his bonded at great distance. Surprisingly, Moltar was keeping to the cliffs of the Orenthal Mountains while tracking the trolls' movements.

"Shuran!" Moltar growled with a smile and a swish of his massive tail. "I am glad you have decided to join me. Are we to attack then?"

"No, my feisty friend, we are only going to watch briefly then head back to the Vault," Shuran said, noticing Moltar's disappointment. "We must not give away the Vault's location so easily. These mindless creatures are likely watched from afar."

Shuran was intoxicated with Moltar's exuberance and playfulness. It was amusing to watch a beast the size of a large dwelling, scamper about like a house cat. Once Moltar dropped down from his perch, Shuran mounted his trusty bonded drakkon and they headed out to circle the trolls while cloaked.

The trolls were making good time traveling, and heading almost directly toward Durangug. Shuran sent a mental message to Gregoran and Jade before the four turned south and headed to an area that was at least two days from where the trolls were.

"I think it time we take advantage of the volatile times of the unbalance," Shuran started.

With unspoken acknowledgment, Jade and Gregoran landed beside Moltar and Shuran. The four of them combined force to create one large pull on the earth and rock before them. They created an obstacle to slow the march of the troll legion. The upraised ground before them now, would cause a delay but not deter the trolls' approach. Shuran was not expecting anything more than extra time.

In Durangug the rest of Shuran's growing followers, busied themselves preparing a spell to ward off, not only the trolls, but any unwanted travelers. The casting was rather complex, as it involved storing the spell in the gugtu surrounding Durangug. Additionally the spell would be linked to the Emmuku'Gu for powering it indefinitely.

When Shuran arrived back, all was ready to cast the spell of enchantment. The as yet incomplete Zidu'Si, gathered in a circle and joined their minds as one. Drawing on the strength of the drakkon, they called forth a ball of pulsating energy. Orian established an aura of influence that settled over the great glowing sphere. Shuran called to the Emmuku'Gu and created a line of energy, linking the sphere to the great flow of power in the earth. As one, they moved the spelled sphere into the ground and joined it to the gugtu surrounding the area.

As the spell anchored to the special stone, it spread through it and a bubble of influential energy rose into the air and covered the ruins of Durangug. To an outsider, the area would seem uninteresting and they would be compelled to avoid entering. With this task complete they could focus on planning the next leg of Shuran's quest to rebuild the Zidu'Si.

"Why are we not all going north?" Mallick inquired.

"There are too many plans and tasks to undertake for us all to leave. We have the link to maintain communication. Moona needs help with the weapons for the magurmu as well," Shuran answered.

"I thought while I am here I might also look into these statues. They are all old Gods, I am curious why they are among the treasures in the Vault," Mallick said.

Shuran nodded as he looked at the various statues ringing the chamber. He was also curious about the significance of their presence. He spared them only a fleeting glance as his mind was brought back to the task of preparing the hunt for the home of the giants.

"According to all we have discovered, the giants refer to themselves as the Gula'Lu. I suggest you remember that, in case they are slighted the same as using the term dragon," Mallick said, as Jade huffed at the common-tongue word for drakkon.

Gregoran and Jade would stay behind to continue watch on the trolls and the surrounding areas. Mallick would continue his research into the old Gods as well as help Moona and Codge with the weapons.

"I plan on stopping to check on Aknard in Duranekur, he can return here with trusted comrades to assist with the bombs and stock the other magurmu," Shuran said.

"Some of the dwarven clans still worship Damkianna, perhaps they can add to what the statues are doing here," Avrank suggested. "Aknard already knows of Durangug, if not its actual location, but as for any that accompany him, they will need selecting."

"It is good you are accompanying Shuran and I north then," Orian smiled.

"Great! The smallest of dwarves out hunting giants, what could go wrong?" Avrank grimaced.

The remainder of the evening was spent preparing for the trip north into the frozen lands beyond the Orenthal Mountains. No known maps existed of the realms outside Aurderia. Any travelers brave or dim enough to venture into the glacial terrain, never returned to boast of their exploits. If any ancient maps existed, they were not found. Shuran, Orian, Avrank, and Moltar would rely on their sense of Essence and being able to search from the air.

"This time of season is harsh with the winds blowing from the North, perhaps you should wait until the time of new growth when the winds pass?" Gregoran suggested.

"Time is not on our side, we have no information on the cities of the Badur'Lu or Lil'Du. Our best option is to go now with what little we have." Shuran was trying to convince himself.

"I can fly the winds," Moltar proudly added. "With the bond of my Lugaldur, I can manipulate the winds some as well." Moltar was feeling more confident in himself than Shuran was in his control over air and wind. Moltar could sense this and gave Shuran a feeling of reassurance through their link.

"Come over here my boy." Moona took Shuran by the arm and pulled him away from the others for one of her little talks.

"We will be fine Moona," Shuran reassured her.

"Now just you listen, mister not yet all powerful Shin-for-brains! I want you checkin' in every day, twice at the least!" Moona was more serious than usual.

"Moona, you can get updates through the link I share with the Zidu'Si-"

"I will be hearing from you directly or you'll be havin' a great deal more than the Order to fend off when you get back!" Moona meant business. She was worried about Shuran and things were just getting worse in Aurderia.

"You got that evil bastard what use' to be my sprat all worked up now. That with what was your twin sister 'll be causin' more trouble, an' lookin' for ya!" Moona reminded him.

Shuran acknowledged her feelings and tried to sooth her as best Moona could ever be soothed. He left her to go about finishing his preparations for the journey.

The sheltering tents were checked, and foodstuffs were packed and set to the side. As had become the standard, those venturing on this part of his quest would travel light and call forth what was needed from the Vault.

Shuran turned to the notebooks of the Zidu'Si from over five thousand years past. He knew that the Gula'Lu had a gug weapon among the Vault's contents but wanted to know more about it. Of the remaining weapons, it was the strangest.

The simplest to understand was the gug wand of magic for the human weaver, the Gidri Zisura. Where the Kibir'Zisu was the trident of power for the Badur'Lu and the Shi'Imbi was the staff of Life's Wind for the Lil'Du, the A'Baddasu was a more of a mystery. This weapon was the Gauntlet of Strength, which on a normal person would be mighty. The Gula'Lu were said to have been a much larger and stronger race of man. Shuran could not comprehend how much more force this weapon would yield on the arm of a giant.

Examination of the weapon and reading the notes on its past use left him with even more questions. The design was made to allow the gauntlet to bond to its wearer, but it seamed to Shuran that it would not fit his image of the arm on a Gula'Lu. It looked to fit a much smaller arm, but Shuran would not doubt the magic of the weapons unwarranted. He placed the A'Baddasu back in the cradle made to hold it in the weapons room.

Shuran slept restlessly that evening, visions of death and destruction filled his night. He saw himself standing atop a mountain and the land all around him split and broken with molten rock flowing freely over all of Aurderia.

The next vision would see him atop Moltar as waters from the Great Sea drowned the lands. From the West and South, waters from the Great Sea rose hundreds of paces into the sky. In motions slower than normal, Shuran watched as the mountain of water laid waste to the shores and carried its destruction inland for miles.

What finally woke him was the image of a star exploding in the night sky and setting Ersetu to ash. It was his sister's star.

Shuran arose drenched in sweat. He did not know what to make of his visions. He felt somehow that these were possible outcomes of what may become of Aurderia, but he was the most confused about the stars from the prophecy. He had not thought on them since hearing of the prophecies surrounding he and his sister. To most, these stars were just a symbol of the birth of twins who would be linked to the future of Ersetu. Shuran was no longer convinced that this was the true nature of the bright objects dominating the night skies.

The stars tracked the evening sky as Utu waned. Shuran noticed how the once dimmer of the twin stars grew in brilliance as time past. They were born to the sky of equal brightness then one diminished in brilliance at the sacrifice of Tianna. That same star grew brighter to nearly the same shine as its twin. What this ultimately meant, he was without the knowledge to understand.

"You slept in fits last night my boy. What troubles you?" Codger asked when Shuran approached the hearth.

"I had disturbing visions of the destruction of Aurderia, and of the twin stars of prophecy," Shuran answered. "I cannot help but wonder at their connection to the balance and our birth."

"I have often wondered what the stars had to do with all this as well," Codger said. "Have you noticed that they grow greater in brightness once again? What would cause a star to nearly wink out then become bright again? That has had me thinkin'."

"What have you been able to determine about their importance?" Mallick asked as he came to the dining area to join them.

"He ain' got no thoughts in his addled ol' brain!" Moona answered for Codge. "The ol' fool thinks they are gettin' closer. I milked yaks got more sense than ol' Codger!"

Shuran was not so certain that Codge's summation was too far off point. Why would a star burn bright, then become dim only to return to brightness again? Shuran could not answer, but he knew the closer you got to a fire the brighter it seemed to burn. The rest of his vision was not easily understood.

"Seems I remember some reference to purification from the heavens," Mallick interjected. "I will have to retrieve my ring to find it again." Mallick took to removing the ring while not requiring immediate access to knowledge. He was still mastering his access; wandering thoughts would often cause a flood of information when he did not concentrate.

Shuran instructed Mallick to use the time he, Orian, and Avrank would be away to find what he could about the stars in addition to the statues. Time was not halting, so Shuran continued preparations for the journey north. They would be leaving before mid Utu.

They ate a hearty breakfast and spoke of lessor concerns such as the weather and when the winds might change. On more than one occasion during the meal, a pork sausage or piece of fruit would disappear from the table, stolen by the quick tongue of one large red drakkon.

Moona would curse and shake her fists at the young playful beast, but it was for show mostly. Moona had a family to look after and like it or not, Shuran's new 'pet' was as much a member as any. She was concerned about Shuran heading out into the unknown, but she could see the vehemence of Moltar's loyalty and love for Shuran, so she felt a small bit of comfort that the beast would do all possible to keep her boy safe.

Chapter Three

After saying their farewells, Shuran, Orian, and Avrank, climbed atop Moltar and settled into the new rigging. Orian and Avrank joined their skills to create a multi-function set of straps and satchels that could be converted to temporary saddles.

"Is everything secured?" Moltar asked anxiously. He, for some reason, enjoyed carrying the un-bonded Zidu'Si. Most drakkon would only carry their Lugaldur.

"All ready Moltar, the 'Turd' is strapped and settled," Orian jested.

"Stuff gug up your backside, shoe boy!" Avrank retorted.

With a snicker, Shuran patted Moltar and shared his thoughts of getting underway. The sudden lift drove the air from both Orian and Avrank's bantering. All Shuran could hear was the wind rushing past his ears and the excited hum of Moltar's joy at taking flight. They flew low until well out of possible view of the approaching trolls, and they passed the southern foothills of Orenthal. Their flight path would take them around to the glacial pass with a stop at Duranekur.

***

Mallick sucked in his breath and emptied his mind before slipping the jeweled ring upon his finger. He found that the scrambled images and words were easier to comprehend when he focused on the ring. As he opened his eyes and gazed upon the ring, he traced the facets of the gleaming stone at its center. It was the size of his thumbnail, white with flecks of gold, silver, copper, and small chips of every known gemstone.

As his gaze moved across the setting, he noticed something for the first time. The setting did not sit centered on the band. It was offset by the full width of the band itself. The look of the ring now appeared as though it were part of a nested set. As this thought narrowed and focused in his mind, information poured into him so quickly, he caught his breath and stumbled.

"Mally! What is it?" Moona ran to his side to help him back up from his fall.

"It is incomplete!" was his reply as he hastily took the ring from his finger. "There is another ring that completes this as a set, I felt it."

"Where is it?" Gregoran asked.

"I know not, perhaps lost here in the Vault."

Mallick set about searching the vault for the lost band that completed the Mudutu'Har, Rings of Knowledge. He saw the rings were worn together from the flood of images he received, as a balancing system to control the flow of information. When separated the simple band, provided a flow of information to a secondary wearer.

While Mallick searched, Moona and the others began creating vessels for the exploding devices, Padiri'Bur. Codger took the Mellamu Nanna out to the coast with Moona to collect sand to make glass containers fashioned after something found in the Vault library. The only glass ever seen in Aurderia was from ancient structures or naturally found from lightening strikes or dragon glass shards. Now that they had the library, many ancient technologies would be re-introduced to Ersetu.

Gregoran and Jade made their way north to check on the progress of the troll legions. With the spell for cloaking Shuran gave them, they were able to fly around the horde and estimate their numbers better. Gregoran was able to count them in the thousands. Much like dwarves, trolls were divided into clans. Unlike dwarves, troll clans normally did not mingle.

Something was calling them together.

***

Shuran and companions arrived at the gates to Duranekur by early evening. Vraduun sent a greeting party to meet them. The goat drawn carts were not needed. Although Moltar was too large to fly within the vast tunnels, he moved faster afoot than the now scrambling goats.

Moltar looked after the running game with hunger. He was tired and famished after their long flight.

"Do not worry bonded, I am certain the King will have plenty of game for you to feast upon when we arrive at the palace," Shuran assured his beloved drakkon.

"I hope they have something that smells better than those hairy creatures that just run off?" Moltar answered. "I may be a drakkon, but I do have standards."

Moltar lumbered quickly along the tunnels with his passengers. The trip that last time took past a turn to travel, now took less than one-third that time. The sudden appearance of a drakkon of Moltar's unnatural proportions played on the already overactive imaginations of the dwarves assembled around the town. Where most drakkon would have been a disappointment to how most picture the legends of dragons, Moltar presented them with more than they dreamed.

"I will not make it past these buildings without damage, Lugaldur," Moltar expressed. "This chamber provides room for flight is there room to land at the palace?"

"You could land within the palace grounds easily enough, should there be no assembly present," Avrank answered.

Moltar spread his enormous wings to the awe of the dwarves that scampered away. With one large heft, he took to the space inside the vast mountain chamber. Within moments, he was circling the palace centered in the dwarven Capital City. Much to the dismay of the palace guards, Moltar landed on the grounds within the closed gates, in front of the main entrance to the royal seat of power.

"Stand down guards, these are honored guests and family." Levdrianda, Queen of the dwarves, came out to meet the royal guests. She smiled to herself as she passed the guards huddled together beneath

Moltar's shadow.

Avrank barely finished unstrapping himself from the saddle, when a set of earthen steps lifted from the ground and to his side next to Moltar.

"I thought you might dismount with more dignity than being carried off by an elf," Levdrianda said as she approached the base of the steps. "You are still royalty after all!"

"Thank you, mother," Avrank replied with an embarrassed look. "Where is father?"

"The king is feeling unwell at the moment, but I am here to receive you," came the bitter answer from Brakvar as he exited the palace. "Why have you come?"

"Brakvar! What is wrong with you? Your brother, as well as Shuran and the Zidu'Si, are welcome any time they wish!" bellowed Vraduun as he lumbered and coughed in the palace doorway. "Please come inside, those able to fit the doorway." Vraduun was marveling at the size and beauty of Moltar. "Magnificent!"

"I shall send for the heartiest of my herd to feed your hunger, mighty drakkon," Vraduun said to Moltar.

Moltar puffed up with pride.

Hugs and words of greeting were shared among all, except Brakvar, who exited the gates at the appearance of Vraduun. The rest of the assembly left Moltar to settle in the grounds and entered the palace to have dinner and discuss matters.

The royal dining hall was set for a feast when they all arrived. Vraduun anticipated his guests, having received a message by communication stone. The table was set with all the best the royal cooks could provide.

While the others dug into eating and talking, Shuran noticed that the King was not his usual self. Where he would normally be drinking and eating with mirth, Vraduun sat back and picked at his food, not getting overly involved in the conversation.

Vraduun noticed Shuran watching him and forced a smile and nod. He waved off concern, but he knew that Shuran would insist on knowing what troubled him.

"Shuran, Avrank tells me you seek spiritual guidance from some of our followers of the ancient Gods," Vraduun stated, attempting to draw attention away from his condition.

"While true that I wish guidance, it is more a matter of knowledge of the Gods, rather than anything of a spiritual nature," Shuran answered. "I believe there is some connection between these 'Gods' and Durangug, beyond religious practice."

"Do you not follow the Gods, Shuran?" Levdrianda asked with a hint of disappointment.

"I find it difficult to believe in the teachings written to suit the followers agendas, and their explanations for things they did not understand." Shuran was a bit terse in his response. "There have been multiple religions and belief systems, formed and forgotten, over the history of Ersetu. Why should one religion be right while another one wrong?"

"Do you not have faith at all, Shuran?" Levdrianda asked pointedly.

"In the Gods and their man written laws of sentience? Not entirely…" Before Levdrianda could interrupt, Shuran continued. "Do not take my word as denial. I find much of the basic system of beliefs in a number of the religions, palatable. What I find distasteful is justifications in each, to name another wrong or false. The atrocities committed by zealots in the name of their gods is abhorrent."

"Belief systems change over time, it is true. It is my feeling that as we grow and learn, so do our beliefs," Levdrianda started.

"Bah!" Vraduun voiced. "Most people in this world believe what suits them and hide their ignorance behind whatever religion best supports their prejudices! Besides, religious doctrine like historical accounts are written in the opinion of the one holding the pen!"

Levdrianda began to offer more on the subject before a wave of Vraduun's hand put an end to the discussion.

"Best to leave the philosophy to the philosophical," Aknard said as he entered the room and joined them for dining.

"Uncle, how are you?" Aknard asked.

"I am well young Turd, I mean nephew," Aknard corrected himself. He knew Avrank disliked being referred to as Turd, now that he was Zidu'Si. "A far shake better than my troll-headed brother."

Vraduun grunted and gave a quieting look to his brother.

"So what is this I hear about weapons for the magurmu?" Aknard asked, changing the subject.

"Moona has created a two trigger device to attack the death walkers while in flight," Orian said. Orian explained to them how they worked and the expected results. He explained how they were supposed to work by the second trigger coming into proximity with dark forces.

"Damkianna protect us! That sa'nua old woman will blow everyone up! What they are supposed to do and actually will do may be something altogether more tragic for us all!" Moona intimidated Aknard and it showed.

"Moona is not crazy, just enthusiastic. You will likely have a chance to test the padiri'bur after you arrive. There are trolls heading south in the area of Durangug." Shuran explained to them the events leading up to the spelling of the area. He also advised them on how best to counter its effects for their trip there.

Aknard was happy about getting weapons for his fleet of magurmu but not so about seeing Moona again. Aknard motioned for Shuran to follow him out of the dining hall, when Vraduun was not looking. He excused himself from the table and slipped out the side exit toward the private mushroom gardens.

Shuran quickly got up to follow him with a nod to Queen Levdrianda. He looked to the King, but Vraduun was nodding off in his seat. Something was not right, and Shuran sensed it.

"Shuran, over here!" Aknard whispered from the shadows of the garden.

Shuran followed his voice and gazed at the dozens of varieties of mushrooms growing in the garden. There were large groups of small and colorful types of mushrooms as well as some that nearly reached Shuran's shoulders. He found Aknard sitting beneath one of the large mushrooms drinking from a flask.

"How long has Vraduun been ill?" Shuran was not going to dance around the issue.

"From what I have learned, he fell ill only in the last two cycles. His appetite left him, followed by weakness and occasional episodes of hallucination."

"The last symptoms could be from lack of nourishment. I would like to examine him, but I am not sure he will approve." Shuran wondered at how he might persuade the King to allow him to check his system, but Aknard agreed that Vraduun would be too proud to concede.

"There is more…" Aknard began in whispered tones. "There is talk of Dark Dwarves deep in the mountain."

"Dark Dwarves?" Shuran asked. "What on Ersetu do you mean? Am I to understand that there are dwarves who follow the Order?"

"Follow the Order? Not exactly or I should say, we do not know. All we can say is that there has always been a clan of dwarves that found the darker ways of life more appealing. It would seem as though they have resurged after hundreds of years. I do not find it coincidence that it should happen now." Aknard showed a look of disgust and suspicion.

"You suspect they are involved in what has befallen the King?" Shuran asked.

Aknard turned to Shuran with a look of doubt. "I am not certain it is them directly, for I fear it may be closer to home."

"Surely you do not suspect Brakvar? I know he has no love for most and especially not Avrank but to poison his father?"

"I did not say that… Exactly, but that nasty little upstart has been sour since Avrank was elevated in the eyes of the elders. He has also been acting odd and sneaking around. I hate leaving at this time." Aknard was deeply upset and concerned.

"Perhaps I should leave Avrank here while I travel north. Through the Zidu'Si link perhaps we can both observe and learn more," Shuran suggested.

Aknard lightened at the suggestion and joined Shuran in walking back to the royal apartments. "In the morning I will head to Durangug with those who can be trusted."

"Thank you. I will provide your vessels with the cloaking spell so you may approach without notice to the trolls."

Aknard's usual smirk spread broadly across his face at the thought of target practice on trolls. But mostly he was thrilled at having a cloak for his fleet of flying pirate ships. He motioned for Shuran to join him in a toast as they sat back down at the dining table.

"Aknard, Avrank has just heard from your contacts with the dwarven followers of the old Gods," Levdrianda mentioned as she looked at him and Shuran sideways. "They will meet with you on the morrow in the depths of the forgotten mines outside the ruins of Badgaldingir."

Shuran noticed Vraduun's absence. He began to speak when Levdrianda turned to him.

"My husband is not well Shuran. He would not speak honestly about it, but I fear some darkness stirring in Duranekur," she began. "Vraduun will not seek proper medicine or examination."

"The King is even less likely to allow an Essence based exploration of his system either, I wish to have Avrank stay here while Orian and I venture north. Perhaps he will have better results with the effort?" Shuran looked to Avrank, who was visibly relieved at not venturing to the Frozen North, and yet shaken by the thought of something happening to his father, King Vraduun.

"I will do what I can. Moona perhaps might provide medical concoctions," Avrank replied.

Those remaining in the dining hall shared good wishes and departed for their bedchambers to retire for the evening.

Chapter Four

Shuran departed the Royal apartments and headed out to the courtyards to see after Moltar. He arrived to find Moltar hunched before a large group of dwarven sprats.

Moltar was sending small smoke rings from his nostrils to the delight of the dwarf-lings.

"It would appear you have made some new friends," Shuran spoke as he rounded Moltar's enormous form.

"We have been playing games and roasting mushroom caps," Moltar grinned.

Shuran returned the smile as he watched the young dwarves climb Moltar's tail and scurry along his back only to slide back down along his wing. Witnessing this moment of joy allowed him to lighten his heart and the weight he carried. Shuran sprinted up Moltar's tail and joined in the game.

After the last of the dwarf-lings was taken off home, Shuran sat back against his friend and relaxed for the first time in many moons. As he scratched Moltar below his jaw, Shuran began to drift off to slumber. His state became so eased that his normally warded mind was opened up for the first time in many moons.

The vision was more fragmented than any that preceded it. Shuran looked down upon himself from high above. He watched as his own body fought with Bastien. The next moment he was holding a golden dagger to Bastien's heart. The dagger had a gem on the end of the hilt, which changed from clear to black then brilliant green.

In the following moments, he stood with Bastien at his side fighting with Mallick. The three locked in a struggle of will until they all three were drawn together as one. Three rings blurred across the edge of his now foggy vision. Shuran struggled to bring them into focus and the three blurred bands combined to form one ancient jeweled ring of gold. As Shuran strained to read the symbols on the band, he was snapped out of the trance.

"LUGALDUR!" Moltar bellowed into Shuran's mind. "You must wake from this vision." Moltar could sense danger from his link to Shuran. He could also sense that Shuran's mind was vulnerable in its now unshielded state.

As the darkness dove in to seize on Shuran's unprotected shi, Moltar acted on instinct. Instantly Moltar's mind surrounded Shuran's. The effect was a shield beyond anything Shuran had constructed by his own strength. As the darkness slammed into the barrier, Shuran and Moltar winced at the high-pitched screams and howls that resulted from the impact.

Shuran was revived by a splash of icy water, to find Orian and Avrank standing above him with looks of both worry and anger.

"What are you doing leaving yourself so open to attack!" Orian's expression was for the first time showing true emotion. "You nearly had your mind taken by darkness!"

"I was tired and fell asleep…" Shuran started then remembered the barrier and turned to Moltar, who was snoring to his side.

"He is fine but will sleep most of the night and day next," Avrank said. He noticed Shuran's confusion and continued. "We felt the attack, though much less than you and Moltar. That barrier he constructed likely saved your life."

"How would the Order even know you were here? They could not have scried you so quickly after you let down your defenses unless they were constantly doing so." Orian was now less angry and more agitated. "Someone has informed the Order you are here!"

"I have never felt this kind of attack from the Order before," Shuran expressed as he rubbed his fingers on the sides of his head.

"We have little understanding of what your sister and her cronies are fully capable of," Orian interjected. "They side themselves with the dark and may have gained more from the unholy alliance."

"Come, you need food and rest before we go to the old ruins." Orian reached out his hand to steady Shuran on his feet.

"The vision-" Shuran started.

"We saw it as well, we all did," Avrank said as he indicated the flashing communication gem on Shuran's arm band. "Moona would like a word."

"Tell her I am sleeping it off," Shuran said with a boyish voice. He knew he was in for an ear chewing.

"That old woman could smell a lie even from this distance. If I ever wish to step foot within her reach again-" Orian began.

"OK, ok, I'll take my tongue lashing like a man. At least she is not here to-"

WHACK! Avrank struck Shuran from behind with a stick. "That is from Moona."

Even Orian could not hold his laughter as the three headed back to the royal apartments.

Long after Shuran faced the wrath of Moona, he met the others for a morning meal in the dining hall. He was not at all rested, even though he had slept several hours. The vision that felt like only moments had lasted most of the night. Orian and Avrank came to him only an hour before what the dwarfs considered morning in the depths of the Orenthal.

"You look no worse for it Shuran," Levdrianda giggled as Shuran sat beside her at the table. "I understand that Moona can be quite harsh."

"She is overly protective and equally corrective." Orian was among the others grinning at the table.

"It would appear that my scolding has been spread like gossip at a garden party." Shuran could not hold back his own grin.

"Experience, my dear friend, is a school oft attended by fools," Vraduun chimed in as he entered the room. "You should learn not to ire your Moona."

"You look better this morn," Shuran said as he stood to greet the King.

Vraduun grunted and motioned for all to sit. "Better than the past few days, thanks be to the pestering of my youngest son."

"That, and a mix of herbs from one of Moona's medical belts," Levdrianda said smiling. "I must say I am liking this Moona woman more each day. I cannot wait to meet her."

"Be careful what you wish for my Queen, her tongue is sharp and her opinions abundant," Shuran said between mouthfuls of food. His hunger was fierce this morning. He could only image Moltar's need when he wakes.

"Do not fill yourself over much Shin'Ar, we have a long walk through the Orenthal to reach the old tunnels. You will cramp in your gut by the time we reach the halfway point." Aknard was eating a light portion of food, but the same could not be said of his drink.

"And you will be stopping to water the rocks every half hour should you continue to drink so," Levdrianda pointed out. "It will not be so bad will it?"

"There is a reason no one goes to the old tunnels my Queen. The dark dwarves are down there as you know and they do not take well to passers-by." Aknard was nervous and could not hide it.

"You shall be in the company of Shuran Shin'Ar and one of his Zidu'Si. You have little to fear of some cult of recluse dwarves!" Vraduun barked from his end of the table. "I should have warranted them out decades ago."

"Still, few outside the worshipers of the old Gods ever return from venturing to those depths. It is said that Shadow takes form among the abyss and doorways exist to the Netherworld." Aknard took another healthy draw from the barrel to fill his cup.

The King grunted as he ate, but the others were not so quick to dismiss the gloom of Aknard's assessments. The rest of the meal was eaten in relative silence before the King began to tire again and he excused himself to go rest.

"I am glad to eat but I still need my rest," Vraduun said as he kissed his lady wife and bid the others good day.

"Continue with the herbs Avrank, we shall return soon and then be off to find the Gula'Lu. Please see that Moltar has plenty to eat when he wakes." Shuran excused himself and then, along with Orian and Aknard, headed off to the depths of the Orenthal Mountains to find the old worshipers.

Aknard lead the way from the Capital City of Duranekur, into the dark caves beyond that led into the deeper settlements and ultimately the ruins of Badgaldingir. The old fortress city is surrounded in myth and mystery. Aknard told them the stories as they travelled into the depths.

Badgaldingir was discovered thousands of years ago when a clan of dwarves was mining the deepest veins of gold ever discovered. It is said that when they broke through the thin wall of rock and laid eyes upon the fortress, they immediately fell to a knee and gave up all natural dwarven desires for mining and digging. The dwarves saw something there that caused them to begin worship of the old Gods again.

"No dwarf outside their religious order knows what lay within the city walls, they forbid entrance to non-believers," Aknard said. "They do not even surface to Durangug much, only rarely for trade."

Shuran and Orian kept silent as they continued on. The trek was strenuous as they took steep declines and rough paths that wore away with age. They could tell these ways were seldom traveled. The darkness seemed to swallow up the light given off from the glowing orbs Shuran and Orian created to illuminate their journey.

The three continued on for nearly a day with only breaks occasionally to rest, drink, and take a bite of cheese or bread.

Shuran thought they would walk to the other side of the world before the ground finally began to level out. Shuran stopped as he listened to the absolute stillness of their surroundings. He reached out with his shi, searching, until at last he found what he hoped for since leaving on the journey. He sighed in relief.

"What is it Shuran?" Orian asked puzzled.

"We will find it faster to return than the journey down. I have found an unbroken line of the Emmuku'Gu."

After he had said his words, Shuran felt a presence while his shi was extended. It was something he had never felt. Something deep and ancient, dark and corrupt itching at his senses. It felt him as well and stirred.

"We have to move!" Shuran whispered urgently. "Something is down here, and it does not wish us well."

Without further explanation, the three of them ran further down the tunnel that stretched out before them. The shadows began to move and coalesce into a foggy dark mist that followed after them. The dark fog gained on them as they ran for an opening at the far end of the tunnel.

As they dove through the tunnel, their ears popped and they had felt dizziness before darkness began to take them. The last thing Shuran saw was a bright spot before his eyes and then a flash of light. He sank into unconsciousness.

Shuran woke soon, to the sounds of water spilling and night creatures buzzing and chirping. He sat up with a start that threatened to pull him back down as his world spun. As his vision began to return, he could make out the forms of Aknard and Orian sitting nearby. They were with another figure, a dwarf it seemed.

The dwarf motioned for him to come forward and reached out to hand Shuran a cup of water from the fountain they sat near. He lowered his hood and looked at each of the newcomers in turn.

"Long ago, before the first Orenthal Mountains came to exist, The Gods of Ersetu lived among the children of the world. They called Badgaldingir home," he said as he gestured around. "Welcome Shuran Shin'Ar and friends. You are safe here." The white-robed dwarf crossed his right arm to his forehead palm out, and tilted his head back to look up.

Shuran and the others followed his gaze to find above them a dome of light radiating down upon the chamber they were now in. There were no clouds. Utu was not seen shining above, yet the place they found themselves in felt as though they stood out among the surface.

"What is this place?" Shuran asked. "Are we somehow out the other side of Ersetu?"

The dwarf just laughed and stood. He motioned for them to follow as he walked off toward the large building that stood opposite the fountain they drank from. All around them, buildings stood as if only recently erected. Strange trees, flowers, and plants grew in abundance at every turn. This place was unlike anything they had ever seen.

As they walked to the building, Shuran was surprised to feel energy pulsing from every stone. He reached out his hand to touch the masonry. The dwarf grabbed his hand just before he touched it.

"I should not do that if I were you. They do not like uninvited intrusion," the dwarf smiled as he released Shuran's hand. "Follow me and all will be explained as they have instructed." The dwarf led them into a grand, central gathering room where dozens of other similarly robed dwarves busied themselves with menial tasks.

"Please sit and nourish yourselves. It was no small journey to reach us from above. I expect you are all quite hungry." The dwarf guided them to a large table that held platters of strange looking fruits and vegetables, the likes of which the three had never seen or heard of. "You will find these items very pleasing."

"What are they?" Orian asked.

"The grounds of the city provide for our needs. We tend the gardens and this is the bounty of our work," the dwarf answered as he took up a green object that had a coating of hair on its skin. He sliced it open to reveal the bright green and juicy flesh of fruit inside, before taking a bite.

"You mentioned our journey from above…" Shuran began. He continued when the dwarf nodded. "So we are still below the Orenthal Mountains?"

"In a manner of speaking," The dwarf acknowledged. "I understand your confusion. The light comes from the Emmuku'Gu. It surrounds this place, protecting it." The dwarf suddenly blushed and fumbled as he placed his fruit down. "Where are my manners? I have not introduced myself. I am Dravard, leader of the Entar'Lu."

"Caretakers? So you look after Badgaldingir?" Shuran asked.

"They said you would know the ancient tongue," Dravard said with a look of admiration.

"Who are 'they'?" Orian asked.

"I cannot say." Dravard held a tight stare.

"You do not know, or you will not tell?" Aknard asked with irritation.

Dravard saw Aknard's frustration and softened his expression. "What I mean is that it is not my place to say. They will speak when they wish and reveal what they please." His tone left little doubt that there would be no more answers to the question.

"How is it we were allowed to enter the city?" Aknard asked.

"Because they wished it. You were expecting to meet someone, were you not?" came the cool reply.

"An acquaintance said I might meet someone who could tell Shuran about the old Gods. We were to meet outside the city," Aknard answered.

"I am afraid you were led down to the depths falsely. Had they not warned of your presence and bid us assist you, I am afraid you would have been consumed by the Shadow." Dravard whispered to a passing dwarf and sent her off.

"I have sent for a scholar to answer what questions we are able. Until he arrives, you are welcome to explore the courtyard and this hall. Please remember not to touch anything without invitation." Dravard got up to leave.

"How do we know if an invitation has been extended?" Shuran asked.

"You will know." Dravard laughed as he exited the hall.

Chapter Five

Shuran had far too many questions on his mind to continue eating. Although the many odd fruits and vegetables were delightful, he found himself in need of guidance. He exited the hall to go back to the courtyard so he might contact Mallick. When he attempted to send a message, he found that his communication stone would not activate.

"You will find that you are unable to work much Essence here young asipu." An ancient looking dwarf sat below a white tree with drooping branches that swayed in the unnatural breeze. "Please join me. My name is Zakbravan, but you can call me simply Zak."

Shuran approached the old dwarf and took the offered seat beside him. Shuran noticed the dwarf eyeing his wine skin and offered it up.

"Oh, I would be ever so grateful should this be dwarven brew!" Zak said with a glint in his eye.

"It is. From the King's own stores," Shuran answered.

Zak took a deep drink from the skin and snorted with delight. He helped himself to another before passing it back to Shuran.

"Keep it. I take it Badgaldingir does not supply spirits down here," Shuran said as he gazed off at the mysterious creatures and plants that filled the large courtyard.

"Oh, there be a few of us what brew a few things from the fruit and tubers that grow, but none has much kick." Zak was openly thankful for the skin. "I hear you are looking for knowledge of the old Gods eh?"

"Yes, I am to meet with a scholar to get what answers 'they' see fit to allow." Shuran's tone gave away his frustration and confusion both. "I do apologize, I mean not to take things out on you friend."

"Don' bother yourself about it… and friends we are." Zak raised the skin in salute and took another drink. "Now ask away."

Shuran looked to Zak confused at first before realization set in. "You are the scholar then?"

"Indeed I am Shuran Shin'Ar, and I shall answer what is allowed and perhaps more," Zak said with a wink. "But first let us speak of how I come to know so much shall we." Zak set down the skin and pulled out a long pipe. He lit it and took a long draw.

Shuran could not help but think of Moona. This Zak was just as feisty and was probably going to bend the rules. He smiled.

"First, I ain' as young as I look," Zak said as he grinned and all the wrinkles of his face became exaggerated. "See, I was the first to break through the wall of that tunnel you came through over twelve thousand years ago." Zak could see the shock in Shuran's expression. "Badgaldingir provides and sustains, my boy."

Shuran sat back and took a drink from the skin himself as he prepared for Zak's tale.

Sixteen dwarves were among the crew that ventured so deep into the mountains in search of the source of a mighty deposit of a rare and pure gold. Small veins had lead them deeper than any dwarf had ever mined. When they reached the end of the tunnel and broke through to a chamber they saw nothing but darkness beyond. The darkness surrounded them as they entered the chamber.

They heard whispers and the shadows seemed to tug at them until finally a bright flash of light chased the shadows and bathed them in a warming glow. When their eyes finally adjusted, they gazed upon the mighty city of the ancient gods, Badgaldingir. The dwarves did not know at first what they had found until the voices spoke to them and led them inside.

What they discovered was truth. The voices told them of the great split among the Gods and a war that led to the first fall of balance in Ersetu. The Gods fought among themselves and most of the Telukukal perished in the process, victims or tools of the Gods. As the Gods warred, the lands began to tremble and change. Valleys filled with sea, lakes emptied into the earth, and the face of the land was altered.

"That is when this city was swallowed by Ersetu and the Orenthal grew to cover the north of what is now Aurderia," Dravard said. "All of the old cities, villages, and temples of the Telukukal were destroyed or swallowed by the great changes that took hold of the lands."

"So there are more cities of the Telukukal buried throughout Aurderia?" Shuran asked.

"When I speak of the cities, know two things. All of Ersetu was effected not just what is only now Aurderia. The Gods war and the balance affect the entire world."

"And the second thing?"

"You confuse the Telukukal with Gods," Dravard started. "The very name means 'First People', they were the children of the Gods."

Shuran was more confused than before he arrived in Badgaldingir. He tried processing the information that Zak provided, but every answer spawned more questions.

"I apologize my boy, it has taken me and the remaining members of my crew many millennia to understand what I have told you thus far." Zak was trying to console Shuran, but saw it was not working. "Perhaps you will begin to understand, or mayhap the Gods will speak to you in time."

"Have you heard of the compendium?" Shuran asked as the thought suddenly entered his mind.

"Ah yes, the ancient collections of the Gods knowledge, I know of it." Zak answered.

"Is it here, in the Badgaldingir?"

"Would be a good place for it, but no it is not. We only know of its existence and that it is hidden even better than Badgaldingir."

"I need something more if you can answer two more questions?" Shuran asked not showing any defeat from Zak's previous answer. Shuran continued at Zak's nod. "Is Durangug a city of the Gods or the Telukukal?"

"Both, the Gods left it and others like it for their heirs to repair the world, though I do not know the why or how," Zak answered. "And your other question?"

"Damkianna, was she a God or Telukukal?"

Zak was surprised by the question. Before he could answer he was stopped. "I am unable to answer," Zak said with a blink and slight nod.

That was answer enough for Shuran.

Shuran escorted Zak back to the hall where he found his friends and Dravard.

They were discussing the lives of the Entar'Lu and what their lives were like. Orian and Aknard shared stories of life on the surface and the history of things that the Entar'Lu did not know about.

Shuran turned to Zak when he recalled something Zak said. "Zak, you mentioned earlier something about those of the sixteen who remained. What became of them?"

Zak paused for a moment before responding. "They could not bare the isolation, and for a few their desires for the gold we originally searched for, caused them to leave. They never made it past the Shadow."

Shuran stepped away from the others and headed to a recessed section of wall several paces away from the sitting area where the others remained talking. He was drawn to the pulses of energy coming from the alcove. He stepped within it and was bathed in light.

"So they died when they left, how are we to get back without meeting the same fate?" Aknard asked.

"I did not say they died. They were taken by the Shadow and now serve it." Zak spoke with sadness in his words.

It was then that they noticed Shuran's absence. A moment of looking brought their attention to the glowing form of the Shin'Ar mumbling to himself in the alcove. Aknard stood to go to him.

"Do not approach, he is unharmed. The voices speak to him."

Dravard said.

Shuran stood in the alcove motionless in a trance, as the only thing moving were his eyes and lips. That is what the others saw. What Shuran experienced was something all together different. Shuran stood alone surrounded by a flow of energy that filled him with a sense of serenity. The flow reminded him of the way the Emmuku'Gu looked when he entered it. He waited for what felt like an eternity before he heard the voices. They were androgynous and commanding, yet comforting and gentle. Shuran appeared as a small boy, more representative of his true age.

"Shuran of the Shin'Ar, you carry a great responsibility. You must face many challenges and will experience pain and loss before your task is at an end. The greatest challenge will be facing yourself," whispered the voices.

"Why has this fallen to me?" Shuran shouted. "I am still but a boy."

"You are more than you seem, and you chose this for yourself. All will be revealed in time, but you must discover things in your own time. We will always be near to guide you," the voices spoke.

"But what do I do next?"

"Save the one called Bastien. Complete your Zidu'Si. Face the Shadow many times. The rest will come as it must before you rejoin the rings and save Ersetu." The voices faded and Shuran was standing in the alcove, blinking back the spots before his eyes.

"Shuran, are you well?" Orian asked.

"I am unharmed, but I am no less confused than ever I have been."

Shuran relayed the words spoken to him. No one was able to provide insight into them except one thing. The voices referred to him as Shuran 'of the' Shin'Ar.

"The translation of the title 'Shin'Ar' has changed over time. Originally it meant 'Lands of the Watchers', being the place where the first guardians of man hailed from. It changed over time to mean 'Watcher of the Lands'." Zak explained.

"Does that mean Durangug was originally called Shin'Ar?" Orian asked.

"Not exactly, Shin'Ar was any place where a Telukukal was left to look over the land and continue the work of the Gods. Durangug is but one such place." Zak completed his explanation with a pat on his belly. "I am hungered beyond words. Shall we…" Zak motioned for them to head to the now set table.

They ate and continued with small talk before Shuran finally brought up another question.

"Are the shadows the work of the Order of Chaos?" Shuran asked.

"I should think it the other way round my friend," Zak answered. "The Order has not always been, neither has the Followers of Light. They are products of what has always existed."

"There can never be one without the other. Where light shines there can always be found the Shadow," Dravard whispered as though speaking prayer. "Time has come where you must leave us and continue on your journey Shuran Shin'Ar."

Shuran was not at the least put off by the abrupt dismissal. He, Orian, and Aknard were more than happy to head back home. Shuran stood and returned Dravard's and Zak's salutation of outward palm to his forehead.

"Ah, how are we going to get past the Shadow?" Avrank asked with a nervous tone to his voice.

Shuran looked up when they reached the courtyard. "By Emmuku'Gu my friend, hold on tight." Shuran answered as he held out his hand.

With a final nod and smile to Zak, Shuran closed his eyes and reached out to the Emmuku'Gu. He held tight to his friends and entered the flowing rivers of energy that circled the entire inner-world of Ersetu. With the thought of Duranekur in his mind he followed the flow that lead them up and out of Badgaldingir.

Just before exiting the river of power, Shuran heard a voice from the light. "Remember Shuran of the Shin'Ar, out of the darkness comes the light." And the voices were gone.

Shuran stood in the Royal courtyard a few paces from where Moltar was feasting on a large spread of prepared beasts. Orian stood to his left. Aknard was bent over vomiting to his right. Shuran laughed and patted Aknard on the back. "It takes getting used to my friend."

"I will stick to sailing my boats!" Aknard managed between heaves.

"LUGALDUR! You have returned!" Moltar came bounding over to greet Shuran and proceeded to drag his slobbery forked tongue across Shuran's face.

"AG! That was disgusting. There was still meat in your mouth." Shuran wiped his face and laughed at Moltar's unchanged posture of happiness.

"I only woke a short time ago, Avrank brought me the most wonderful beasts for dinner. He even had that smelly hair removed and they soaked the meat in something before cooking it." Moltar said before a hiccup and burst of flame escaped his maw.

Shuran knew he could have channeled power into Moltar to revive him before leaving for the depths of Orenthal, but leaving him unattended among the dwarves would have been more trouble than he wished on any but his enemies.

"I believe your pet is drunk, Shuran," Orian joked.

Shuran patted Moltar on the snout before heading into the Royal apartments. When he and the others entered, they found Avrank, Levdrianda, and Vraduun dining.

"Shuran, Orian, Uncle, you have returned. Did you find the information you were after?" Avrank exclaimed as he got up to greet them. "Did this contact have information on the Gods of old?"

"The contact was a false lead. We were pulled into a trap." Orian said.

After the initial shock had worn off, Shuran explained to the Royal Family what they encountered in the depths of Orenthal. He left out the parts of his conversation with the voices in the light and their final message.

"So the rumors of Dark Dwarves are true. I had hoped that it was only a matter of traitors who spied for the Order. This is most unpleasant and disheartening." Vraduun was taking this news personally.

"These dwarves are servants of Shadow my dear, we do not know that they do so willingly." Levdrianda tried to make Vraduun see reason.

"Perhaps the first ones fell in their departure from Badgaldingir, but it was greed and desire for gold that drove them. Others have likely fallen for similar reasons or worse." Vraduun was looking even less well suddenly as the thoughts of his kin becoming tools of this darkness seeping up from the abyss, crossed his mind.

"There is darkness in us all Vraduun," Shuran started. "It is only when we cast doubt upon and conquer it, do we see the light. There will be many more taken by Shadow before this war ends, it is our task to shine that light for them to see their way back." Shuran was just as shocked as the others at the wisdom that came from his words.

"Well said Shin'Ar." Orian was now more assured of his position among the Zidu'Si after Shuran's statement.

"While you were unreachable, some of the Northern clan dwarves came with information on what may lay ahead for you in the Frozen North." Avrank continued and told them of the rumors and whispers of the treacherous ice fields and winds. It was also shared that some have heard tales of the ice being alive and attacking those foolish enough to venture within its reach.

"How has your health been, Vraduun?" Shuran inquired.

"I have been getting better slowly. The herbs have helped, though the taste is less appealing than licking a yack's arse!" Vraduun laughed.

Shuran was not entirely convinced. He studied the King while they spoke more. Later he spoke with Avrank and told him to watch for his father to begin declining again.

"Keep a record of who he sees and samples of his food and drink should he fall ill again after I leave," Shuran told Avrank.

"Do you suspect poison?"

"I have no thoughts, other than the fact that something is not sitting well." Shuran was not prepared to share more.

Chapter Six

Shuran just noticed that Brakvar was not in attendance and realized he had not seen him after he first arrived in Duranekur. An inquiry confirmed that he had not been seen by anyone since then, other than his chamber man. Shuran knew that Brakvar did not care overmuch for him or the Zidu'Si, but that did not excuse his behavior especially as the new heir apparent.

Avrank did not know what to think of Shuran's questioning of his brother's whereabouts. He also did not know what he felt himself. As much as his relationship with Brakvar was difficult at times, he did not believe him capable of involvement in a plot against his father.

The flashing of the red gem on his armband interrupted Shuran's conversation with Avrank. He was receiving a communication request from someone, likely Mallick. Shuran had recently adjusted the spell on the communication stones to allow synchronous communication. The receiver or sender only need use the spelling word once, and they could speak as if in the same room. Each stone received the new spell by sending it through the communication link as an upgrade of sort.

"Kin'Su!" Shuran intoned to open a line of communication.

"Shuran, it is me Mallick. I have information on the Gods of old as well as something else of the dark." Mallick had a tone to his voice that lent urgency to what he had to share.

Mallick spoke of the Gods as having worked with their children to fight off the darkness that was spreading across Ersetu. There was a reference to a great failure of the Gods that spawned a threat to the balance of light and dark.

"I believe what you reference is known as the 'Shadow', and the 'children' are actually the Telukukal." Shuran shared what he learned while visiting the lost city of Badgaldingir.

"BADGALDINGIR!" Mallick yelled in excitement. "I have recently read information on such a place, but from what I gleaned, I thought it appeared as a floating city in the clouds."

"I assure you it is a sunken city, buried under the Orenthal for thousands of years." Shuran paused for a moment realizing that Mallick had said he 'read' about the city. "What do you mean you read about it? Why are you not using the ring?"

"It is not working properly. It is as if suddenly I am unable to properly filter the information. It comes to me broken and fogged. I found a reference to another band that should be paired with it."

Shuran did not know what to think of this new information at first. "Are you certain? And it is just a pair?"

"Yes… why do you ask?" Mallick asked.

"Nothing… where is this other band?" Shuran was thinking of his correlation to the visions and prophecy of uniting three rings.

"We cannot locate it. It is not here in Durangug. I fear someone has it and perhaps wearing it."

This additional piece of the ever-growing puzzle was more disturbing than any other. Shuran advised Mallick not to wear it until he returned and they could figure this out together. He also inquired if he knew anything more about the Shadow.

"The only thing I have, thus far, found is a name… The Gizzu'Su. This is what the ancients called the darkness, shadow people," Mallick said with a mysterious tone trying to intone humor to his response to lighten Shuran's mood.

"Mallick, I need you to focus on finding everything you can about the Gizzu'Su, the rings, and everything on the ancient Gods. I think the Order of Chaos are marionettes and these 'Gizzu'Su' are the puppet masters."

Shuran ended his conversation with Mallick after advising him that he and the others should soon expect the fleet of magurmu to arrive for weapons. From the corner of his eye, he caught a movement that drew his attention. When he looked there was nothing there, but he swore to himself he saw movement in the shadows.

Brakvar entered the room and greeted his father and mother. He ignored Shuran, who eyed him with suspicion and his brother who now had a look of doubt in his eye. Orian he glanced at sideways and winked.

"My Father, Mother, and others… I do apologize for my absence, but I have just come from a long trip to the outer clans gathering information to help Shuran Shin'Ar with his quest to find the large hairy freaks from the North." Brakvar spat each word with a venom that even his parents could not mis-interpret.

"Speak plainly boy, your flowery words are not scented with an aroma we care to smell!" Aknard was not pleased as he spoke.

Brakvar was not in the least perturbed by the rebuttal. "I only wish to share what I have learned about the passage through the Frozen North."

Levdrianda was upset with the way her eldest son and husband spoke as of late. There was a disconnection she could not understand and was worried about her family. Her youngest child was now among the Zidu'Si and thrown into the face of danger from the darkness and her eldest had become a vindictive and sour reflection of his once loving and honorable self. She broke down and left the room.

"Do you see what you do to your mother? Spit it out and be away from my site!" Vraduun was also not his normal jovial self.

Shuran could sense a rift forming in the royal family and he could not help but feel that there was a plan in motion. A plan that involved something to do with the Gizzu'Su.

"I hear that there are great winds from the North and they are much more fierce this season than in many seasons past. I am afraid that even your mighty dragon will not be able to speed your progress," Brakvar said using the dragon term as a purposeful slight.

"Even if the wind is too strong, we will make better speed upon his back as his stride is far greater than a man," Shuran replied.

"Perhaps, but then there are the ice falls and caverns to deal with. Also, you may encounter the Tal'Ba-ad. The ice demons!" Brakvar's evil smile had spread across his face before he began to laugh maniacally.

Vraduun's swing of his arm was so sudden that no one had time to register the action before Brakvar was already lifting himself from the floor and wiping the blood from his now down turned lip.

"You will regret that… Vraduun!" Brakvar left the room without shedding a tear or showing any emotion besides hatred. He clutched upon a neck chain holding a plain grey looking pendant in the shape of a cube.

After Brakvar had left the hall, Shuran and Orian looked at each other with knowing glances before moving to the King. Avrank stood to the side not understanding what had just transpired.

"That… is not my son!" Vraduun spat as tears welled in his large dwarven eyes. "I do not know what has come over him, but he has changed since named heir apparent."

"No father, he began changing the day I was named heir apparent," Avrank said as he approached.

Shuran was only half listening. He walked to where Brakvar had fallen and touched the spot of blood left on the floor where his now split and swollen lip had met the granite tiles. He touched the blood and lifted his hand as he rubbed it between two fingers and closed his eyes. As he suddenly opened his eyes, he turned, then eyed the king and his youngest son, but said nothing.

Orian just nodded when Shuran noticed he had watched his every move.

"My King, we must leave without haste for the North before the weather turns against us. I do regret what has transpired, but matters have become quite urgent." Shuran turned to Avrank and pulled him aside.

"Stay by your father's side and keep Brakvar away from him. If you see your brother again, hold him until I return and use a cell of gug!"

"I do not understand!" Avrank was confused.

"I cannot be certain, but I do not believe that thing that just left was your kin. I do not think he was a dwarf at all." Shuran said nothing more before nodding to Orian and the two exited the hall leaving Avrank with a questioning look and feeling abandoned.

Outside the Royal apartments, Shuran called for the guards to assemble and then called to Moltar to prepare for departure. He gathered the guards and told them that Brakvar assaulted the King and was wanted to be found and captured.

"Shuran, do you not feel that you should share your suspicions with the others?" Orian asked.

"Do you understand what is happening here? Are you of the same mind?" Shuran asked.

"Of course Shin'Ar, but why not share the same thoughts with Avrank at least?"

"He is of the Zidu'Si, he should have understood and felt my sense through the link as you did, but failed to… why?" Shuran asked with a look that told Orian all he needed.

"Because his judgement is clouded."

"Precisely, this is why we must let him find the truth for himself. We cannot delay our journey and for now, we have Avrank's loyalty to his father as a means of keeping him safe. This impostor is a distraction and a spy, likely sent to delay us with the King's illness."

Without another word, Shuran mounted Moltar followed immediately by Orian. They flew up over the city and landed at the large tunnel that exited Duranekur on the North side of the Orenthal Mountains. As they lumbered along the unfamiliar passage, Moltar slowed so that Shuran could view the frescos on the walls. They were new and many pictured events involving Shuran and what had transpired since he was born.

"History being recorded, at least here in Duranekur, it will reflect what has truly transpired," Orian said.

"What do you mean?" Shuran asked.

"History is usually retold by the victorious. Should we not prevail, here the truth will be remembered."

"Your confidence in me is overwhelming my friend," Shuran replied with a smirk.

***

Brakvar sat in a hidden chamber wiping the blood from his lip. He was not in the least bit happy at his own behavior, but emotion somehow prompted his actions. This was not how things were supposed to play out. He laid the cloth down on the table and turned to the mirror in the corner of the room.

"Things are not working as we had anticipated. I need to alter in order to get things back in line with your plans," he spoke to the mist in the reflection.

"Move to the alternative plan then, but do not hesitate. I have seen the way you have wavered with feelings for the Aurderians, you are part of a greater purpose now. Do we understand one another?" the irritated female voice spoke from the misty reflection.

"Understood, I will adjust in order to change the course of things." Brakvar covered the mirror in the chamber and walked over to the cupboard. He opened the door and stared into the shocked eyes of his captive, the true Brakvar.

"Remember nothing… Luh'Sa!" he spoke.

The restrained form of Brakvar slumped over and his memories of the past cycles in captivity were washed from his mind.

The false Brakvar waited until late in the evening when the royal apartments were quiet, before moving the unconscious dwarf. He levitated the body down the darkened hallways until he reached his apartment. He did not want to risk waking the chamber attendant, so he left Brakvar outside the doorway and then vanished into the darkness.

Brakvar awoke soon after, completely disoriented and in a state of hysteria. His screams brought half the royal staff running to his aid. His personal attendant opened the apartment door to find Brakvar huddled in the archway, shaking and rocking while he sobbed.

Avrank, who's room was just down the hall, came running up to see what was happening. He saw his brother rocking and sobbing in a huddled mass.

"What is the meaning of this?" Vraduun shouted as he and Levdrianda approached the scene. He also looked down at Brakvar and noticed his trembling. "Are you finally coming to your senses about your behavior of late?"

Brakvar just looked up at his father with questions in his eyes but did not say a word.

"Father, I do not think it has been Brakvar we have been dealing with." Avrank pulled his father to the side.

"What are you about Avrank, of course this is Brakvar."

"This dwarf likely is our Brakvar, but the one you hit today was not. Look he has no mark or split lip."

Vraduun looked and after a moment, saw the truth in his youngest son's words.

Avrank told him about what Shuran had said earlier in the royal dining room. He also repeated all the actions and absences that have been outside Brakvar's normal behavior. The pieces were beginning to fit and the King was seeing it clearly for the first time.

Vraduun ran to his son huddled on the floor and pulled him into an embrace. Brakvar held tight and began to mumble.

"What is happening, why do I not remember how I got here?" Brakvar whimpered.

"You are going to recover, what do you last remember?" Vraduun asked.

"We returned from Durangug with the Shuran human, then…" Brakvar stuttered. "I do not recall after that."

"For that long? GUARDS!" Vraduun waited until his guards appeared. "I want the entire palace searched for anything or anyone out of place. When you finish, expand to search every last part of Duranekur."

"Do you truly expect to find this impostor?" Levdrianda finally spoke up.

"No, but we might find a clue as to who is behind this. Be they Chaos zealots, Shadow worshipers, or Damkianna knows what, I will have answers for this."

Avrank stood watching his parents fawn over Brakvar. He noticed for the first time that Brakvar was not the emotionless and hardened dwarf he always played. For the first time, he saw the brother he knew when he was a dwarf-ling. Avrank smiled as Brakvar smiled in return.

Chapter Seven

The winds from the North whipped toward the peaks of the Orenthal Mountains. Gail force icy blasts made flight from off the cliff face impossible. Moltar, in spite of his massive size and strength, was unable to lift off from the ledge without being forced back down. Eventually he, with his passengers, slowly crawled down the face of the mountain to lower elevation where the wind blew weak enough for him to take flight.

The trio headed into the Frozen North with only clues and the hope that Shuran could eventually sense the Gula'Lu when they were near enough. The bitter cold was not an issue, since Shuran cast a shield of heat around them. He attempted to create a bubble to keep the winds away, but that proved a poor idea. The wind pushed against the shield and forced Moltar's momentum forward to a near standstill.

The best Shuran could accomplish was a filter of sorts. The shield slowed the winds and warmed them. The result was a slower progression, but at least they were no longer being pushed backward. Shuran had to tap into the power flow of the Vault to feed energy to Moltar as he was exerting himself far more than necessary to make any measurable progress.

Hours past and they only made a few hundred leagues of distance. Moltar was exhausting himself to the point where he would soon damage his body beyond simple magical healing. Shuran could not allow him to continue on, even though he knew Moltar would keep going if nothing more than to get his Lugaldur where he intended to arrive.

"Moltar!" Shuran sent through his link since the wind prevented spoken communication. "We need to land and rest. There is an area just to our left that will allow a break from the wind." Shuran then sent a mental message back to Gregoran and Jade to have wild game available in the Vault so he might call it forth for Moltar.

Moltar fought against the high winds for nearly thirty minutes before finally landing in a partially protected area. It was a sunken section of ice that was blocked from the winds blowing from the North. Upon landing, Shuran dropped the connection to the Vault and the flow of power that it provided. Immediately both Moltar and Shuran felt a wave of exhaustion come over them, forcing them to settle on the cold hard ground with an unceremonious buckling and thud.

Shuran had been channelling the power to Moltar so it burned through him and ate away at his inner strength. Although he was tired beyond normal weakness of wielding, Moltar was nearly dead on his gargantuan feet. They both settled upon the icy ground and drifted off to sleep. Even though tapping the Vault allowed virtually unlimited strength for a spell or weaving, it came at a cost.

"Mallick! Can you hear me?" Orian shouted over the howling winds.

"Yes, I hear you. Are you all well?"

"Shuran and Moltar are sleeping, but they will need food and drink when they awake." Orian continued to relay the difficulties they had experienced. Mallick assured him they would have what food and drink would be needed for them all within the hour. Gregoran and Jade were already out hunting. Orian closed communication and called forth a warming ball of flames from his limited abilities with fire elemental Essence through the Zidu'Si link.

Shuran slept for just short of an hour before waking. When he finally

50

arose he called forth a source stone to bolster his strength, but he needed food and drink. Shuran focused on the Vault and found ample sustenance ready for transport. He retrieved food and drink for Moltar as well as him and Orian.

"Good morning Shin'Ar!" Orian joked.

Shuran grunted, but he did so with a half grin and a nod. He took a strong draw from a wine skin and then called forth wood and stone from the Vault to make a fire building upon the meager flames started by Orian. Shuran laid the stone on the icy floor to place the wood over. He knew that the heat would begin melting the ice and used the stone to keep the wood dry as long as possible.

"We will need to move on soon, I do not wish to remain upon the ice in one spot for long," Shuran said as he lit a fire with a word. "We will rest and forge ahead once I get a sense of direction."

As the three sat resting and eating a light meal, Shuran extended his shi out into the frozen expanse that lay ahead of them. He found nothing but empty ice fields all around them. His only choice was to continue north. He was about to suggest they prepare to leave when the first crack formed in the ice below their feet.

"Shuran, the ground opens!" Orian shouted over the sounds of cracking ice reverberating off the walls surrounding them.

"Yes, I see it, we need to get moving-" Shuran's words were cut off as the ground split apart and they all began sliding down through the opening below them.

As they slide through twists and turns of the huge circular tunnel that opened at their feet, Shuran had to use all his concentration to move himself out from in front of Moltar. He feared hitting a wall and being caught between it and Moltar's bulking form. Orian had managed to slide out just to the side of Moltar and prepared to climb atop the drakkon as well. Neither Shuran nor Orian made it as a hole too small for Moltar came up before them. They fell into the gaping opening as Moltar slide past.

Shuran and Orian continued to slip and slide through the new smaller tunnel. As they followed the bends and curves, Shuran vaguely noticed images in the ice. He passed them off as reflections of himself and

Orian as they traveled the tunnels. They were too distracted to attempt to slow themselves. They also did not take notice of why this deep ice tunnel was somehow illuminated.

Shuran was both concerned and bewildered by the shouts of Moltar's panic in his mind. His voice was getting fainter as Lugaldur and drakkon grew more separated, traveling different tunnels. After what seemed an eternity, Shuran and Orian slid to a halt deep below where they fell through the ice floor. They now stood at the edge of a vast cave with a dirt floor.

"Under different circumstances, that might have been enjoyable," Orian said as he moved further into the cavern and sent a globe of light from his palm. He levitated the orb high above them and out toward the center of the cavern.

Large stalactites of ice clung to the cavern ceiling, glistening from water streaming along their sides to drip into pools below them. An unnatural breeze blew through the cavern. What began as a biting cold, quickly turned to warm and stale strong wind in the opposite direction.

"I do not like the feeling I am getting here Orian," Shuran said. "This place does not give me anything good to cling to, yet I sense no trace of Shadow."

"The wind seems strange as well-" Orian was cut off by the sound of scrapping that seemed to originate from the far end of the cavern.

Shuran reached out toward the source of the noise with his shi. His immediate reaction was a look of confusion, then one of shock. Something was alive deep in the cavern, and it was aware of their presence.

"Something is coming, and it is massive," Shuran whispered as he pulled Orian behind a cropping of large boulders. He peered around the side of their hiding place to see the beast undulating forward.

The beast's appearance was a gargantuan sized worm of sorts, except that it was covered with fur. And then there was the mouth. The front of the furry worm was a circle of row upon row of razor sharp teeth that moved in a back-and-forth sawing motion as the creature moved forward. The strangest characteristic of the beast, it glowed.

"What on Ersetu is that?" Orian asked.

"I have no thoughts, but I would not like to meet the business end of that thing. By the looks of those teeth, I would venture to guess that this thing is responsible for making that tunnel we slid down." Shuran then thought back to the first tunnel they slid through and could not help sending the mental image he formed to Orian.

"Damkianna! This must be a baby if what you are thinking is true. Do you suppose those tunnels are some sort of trap? I know of several creatures in the woodlands of Entensiama, that burrow below the earth and wait until unsuspecting prey falls within their grasp."

"Perhaps, but I do not sense hunger or malice in the creature. It is more a sense of curiosity." Shuran noticed just then, that there were many other holes along the ice walls of the cavern. He was in the middle of pointing this out to Orian when he heard a rumbling noise from above.

The ceiling of the cavern began to shake as many of the smallest icicles fell to the ground. Soon after, several of the larger stalactites came crashing down. Several more creatures came sliding out of the other holes in the walls and made a fast path for the place where the first one appeared. Following their exit came a reddish glow in the side of the cavern wall.

Shuran smiled as he had sensed Moltar before he saw him. He could feel Moltar's desire to get to his Lugaldur. Shuran sent back a feeling of confirmation that he and Orian were well. He included images of the fur-covered saw-mouthed creatures fleeing as he and Orian made their way in the same direction the creatures departed.

By the time they reached the tunnel where the beasts exited, Moltar was breaking through the ice from a high point in the wall. Fire and water burst forth from the entry point he made. Moltar jumped from the hole as jets of steam accompanied his exit from the newest hole in the walls. With wings spread he drifted down to the cavern floor and landed before Shuran as the last of the furry worms escaped. Something followed into the cavern through Moltar's new tunnel.

Chunks of ice fell from the hole as a much larger creature slinked down into the cavern. The beast outsized Moltar by more than half, the falling ice was a result of the worm's teeth increasing the tunnel girth to fit its own bulk.

"Lugaldur! The beast followed me as I made my way through the ice. I forced it back with fire in the larger tunnel, but it gave chase." Moltar moved to block the creature's approach, but it paused and turned its head toward the tunnel the smaller creatures traveled from the cavern.

Shuran was preparing a volley of low volt strikes when Moltar stopped him.

"It is a mother! It only cares for the well-being of its young." Moltar sent her thoughts of peace and understanding. "She will leave us be, but we must leave here."

"How can you know this?" Orian asked.

"She spoke to him... in a manner of which I can barely comprehend," Shuran answered. "I could see, rather than hear what they communicated."

Moltar nodded, then began moving in the direction the creature indicated was a way out of the ice caverns. He continued to explain what else he learned from his communication with the beast.

They are slightly intelligent creatures. They burrow through the ice, feeding on the tiny luminescent animals that live in the ice. They do not normally attack anything as they are left alone by other creatures that lived within the frozen lands of the North.

"What other creatures live up here?" Orian asked.

"I did not get that information. The only important information shared, was heading in this direction would take us toward similar man creatures. I can only assume the image shared was supposed to represent a Gula'Lu," Moltar said as they walked along the ice tunnel. "They also shared their distaste for man flesh, but have been forced to protect themselves."

"I imagine their fur would be useful in this bitter cold. That explains some of the tales of the ice eating up travelers." Orian shivered and wrapped himself in his cloak against the cold air.

As they walked along the icy tunnels, Shuran felt a wave of unease. He sensed as though he were being watched, but felt he was not being scried. He double-checked his mental shields, just to make certain he could not be attacked mentally.

"Did you see that!" Orian said and pointed to the ice wall.

"I see nothing. What was it?" Shuran replied.

Orian squinted and shook his head. "Nothing… I must have imagined it, or it was my own reflection distorted in the ice."

Shuran was in the lead as they exited the ice cavern, and entered the crevasse maze. The great warren was made from the broken glacier that covered the lands north of the Orenthal Mountains. Hundreds of fissures spread through the massive ice sheet, creating a natural labyrinth. Wind blew in gusts at un-even intervals as bursts of icy air from high above funneled down through the narrow passages.

"Perhaps now we could make for the surface of the glaciers and take flight?" Shuran suggested to Moltar.

Moltar suggested they climb atop his back and strap in so he could take to the air. He struggled to leap from the ground as the wind seemed to protest his attempts. Moltar's strength was no match for the force of the air pushing back on his massive body and wings. An alternate attempt to climb the ice proved equally fruitless, as his claws could not gain purchase on the slick walls.

"I am sorry Lugaldur, I cannot achieve a grip on the ice nor take to the air. Perhaps further on it may be possible." Moltar bowed his head at disappointing his bonded.

"Do not blame yourself beloved drakkon, it is I who has neither knowledge nor understanding required to manipulate the ice or air," Shuran answered with a loving look and scratch of Moltar's neck. "We will forge ahead and perhaps find a better place to head to the top of the glacier."

Off they set down the myriad of paths, looking for the best way to reach the end of the ice fields. They had no means of knowing which paths to take in most circumstances. Shuran would reach out with his shi, but more often than not, he could not sense anything beyond more paths. They wandered for two days, and yet gained little advance in their march north. Often times they would encounter a dead end, forcing them to retrace their steps and try another path.

Although it was well into the evening, Utu was still clutching to the sky and shining a dim light over the North. The light cast eerie shadows throughout the crevasses, as it hit every wall of ice. Wind blew into the passes, carrying ice crystals that glittered in the struggling rays of light, adding to the odd feeling settling upon each traveler. The feeling of being watched strengthened.

Shuran and Orian had dismounted Moltar so he might heat himself without burning them. They each cast warming shields around themselves as well. They traveled on far enough to finally come across a clearing in the labyrinth. The sight before them was daunting. Uncountable paths led out of the clearing. At this point in the journey, they were so turned around it was impossible to decide which route to take.

As they entered the clearing, Moltar took to a fast run once Shuran and Orian climbed upon his back and strapped themselves secure. He did not think to explain what he was about. Head low and wings tucked tight against his body, he ran along the edges and hugged the walls. He gained speed as he ran with the swirl of wind and started for an updraft of wind. He leapt into the air and whipped his wings out in a sudden motion and gained lift. That is when they were assaulted by more than the winds and ice.

Chapter Eight

Aknard in his leading magurmu passed the boundary of the deterring spell that covered Durangug. Seven additional airships followed his descent into the clearing where Codger stood directing them. As they landed, each ship's crew lowered long poles from the sides of the vessels and secured them into a brace. Each pole angled down to the ground and once locked into the braces, provided a means of stabilizing the ships into a dry dock.

"Very clever, you old pirate!" Codger exclaimed as he admired the addition to the plans he gave Aknard. "I will have to copy that little addition."

"I can have my crew work it into your vessel while we are here." Aknard clasped Codger's hand in greeting and gladly accepted the tankard of ale offered to him. "Now, where are these little death bombs I been hearin' 'bout?"

"Moona has a good number ready, but there is much work to do." Codger pointed the way toward Moona's workshop.

Codger took Aknard and a select number of dwarves and smugglers to the ruined tower, where Moona had set up an assembly room for the weapons. Since the others would not be allowed to enter the Vault, they needed a sheltered area to do their work. Moona had been using earth essence, powered by crystal, to call more sand from the far shores. She had a great number of awaiting glass containers.

"Is this all the help you brought!" Moona screeched as she exited the tower.

"Easy Moony girl! The others are working on adding a portable dry dock to the Mellamu Nanna," Codger answered.

"Fiddle-farts! Well, don' just stand there! You men and dwarves follow me and do as I tell ya!" Moona set all those present to work. She setup stations for men to work at, around the tower outer walls. She had a brewing table in the center of the space, where she made the ingredients for the devices.

Once each man knew their part, assembly began in earnest. More workers came in after they completed fitting the Mellamu Nanna with a mobile dry dock. They were eager to test the padiri'bur on the trolls that passed the area just that morning.

They worked through the night and well into the day following. All the magurmu were full to capacity of padiri'bur and a stockpile was left in the tower to later be taken into the Vault.

Moona busied herself making as many padiri'bur as possible. She did this in part to prepare for the inevitable battles ahead; she also did so out of worry that there had been no word from Shuran.

Gregoran assured Moona that Shuran would be fine, although he could not connect mentally, he could still sense his shi on the edges of his own mind. The link of the Zidu'Si not only joined their abilities to the Shin'Ar, but also his mind.

***

Shuran was alone when he awoke. His vision was blurred and he could not move. His body was pinned against a wall of ice where his arms and legs were encased in ice, holding him firm. A panic took over him. He could not clearly see his surroundings. He could not locate Moltar and Orian. He could not sense them or anything else. He attempted to call fire to melt the ice; it was fruitless.

"It stirs," hissed a deep and menacing voice.

"Who is there?" Shuran asked.

"You do not belong here, your kind agreed long ago to leave us and our land untouched."

"What do you mean?" Shuran was confused, but his vision was clearing.

"Your molestation of Ersetu has unsettled our home. Have you come to answer for the crimes of your kind?"

"My kind? I do not understand. Who are you?" Shuran could now see the being before him.

Shuran was looking into the face of what appeared as an ice sculpture. The ice creature was not alone. There were hundreds of the same creatures filling the clearing that he, Moltar, and Orian had entered. They took varying shapes and sizes. Some resembled men, others were shaped like animals and still others, beasts Shuran had never encountered or heard of but they all had the same yellow glowing eyes.

"Do not feign ignorance. Though you are young, we feel the mark upon you. Our home has been falling and it is the makers who are to blame. You shall stand in judgement!"

"Where are my companions?" Shuran demanded.

"They will stand in judgement with you."

The ice beings stood apart to clear the view for Shuran. He saw Moltar and Orian both completely encased in ice on the other side of the clearing.

"What have you done? We have not attacked or molested you. We only wish to find the Gula'Lu." Shuran shouted as tears began to turn to ice as they fell from his eyes.

One of the ice creatures moved forward to examine the frozen tears. The ice creature raised its hand to Shuran's face and collected a tear as it fell. It took the tear in its palm and looked upon it closely before moving back to continue studying the small symbol of emotion.

"The Gula'Lu are not here, they respect our home and do nothing to destroy. They are not like the rest. You must answer for the damage to our home."

Shuran was beyond confused, he was defeated. He did not understand what was happening. He could not call upon fire element, electric, or earth. He could not reach out with his link to the Zidu'Si or his bond with Moltar. He could only assume that the creatures before him somehow prevented his abilities.

"What are you?" Shuran asked.

"Do not speak an insult upon us. The Tal'Ba-ad will not continue to allow you to destroy our home as you poison Ersetu with your taint, Telukukal!" The lead Tal'Ba-ad now stood inches from Shuran's face.

"I am not Telukukal, they have been gone for thousands of years. I am only new to the world."

"LIES!" The Tal'Ba-ad raised its frozen hand to strike Shuran. It was stopped by the Tal'Ba-ad that gathered Shuran's tear.

"Hold! There is something here," it said, showing the tear to its comrade.

"What is this? We have no concern for displays-" It halted as it stared into the tear that sparkled in the palm of its comrade. "What is this concern you show for a beast and an elf man?"

"They are my friends, my bonded, and my Zidu'Si," Shuran answered.

"ZIDU'SI! Then you admit you are Telukukal!"

"No, I am newly birthed and only now rebuilding the Zidu'Si, so we might defeat the Shadow and restore balance to Ersetu." Shuran now spoke with an urgency he hoped registered with the Tal'Ba-ad.

Shuran conversed with the Tal'Ba-ad leader for some time. The Tal'Ba-ad spoke of the Telukukal and their masters causing Ersetu to become poisoned and begin a pattern of destruction. Shuran talked of the prophecy and his part in it. He explained how one sister was sacrificed and another turned to a tool of the Shadow. He continued to explain all that had been happening in Aurderia.

"If you speak true then you cannot be of the Telukukal, but you bare the mark."

"What is this mark you speak of? Is it something to do with my abilities of seven bloodlines?" Shuran inquired.

"No, there is more to you than that young asipu, we know not what it means." The Tal'Ba-ad leader lifted his hands and Shuran was freed from the ice.

Shuran quickly slowed his fall from the height he was held, with his limited abilities with air. He immediately ran to his friends, who were freed at the same time. Shuran checked after them as they awoke from a sleep of sorts. He then returned to the Tal'Ba-ad leader.

"Your race, the Tal'Ba-ad, it means ice demon. Are you truly demons?" Shuran asked.

"Demons?" It laughed. "Not in the sense that your kind has come to understand. We are not of the making of your Gods, we were here before they came from the heavens. It was the tampering of the Telukukal that caused us to take form."

"Why do you call yourself demons then?"

"That name was given us by those before you, we have no need of titles, but we rallied against their deeds so they gave us this name."

"I am sorry for what has happened to your home. I cannot speak on the intentions of the Telukukal or their masters, but I know they were only attempting to fix what happened to cause the balance of Ersetu to break," Shuran said.

"We shall see if your intentions stand true, we wish nothing more than to see the Shadow purged of the darkness and the Emmuku'Gu drained of the light."

"I do not understand?" Shuran questioned.

"We believe you will understand in time once you understand what you truly are."

Before Shuran could question further, the Tal'Ba-ad leader motioned for some of his brethren to come forward with Moltar and Orian.

"When the time comes, young Shin'Ar, the Tal'Ba-ad will stand by your side. But do not take over long, we wish our lands restored so we might return to our true form and be free of this corporeal existence."

Shuran nodded. He could not think of anything more to say at the moment since he was still unsure what all had truly happened. He climbed upon Moltar and drew power from the now reconnected Vault and refreshed Moltar's and Orian's continence.

"Can you assist in telling us the correct path to find the Gula'Lu?"

Shuran asked.

"We are bound by trust to not reveal their home but we can assist in getting you to the air. You will easily find your way should you continue north."

The Tal'Ba-ad all converged into a bridge of ice that rose well beyond the surface of the glacier.

Moltar did not waste time with good-byes. He charged forward full speed and climbed the ice-bridge into the air. Once at the apex of the frozen structure, Moltar leapt high into the air and spread his massive wings. He immediately caught the wind and raised high into the sky.

Shuran raised a shield of warmth around them as they headed north into the cold thin air. He afforded a glance back at the clearing to find it gone, replaced by a solid sheet of ice. As a question formed in his mind, a voice intruded upon his thoughts.

"Remember Shin'Ar, though we reside in the Frozen North, the whole of Ersetu is our home. Keep to your task and we shall stand by your side. Not all 'demons' serve the Shadow."

"Shin'Ar, what exactly happened back there? I recall Moltar attempting to take flight and then coldness surrounding me." Orian asked.

"You both got turned into ice sculptures and I was questioned by the Tal'Ba-ad," Shuran said matter-of-factly.

Shuran explained what occurred during their time spent on ice. He spoke of everything that was shared except the part where he was told he was something more than a seven bloodline born man. It was not the first time he felt there was more to his being, but until he knew something for certain, he would not speak of it openly.

The three of them flew for several hours before they finally caught sight to the end of the glacier. Beyond the ice was a vast forest of pine trees that spread out along the entire horizon. They had to decide where to turn in order to seek out the Gula'Lu. Their decision became clear when Moltar called out a depression in the landscape that seemed out of place.

Moltar angled toward the area but was becoming tired. He signaled to Shuran he needed rest and then headed to the ground so they might rest and have a meal.

"I am sorry Lugaldur, but I am hungered beyond belief and I must have true rest aside from strength from the Vault or crystals."

"I understand my friend, perhaps there is game in these woods that might provide a decent meal. I think it also past time I send word back to our family," Shuran responded with a worried look.

"Shall I have a needle ready to sew your ear back on Shin'Ar?" Orian joked, knowing Moona would chew the appendage off.

Shuran just offered a forced laugh in response.

Shuran completed his communication with Moona and Mallick. The distance was too great to have full mental communication so he used the communication crystal. He also attempted to contact Andra but received no response, which was unsettling. Shuran then called forth some food items to stave off immediate hunger, while Moltar stalked some wild game he sniffed out.

The group ate well and rested far into that evening. The temperatures were still cold but not intolerable. Shuran and Orian laid their bedrolls next to Moltar, who lowered his wing to cover them and his internal heat kept them comfortable throughout the night.

Chapter Nine

The Great Hall in the New Draven Commons House was full to capacity as citizens from all over Aurderia arrived to seek an audience with the new Great Council. For uncounted centuries, the council met in private and kept themselves unidentified by the people they ruled over. Now that they no longer hid themselves away, people arrived in the hundreds both out of curiosity and outrage over what was becoming of their lands.

Farmers, crafters, and tradesmen alike were fighting to make themselves heard. They all had lost much, not only to the seizure of goods by the Council, but also from the destruction by soldiers and death walkers.

"We demand restitution!" shouted one group.

"What are you doing to protect the common folk?" screamed another.

This went on for many minutes before the Council finally appeared and took their seats upon the dais. Vardoran took the center seat, with

Salmetu and Penelle seated to each side. Scholars filled the remaining seats from what remained of the Academy. The member from Drakkfoth, the Baron Fallon De Drakk was no longer serving the council, and Nagutan had yet to resurface. The two empty seats did not go unnoticed.

The shouting in the hall became that much more fervent. Calls for full council and re-appointments were the loudest protests amongst those in attendance.

Vardoran raised his hand in a waving gesture and called them to silence, "Nime'Gar!" he spoke, and the room went quiet. "You shall show patience and respect when in the presence of the Great Council."

"We have allowed this audience at our pleasure and shall call it at an end should outbursts continue!" Salmetu spoke in an echoed and irascible voice.

Vardoran and Penelle both glanced at Salmetu with caution. Her moods had been quick to ire and she was showing signs of instability. Now was not the time to alienate the commoners, they needed them.

"We, the Great Council, understand the hardships that you are all facing. We all share a common threat to our way of life and the prosperous times that have favored Aurderia for centuries," Vardoran began. "There has been a great undoing of the balance, this much is widely known. What has been kept from you all is a name to the scourge behind these difficult times."

"An Anzillu, named Shuran of Rivenwood, calls himself Shin'Ar Reborn. He has been building a force called the Zidu'Si, with members from the Drakkian, Elf, and Dwarf races of man. These abominations, wish to usurp the Council and destroy our way of life. They wish nothing more than to erase humanity from the face of Ersetu!"

Cries of panic and outrage filled the hall and rose the level of urgency for action. The people of Aurderia were beginning to react to Vardoran's words. He had them eating from his palm and would see that he turned them all against the Zidu'Si and the non-human races.

"You see no Drakkian Council member among us. No Dwarf of Elf stands with the council to aid us against the threat of the Anzillu," Salmetu added.

Vardoran nodded to Salmetu, but he held a look that requested she remain silent. The look she returned was of no comfort to him. He continued on to speak of the atrocities committed by the Zidu'Si. He blamed them for the destruction of entire settlements and villages. He spoke of them casting human shi from their bodies and creating walking dead to use as soldiers.

One man spoke with nervousness coating his words. "I have seen these death walkers you speak of. They destroyed Elmwood, but they marched with soldiers of the Land's Guard. I never saw any Elf, Dwarf, or Drakkian amongst them!"

"You see, they turn humans into their tools so they might spare their own kind. They hide in the background and turn us against one another!" Penelle reassured the man.

"Then how do you explain the soldiers, and it was the Inquisitors as well that came to take away our weavers long before these death walkers!" The man was getting more courageous with his words.

"Another trick of the Anzillu scum. They made you believe you saw the Inquisitors. They only wanted to strip you of your Essence users, to leave you weakened of magic," Penelle added.

"I do not believe you! The Council has taken our strongest weavers for as long as any can remember. How do we know it is not you behind this?" Those were the last words the man would ever speak.

Salmetu stood in a fury and held her hands out toward the man. "KAR SHI!" she screamed.

The man began to convulse as his shi was pulled from his body. It paused briefly and turned to watch its own body fall to the ground before being absorbed by Salmetu's Chaos fed rage.

The audience chamber had become deathly silent for one fleeting moment before pandemonium broke loose and the commoners scrambled to get away from the council. Many people had escaped before the hall was sealed off by magical means. Just as many were trampled under foot by those seeking escape. The many who remained were corralled and taken to the dungeons at the Academy. They would become the newest recruits to Salmetu's army of the dead.

"Are you mad?" Penelle asked when the chamber had been cleared.

"Watch your tone kashshaptu!" Salmetu threatened. She did not like Penelle in the least and cared even less for her challenge.

"She is correct in her assessment Salmetu. What were you thinking? We had them where we needed them. Now they are lost to us!" Vardoran was angry and showing it without concern for Salmetu's volatile state.

"The people are required to provide goods and services, the death walkers are of no use in such things. If our goal is to eradicate all non-humans from Aurderia, then we should not deplete our own people," said one of the Academy members.

"Our battle is against the enemies of the Order, we may have allies among the other races, we simply do not wish them to interfere with Aurderian affairs," Vardoran pointed out.

"They are all nothing! We shall do as we please. Do not question me again!" Salmetu said pointedly before disappearing in a cloud of brackish smoke.

Vardoran and the other members of the Great Council were dumb stricken. They mumbled and became uneasy as they began gathering their things in preparation to leave the chamber. Salmetu was becoming increasingly unstable and thus escaping Vardoran's control.

A messenger arrived for Vardoran and presented him with a scroll bearing the seal of Drakkfoth. He opened the parchment to read the message it contained. When he finished, he smiled and set the scroll alight before turning back to the chamber.

"I am concerned at her stability Vardoran," Penelle said as the other members of Council left hurriedly. "She grows more unstable as the days pass. I fear that soon she will be without any sense of control."

Vardoran smiled calmly and approached Penelle. "I see it, but I believe I know how to focus her and get her back on task," he began. "What we need are spies among the races to bring us news and help guide our actions. Salmetu has already expressed managing some work amongst the Dwarves. What we need is to infiltrate the Elves and Drakkians."

"What work was done with the Dwarves?"

"She did not elaborate. All she said was that the seed of distrust and dissension has been sewn." Vardoran went to the side table and poured two goblets of wine. He returned to Penelle and offered her one as he continued. "I have allies still, among the Drakkians, and will use them for information and a little surprise I have in mind. Can you work on the Elves?" he asked Penelle.

"I can see what I can do. What do you have in mind for the Drakkians?"

"I plan on stealing away the one prize they think we do not know about. I will have Salmetu's mother captured and brought here, as our… guest." A wicked smile spread across his face.

"But I thought the mother died giving birth?"

"We all thought this, but the Baron had her moved when the ceremony ended. He and his kind nursed her back to health. I shall bring her here to temper the child within Salmetu so we can get the priestess to focus on matters without killing everyone." Vardoran finished his wine and went to pour another. "I find it an added bonus that we will take away Shuran's mother so soon after he has been reunited!" Vardoran laughed.

"Do you think it wise to toy with the Shin'Ar emotionally? We are already without knowledge or comprehension of what he can wield. This might make bad matters even worse!"

"If he was so terribly powerful, we would not be having this conversation. He spends most of his time hiding like the child he truly is," Vardoran stated.

"Is he hiding or getting stronger?" Penelle questioned.

"I do not know, no one yet seems to know what he is doing or where he calls home. But I know someone who might, and she will soon be here to answer our questions. One way or another we will have the information we require and a handle on Salmetu."

What Vardoran implied concerned Penelle. She had her own agenda and although Sulura played no key role in those plans, harm to her could cause more problems than good. She had hoped to move forward with her own plans, but now she had to keep a watch on the boiling cauldron brewing in New Draven.

An odd and sickly looking black cat sat below the table watching as Vardoran and Penelle left the room. It waited as they exited the room before padding out from its hiding place and following out behind them. The strange little creature navigated the labyrinth of long halls, following the instructions of its master.

***

Salmetu paced her room mumbling to herself. She seemed at odds with herself. She was not bothered by her display in the Great Hall, but she was not pleased with the outcome.

"Priestess, you will wear a hole in that rug should you continue pacing so," said Bastien with Telalsu's voice. He still had difficulty controlling the will of the young man, but he was gaining a stronger hold as the days past.

Salmetu turned at him with daggers in her eyes before her expression softened and she approached him to stroke his hair.

"It is difficult dealing with inferiors my pet. Moreover, I have conflicted feelings about what to do about Shuran as well. Vardoran and the Council are yet another agitation I am burdened with daily."

"If they vex you then eliminate them," Telalsu suggested.

"Oh, you are a wicked thing!" she giggled. "How refreshing, but alas I have need for them yet. There is more I need to learn and as unfortunate as it may be, Vardoran is key to my gain in knowledge."

"And Penelle, she can be of no use, can she?"

"Her part is to keep Vardoran's lustful old eyes distracted from my form. She currently has his attention in that respect and it suits me. Once she is no longer playing that role, I will do away with her."

"I have a suggestion on hastening your learning should you wish to hear me, my Queen," Telalsu spoke with a devious tone.

Salmetu listened to Telalsu's suggestion and delighted in what he told her. The two of them stood and left the room.

One of the Council members backed into the shadows of the hallway where he had been listening to their conversation. Behind him sat the emaciated black cat with an oversized head and red eyes, silently watching and listening.

***

All throughout Ersetu, the ground began to tremble. A great disturbance in the balance opened chasms and swallowed large areas of earth. The Foresworn Territories were hit as hard as any other part of the world.

"NABUSA! The trembling grows worse as the days progress. What is your council?" inquired a fearful Guardian.

"Gather the rest of your Guardians back to the Territories, I have work for you. I shall call you to action in the coming weeks," she answered calmly. "Send Andra to see me immediately."

Nabusa sat alone in her dark chamber staring at a large mirrored table. Images raced across the mirror, showing her the destruction taking place around much of the world. She wore a look of consternation as the various scenes played across the scrying glass. Something was acting upon the balance that she did not understand.

Her visions usually provided her insight into the workings of the Essence, but she was not receiving them as of late. Nabusa resorted to scrying spells and information gathered from the Guardians. There was once a time when she would have visions without the slightest effort, at times it would feel as though they were meant for her intentionally. She always assumed the Gods wanted her to enact their will, but lately the Gods did not send her instructions.

Andra arrived to find Nabusa unsuccessfully scrying for images of Shuran and Salmetu. He had been prohibited from returning to Aurderia until Nabusa wished it. He was torn between loyalty to the Foresworn, and the love he came to feel for Shuran and his motley crew.

"You wished to see me?" he asked as he slowly approached Nabusa.

"Come. Sit with me my child, there is much to discuss," she answered without looking up from her scrying. Frustrated, she finally abandoned her attempts at locating the two objects of her attention and turned to Andra with a motherly look. "It is time you return to Shuran's side my child."

"Forgive my ignorance, but why now? I thought my part in your vision was at an end?" he asked without expression.

"Things change Andra, and I am afraid that we are losing our hold on Shuran. He is lost to my vision and soon I fear his own desires will prevent him fulfilling the prophecy."

"I do not understand. Have the visions changed?"

"I no longer receive visions of the prophecy. This is not necessarily an ill omen, but coupled with my inability to locate Shuran or his sister Salmetu, I must have answers. You will use his trust to get the information we desire." She turned from him a moment to retrieve a package from her side. She unwrapped the package to reveal the pendant Shuran had made and given Andra containing a communication stone. The stone was flashing.

"It would appear that the boy has been trying to reach you. You will go to him, but do not answer his call until you are back within Aurderian borders."

"And what do I say of my failure to respond?" Andra asked.

"You were on business of the Guardians, that will be sufficient and not entirely deceitful."

Andra accepted the pendant that Nabusa had insisted he hand over when he last returned home. She had deemed it too risky to communicate with the boy while back in the Territories, for fear he would be able to locate their hidden city. Andra was not certain what it was all about, but he felt he was not being given all the information on what Nabusa had planned for Shuran. More than the fulfillment of prophecy was at stake, she just did not share with him what else that meant.

After Andra had left, another guardian entered from the darkness of the room.

"Follow Andra but do not be discovered. I want regular reports on his movements. I need to make certain there is no faltering in loyalties to the Foresworn," Nabusa told the Guardian, as she handed him a satchel.

The Guardian peered inside and gasped at what he saw inside.

"You will do what must be done if it becomes necessary." At Nabusa's final words, the Guardian left her. Nabusa went back to her fruitless attempts at scrying the twins of prophecy.

Chapter Ten

"Get those boats in the air!" Aknard called from the deck of his own airborne magurmu. We be wantin' to circle around and take on some trolls from south o' their advance."

"Are you sure this wise?" Mallick asked Codger as they looked on from the ground.

"I don' like stirrin' trouble any more 'en the next dwarf, but them trolls is too bent on gettin' south which means they march for New Draven!" Codger answered.

"No, that is not what I mean, sending Moona off on Aknard's magurmu with them is what I refer to."

"Oh, she insisted on seeing her work in action for a test run. 'Sides she can look after herself."

"It is not Moona I am concerned for," Mallick said smiling as he watched Moona barking orders and taking charge of Aknard's vessel.

Aknard stood there, mouth agape while Moona took over.

"Serves the ol' pirate right. Should o' never spoke on how grouchy she was this morn." Codger laughed along with Mallick as they turned to head back to the tower.

Codger, Mallick, and Gregoran worked on moving the stockpile of padiri'bur into the Vault. They would spend most of the day at the task while Jade hunted game and rested from the nights spent patrolling and keeping watch on the troll's movements.

Once they completed moving all the Padiri'bur, Mallick went back to researching what he could about the Rings of Knowledge and attempt to track down the missing band that completed the pair. He found himself wishing, not for the first time, that the Zidu'Si of old had kept personal journals and left them at Durangug. Without second hand knowledge from personal recordings, there was likely no way he could track down the absent mate to his ring.

The ring gave him trouble at times and he felt as though something was missing. So many questions remained unanswered, least of which was what else the ring might be used for. Mallick often thought that, though knowledge was power, an Essence created ring was somehow overkill when it came to gaining wisdom. He tried many times to push spells through the ring, only to end up burning his finger. He continued his research and scanning the library for answers that eluded him.

***

The magurmu caught up with the trolls a few hours after they departed Durangug. The fleet intentionally flew out over the Great Sea and out of sight from the trolls so they might overtake them and approach from the South. This was done in order to prevent them or any weavers watching their movements, of suspecting they came from anywhere other than the south of Aurderia.

The ships were cloaked as they approached the trolls and spread out just in front and above the advancing army. Man and dwarf alike gathered on the decks of their respective flying ships, ready with padiri'bur in hand.

Moona had seen fit to make certain that there was at least one weaver aboard each vessel. It was more than just luck that Aknard had employed human weavers into his merry band of smugglers, he had told her. 'Having skills in Essence are vital to successful piracy in Aurderia'.

The weavers were necessary to kindle the first portion of the two trigger devices. The second would trigger automatically when in close proximity to the darkness or those influenced by it.

Moona only hoped that the trolls were touched by dark; otherwise it meant they were just nasty mindless creatures that only followed their own desires. Somehow she was not overly worried about that possibility though as the trolls were answering to something in the South, and the only thing to the south was the Order of Chaos and those they controlled or enslaved.

The first volley of the bombs proved effective beyond what Moona calculated. A sudden rocking of the magurmu meant they were far too close to the ground and the detonation zone of the blast. The ships all quickly lifted higher into the sky while sending the next volley. Their lift was too slow, however. The blast still rocked a few ships and thus disturbed the cloak that enveloped them.

Many of the trolls had been looking up and saw the ripple in the sky from where the bombs originated. The creatures had a target now themselves, and began slinging twisted gug stones at one of the magurmu. They hit their mark.

The shields had been down to allow them to drop the padiri'bur. This is what allowed the gug to not only hit the magurmu, but it broke the spell cloaking them, exposing the vessel to more volleys. Rising the shield did not work but fortunately the gugtu lined hull repelled the twisted stones and prevented them breaching the vessel beyond the outer hull. The ships all headed out to sea and retreat since one of them was exposed. The crew took a final opportunity to throw padiri'bur down, but could not stay to witness the results.

***

"How many lost?" asked the crone.

"Numbers are still coming in from the scryers, but it would appear the flying ships managed to take out at least four hundred of our trolls," answered her sister witch.

"What is this spell work used to attack our servants? And where did those magurmu come from?"

"We do not know the answer to either, but it is safe to assume they are aligned with the boy of prophecy. The same flying vessels were reported at the battle of Drakkfoth, but they did not have cloaks or this new weapon at that time."

"Get me Penelle, our sister needs to work on getting us free of this swamp! She takes too long!" The old crone was Penelle's stand in coven leader while she worked her way into the Great Council. The witches grew restless waiting for her return. The fact Penelle had not communicated in weeks was not helping settle their anxiety.

The sitting Grand Kashshaptu took it upon herself to call the trolls from their Northern forest homes. Now that the kashshaptu were so close to freedom from their swampy prison, they were growing ever more restless with each passing day. A witch approached the crone with a scrying mirror and handed it to her. Penelle was reflected within the glass.

"What is so important you must interrupt me? Now is not a good time, things are falling apart with the Council!" Penelle snapped.

"You have not communicated in many weeks sister, we grow worried at your progress."

"Things have been tumultuous to say the least. The priestess grows unstable and I fear unable to serve our purpose." Penelle could see the look of consternation upon her sister witches face. "Not to fear; however, I have discovered someone else who may be persuaded to provide a cure to the curse," Penelle reassured her sister.

"There is more. Our trolls were attacked during their march south from the Northern forests beyond the Orenthal."

"And who attacked them?" Penelle demanded.

"They flew aboard magurmu and released some sort of spelled weapons upon them as they marched. They appear akin to the same flying vessels in league with the Anzillu Shuran," the crone replied.

"This is upsetting, but why are the trolls on the march, they should be awaiting instruction in the North?" Penelle asked realizing they should not be on the march yet.

"They marched at my call. We wish them closer and ready upon your eminent return to the swamps."

Penelle held a neutral expression, but her anger was just below the surface. Her sister kashshaptu was over-stepping her bounds by calling for the return of the trolls. It was not yet time for them to come to the

76

aid of their mistresses. This bold move may be a reaction of fear or anticipation as the second sister stated, but Penelle suspected there was another motive behind her actions.

Penelle breathed deep before responding, "I will contact you soon with news on my progress with this new possible source for a cure." She immediately closed the spell in her mirror, just as a knock came to her door.

"Yes, who is there pounding incessantly upon my chamber door?" she asked standing in a fury and flinging her mirror onto the lounging bench.

"Madam Penelle, I have some information that you may be interested in," the man said from outside the door.

Penelle recognized the voice, but she could not place it. She crossed the sitting room and opened the door to find a councilman from the Academy holding a sickly black cat.

"What is so urgent that you visit my private chambers, Councilman?"

"It involves the odd behavior of the Councilwoman, Salmetu, the Priestess," he answered in a hushed tone, stressing the reference to 'the Priestess'.

The Councilman addressing Salmetu as 'the Priestess' threw Penelle. It was not common knowledge to those outside the Order of Chaos, Salmetu's true purpose and role in the new established ruling class. This man from the Academy was a member of the Great Council, but to her knowledge, not a member of the Order. Still, there was something about this man that struck a cord of familiarity she could not explain.

"What is it you wish to tell me?" she asked as she offered the man entrance to her room.

"I cannot stay madam, but I will say that if you wish proof of the instability of the young woman, you need only enter the deepest level of the Academy catacombs." The man handed her a piece of paper and pointed out the location on a drawn diagram. "There you will find a crack in the foundation where the Priestess visits as we speak." He turned to leave.

"What is it you are saying?" Penelle said, studying the drawing and somewhat familiar scroll written upon it.

"Go there and see for yourself. It will become clear when you witness the corruption for yourself." With this statement, the man quickly strode down the hall. The black cat followed closely behind.

Penelle walked after him. When she rounded the corner he had just turned, he was nowhere in sight. Her eyes narrowed as she headed back to her room. Something burned on the edges of her mind about this man, but she could not place it. She quickly dismissed the itching feeling and put it out of her mind. She had to see for herself if what he spoke of was true. She left the building and head to the Academy to investigate the catacombs.

Penelle took up the map again and studied it before committing it to memory and discarding it into the fireplace. With a determined look, she quickly changed her voluminous skirts for something less obtrusive and headed down into the dark and gloomy bowels of the Academy.

***

Salmetu stood before a crack in the floor. She could see that this was a new break in the foundation, likely caused by the latest series of earthquakes. As she moved closer to the fissure, she began to feel the darkness emanating from deep within. It called to her. It was familiar to her. She longed to connect with it.

"It calls to you Priestess. You feel it, I can see it in your eyes," Telalsu said.

Salmetu did not look up as she nodded in response. The familiar feeling of what lie within the crack was unmistakeable. She knew by instinct that she already had a link to this darkness.

"What is it, pure Chaos? I feel connected to it," she asked.

"Not Chaos, my Queen, pure shadow. Shadow is the master of Chaos and the ultimate power. It is yours for the taking." Telalsu was doing his best to persuade Salmetu to move closer to the source.

Salmetu's eyes grew wide as she knelt down and the shadowy fog lifted from the abyssal darkness and drifted up to her. It began to surround her. Salmetu took in a breath and the wispy darkness filled her. She reveled in the cold emptiness that overtook her. All the conflicts she had recently dealt with, seemed trivial compared to what she now felt.

Telalsu stood watching the Priestess taking in the Shadow. This had been part of his task since he was summoned forth by Vardoran. The old fool believed he called the demon forth, when all he did was open a door allowing the demon warrior to enter the corporeal realm to do his true masters' bidding.

Salmetu's eyes went completely black. She tilted back her head and let loose a scream of pure ecstasy. When finally her cries abated, she gathered her composure and took in her surroundings. She stood and offered her hand to Telalsu, who bent knee and kissed her knuckles.

"It is good to see you again, faithful servant," voices came from Salmetu's mouth. She bid Telalsu sans Bastien stand, and escort her back to her chambers where she might prepare for what was to transpire.

Penelle stood in the darkness, cloaking her presence as the demon possessed Bastien and whatever now wore Salmetu as a vessel, walked down the halls past her. She had never been a zealot among the Order of Chaos, nor had she favored anything that the Followers of Light represented, but what she felt as they passed was completely void of anything earthly. A coldness shivered through her body as utter dread filled her. She took a final look at the crack in the floor then quietly headed back to her rooms.

As she left the lowest levels, the black cat appeared from the dark and watched her leave. After licking its paw and wiping its face, the cat returned to its imp form and ran off in the opposite direction.

Chapter Eleven

◁𐎛

Shuran was the first to awaken in the early hours of the morning. He heard the unmistakable sound of branches snapping under weight of something moving about the forest. It was not long before Moltar stirred, and when he stood at the sound of more cracking in the distance, he unceremoniously dumped Orian from his nestled position into the bramble off to his side.

Orian stumbled free of the bushes and expected laughter from Shuran and Moltar at his situation, but found them intently listening to the woods. Being a creature of the woodlands himself, he knew to stand still as possible and wait. His wait was not long before the sounds returned.

"Something watches us at a distance, Shin'Ar," Orian whispered.

"How close?"

"One-hundred-twenty perhaps thirty paces off to the South," Orian answered.

Shuran began to peer off into the woods, but saw nothing.

Orian patted him on the shoulder and indicated he should look the opposite direction.

"You forget we traveled past the northern-most point of the world Shin'Ar. North has now become south."

Shuran refocused his attention to the south of their position. He could not see anything, but he felt that Moltar could since his eyesight was measurably better than any man, even elf.

Moltar mentally indicated that they pack up their things and mount his saddled back.

Shuran chose not to waste time, he sent their unpacked items to the vault, and they climbed atop Moltar, and then took to the sky.

They flew low over the tops of the trees in the direction they heard the noises. After circling the area for several minutes, they came in for a tight landing between the trees. Moltar's bulk took more than a few branches down with them as they landed.

There was no sign of their observer aside from the broken branches they found. Orian went to look at them while Shuran tended to Moltar's minor cuts to his body and wings from the landing.

Orian returned quickly with one of the broken limbs. He showed it to Shuran and saw that his Shin'Ar noticed the same thing he had. The sizable tree limb was broken intentionally. Someone was trying to draw them to this area.

"Is there any other sign of people around?" Shuran asked.

"Not that I can tell Shin'Ar. They appear to have left the area," Orian answered.

"They went that way," Moltar said pointing with his head. "I can still smell her."

"You can tell it was a female?" Shuran asked. "How?"

"There are differences between male and female in all man races, Lugaldur," Moltar said winking at Orian. "I can tell."

They all walked off in the direction Moltar indicated. They tracked the movements and scent of the female to a massive outcropping of boulders. As they made their way around the boulders, they found the entrance to a cave. It seemed artificially created as they recognized unmistakeable tool marks.

"Do you suppose she went in there?" Orian asked.

"Smells like it," Moltar said.

Shuran and Orian approached the entrance. Moltar would not fit so he would stay outside and watch the entrance and guard their back.

"Be careful Lugaldur. I will be unable to get to you without tearing apart these rocks, but I will should you need me."

"I have no doubt you would, my bonded. We shall look inside and return soon."

Shuran and Orian entered the structure to find man-made steps that led down into the ground below the boulders. Orian was about to create an orb of light, when Shuran stopped him. There was a light coming from below, it flickered like flame torches.

They paused at the bottom of the stairs and waited before stepping into the light of the torches they confirmed were illuminating the space before them. They finally left the stairs to find a tunnel leading off into the distance. There were more torches lighting the way down the passage. They also passed a pool of what looked like liquid metal.

Shuran looked into the pool and saw his perfect reflection staring back at him. He felt no heat from the molten metal pool.

"What is that?" Orian asked.

"It is a metal of some kind, but liquid and cool. I have never seen anything like it," Shuran answered. "Have you noticed-" Shuran began while looking up.

"The distance from the floor to ceiling? Yes, I have. It is not like an average man to build tunnels to twice his height," Orian answered.

"Shall we?" Shuran motioned for Orian to lead the way. He then sent Moltar a mental communication of their situation and advised him to wait them out.

Orian led the way down the grand tunnels. They were by no means as sizable as those of the dwarven making in Duranekur, but from the look of it, they were not built as grandiose passages to some royal seat of power for an entire race.

The walls of the tunnel were veined in rich ores of metal. Broken lines of silvery metals, mingled with those of golden, copper, and darker metals of unknown kinds.

"This is odd," Shuran noted.

"What is Shuran Shin'Ar?"

"I thought copper was a patina green in its raw ore state. It appears that all these metals are veining the walls in a refined state." Shuran ignored Orian's incessant use of his formal title.

"I am not knowledgeable in metals but I believe you may be correct."

"Your master is correct elf," came a voice from behind them.

Shuran and Orian turned to find themselves face to hip with a gargantuan woman dressed in the leathers of an odd skin. She looked down at them from nearly twice their own height. Her hair was pulled back behind her head save one lone strand that dropped forward over her furrowed brow. As tall as she was, and dressed as a woodsman, she still gave off a regal beauty that struck Shuran deeply. Her skin shined a silvery luster. He wondered at the use of skin paints or if it was her true skin.

"Pardon me madam, we are not intruding are we? Though I suppose it was you who lured us to this tunnel," Shuran managed to stutter out.

"Ease your concerns young human. You and the elf are in no danger from me. You are expected in the valley. Please continue and we can speak freely on the way." The Gula'Lu woman urged them to continue along the passage. "My name is Daraeszag, but you may call me Dara. I am fifteenth daughter to the forty-fourth wife of King Awilzag," Dara said.

"Forty-fourth wife?" Orian asked.

"Yes, I know so few wives in his long life. He really should consider taking a new one. At least that is what his advisors say. I do not understand the desire to wed myself... Here I go babbling on again. Father always says I need to learn when silence is favored. I just can not help myself sometimes-"

"Pardon me Dara, but I did not get to introduce myself or my companion," Shuran interrupted offering his hand.

"No need Shuran Shin'Ar. You, Orian the Elf, and Moltar the drakkon have been watched for some time now. We have been expecting you since your release from the Tal'Ba-ad," Dara explained. "You will excuse my not receiving your outstretched hand, we Gula'Lu avoid skin contact with outsiders."

Shuran was not certain if this was to avoid contamination from outside illnesses, or simply a slight on people outside their own race.

The three of them had continued on for many hundreds of paces before natural light began to fill the tunnel. Dara followed them from the passage out onto a ledge that overlooked an immense valley. Looking around at the valley slopes, it appeared to Shuran they had thousands of feet more travel ahead of them to reach the valley floor. He sighed heavily at the thought.

"Oh, not to fret young human, we will not be walking down. Follow me if you will." Dara led them off around the corner of the ledge where they were greeted by a large cage of metal and glass.

"Damkianna, what on Ersetu is that!" Orian exclaimed.

Dara just laughed then opened the door and pushed them in as she followed. She closed the door fast behind her and reached for a lever and released it. Instantly the iron cage lurched forward and began gliding along a set of iron made ropes descending into the canopy of trees that grew beyond even the size of those in Entensiama.

Shuran and Orian ran to the sides of the large cage to peer out the glass sealed windows out on the view of the valley.

Dara just laughed at their excitement.

"You laugh as though this was anything less than amazing. It is beyond the grandest feat of Essence wielding I have ever witnessed or read of," Orian expressed.

"This is just a mover car, and a rather old one at that. I do hope it does not stick again," she replied with a grin. "This is nothing new to the Gula'Lu, we have made use of such things for thousands of years."

Dara explained the workings of the cable car system that allowed the Gula'Lu to traverse the vast expanse of their valley. The system used a series of iron towers with spans of steel cables lined with cooper, running between them. The cables anchored into the ground near a source of the Emmuku'Gu, that sent electric charges through the cables and allowed the wheels and pulleys to spin, moving the cars around.

"It is all a bit more complicated, but I am not the one to explain in detail. Our tinkerers are the ones to ask about how they all work." Dara pointed outside to the sky above them. "There is the true masterwork of the Gula'Lu. The mundane shield over the valley." Dara pushed another lever and the car burst forward at such a speed, that Shuran and Orian fell back against the far walls.

Once they steadied themselves, Shuran and Orian moved back to the windows to watch their progress down toward the valley floor.

"What do you mean, I sense no shield?" Shuran asked. Then he noticed the iron framework that spread across the entire valley.

"That is because it is mundane, silly human. It is a series of double view mirrors. From the outside world, they are angled to reflect all the trees surrounding the valley. Unless you were directly over the area and looked down, you would not know it was there. Your flight brought you close to the spot."

"The odd dip we saw in the canopy!" Orian gasped.

Dara nodded affirmatively. "The framework allows for channeling rainwater and air as well."

"Moltar! He will be tearing apart the entrance to the passage by now!" Shuran exclaimed.

"Not to worry, he was gathered as I greeted you and taken on ahead to a more sizable entrance. That is one large drakkon you have there. I did not think they grew to that size," Dara stated.

"They do not normally," Shuran said. "He is only this size due to his bond with me, and is not yet fully grown."

"But you are not a Drakkian, I think what they teach in our classes of outside life is in desperate need of correction," Dara complained.

"Drakkon traditionally will bond only with a full-blooded Drakkian, but I am of seven bloodlines and Moltar chose to bond with me. The unique union produced a stronger, larger, and more powerful drakkon than ever before," Shuran explained.

They continued to share stories of the outside world and Shuran told his part in the prophecy. The trip to the valley floor took over an hour on the cable system. When they finally came to a halt, Shuran saw Moltar hopping from foot to foot, to foot, to foot, waiting for his Lugaldur to exit the iron contraption.

"Lugaldur!" Moltar shouted as he scooped Shuran up with his tail and proceeded to lick his face.

86

"MOLTAR! Easy, I am fine, please place me down," Shuran shouted. Shuran could see Moltar's disappointment at being scolded. "It is all right my beloved, I am happy to see you as well, but we are in the company of the Gula'Lu and must restrain our excitement."

"Your beast seems a bit excitable, he does!" Boomed a voice approaching from a large set of doors to a gate. "Welcome to Edinzabar, Shin'Ar and friends. I am King Awilzag, if you would please follow me, the Elders Council await you within," he said and pointed the way to the gates.

As they walked to the entrance, Awilzag kept observing Moltar. He would walk around him in long strides, looking at every inch of the drakkon.

"You are young yet are you not, drakkon?" Awilzag asked Moltar.

"I am still technically considered a youth among my kind. I will not be fully grown for perhaps twenty years," Moltar answered. He was feeling a bit self-conscious.

"You speak as though you know the drakkon breed, King Awilzag," Shuran inquired.

"I was there when they were first crossbred into what they have become. But it has been quite a long time since I have seen one myself; amazing beasts, and smarter than the average human." Awilzag made his statement without a tone of malice. It seemed as though it were common knowledge. Awilzag resumed his place at the head of the procession.

Shuran noted the same silvery shine to the King's skin that Dara had. His hair was black with streaks of silver throughout. Awilzag's height was a head taller than Dara, but he had the same chiseled frame and thin waist. Shuran could not help but wonder where the tales telling of the strength of Giants came from. He could not imagine these tall, thin people being much stronger than an overly built large human.

The procession arrived in the middle of a vast courtyard. There were hundreds of Gula'Lu awaiting their arrival. The image was surreal. The Gula'Lu were all the same, towering beings, with silvery skin and thin frames. The assembly remained completely quiet as they stood observing Shuran, Orian, and Moltar enter the center of the yard.

The one thing Shuran could not determine was the age of any one of them, not precisely. If what Awilzag said were true of being alive when the drakkon were first cross-bred, then he would be thousands of years old. He did not appear any older than a human in his late prime.

Awilzag must have read the thoughts in Shuran's mind.

"Although we do not age as the other races of man, I assure you we are more ancient than we appear," Awilzag told Shuran. "We are the oldest of the races, first created and we shall be the last to fall."

"I mean no disrespect, but why have you stayed away from the rest of the world for so long? Most do not even believe your kind ever existed."

"That will become clear in time. Should you prove worthy, many things will be explained." Awilzag ended their discussion as he halted before his people that attended their arrival.

"We have brought the man Shuran and his companions before the assembly to test his worth and decide what part we shall play in his prophecy," Awilzag began. "Who shall stand as Geshtu'Bad?"

Long silent moments passed without a response, then Dara stepped forward to answer.

"I shall teach the man our ways. Should he excel and show intelligence he will prove his title, Shin'Ar, before the assembly." Dara glanced down at Shuran and winked.

"So be it!" Awilzag turned to Shuran, nodded, and then walked off between the other Gula'Lu, who simply turned and left.

"Not a talkative bunch," Orian stated.

"We do not get visitors, ever, most simply have no interest in the outside world," Dara pointed out.

"But you are different in that respect?" Shuran asked.

"I am not foolish enough to believe that what is happening outside our lands, will not find its way here in time. The ancient powers at work know where we are and will not simply ignore us." Dara caught herself saying more than she should.

"You speak of the Shadow then?" Shuran inquired.

Dara's silence confirmed the answer Shuran already assumed.

She took them to a large building. It was massive but plain in structure. There were many similar structures throughout the valley. They were framed with beams made of iron. Blocks of hard stone were stacked around the sides to form straight walls and the roof was made of more beans with smaller blocks of equal dimensions slid into channels.

Inside they found beds, a table set with food, and a large pile of white fur in the corner that looked like that of the furry worm creatures.

Dara noticed Shuran looking at the fur. "It is of the Zibu'Mawur, we harvest the pelts and teeth when we find one that has passed from the world. The meat is beyond disgusting. But the fur will keep the cold of the glaciers at bay and the teeth contain special properties passed on from the creatures they eat." Dara indicated they should sit and eat.

"What kinds of properties are in the teeth?" Orian asked.

"All in time my friends. I shall leave you to rest a bit and eat. I will return in two hours time to begin your lessons Shuran. This is so exciting!" Dara spun on her large booted feet and left the building.

"Did that giant girl just skip?" Moltar asked.

Shuran and Orian had to stand on the chairs in order to reach the table as they were half the size of Gula'Lu. Moltar, on the other hand, easily lowered his head and snatched a sizable leg of some sort of roasted beast and settled into a hearty meal.

Chapter Twelve

Dara returned in the two hours she had promised, and she was ready to get started.

"Are you ready Shuran?" Dara asked as she entered the room. "I am afraid Orian and Moltar will not be allowed to follow along in the training, but they are free to explore the valley. Have you rested enough?"

"Better than I have in a long time. For such a short rest, I feel as though I woke from a full night of sleep!" Shuran told her.

"That would be the air. Down here in the deep valley there is a higher level of breathable oxygen than on the surface. We also increase that by having the glass shield over the valley."

"I could fly for days breathing the air in this valley!" Moltar exclaimed. "Orian, let us go for a ride."

Orian shrugged and climbed aboard Moltar, who then lumbered out the doorway getting stuck for a moment when his hind legs got caught. With a squeeze, he finally got through and immediately took to the sky.

"I think he over indulged on the rich meats you provided!" Shuran said with a grin.

Dara looked skeptical.

"Let us be off then. First I will take you to our metal working structure. You will learn the basics of metals and their properties," Dara said as she led him from the building.

"And then?" Shuran asked.

"One step at a time human."

"You do know I am not entirely human, Dara."

"That remains to be seen. Once your lessons are complete, the assembly will judge that and we shall decide whether or not to get involved."

Dara took him to the metal works in relative silence. As they made their way through the forest, Shuran was amazed at the sizes of all the flora and fauna. He suddenly felt small and insignificant. Bushes along the path were loaded with flowers larger than a shield. There were berries growing that were the size of a full-grown man's head. What caught his attention the most was the enormous birds flitting from one flower to the next, drinking up the nectar with tongues longer than his own leg.

"Is everything so big here?" he asked.

"I would ask if everything is so small everywhere else." Dara wore a grin from ear to ear.

Before long they emerged from the forest into a clearing that teamed with activity. Gula'Lu were moving about in an almost orchestrated manner. They entered from one side of the clearing, leading large metal carts that rolled along on rails laid in the ground. Each cart was loaded with chunks of various refined metals.

Dara saw Shuran's questioning looks and began his lessons. She told him how the Gula'Lu attune themselves to the song of the metals. They reach into the ore and coax it out. Metals are very much like everything else on Ersetu. The tiniest of particles makeup everything and only adding or removing a single pair of these particles can drastically change something.

"All metals, save one, have all the same basic properties. They are shiny, have high melting points and are dense. They become malleable, ductile, and are excellent conductors of both electrical and thermal energies. They are also all solid at average temperatures except mercury, which is a liquid metal except at far below normal freezing temperature."

"I think I saw this mercury back in the passage we followed to the valley," Shuran noted.

Dara nodded and continued his lessons. She told him of the special group of metals referred to as royal or nobles. These select metals resist the oxidation and corrosion of moisture in the air. The other metals are considered base metals because they more readily corrode, discolor, and rust.

Dara led Shuran into the metalworks and began handing him bars of different metals and had him examine them and repeat what he observed and felt.

Though Shuran already knew some of the principle science of what made things, and had explored the workings of many things from human, plant, rock, and animal, he had never delved deep enough to find the core of what held everything together. He continued to probe deep into the metals and ore samples until he was able to find the tiniest part that separated them from one another. He looked up and smiled.

"It is amazing," he said. "This nugget of gold is so different, yet so similar to this silver piece."

"Explain what you discovered," Dara said.

"The gold is much heavier, and, of course, there is the color, but there are the particles that bind the metal together. I see thirty-two fewer pairs of particles in each of the building blocks of the silver."

Dara was visibly impressed with Shuran's quickness in grasping this knowledge.

"Can you take these particles and move them around?"

Shuran focused on the silver in his palm. He mentally tugged on several of the building blocks until he pulled them free from the silver. He saw and felt it getting smaller. He then broke the blocks apart and began adding thirty-two of the pairs to each block within the silver. It was difficult at first, but he soon mastered the art of manipulating the metal. He had transmuted the silver into gold.

"Very good, now I want you to focus on the gold. Listen to its song and join it. Once you are singing with the gold, call a pair of particles to each of the building blocks," Dara instructed.

Shuran concentrated and attempted to 'sing' with the metal. It was difficult and he began to sweat from concentrating. He began calling for particles to join in the song, and was surprised when they started to join. Suddenly the gold in his palm puddled into the liquid metal called mercury. He stood, staring in wonder at the liquid metal in his palm that was so different from gold, but only the tiniest thing separated the two metals.

Dara laid a flat stone on the ground and motioned Shuran to pour the mercury on the slab. After he did so she dipped her finger into the metal and separated it into beads that kept rejoining into a single pool. Every time she would force them apart the mercury would join back together on the flat surface of the stone.

"Do you begin to understand, Shuran?" she asked as she watched the light in his eyes.

"I believe I begin to. But when I called for the particles to join the gold, where did they come from?" Shuran asked.

"From all around you they came. The particles in everything are the same, it is a simple matter of knowing the number of particles required to make up one single building block. It is no different really to transfer this knowledge from metals to other things." Dara knew she had overstepped her lessons but was not concerned. Shuran had to learn or he would not pass the tests.

"Dara..." Shuran started. "I have the ability to 'shift' into other creatures, does this perhaps help in my quickly understanding all this?"

"Learning this information would explain that more than likely, but I think there may be more. You are also part Gula'Lu, if the prophecy is true and you are of seven lines of man. This is also partly responsible."

"With each race I bring back to the Zidu'Si, I learn what being that race is about and wield their power, what is it like for you being Gula'Lu?" Shuran asked.

"You should ask what metal truly encompasses. You will have to discover that on your own, but I will warn you, do not attempt to turn to metal lest you lose yourself to it."

"How so?"

"There is a place deep in the valley where we have a shrine to the man of gold, it is a living statue. Long ago a Gula'Lu tried to change his silvery skin to that of gold. He was foolish and prideful. His motivation was to stand out from the rest of the Gula'Lu. His folly was that he forgot the main property of gold. Do you remember Shuran?"

"Gold like all but mercury, is solid at all but extreme temperature?" Shuran replied.

"Precisely, once he started the change it spread out of control and he turned to gold. He is trapped inside."

"Could you not melt the gold or coax it free?"

"The gold bonded with his flesh and all but his shi is now lost. The Gula'Lu do not have the kind of ability necessary to rebuild flesh from solid metal and to melt him would release his shi but he would not be able to reform," Dara said with a single raised brow. "That is beyond our capabilities."

"I will leave you to explore and learn. I must rest. You will need to return to the main clearing by the setting of Utu to stand and be tested." Dara left Shuran, and went back to the forest.

Shuran spent the remainder of the afternoon wandering the valley until he came upon a silvery river. Mercury, he realized as he watched it flow in multiple directions. He was unsure, but he thought he felt intelligence in the liquid. He began to reach toward the surface and saw that the mercury moved away from his hand.

"I would not do that if I were you, young human," Awilzag said as he approached from the trees. "It would be rude to wake another from their slumber, do you not agree?"

Shuran wore a look of confusion that seemed to amuse the otherwise stoic King of the Gula'Lu.

Awilzag responded by simply placing his right hand into the palm of his left and allowed it to transform and pool into a puddle of silvery liquid. He quickly reformed his hand and returned his arms to each side.

"Come, it is nearly time for your test. Dara reports that you may just yet prove worth, but it will be ultimately up to one who shall decide if the Gula'Lu will rejoin the Zidu'Si."

Shuran followed Awilzag back to the building where he found Moltar and Orian outside sitting. Moltar was eating again while Orian spoke to

Dara.

"Why do you sit outside?" Shuran asked.

"Because your pet has eaten so much that he can no longer fit the already sizable door!" Orian joked.

"I cannot help it, I am hungry beyond words, Lugaldur!" Moltar said with his mouth full.

"Moltar, you have grown considerably since we arrived. I would venture to say you could even carry a Gula'Lu now!" Awilzag said as if knowing this would occur.

"The rich air here is why everything grows so large. Moltar is especially affected due to his bond with you Shuran. I should expect the longer he stays, the larger he would become. If not for the fact he would eat us into starvation, I would be interested to see just how large." For the second time, Awilzag showed a slight smile.

"Time to ready for the trial Shuran. Please follow us into the clearing where you will be put to test. Put these on your wrists." Dara handed Shuran two wrist cuffs.

He could tell from the void within the metal that they were constructed of gug.

"You will not be allowed to wield Essence, a true Shin'Ar would not need anything but what you learned here today," Awilzag said as he led them off.

"I do not like this Shuran Shin'Ar," Orian complained.

"Do not interfere, my friend. If we are to gain their support, we must do as the Gula'Lu wish."

When they reached the center of the clearing, it seemed as though all the Gula'Lu finally came out to witness the testing. Thousands of the giant man-like beings stood silently waiting for something or someone.

Shuran noticed a large basin placed next to the chair that King Awilzag now occupied. As he watched and wondered what was to occur, a pillar of mercury lifted from the basin and began building up into the shape of a female, a Gula'Lu female. Shuran glared at Orian when he made a low whistle sound.

The process took only moments, before a fully formed Gula'Lu woman stood naked before the assembly. She remained standing while two other females came up behind her and draped a robe over her silvery bare body. She stepped forward and stood before Shuran.

"Shuran, claimant to the title Shin'Ar, you will stand in a trial to your worthiness of the duties and responsibility. I am Gimagala, first Gula'Lu to serve the Zidu'Si. Should you be worthy, our people will serve again."

Shuran was shocked to find that one of the original Zidu'Si still lived. Only when she continued did he bring his attention back to the matter at hand.

"Who will stand against this human, and test his true nature?" Gimagala asked the assembly.

"I shall stand!" Dara said as she entered the clearing to stand next to Shuran.

"Then let it begin!" Gimagala said as she took a seat next to Awilzag. "You will take a single blow from the strength of the Gula'Lu. If you survive, you shall be deemed worthy."

"Remember your lessons. Let me know when you are ready." Dara stepped back and readied the massive sword she held at her side.

Shuran was in shock. Dara had spent the day teaching him of the properties of metals. Now she stood ready to kill him if he did not pass this test. The gug around his wrists prevented him from wielding or weaving Essence. He tested them again and found that the loadstone absorbed his attempts. METAL! He thought to himself.

Dara saw the look of comprehension in his eyes and took that as her signal to strike. She hoisted the grand sword and lifted it above her head. In a single motion, she brought the blade down toward Shuran's head.

The world went into slow motion for Shuran. As he watched the slow, deliberate motion of Dara's swing, he raced through all he had learned that day as well as everything he already knew. He could not shield himself. He could not call elemental Essence to effect the sword or his surroundings. He could, however, affect himself.

Shuran focused on the gug braces around his wrist. He joined in their chaotic melody and began to sing. The particles of his body began to vibrate and sing along. Slowly his body started to change and harden. He was becoming gug and it was spreading fast. He remembered too late, Dara's warning about changing to metal, but also remembered that the

Gula'Lu could turn to mercury. They could not manipulate themselves beyond this ability, but Shuran could.

He released the restraint of the transmutation and gathered his shi into a shielded part of himself. The world moved back into real time.

To those watching, they saw a sword falling and a man turn into a dark metallic statue. The sword fell upon Shuran's hardened and raised hands. The force of the blow met the gug made man statue with such a clanging noise that even the expressionless Gula'Lu cringed. The sword shattered where it impacted the statue, and the still metal form of Shuran stood firm.

For several breathless moments after the sword fell to the ground in countless pieces, the crowd waited in silence.

Orian was near panic and was trying to free himself of Moltar's hold, to go check on his Shin'Ar. He could not understand why Moltar was not already upon his Lugaldur. When he looked up, he saw a gleam in Moltar's eye that told him it would be well. When Moltar loosened his grip, Orian settled down and waited.

Slowly, Shuran struggled to free his shi. He was solid metal, and worse, he was gug. He fought against the tightening on his shielded shi, until he realized he was still singing with the metal. He quickly changed the vibrations of the gug and set about returning every building block to its original state. It was slow at first, but then suddenly it was as if every part of him was returning to normal of its own accord.

Shuran stood before Dara whole, and lowered his arms. The gug wristbands fell to the ground in a pile of fine powder.

"I knew you could do it, Shin'Ar." Dara winked at Shuran.

"What have you learned, Shuran Shin'Ar?" Gimagala asked.

"To understand the element and become like it is to remain solid and strong like the noble metals but remain malleable to change when required. I can choose to become a weapon, a tool, or ornamentation but must do so with purpose and truth while not losing myself in the process."

Gimagala stood and walked over to Shuran. She placed a hand on his shoulder and lowered herself to look him in the eyes.

"You look so much like he. I thought I would never see your return," she said with silvery tears in her eyes. "I failed my Shin'Ar, but my daughter will not." Gimagala motioned for Dara to step forward. "If you will accept her, Daraeszag stands ready to serve the Shin'Ar, bringing the Gula'Lu back to the Zidu'Si."

Shuran turned to face Dara and with a slight intake of air, he called forth the A'Baddasu, Gauntlet of Strength, from the Vault.

"Wear this and use it well, sister of the Zidu'Si. Your strength and knowledge will join with ours, as you will gain from our abilities and knowledge in return," Shuran intoned.

Dara placed the gauntlet on her arm and it instantly transformed in size and shape to fit her like a second skin. At the same moment, she was flooded with the abilities of the other Zidu'Si, and her strength and knowledge joined theirs.

***

Across the world back in Durangug, Mallick and Gregoran were sitting at the table eating with Moona, Codger, and Aknard, when they sat stiff suddenly and began to sparkle with a silvery shine.

"What in the name of Damkianna happened to you two!" Moona screeched as she dropped her cup of wine. "Ya' look like a couple o' fancy candle holders!"

They just laughed and drank as the sparkle began to fade.

Chapter Thirteen

Penelle was sitting alone in her room trying to decide what to do with the new information she had. She was unsure what it meant or even what she saw. She remembered the warnings from thousands of years past, to stay away from the shadows. And although the witches did not agree with the Followers of Light, they remained self-serving and followed no other direction but their own, staying clear of the Shadow. She had to talk to Vardoran.

Vardoran was sitting in his own chambers reading through ancient tombs when Penelle knocked upon his door. He invited her to enter and asked her to sit while he retrieved goblets of wine. He could see in her eyes that something troubled her.

"What troubles you Penelle," he asked in his best attempt at being a concerned gentleman.

"I have just recently observed something that upsets me beyond anything I have witnessed in my vast years," she began. "I went down to the catacombs to witness Salmetu, taking in Shadow!"

"You saw her taking the shi from one of her prisoners?" Vardoran asked plainly.

"No! She was absorbing SHADOW! Directly from a crack in the foundation of the deepest levels, she breathed in the darkness like it was air!"

"What are you talking about Penelle? What is this talk of shadows?"

"Not 'shadows', Shadow, as in 'The Shadow'!" She was frustrated at his ignorance. "Sometimes I forget how young you actually are. This 'Chaos' you worship, have you never wondered what directs it?"

Vardoran just returned a look of confusion mixed with curiosity.

Penelle explained that she was tipped off by one of the Council members from the Academy. He brought her a map and told her that she might find the Priestess down in the catacombs. She described the scene that played out before her and then explained the balance of the light and the Shadow. They are opposites that must remain in balance at all times. These powers have existed as long as living history and before. They control both the beginning and the end, creation and destruction, harmony and chaos.

"I still do not understand. There is Creation, and there is Chaos," he muttered, not taking her meaning.

"Oh, you fool; those are but results, and they are not the power behind anything. Shadow and Light, They are the opposing forces of the universe. This is where the old saying in your religion comes from Vardoran, 'There is power in shadow'! Chime any bells for you yet?" She was now more frustrated and angered than frightened.

"That is just a saying, symbolic in meaning." Vardoran stood to answer another knock on his door.

"Your guest has been settled in the room you requested sir," the soldier said.

"Penelle, care to join me for a visit with my honored guest?"

"Vardoran! Have you heard a word that I spoke?"

"I think you are over reacting sweet Penelle. Salmetu will be well in hand when she meets our guest. Come, let us greet her warmly." Vardoran led her out of the room and down the hall.

He inquired about this Council member that brought her the drawing and instructions about where to find Salmetu in the bowels of the

Academy. He did not recognize the man she described but her passing mention of an odd looking cat struck a chord of familiarity. He would look in on Nagutan when the time permitted and he was able to locate his old mentor.

Sulura was waking from her drugged sleep when Vardoran and Penelle arrived.

"Good, you are waking. Welcome to New Draven, Sulura," Vardoran said.

"Where am I, and who are you?" she asked.

"I am Vardoran, and this is Penelle. You will be our guest here in New Draven."

"A guest is not drugged and carried away against their wishes. I do not care to remain here," Sulura said defiantly.

"I think you will change your mind when Salmetu arrives, my dear." Vardoran's expression changed from warm to smug.

Sulura became quiet and sat down. She was reeling with emotions. She knew that Salmetu was overtaken by darkness, but she hoped that there was yet a chance for her salvation. She was not sure how she felt about seeing her daughter. She did not have time to think.

Salmetu came walking slowly through the door. She heard that her mother had been brought to New Draven, but she had to come and find out for certain. She believed all this time that her mother was dead, taken by the Followers of Light. She turned to Vardoran.

He saw the full blackness of her eyes when she looked at him. He felt she was looking straight through him.

"You told me the mother died during birthing, Vardoran. What is the meaning of this?" Her anger balanced on a precipice of a full rage.

"We were deceived I am afraid sweet child. The Baron of Drakk himself took your mother in and saw to her recovery, which as I understand it, took many years." Vardoran was soothing her as best he could.

Penelle was not about to stay for what might happen. She leaned in close to Vardoran.

"The Shadow you fool. Research it," she whispered to him. "If you will excuse me Salmetu, I will leave you to your reunion," she said as she gracefully left the room. Once she exited the room, she quickened her pace.

Salmetu glared after her. "I do not like that woman."

"She is harmless, Salmetu," Vardoran assured her.

"No woman is harmless, especially a kashshaptu and more pointedly that particular witch." Sulura finally found her voice.

Salmetu turned to her mother and was suddenly carrying herself as a child. The darkness left her eyes, and she began to tear.

Vardoran caught the sudden change in her stance and personality. Believing he had tamed the unruly nature of Salmetu, he departed the room to leave them alone. And yet as he passed the Priestess, he could swear he saw a wispy tendril of darkness whip out from her body and attempt to touch him. He quickly withdrew and headed back to his chambers.

"Mother? Is it truly you?" Salmetu asked timidly.

"Yes, but is anything of my child still left within you?" Sulura answered.

Salmetu recoiled as though she had been slapped in the face. She became defiant.

"I am completely your child, mother. Just as much as that wicked boy Shuran is your son!"

"He is no more wicked than myself, child. What has become of you since taken from me? You leech the shi from innocents and transform them into living corpses. How is this not wicked?"

"I will no longer practice that art mother, of that you have my promise. As for Shuran, he defies the rule of Aurderia. He cavorts with Dwarfs, Elves, and Drakkian alike. Uggae knows what he is up to know."

"Do you know who Uggae is, Salmetu?" Sulura asked upon hearing her daughter use his name.

"Of course mother, he is the one true and benevolent God. He directs me, and I follow his word."

Sulura cast down her eyes to hide her tears. Her daughter was lost to her.

Salmetu became outraged and left the room, locking her mother within. She headed back to her room and began to pout. She had not behaved so in many years. Her mother had rejected her. Salmetu's anger surfaced as she began to fling spells at everything in sight. Finally, her anger abated into sobbing. She was upset with feeling hurt, at feeling anything at all.

Sulura continued to cry for her daughter, when Tianna appeared beside her.

"Do not cry for the shell of what was, mother. There is still some light left buried deep within her," Tianna said. "I am here with you and shall keep you company."

"Oh, sweet Tianna, what is to become of my children? I fear they will destroy one another."

"That is not how it is destine to play out mother, Shuran will save her. He will save us all."

They talked for some time, taking comfort in one another.

Vardoran grew tired listening through the door and finally barged in to see Tianna evaporate and Sulura stand in shocked surprise.

"What was that you have been speaking to? What was she talking about? I must know everything." Vardoran had a look of desperation in his eyes. He approached Sulura and called an iron poker from the hearth. He heated it with the word 'Ma', burn.

***

Moltar's added bulk, while in the valley of the Gula'Lu, proved more than enough to accommodate Dara's added weight. He was surprised that, in spite of her size, she weighed little more than Shuran and Orian together. Departing from the valley, Moltar was able to gain great height and was able to use the strong winds to push them along. They were able to reach the Orenthal Mountains in less than two days flying straight through.

Shuran and the other two riders slept upon Moltar's back when rest was needed. Shuran used Essence to slow their metabolism so they would not require food or have an urgent need of a stop to relieve themselves. He knew that if they landed once over the glacial ice sheet, they would not get back in the air regardless of Moltar's new size.

As they approached the mountains, Shuran pushed out with Essence as best he could to force them to slow using his limited ability with air.

He had little to no effect on their speed.

Moltar needed no help. He communicated back to his riders to hold on tight. He angled his wings and pulled his body on an angle to add friction and reduce his natural lift. They began slowing but not enough. Moltar told them the fit would be tight, and at the last minute he tucked in his wings and dove into the North-facing tunnel to Duranekur. He lowered his legs and ran with the momentum until he could come to a skidding halt.

"Good for us the dwarfs do everything on such a grand scale," Moltar said indicating the size of the passage they now lumbered down toward the capital.

Dara jumped down from Moltar's back and walked along the passage admiring the frescos being added to the walls of the Northern Passage. Her long legs afford strides that could easily keep up with Moltar's relaxed pace. She was amazed at the beauty of the artwork.

"These are beautiful!" she exclaimed.

"Do the Gula'Lu not paint?" Orian asked.

"No, we create art through working metal and music from instruments we fashion. Next time we are in Edinzabar, I will take you to the metal gardens. All the plants and flowers are sculpted from various metals. It is amusing to watch the birds attempt to get nectar from them."

"Avrank will be meeting us at the far end of the entrance to escort us to the palace. Prepare yourself Dara. Where your people are content to stand silently and observe, the dwarfs are the extreme opposite," Moltar told her with a snort.

They made quick time completing the journey through the passage. Only a few dwarves were present, busying themselves with painting the new frescos. They stopped to gape at Dara and Moltar's new size, but did not follow.

Avrank was waiting as expected when they arrived at the other end. What was not expected was that Brakvar was with him, and he was smiling.

"Avrank?" Shuran said questioningly as he looked at Brakvar.

"It is my true brother Shuran. Much has happened while you were away. I tried communication, but was unable to reach you," Avrank assured him. He nodded to Orian and then his eyes met Dara's. He was frozen in place and stammering over his words to introduce himself.

Orian stepped in and made the introductions. "Daraeszag of the Gula'Lu, may I present the Heir Apparent, Brakvar of Duranekur. And this is his stumpy little brother the fool apparent, Turd!"

Everyone except Dara and Avrank was laughing as they exchanged bows and headed toward the palace.

Avrank stood alone still stunned by the silvery image of beauty that was now burned in his vision.

"AVRANK!" he said as he ran after them. "My name is Avrank, not Turd!" He followed behind Orian trying to kick him in the back of the ankle but kept missing, much to the amusement of Dara. Finally, he called upon the earth to lift before Orian's feet, causing him to fall on his face. "Watch your step shoemaker, perhaps it is past time you craft yourself a new pair of boots."

Avrank winked up at Dara who continued to giggle.

They made it to the palace without too much distraction since there was no formal announcement about the arrival of visitors. Because they approached from the backside of the city, there was also less chance of running into any dwarves this time of their day. They would all be working or in the marketplace. The group made it to the Royal Palace to find Vraduun and Levandria waiting to greet them.

Levandria nodded to Shuran and Orian and rushed past them to greet Dara.

Vraduun just grimaced at her snub and shrugged it off to Shuran, who was not in the least put off.

"Welcome to the Dwarven Capital City of Duranekur, I am Queen Levandria. Please come into our home and join us for a welcome feast."

"Thank you for your warm greeting. I am Princess Daraeszag, Fifteenth Daughter to the Forty-fourth Wife of King Awilzag. You must call me Dara though," Dara responded.

"Then you should call me Levi!" Levandria said as she led the Gula'Lu princess past Vraduun and the others. As she past her husband the King, he cleared his throat. "Oh, and this is my husband Vraduun, the King. Come along Dara, we have a wonderful evening planned!"

"Looks to me as though we are in good company my King," Shuran said grinning at Vraduun.

"And the best of company it is my boy come let us get good and drunk, for I fear we shall be snubbed the entirety of the evening!" Vraduun slapped Shuran on the back, as far up as he could reach, and they all followed the women into the Royal Hall.

Before they all sat down, Brakvar pulled Shuran to the side for a private word. He appeared humble and friendly. He had been thinking about what to say to Shuran since he heard that he would be returning this night.

"Shin'Ar, I wish to express both my apologies and my gratitude for all you have done for my family. Moreover, I am deeply sorrowed by the actions of my impostor," he managed.

"Brakvar, you are not responsible for the acts of your doppelgänger. It alone awaits judgement for what transpired while you were... Where were you?" Shuran asked.

"I was being kept in an old secret room in the Royal Apartments. I have missed much, even being named Heir Apparent. I have no memories since we accompanied you here for the first time from Durangug."

"That would explain the subtle changes in your personality. This impostor was good, but it got sloppy," Shuran added.

"Do you think it will return?" Brakvar asked.

"It will turn up again somewhere, but I doubt it will be here in Duranekur. I do not think you or your family were ever in any true harm. I believe it meant to draw me away from my path."

Shuran and Brakvar quickly finished their conversation and clasped hands. They joined the others at the table. Shuran noticed that Levandria had Dara cornered in conversation. He sent Dara a look of sympathy. Shuran then joined Orian and Avrank on the other side of the table where they were already hitting the cup. He poured himself a goblet of watered wine and sat for the evening meal.

"You just missed it Shuran!" Avrank chuckled. "Apparently, only Dara is allowed to call my mother 'Levi'. Father called her that and she growled at him. I mean she actually growled!"

"She has only sons and a husband, can you not understand her pleasure at finally having female companionship without a formal state dinner!" Brakvar added. "Besides she is Zidu'Si now correct? That makes her family of sorts."

"How did you know she was Zidu'Si?" Shuran asked him.

"I was with Avrank when he began to 'sparkle'. I have to admit it looked good on him, drew attention away from his height!" Brakvar said jokingly.

"Too bad I missed that. I would have given anything to see a sparkling 'Turd'!" Orian said laughing. His laughter ended abruptly when the floor beneath his chair, lifted to throw the chair backward.

Chapter Fourteen

Sulura could no longer hold back her screams.

Vardoran kept repeating his questions, and applying the hot poker when he disliked the answers. He wanted to know what the wispy creature was that he saw leave the room. He wanted to know what they were discussing.

Sulura would not give him answers.

Tianna appeared in Salmetu's room. She saw her sitting in the corner; her room was in ruins.

"Salmetu!" Tianna whispered.

"Go away specter! I have no time for your games now."

"You must go to mother. Your old man teacher is burning her!"

It took a fraction of a moment for this to register with Salmetu. The Shadow disappeared from her eyes again and she was up and running to her mother's room. When she got there, the door was locked from the inside. She blasted it open.

Salmetu immediately held out her hand and called the hot poker from

Vardoran's hand. Her other arm flew into the air, and Vardoran went flying across the room. She crossed to her mother and without a word, healed her burns.

Sulura was now unconscious.

Salmetu put Sulura on her bed. Then she moved her attention to Vardoran, who managed to escape the room while she was looking after her mother. Anger floated over her features, Shadow filled her eyes and rage filled her heart. She left her mother resting to track down Vardoran.

Vardoran made his way to Penelle's room. He made it there in time to see her exiting.

"Penelle, you were right, she is taken!" Vardoran was talking frantically and out of his mind.

"What are you going on about you old fool? I warned you and now you come running-" Penelle stopped mid-sentence when she saw Salmetu coming down the hall.

Salmetu was floating on Shadow mist. It lifted her from the floor and carried her toward her target. Tendrils of shadowy smoke formed around her and began reaching out ahead of her toward Penelle and Vardoran.

"How convenient, we can eliminate both of you now!" Salmetu was speaking with multiple voices.

Penelle opened her door and ran in with Vardoran at her heels. She did not know what to do. Quickly she ran to the hearth and laid logs out for a fire.

Salmetu burst through the doors and headed straight for Vardoran. "Wait your turn sweet Penelle, we will be with you soon enough, kashshaptu!" Salmetu was now in the center of the room. She hovered several inches from the ground floating on the same shadowy smoke. Her eyes were completely black and her expression blank. Tendrils of shadow reached out from behind her, and grabbed Vardoran. They lifted him from the ground and pinned him to the wall.

"Please do not kill me," he whimpered.

"We will not kill you Vardoran, though you may wish we had once we have finished with you!" Salmetu said with many voices. She began laughing madly then reached forward with her hands and placed them over his eyes. As Vardoran screamed, Salmetu opened her mouth and

Shadow poured out and into Vardoran's, choking his screams of protest.

Penelle finally got the fire going as she watched Vardoran go completely still. She inched her way to her bag and grabbed it. As she got back to the hearth, she cast her spell just before the black eyes of both Salmetu and Vardoran turned on her.

They reached for her with the shadowy tendrils.

Penelle disappeared in a green smoke that went into the fire. Penelle appeared at a small fire burning just outside two bridges. Earlier in the day she had instructed her carriage man to take her things and wait with a fire burning at this location. She knew she would be leaving tonight, one way or another. As much as she did not wish to do so this soon, she now had to seek out Shuran immediately.

***

Shuran was ready to leave Duranekur early the next morning. He was one step further along in his quest and wanted to get moving on to the next. He spoke with Mallick earlier and advised that they would be back in Durangug before that afternoon. First he had to meet Vraduun for breakfast and talk about what happened while he was in Edinzabar. The previous evening was far too jovial, and 'Levi' would not hear any dark news or talk of dreadful things while she entertained Princess Daraeszag.

Dara was enjoying the experience of anything not Gula'Lu. Everything was new and exciting.

Avrank, Brakvar, and Orian joined Shuran and Vraduun for breakfast. They spoke of all the events that happened over the time since Brakvar had been replaced. The only thing they could come up with was that the impostor had arrived undetected into Duranekur sometime before Shuran's first arrival.

"Only a shifter could have done this. It is the only explanation," Shuran insisted.

"A shifter?" Vraduun asked.

"There is a race of beings, offspring of the Foresworn that escaped the Sikil'Mah. They continued to have children, but something was different about them. They have no identity of their own per se. They can shift into any living thing they come in contact with and have some abilities with weaving."

"How do you know this?" Orian asked.

"Because I am living today due to the aide of one of them. Andra, he is a shifter. He was sent to make sure I escaped when my sisters and I were born. Once, before I sent him home from Durangug, Andra allowed me to examine his physiology."

"So are you saying it was this Andra person?" Vraduun asked.

"No, but it was likely one of his kind, or something similar to it." Shuran was troubled. He did not want to think that Andra was involved or had any knowledge of this. "Then there was the cube pendant that the impostor was wearing that last night. It was the first time I noticed it, but I am certain that it was always on its person."

"Gugtu! A keep-safe, like the one you made of the Vault," Avrank said.

"Precisely, the shifter could only become someone smaller, by storing the extra part of itself in a keep-safe," Shuran told them.

"This is all getting far too complicated. What is there to gain by this for these creatures?" Vraduun asked.

"That is a good question, and one I plan to find answers to!" Shuran said.

"And now there is news of dwarves gone missing in the mines," Vraduun added.

Shuran had looked at Vraduun for a moment before he got up. "Seal the mines! The Shadow is likely on the move. I will visit Badgaldingir and let them know they will be closed in for the time. Vraduun, may I have some of your private brew to take them as a gift?"

Vraduun made sure Shuran had what he needed. He then ordered the mines evacuated and prepared them for sealing. When the barrels of dwarven ale arrived, the King sent them out to where Shuran had instructed and would be awaiting them. Vraduun accompanied them along with Avrank. Orian, Dara, and Brakvar were overseeing sealing of the mines.

Shuran tapped into the Emmuku'Gu, as he began to extend his shi into the flow of power running through Ersetu, he called out to the 'Voices'.

"I wish to travel to Badgaldingir. I must advise the Entar'Lu of our plans to seal the mines, and take them a gift," Shuran asked. He waited several long moments for a reply.

"You and the Zidu'Si may travel freely to Badgaldingir, Shin'Ar. It is your right," they told him.

Shuran then took Avrank by the hand and reached out his shi to surround the barrels, and then they were gone. They sailed through the flow of power with ease. Moments later, they arrived in the courtyard near the fountain.

Zak was there sitting in his spot under a tree. He stood in shocked surprise when Shuran, along with a small dwarf and stacked barrels materialized only feet away from him.

"Shin'Ar! Good heavens, we were not expecting you," Zak said, wearing a friendly smile.

"Sorry for the sudden arrival, we do not have much time. The mines are being sealed and you will have no means of departing Badgaldingir for some time," Shuran told him as he greeted him in the customary way.

Shuran presented him with the barrels of brew, compliments of the King. He also introduced Avrank, Prince and Zidu'Si. After greeting a few more of the caretakers, Shuran prepared to leave.

"Shin'Ar, you will not be able to stop the Shadow at all by simply filling the shafts and collapsing tunnels. You must use gugtu to hold it at bay. It will not stop them indefinitely, however," Zak told him.

"Because they twist it, do they not?" Shuran asked, already knowing the answer.

Zak simply nodded.

Shuran and Avrank stepped back into the Emmuku'Gu, and exited near where the mines were already being sealed. Avrank settled himself after two quick trips through the Emmuku'Gu. He was not as accustomed to it as Shuran.

"Dara, I need your help," Shuran said as he stepped forward. "We need to transmute the stone and ore that we collapse as well as the surrounding area."

"Shin'Ar! That will take more strength and will than we have," Dara protested.

"You have not yet experienced the bolstered strength of the Zidu'Si.

It may not yet be complete, but we share strength with our bond. I also bring the power of Durangug," Shuran said with a smile.

He gathered the present Zidu'Si including the larger and stronger Moltar, and then communicated his need to Mallick and Gregoran.

As one, the Zidu'Si reached into the mountain, led by Shuran and Dara. They began twisting and manipulating the particles that made up the rock, ore, and minerals. With a great deal of strain and concentration, they locked the image of what they wanted to happen into their minds. Then Shuran tapped the power of Durangug. Energy and strength flowed through him and into the Zidu'Si.

Deep inside the mountain a transformation began to take place. Rock and metal began to melt and flow. Particles moved from one building block to another and flowed through the space to small to see. Slowly at first, the molten material began to change. It resisted and the Shadow moved in to fight what was happening.

Shuran could sense the dark presence of Shadow and instructed Dara to take the lead while he held them off. Shuran pushed his shi forward to face the Shadow. His disembodied self stared into the murky void of the Shadow and went numb.

Moltar sensed through his separate link to his Lugaldur, that he was in trouble. He pulled his shi from his body and merged with Shuran as he did, not so long ago and threw up a shield. This time, however, Moltar had the flow of power from Durangug to help. He pulled with the might of a mountain on the flow of raw energy and pushed back the Shadow until Dara and the others finished transmuting the molten flow of materials.

Shuran refocused with Moltar's presence. Together they remained strong enough to allow the formation of gugtu. Shuran felt something, however, something familiar as the Shadow brushed against his shield. It was tainted and malformed, but it was there. The Shadow was flowing with shi. Thousands upon thousands of shi swirled within the Shadow. Shuran was becoming overwhelmed when Moltar finally pulled him back.

The seal was complete. The Zidu'Si all let go of the collective and Durangug flowing between them. All of them were exhausted but still on their feet.

"Moltar, the Shadow, it was-" Shuran started.

"I felt it as well, Lugaldur," Moltar interrupted. "Should we tell the others"

"Yes, but not yet, I need more information and we must get back to Durangug."

"That was beyond amazing!" Dara exclaimed. "I do not believe that even the entire population of Gula'Lu could have accomplished such a transmutation in such a short time."

"What we just did, what was that?" Orian asked.

"We used the Essence of metals and transmuted the entire base of the Orenthal into a gugtu seal to hold the Shadow at bay!" Shuran explained.

"And what happened when you were in there with us? It seemed as though you were getting pulled away," Dara asked.

"The Shadow, there is something there we all need to discuss. But not now, for now we must gather in Durangug and figure out our next move." Shuran was both excited to have another piece of the puzzle and yet disgusted by the taint that surrounded the shi in the Shadow.

Shuran and the Zidu'Si said their goodbyes to the Royal family and made their way to the area where Shuran and Avrank left for Badgaldingir. Shuran told them they would travel back to Durangug by Emmuku'Gu. Even though it was a waste of energy when they could have flown, Shuran did not want to overtire Moltar. In spite of his added size, there was no easy way to accommodate four riders comfortably, and Avrank refused being strapped to anyone but Dara. Shuran did not even ask her to entertain the notion.

Avrank was smitten with the Gula'Lu Princess.

Chapter Fifteen

Penelle huddled in her carriage, still shaken by the encounter with Salmetu. The closest settlement, unmolested by the death walkers, was Middleton, so that is where she headed. She had instructed the driver to get as much distance as possible before the horses required rest. She wanted distancing as far away from Salmetu as possible. She was not certain, but Penelle felt that so long as she was out of Salmetu's way, then she would be safe from her coming after her. As her carriage moved along the trader's roads from Two Bridges to Middleton, she felt them slowing down.

Penelle moved to the window of her carriage to look out the window. When she pulled back the curtain, she saw that they were not stopping to rest the horses; they were in the midst of a caravan.

Hundreds of people were leaving the Capital and surrounding settlements. Word of Salmetu's outburst had spread quickly it appeared. The people of Aurderia did not feel safe and were trying to get far from the source of their fears, Salmetu and the Order of Chaos.

Penelle traveled through evening with the crowds of refugees. She did not do so out of some feeling of empathy or common purpose. She had no choice since her carriage was unable to go around them. She decided she would travel as long as required until the travelers began to set camp for the night. Once the roadways were clear enough she would have her driver move far to the lead and only rest a short time before forging ahead.

Several long hours past before she was well ahead of the now breaking crowds. When Penelle felt there was enough distance, she ordered her driver to pull off and set up camp. As her driver looked after the horses, Penelle prepared a fire and brought out provisions from the back of the carriage. Though she had a driver to do these things, she welcomed the tasks as a distraction from thoughts of her disintegrating plans.

"Mind if I share your warm fire, Madam?" the man said as he approached from the road.

Penelle was not normally surprised, but being on edge, she jumped and a muffled scream threatened to escape.

"What are you doing out here Councilman… What is your name again?" she asked as she composed herself.

"Escaping the madness of the Priestess, same as anyone else with sense enough to leave," he replied, stroking his bizarre cat.

"You risk your safety, leaving the Council. Why make such a choice? It appears you left with nothing but that bag at your side and the ugly creature you carry." Penelle was studying the Councilman. She was getting the feeling she knew him again, much as she did when he warned her of Salmetu's activities.

"All I need for now is in this bag, and my pet can see after himself. As for the Council, there is, or soon will be no Council. Salmetu is mad with power and does not share it."

"How is it you come to know so much about Salmetu and her behaviors?" Penelle asked while keeping a close eye on the man.

"Things are much easier to see when one is looking," he answered. "I learned a long time ago, that I must not forsake observing the present while calculating my future from lessons of the past."

"I am not certain I follow your meaning," she said defensively. "You never did tell me your name."

"We have already met my dear, you simply have not been paying attention." With a wave of his hand, he dropped the spell. Nagutan took a seat on a log near the fire Penelle had started.

"That is why you seemed so familiar!" she exclaimed. "Why did you do this, and what happened to the Councilman you impersonated?"

"Come now my dear, with all the time you spent in the marshlands, you did not learn to play the game better?" Nagutan gave her a look that spoke volumes.

"There was no other Councilman, you and him, are one and the same. But how have you maintained the spells within the gug-lined walls of the Academy?" she asked.

"You disappoint me my dear Penelle. You are not the only one who knows Blood Magic."

Penelle had studied him for several moments before everything became clear. She stood and readied a spell.

"YOU!"

***

"'Bout time we got more women folk in this odd-ball crew of misfits!" Moona said, as she looked Dara up and down and way up. "You small for your race child?"

"I am of average stature, and I am also three thousand years of age," Dara answered. Seeing the shocked look on everyone's faces she continued. "The Gula'Lu have always been the longest lived race of man. We were given this by the Gods, to prevent the Shadow from taking our shi to the Netherworld and adding it to their strength."

"What do you mean when you say the Shadow takes shi?" Orian asked.

"You truly do not know anything about the Shadow?" Dara asked with concern. She looked to Shuran before continuing. After he had nodded, she continued. "There is no written history of where the Shadow came from, but it has been around for as long as my people can remember. It feeds off the shi of man and the stronger the shi, the more it adds to the Shadow's strength. Due to the abilities given the Gula'Lu by the Gods, we were granted lives free of natural death to keep us from the Shadow."

"How does the Shadow take the shi from someone?" Avrank asked.

"To the living, the Shadow is seductive, it plays on desire as well as fear. It can take a man's emotion and twist it into hate. The smallest amount of darkness in the soul is a way in. Once the Shadow finds a way in, it works on the man, festering and taking over. For the dead, it is uncertain how the Shadow takes the shi."

"Yack scat! Living shadows? Old tales told to sprats to keep 'em outta mischief!" Moona said.

"Moona, I assure you there is shi in the Shadow. Moltar and I both felt it while blocking it from entering Duranekur. The shi we sensed felt twisted and confused," Shuran told everyone.

The Vault remained uncharacteristically quiet for several long moments. It was not until Dara stood and moved over to one of the statues, did the silence break.

"Do you recognize this statue?" Shuran asked.

"Yes, this is the Lord of Earth, Enki," Dara answered. She began walking the perimeter of the room and stopped at each of the occupied alcoves to name the ancient Deity represented.

"So we have: the Lady of the Sky, Hebat; the Lady of Water, Nina; the Lady of Life, Ninti; Damkianna, Mistress of Heaven and Earth; and then there is Nergal." Dara stopped before the largest and most prominent of the statues.

"And who was Nergal?" Gregoran asked.

"Negral, 'is' the Great Watcher," Dara said.

Before anyone could ask further questions, Moltar called Shuran through their link. He could no longer fit comfortably within the Vault since returning larger than when he left.

"We have an unexpected visitor," Shuran interrupted. He headed calmly to the Vault door and began the climb out to the surface with his Zidu'Si, Moona, and Codger on his heals. After he had exited the doorway on the surface, he walked up beside Moltar, who was crouched down with his head level to the man standing in the clearing.

Moltar was growling.

"Easy my friend," Shuran said to Moltar as he placed a hand on the side of his bonded.

"Things have changed here since last I was in Durangug. I might not have made it at all, had I not finally sensed the spell work deterring me from approaching," the man said.

"Necessary precautions in these treacherous times," Shuran responded while looking at Moltar admiringly. "Where are my manners? Moltar here is my bonded drakkon. Moltar, this is the shifter, Andra."

At the name, Avrank began to move forward but was stopped when Dara held out her hand. Moona, on the other hand, would not be so easily halted.

"What do you mean by disappearing for so long, shifty?" Moona scolded. "And you just ignored all attempts at communication from Shuran!"

"I apologize, but my pendant was taken by my… It was kept from me while I was in my homeland. I was not allowed to leave until ordered. Things have not been well in the Territories. The ground regularly quakes and splits open," Andra explained.

"And what of the others of your kind, Andra? Have they been back in the Territories as well, have the Guardians abandoned their charter?" Shuran asked.

"The Guardians were all called back to the Territories some time ago, for what I have not been told. The rest of their kind, I cannot speak to what council they keep."

"So if I were to speak of a shifter taking the form of the dwarf Heir Apparent, poisoning the King, and stirring up discontent, you would tell me you know nothing about this?" Shuran asked.

"In truth I do not, it is disturbing, but not beyond the capabilities of those I answer to. I am confused at many things of late. I am truly sorry, Shuran. If one of the shifters was behind this, I do not know the motivation behind it."

"What motivations can you tell us about?" Orian asked. "You must have learned the art of deception from an elf sir."

"I have always been dedicated to seeing Shuran fulfill his destiny. The prophecy is in the best interest of all on Ersetu," Andra responded.

"Prophecy my fat fanny!" Moona cried out. Moona whacked Codger before he even had a chance to think of a comment.

During this entire exchange, Moltar and Jade sat quietly, listening and watching Andra. As the conversations trailed off, and plans were made to take a meal outside, Moltar finally spoke up.

"You smell odd," Moltar said to Andra.

Andra said nothing.

Moona grumbled in agreement.

Moltar kept his eyes trained on the shifter.

***

"How dare you show your face or any of your faces to me! I should kill you where you sit!" Penelle screamed at Nagutan. "You who walked away free while my sisters and I were cursed and cast out to the swamps to suffer endlessly."

"You forget, it was not I who broke the laws of old. I did not use blood magic to create the trolls. That was you and your coven," Nagutan told her. "I did not teach you those magics for you to defile a race and turn them into ignorant and wild creatures to serve your will."

"You stood there when we were tried and sentenced. You never spoke up in our defense!"

"Defend you? What defense would there have been for your actions? No Penelle, you reap what you sew though I believed the punishment severe in its term," Nagutan started. "This is why I sent the visions to your seer on how to break the curse."

"What are you saying? You sent the means of our release? Why?" Penelle asked. Her anger had been replaced with confusion.

"Oh my dear, there is a great deal more going on than just a balance broken and resurgence of the Shadow, I only hope things work out this time." Nagutan motioned for his cat to approach from the fire where it had been sitting. "Go to Shuran. Tell him what we spoke of earlier and return with his answer," Nagutan instructed the gangly feline.

The imp transformed into its natural form, winked at Penelle, and then disappeared.

"What was that all about?" Penelle asked.

"We must head for Drakkfoth and see to the traitor in the Baron's castle. Someone gave up Sulura to Vardoran and must answer for it. This little addition to the troubles was not part of our designed plan, and it may complicate things."

"What plans? And what is 'our' plan?" Penelle insisted.

"All in good time my dear. Pay close attention." Nagutan said nothing more and smiled at Penelle, who sat glaring at him. "You are more beautiful than ever my wife."

***

Shuran sat talking with Andra, catching him up on the important things he felt comfortable sharing. Although he trusted in Andra's friendship, he did not know what would happen should Andra's loyalties to his kind be tested. Something told him that Andra was deliberately being left out of some greater plan. Shuran told him more about the impostor Brakvar.

"You were correct to implicate a 'shifter' as you call us. There is some of my kind who work in secret for the Nabusa. Only she knows their movements. I have only ever seen one of them on a rare occasion, but they always wore a cube of gugtu around their neck." Andra was torn. He decided then, that he would not be a pawn to Nabusa's game any longer. "Shuran, you have my allegiance. I shall not return to the Territories, but I fear that the Nabusa knew this was coming. They will come after me."

"Then we shall be ready for them," Shuran said and all in attendance agreed.

A growl and a screech sounded in the distance where Moltar and Jade settled for the evening. Moltar had something in his claws.

"I caught a darkling, Lugaldur," Moltar announced as he produced a small black creature.

"Put it down Moltar, that is Nagutan's imp," Shuran said as he approached. "What are you doing here imp? And how did you find this place?"

The little imp stood up from where Moltar had unceremoniously tossed him down.

"My master bid me find you and deliver a message. He told me where to find you, and your spells of determent do not work on the likes of me," the imp told him.

"Speak then. Tell us what he bid you."

"The Council will soon fall. Salmetu has gone mad with power and the people now flee out of fear. Refugees travel to the lands of Drakkfoth and north toward the Dwarf and Elven lands," the imp spoke.

"This is a mixed blessing, Shin'Ar," Orian said. "Although the Elves will not permit them enter Entensiama, they will not turn them from the forests. More allies to fight the dark means less turned to death walkers."

"There is more," interrupted the imp. "Vardoran has allies in Drakkfoth. Through them, he managed to take Sulura, and delivered her to Salmetu. He was punished for harming Sulura for information. Nagutan travels with the kashshaptu Penelle, to Drakkfoth to find this traitor and wishes you meet him there."

"When does he wish to meet?" Mallick said seeing Shuran's shock at the news of his mother's capture.

"In five days, Nagutan will arrive in Drakkfoth near the Stone Forest. He wishes that you met him then."

"Advise your master we will see him there, but I will advise the Baron that there will be refugees arriving in his land. I shall find out why I was not advised of my mother's capture."

The imp nodded and disappeared.

"We shall go rescue your mother Shin'Ar!" Moltar said.

"No, my bonded, I do not believe Salmetu will harm her. If anything, she will likely use her as a means to bring me to her. When I go, it will be on my terms."

Shuran and the others spoke of this news and what should be done. It was late and the early hours of pre-dawn when Shuran sat alone outside with Moltar that Tianna came to him.

"I wondered when you might come," Shuran said, expecting her visit.

"Mother is safe for now, but for how long I do not know. Salmetu is poisoned and tainted by the Shadow. She has taken more of it in," Tianna told him.

"What do you mean by more? Has she done so before?"

"The night of our birth, Shadow entered her at the altar to quench the void," Tianna said almost cryptically. "Now it fills her and she infects others with it, including the old man Vardoran."

126

"So she is beyond saving now," Shuran whispered.

"She is a tool for the Shadow, she can be saved." Tianna paused briefly before continuing. "I must get back to mother. I stay by her side."

"Take her a message, mother… Tell her I will come for her."

"You must not do so until your Zidu'Si is complete. You are not yet strong enough to face Salmetu and do what must be done." Tianna disappeared at her last word.

"What do we do now Lugaldur?" Moltar asked.

"We must see to the safety of the refugees. Beyond that, I just do not yet know my friend."

Chapter Sixteen

Shuran met with the Zidu'Si and shared his thoughts on rebuilding the Britengate settlement. As a group, they decided that they would need to enlist the help of the Elves and Dwarves. Until they knew who in Drakkfoth was allied with Vardoran, they would not include them in their plans. Only the Baron would be advised, along with any of the Drakkon Riders. The Gula'Lu would not be asked to leave their valley, but they would be told.

Shuran decided to spend some time in the Emmuku'Gu. Part of his reasoning was to find a path to Edinzabar, another was to talk to the voices. He wanted answers to questions that were forming as his quest progressed. Shuran had been having more visions and flashes of memories that were not his own. He found no voices this time, and this caused more questions.

That evening as he rested, Shuran had another of his visions. He looked around to find himself standing in an expansive room. Row upon row of shelves and cases filled the space. As he walked the aisles, Shuran noticed that all the shelves were lined with books bound in gold. He approached one of the shelves and looked at the symbols of the binding on one of the books. It read 'Kima Parsi Labiruti' and disintegrated upon his touch.

He moved through the shelves trying to pick up one of the golden bound tomes. Each bore the same title and disintegrated immediately before he touched them. Soon the entire structure of his vision was falling apart before him. He tried to reach out with his will and stop the destruction, but was unable. Soon he stood alone in the dark and voices called out to him. He looked to his hand. It held a jewel-hilted dagger of gold and his sister's body lay bloodied at his feet.

"SHURAN, SHIN'AR!" Mallick yelled, trying to grab Shuran's attention out of a dream. He had been standing there for several minutes talking to Shuran before he noticed that his lifetime friend and Shin'Ar was fixed in a trance and not waking. Mallick finally decided to douse him with icy water.

"What!" Shuran snapped back to reality in shocked surprise.

"Where were you just then?" Mallick asked concerned.

"Kima Parsi Labiruti," Shuran mumbled. "I had another vision, though I am well. Let us make for Britengate, we have work to get underway." Shuran got up and generated heat to dry his under clothes. He performed the task subconsciously as he gathered items to dress and perform his morning ablutions.

Mallick watched with concern as Shuran seemed to walk through his routine, seemingly still asleep.

The Zidu'Si left Durangug that morning after eating. They traveled by Emmuku'Gu since Shuran wanted the others to get used to doing so on their own. It took some coaxing, and Shuran or Orian had to grab hold of their shi a few times to keep them from getting lost, but they were getting the hang of traveling the rivers of power. They arrived in Britengate to find the town already occupied by nearly fifty human refugees.

The people reacted quickly with pick axes and weapons collected on their march from whatever towns they escaped. Essence wielding and weaving became a source of dread for the mundanes of Aurderia. They were rightfully frightened.

Shuran stepped forward slowly and put his hands out in a gesture for them to lower their weapons.

"I am the Shin'Ar and this is my Zidu'Si. We are here to help," Shuran said. He then sensed Orian's thoughts in the corner of his mind. As a single force, Shuran and the Zidu'Si sent out calming feelings to the people occupying Britengate. It was only a matter of moments before they all laid down their weapons and were open enough to listen to what Shuran had to say.

"We need to rebuild Britengate. The force of darkness called the Shadow has taken hold in Ersetu and must be driven back. We are here to help and protect the people of Aurderia, but we must work together," Shuran told them. He continued to speak about how this would be a place of sanctuary for refugees that wish to flee from the darkness. The Dwarves and Elves would be coming to help, and together they could stand against the Shadow.

The Zidu'Si split the folk into groups based on skills, strength, and age. The youngest and oldest of the people were set to less physically demanding tasks like sweeping and collecting wild foods from the forest. The more capable were enlisted for the work of carpentry, clearing out damaged buildings, and collecting timbers and stones. The Zidu'Si used their abilities to move things along faster by lifting beams into place while a mundane hammered or they moved stone so masonry could be sped along.

By early the next evening, there was enough accomplished to put roofs over the heads of those already there. A bakery and an inn that mostly survived the battle with death walkers were both repaired to a useable status so they could cook meals and gather together. That evening the first of the elves arrived followed soon after by Moona, Codger, and Andra with the Mellamu Nanna filled with dwarves.

Shuran instructed Andra to travel by Magurmu with Moona and Codger; he did not want to risk teaching him the ways of the Emmuku'gu. It was not that he distrusted Andra, he simply was unsure of his kind and their motives.

Together they spent the next four days repairing the rest of the buildings in the settlement and started the construction of new housing and barracks with stables. Shuran advised that they needed to have a full working city by the time Salmetu decided to make her move.

The Zidu'Si left the Dwarves and Elves to continue while they went on to Drakkfoth to meet Nagutan.

Moona elected to take charge, much to Codger's visible protest.

***

Nagutan and Penelle had only just arrived in Drakkfoth when the Zidu'Si exited the Emmuku'Gu on the outskirts of the Stone Forest. Shuran took the lead as they stepped through the outcroppings of jagged rocky bushes and trees. In the twilight of early evening, the Stone Forest gave an eerie and mysterious feeling to the secret meeting. The heated ground was already reacting to the fast cooling night and a misty fog floated across the area.

Avrank stopped by a tree that had a face frozen in time, twisted among the rocky bark. He reached out a hand and touched his palm to the side of the tree.

"It still screams even now," Avrank said with tears in his eyes. "The spirit of the dryad is forever bonded in stone with the tree."

"Is it possible to free them?" Shuran asked.

"I do not know Shin'Ar, they may be mad beyond recovery. There is no way to see how they might react, they might turn on us," Orian answered. "They faced certain death to stay with their forest, living without it would likely cause more harm than good."

"Listen to your elf friend Shin'Ar. The dryads would take the first faces they have seen in thousands of years, as a threat. They would tear you apart." Penelle walked from behind a group of trees, followed by Nagutan and his imp.

"And you would know this how kashshaptu?" Shuran said evenly.

"Because I knew these creatures, and their dedication to this forest is eternal."

"Let us get to the reason we have gathered," Nagutan said as he stepped forward. "The Baron will be joining us shortly, but there is something we can discuss before he arrives. What do you plan to do about your sister?" Nagutan asked pointedly.

Shuran studied Nagutan for a moment and felt a familiarity with him that he could not shake. The words came out effortlessly and without thought.

"Kima Parsi Labiruti."

"You are remembering, Shin'Ar. This is good indeed!" Nagutan smiled knowingly.

"You understand this memory? Whose is it?" Shuran asked.

"Your thoughts are your own I would image," Nagutan answered in such a way that indicated he would not entertain further explanation.

The Zidu'Si held confused looks, except Mallick who narrowed his eyes at the exchange. He knew this old man was hiding things, many things.

Fortunately for all, the Baron arrived and interrupted further discussion. He came alone as was requested. There was a howl in the distance.

"Shuran! I did not expect to see you? How is your mother?" Fallon asked.

"I would ask the same question of you uncle, except that my mother is not with me. Why would you think she was with me?"

"Because she told me herself that she was leaving to spend her time with you in Durangug."

Shuran looked to Moltar, who moved his head in and gave Fallon a good sniff. He nodded back to Shuran that it was the Baron.

"What is going on here?" Fallon asked indignantly.

"I apologize uncle, we needed certainty that it was truly you. Whatever it was that told you she was my mother was not. She was taken to Vardoran by a traitor in your castle."

Shuran and Nagutan explained what occurred with Sulura. They explained to Fallon about the refugees fleeing from Aurderia that may enter his lands. Middleton was a border town and Fallon had men that rotated there to maintain barracks on the outside of town. He would send men there to begin covertly directing those who fled, in the direction of Britengate.

"Until those people loyal to the Order are identified, we cannot have any but the drakkon riders or yourself in Britengate," Mallick told him.

The baron felt minor insult, but he understood. He was more angered that there was a traitor in his home. This traitor was a shifter. His thoughts immediately went to Barurbe, his adopted daughter. She was able to shift into a wolf, was it possible she hid other shapes from him. And he had asked her to hide off in the distance, monitoring his safety at this secret meeting.

Shuran must have read his thoughts. "Moltar find the white wolf. Persuade her to come forth."

"That will not be necessary Shuran. I am here, and I am not the one you are looking for." Barurbe stepped out of the mist and into a small clearing the others met in.

"You are a shifter though," Moltar said, sniffing her from several feet away.

"I did not know what I was until two cycles past, when it came to me like a wolf. I felt its kinship immediately. I was deceived of its true intention." Barurbe began to sob.

She explained how the shifter came and told her she was not alone. It made her feel a true sense of connection for the first time. She let it into the castle and soon, her heart. She wondered why he suddenly disappeared. Now she heard the truth of its intentions. She was confused, heartbroken, and ashamed.

"You will not be safe here for long Fallon. I would suggest you begin moving your people to Britengate." Nagutan suggested, knowing Shuran would not object.

"And what will the two of you do?" Shuran asked Nagutan and Penelle.

"That is another discussion we must have. Perhaps on the way to Britengate we can discuss it," Nagutan suggested.

Shuran traveled on to Britengate with Nagutan and Penelle in her carriage. Mallick insisted on driving since he wanted to keep an eye on Nagutan. Moltar stayed with the rest of the Zidu'Si to assist in preparations for moving those who wished, to Britengate or into the Highlands where the rest of the Drakkians settled generations ago.

Nagutan explained how Penelle and her coven were all tried, found guilty, and punished to a cursed undying life in the marshes of the Mist

Swamps. He also explained that their crime was working blood magic and twisting their employed dwarfs into trolls. Not only had they used blood magic, which was frowned upon, but they did so on people and through deception. Three separate crimes compounded the sentencing.

"The punishment was severe. They have been in those swamps for thousands of years." Nagutan seemed to empathize with the kashshaptu.

Shuran was not moved. He wanted to know why they would do this to the dwarves.

"They served us willingly, we overstepped. We needed them to act as fighters, to protect us and be taken seriously. We have had all this time to think on our crimes. The trolls we turned are long dead. We can do nothing to change what happened." Penelle managed to show her remorse.

"And is it you and your sister kashshaptu who call the trolls to service now?" Shuran asked.

"What do you mean? We have not sent the call in hundreds of years!" Penelle lied. She knew her sister witches called them to the swamps.

"The trolls have been active for months, coming down from the North. They now march south toward New Draven in the thousands," Shuran said to Penelle's mock surprise.

Penelle spoke of how the trolls would only come to the call of the kashshaptu, so someone in her coven was working without consulting her. She spoke of her only motivation in the current situation facing Aurderia, which was to gain a means of breaking the curse for her and sister kashshaptu. Using the blood of a seven-born was the only way she knew to accomplish this.

"It is not the only way my dear, Shuran has the power to remove the curse. All he needs is to enact a release upon each of the kashshaptu, and reverse the effects," Nagutan said.

"Although I find what you did reprehensible, I agree that you and your kind have served more than necessary for your crimes," Shuran started. "I will, however, expect answers for why the trolls now march across Aurderia and attacked me so many moons ago."

Chapter Seventeen

Salmetu stood in the Great Hall of the Council House in New Draven. Her hair was flowing back in a nonexistent wind as Shadow poured from her mouth and into the last of the old Council Members. She held the man with one hand around his neck, suspending him inches from the ground. Her eyes were deep black and smokey as she looked up at her latest unwilling follower. When she placed the man down, he joined the others standing behind the large throne that now occupied the center of the dais where the Great Council table once sat.

Telalsu, inhabiting Bastien's body, stood by her side as Salmetu took the throne. He handed her a small crown of gold, jeweled with gems of deep ruby and shards of dragon glass. She placed it upon her head and looked out at the crowd of people in the hall ready to accept her.

Followers of the Order of Chaos and those who have been servants of the Shadow gathered to see the coronation of their new leader. More followers arrived each day. Much of the death walkers were now vessels for the Shadow, and they attended the coronation.

Telalsu stumbled while stepping away from the throne to take his place at her side. Although he quickly reclaimed control of Bastien's body, Salmetu took notice.

"What is your trouble demon? Do we need to find you another vessel?" Salmetu hissed at him in a hundred voices.

"I will not be bested by this human, he will submit."

"Come before me. I will stop this fighting at once," Salmetu ordered. She took hold of Telalsu's borrowed head and she channeled Shadow from herself out toward the body of Bastien.

The Shadow swirled before Bastien's face and began seeping into his mouth. The body had spasmed briefly before the Shadow came rolling back out of Bastien's open mouth and nostrils. It could not take hold.

Salmetu shook with rage. This pitiful human shell was defying the Shadow. She could not understand the resistance. None that she had touched could resist the power of the Shadow.

"Sacrifice…" whispered the voices in her head. "The shi does not give up the vessel, it wants nothing more than returning."

Salmetu finally understood. When the boy, Bastien, stood up to Telalsu and the Inquisitors in Birchshire, he sacrificed himself in a moment of purity. He was protecting his friend. Somehow the shi that would have left when Bastien all but died anchored itself to something. Telalsu could never have this vessel so long as the anchor existed.

"You will go find what holds Bastien's shi to this realm. Find it, and destroy it or take possession of it, then the body will not resist you," Salmetu's echoed voices told him.

"Where shall I begin to look, my Queen?"

"Go back to Birchshire, retrace your movements. The boy had a father did he not? It is likely the father or the Shin'Ar carry an object that holds the shi."

***

Shuran sat in the carriage half listening to Nagutan and Penelle talking as they travelled on toward Britengate. He was exhausted and running on abnu emuq and Durangug energy. He knew he could not keep this up for long without true rest. As he sat thinking, his thoughts began to drift as the rocking of the carriage began to lull him to sleep.

The vision came on fast. Shuran stood before the ancient crystal stones laid out in a circular pattern. He extended his arms out toward the stones, but they were not his own arms.

Strong hands extended toward the crystal structures. They were the hands of a mid-aged man, a ring set on the middle finger of the right hand. Crimson robes fell from his wrists. Slowly the hands began to glow with a white light. Sudden power surged into him from a tapped energy, then flowed out through his hands and into the stones.

The stones rose from the ground and rearranged into the placement of the altar. The stones began to take on the same white glow. As the light intensified, it drove the stones into the ground and the power flowed straight down, deep into the core of the world, where it met the source of Essence.

Shuran woke with a start when Nagutan touched his hand.

"Are you well, young Shin'Ar?" Nagutan asked.

"We need to rebuild the Altar of Creation." Shuran spoke in a distracted manner. He did not say anything else before looking down at Nagutan's hand on his. He looked at the aged hand with one solitary band of metal on a single finger. Shuran put his head back and went back to sleep.

The city of Britengate was more active than in hundreds of years. New buildings were added to those that had been repaired. In the few days since the Zidu'Si first left for Drakk, more refugees arrived and added to the force of workers, rebuilding the deserted city. Followers of the Light returned and the former mood of despair was now one of hope.

The mundane humans in the settlement began to adjust to having magical races around. Since more refugees arrived, many of them were talented in weaving. With human weavers in the mix, the mundanes felt they had representation among the magic users. The sight of drakkon arriving was not as surprising had the new citizens of Britengate not become more accustom to such sights. The old ways of life before the Lalli Mah was returning.

Shuran exited the carriage as rested as he could have expected from days sitting upright. He stood before the city and felt the same hope the citizens had.

"You look like yak scat, sheesh!" Mallick said as he came up beside Shuran.

"You have a gift for stating the obvious my brother. I think it past time I speak to you all about something," Shuran said. "Will you please have the Zidu'Si along with Moona and Codger, assemble in the meeting-house."

"Of course. What about Andra?" Mallick asked.

"I think it best that Andra not be a party to this conversation for now. I need to know for certain where his loyalties reside."

Mallick left Shuran with Nagutan and Penelle to gather the Zidu'Si. The meeting would occur as soon as Gregoran arrived with the kimmane of drakkon and riders from Drakkfoth. Mallick knew Gregoran would be arriving soon since he had communicated his expected arrival.

Gregoran finally arrived with the kimmane. They were two hundred strong and ready to fight. First they needed to create housing and proper fields for the drakkon.

The other Drakkians who would be coming were leading a caravan of wagons with supplies and food. Not all would abandon their home in Drakk for the Baron would travel between there and Britengate to represent his people in both locations.

Gregoran and Jade landed in the middle of the clearing just east of the city. After Gregoran had jump from Jade's back, she flew off to meet Moltar in the distance where Gregoran had pointed him out, huddled alone, upon their approach.

"Why are you not with your Lugaldur?" Jade asked Moltar as she landed next to him.

"He is resting," Moltar said simply without looking up at Jade.

Jade swung her tail around and hit Moltar on the side of his massive head.

"Just because you are now larger than any two of the biggest Drakkon together, does not make you too big for a good knock in the head!" Jade said.

"I am sorry my mother. My Lugaldur is changing," he said as he stood to greet Jade.

"We all change my young hatchling, just look at you."

"That is not what I mean, I sense something else on the edge of our bond. I sense another…" Moltar shared.

"He is the Shin'Ar Reborn. He is bound to change as he grows in strength and ability as you have. Do not worry over much. It is not becoming of a drakkon." Jade smiled at Moltar and gave him an affectionate lick.

"We must go! My Lugaldur calls me to assemble!" Moltar said in haste and took to flight.

In the meetinghouse, the Zidu'Si began to gather. The drakkon could not enter but looked on from windows on each side.

"What in the name of Damkianna is this all 'bout? I got things to do!" Moona complained.

"Shut your crab trap ol' woman! Our boy wants to talk 'bout somethin' he ain' been truthin' 'bout so you're gonna clamp your trap an' listen!" Codger answered in a moment of courage.

Moona looked on in stunned silence, and did not fight back. She slowly turned her snarl into a slight smile.

"I will not coat this conversation with pleasantries and flowery talk. A change has been coming over me. I do not understand it, nor do I know what it represents. I am taking on memories of a time long before I or any of us live," Shuran said bluntly. "I am not certain what any of this means, but I feel it guiding my actions."

"It means you remember who you are, Shin'Ar Reborn!" Nagutan said as he entered uninvited.

"This is a closed meeting! What do you think-" Mallick stood and said before being interrupted?

"It is fine, Mallick. Nagutan speak clearly!" Shuran demanded.

Mallick continued to glare at Nagutan with distrust. He also noticed the band of gugtu on the old man's finger.

"You are more than just the child born to prophecy, my boy. You are the rebirth of my Shin'Ar and I must serve you as I did him." Nagutan said. "You are he and he is you!"

"So much for speakin' clear!" Moona whispered.

"Nagutan explain what your part in all this is. I feel I know you though I should not," Shuran said.

Mallick studied Nagutan closer and recalled something he noticed before, the ring on his finger. He remained silent for the moment. He could not help but share the mental image of the ring with Shuran through the Zidu'Si link.

"I cannot completely explain yet, not without full permission, my Shin'Ar. The effects you feel are memories of your past life reasserting themselves," Nagutan explained.

Shuran looked at Nagutan in confusion for a moment, then realization set across his mind.

"I know you. You were there," Shuran said as pain in his head overtook him. He faltered and began to crumble under the weight of agony and memories. Images of past events, long before his birth, flashed before his eyes. He screamed with a thousand silent voices then suddenly became silent.

Moments passed before anyone in the room gained wits to notice what had happened. Shuran changed in appearance. He was now matured to the age on a man of thirty harvests. His features altered slightly to match his age, but his eyes were different. His eyes were no longer the bright green he was born with, they now shone with a brilliance that was somehow reflecting all colors.

Nagutan approached the rigid form of Shuran. He stood stark still upon the raised platform he had been addressing his Zidu'Si from. As Nagutan reached to touch him, Shuran stepped away.

"What have you done?" Shuran asked as he looked at Nagutan. "What else have you tampered with?"

"I have only done what was necessary to ensure your rebirth and that you would awaken at the prescribed time," Nagutan answered as he backed away. "This was all planned long ago, I only did as I was bade."

"We shall speak of this further in private," Shuran said directly to Nagutan. He then turned to his friends and Zidu'Si before continuing. "As it has become obvious," he glanced at Nagutan, "I have been experiencing visions, memories more to the point, of the past that I was not alive to experience first hand." Shuran again looked at Nagutan to prevent him interrupting. "I am not clear what is happening, but there are elements to these visions that have guided me."

"Why have you not told us of these visions before now, Shuran?" Mallick asked. He was visibly hurt that his adopted brother had not confided in him.

"These things have been happening far too fast. I could not be certain they were not intrusions on my mind, true visions, or simply dreams. I had no intention of slighting any of you by not taking you into confidence, I simply wanted to understand them before proceeding," Shuran assured them. "I do not understand them yet, but they have reached a point, where I must no longer keep my own counsel."

Shuran went on to speak about the visions he had been experiencing. These visions were guiding his actions with a deep need to follow their telling. The latest vision of rebuilding the Altar of Creation created the strongest desire yet. He advised the Zidu'Si that he would be following another instinct, to help cure the kashshaptu of their curse.

After much debate and arguing, the Zidu'Si at least saw the truth behind Shuran's decisions. Moona, on the other hand, was not so agreeable.

"Kashshaptu! You believe you can trust in their sorceress ways?" Moona croaked. "They are as slippery as the swamp eels they eat!"

With a deep sigh, Shuran stepped to the side to receive his scolding. "I am not prepared to fully trust these witches, Moona. I simply do not feel their continued imprisonment is justified."

"HA! You think if them kashshaptu harpies, changed one of your kin into trolls to do their bidding that ya'd be so willin' to forgive and forget?"

"You forget, I am of seven bloodlines, so I am deeply connected to this. Time changes everything. The trolls have become a new breed apart from their dwarven forbears. The dwarves do not even remember the reason for their hatred of the trolls and vice versa. Perhaps it is time these old wounds be healed."

Moona grumbled at Shuran's statements, "I don' like it one bit… but I figure you know best." Moona un-characteristically conceded to Shuran's will and left without further word.

Codger followed after her. "What was that… back there just then?"

"What are you talkin' 'bout codger?" Moona asked in a defeated tone.

"Moony, I know you and you never just give in like that. What gives?"

"He has changed Codge. I know he is still our Shuran, but already he is so very different. I just fear-"

"He ain' our Vardoran, this is different Moony," Codger tried to convince her. "Shuran is special, you know 's much as any what that boy is meant for!"

"Vision and prophecy be damned! I will not just believe that Shuran is a reborn Shin'Ar or prophet!" Moona grumbled.

Codger just stood quietly listening.

"I don' argue he is special, and his abilities grow as fast as he does, but somethin' jus' don' sit right."

Shuran waited until the others had cleared the room before sealing it from eavesdroppers. He cast a simple spell to both keep the sound of their voices within the room, but also obscured viewing. He was certain Moona could read lips. He turned and looked upon Nagutan, inviting him to begin his tale.

Nagutan began his story from the fall of the Zidu'Si. His Shin'Ar made a daring plan to bring balance back to the flow of Essence in Ersetu. His plan was not entirely shared with the Zidu'Si, however, only different pieces were shared with them. As Shin'Ar's Isten, Nagutan was given the most detail, but even that was not complete. The various members were given different instruction that was not for sharing with any other member.

The Zidu'Si of old was torn by duty to both the world and their Shin'Ar. Most of them failed to perform their tasks. The Shin'Ar's ultimate plan was never seen through to fruition. Only the member from the Gula'Lu and Nagutan kept their faith and stayed to see a new plan created, one that would take thousands of years to accomplish. This was why Nagutan and Gimagala were afforded longer lives than even the most long-lived of the races.

"Gimagala was there to collect the shi of the Shin'Ar by using the ancient dagger, Shi'Kar. Affixed to the hilt was a crystal shard of many colors, where Shin'Ar's shi would be trapped and stored until the time of rebirth," Nagutan recited the story as though it had just occurred. "I carried and guarded the stone all this time, until I could see it placed in your hands.”

“The Abnu Emuq! The one I drained as a swaddled sprat!” Shuran realized.

“Yes, I made certain that it was left in the ruins of Durangug, where Codger would find it,” Nagutan confirmed. “I played my part in, seeing that destiny stayed the course my Shin’Ar foresaw. I even went as far as placing the visions in the minds of seers. Prophecy is a tricky business!” Nagutan said with a sly smile.

Shuran was reeling from what he had just heard, but somehow he knew it for truth. “So my life is not my own?”

“You are Shuran, you are Shin’Ar Reborn, you are the son of Sulura and Dalgon. These things are all of you, and make you more than just my Shin’Ar. I sense him in you, but you are not the man he was, only a reflection.” Nagutan was back to his cryptic explanations.

“I still feel myself but with something more. Am I being possessed?” Shuran asked in a sudden horrifying thought.

“No, I believe that only a part of my Shin’Ar was passed to you. When The Shin’Ar gave his corporeal self up for the cause of bringing balance, he surrendered his possible chance of return. His body was not preserved.”

Chapter Eighteen

Shuran was flooded with more memories and realized that his visions were more instruction than foreseeing of future events. As his powers and knowledge in Essence grew, the memories of the prior Shin'Ar were able to reach his conscious mind. He would no longer only suffer the nightly dreams; he was subject to them while awake.

"My only comfort is knowing I am not losing my mind, not yet at any rate," Shuran said.

"It is my opinion that these memories will fade upon completion of whatever task my Shin'Ar has left for you." Nagutan made it clear with his last statement, that not even he knew what was now to come. His job was complete.

"What will you do now?" Shuran asked him, seeing he looked misplaced somehow.

"I would continue to serve the new Shin'Ar, if he will have my council," Nagutan said with a questioning tone.

"I would be ill advised not to take advantage of your experience."

Nagutan removed a simple band from his finger and handed it to Shuran. "This is yours, the only other item left in my keeping to give you now."

Shuran studied the ring and then saw the symbols engraved upon the gugtu band. He immediately recognized it as a mate to the Mudutu'Har, the Ring of Knowledge that Mallick wore. Shuran placed the ring on his finger and immediately felt a connection to the library he never had. That connection was flowing through Mallick, and he knew that his friend would now feel the connection once he placed his ring back on his finger.

Shuran and Nagutan finally emerged from the meeting building to find the Zidu'Si all awaiting their exit. Codger and Moona were conspicuously absent from the assembly. Shuran decided he would have to seek out Moona and talk her down from whatever tirade she was brewing. He shared a mental blending with the Zidu'Si to explain what had occurred. It was easier and safer to do so, rather than a lengthy explanation out in the open.

All the Zidu'Si except Mallick were content with the information. Mallick stepped forward before Nagutan.

"I knew I recognized the ring. Were you deliberately disrupting my connection to the Vault library?" Mallick accused.

"Indirectly I was by having the ring upon my finger. I knew what information you were searching, and at times I prevented or guided your actions. All to fulfill my obligations and make certain things happened as they were planned." Nagutan held up his hands in mock surrender.

Mallick took out his ring to place it on his finger. Shuran stopped him.

"Before you do that I need to borrow that."

Mallick handed the ring over without question, knowing Shuran would have good reason.

Shuran placed the ring upon his finger to nestle with the one he already wore. The effect was immediate. He had full access to the Library as well as other information he did not quite comprehend at the moment. He decided that it would wait for now. He had another pressing matter to see to. He headed to the ruins of the Altar of Creation.

Shuran closed his eyes and raised his hands as he saw in the visions from the prior Shin'Ar. He focused on the memories implanted in his subconscious mind. With a thought, he connected to the force of Durangug and channeled it through his Zidu'Si to himself. He concentrated on the inert altar and poured his thoughts into its repair.

Slowly at first, the altar stone shifted back into place and earth repositioned to support it. Shuran levitated all the surrounding uprights and felled lintels back into position. His brow was wrinkled and sweating as he began the work of repairing the cracks in the altar stone. When he finally completed this, he moved on to the last part of his task, connecting the altar to the core of the Essence at the center of Ersetu.

Shuran reached with all his strength but found he was nearing the limit of his abilities. He would soon damage his Zidu'Si as well if he did not stop. In a last effort, he located a flow of the Emmuku'Gu and built a channel to it. The power flowed into the altar. It was far from the vision but until he could complete the task, it would have to do. He released the power of Durangug and collapsed along with his Zidu'Si.

The Zidu'Si rested for hours after Shuran was up and about. He required less time to recover due to his unique mix of bloodlines as well as his exercise of wielding more Essence than the others, strengthening his constitution. He decided after his conversation with Nagutan, that he needed to speak with Gimagala. He felt there was likely important information that would be gained by finding out her part in the first Shin'Ar's sacrifice.

After discussing his plans with the Zidu'Si Shuran, accompanied by Dara, left first for Durangug. They were stopping so that Shuran could construct a communication crystal for the Gula'Lu. He also wanted some time to speak with Dara alone in order to get to know her people better.

They arrived in Durangug shortly after stepping into the Emmuku'Gu. Within moments, Shuran sensed a disturbance behind him as he and Dara walked toward the Vault entrance.

"You can drop your cloak, I know you are there my bonded," Shuran said with a hint of amusement on his voice.

"Sometimes I think this bond is inconvenient!" Moltar announced as he became visible.

Laughing, Shuran looked back toward his drakkon friend, "I suppose when it comes to sneaking along with your Lugaldur, it would be rather annoying! I should have supposed you would not let me go to Edinzabar without you."

"Yes… Certainly not! That is why I followed!" Moltar did not sound convincing.

Shuran knew full well that his overly grown drakkon's primary reason for tagging along was to take advantage of the effect the valley had upon his size.

"At what point do you suppose you will be big enough my friend?" Shuran asked.

"What? Oh that… I suppose there is the growth effect of the valley. I had not thought of that."

Dara and Shuran simply looked at him sideways as they held their laughter and entered the vault. Moltar waited outside since he no longer fit comfortably within.

Shuran led Dara to his work area where he would construct the communication crystal for the Gula'Lu. As he worked, he encouraged Dara to tell him more of her people and their ways.

"What you will want most to know is of the elders and my mother. She is the only one of the elders still capable of transforming back from mercurial form regularly. The others do not contain the strength of Gimagala, she was granted far more as a Zidu'Si," Dara began.

"What do you mean mercurial form?" Shuran asked.

"You will recall that Gimagala rose up from a basin at the testing, she was carried to the fields in the basin from the Nashi'Zag." Seeing Shuran's confusion, she explained further. "When the eldest among the Gula'Lu are at the point they are failing in health due to aging, they commit themselves to the river of metal souls that flows through the valley. They give up the corporeal form for the mercurial.

Though my mother is capable of maintaining a normal form, she prefers to commune among those of the Nashi'Zag. The elders begin to lose all sense after they have become one with the river. They are prone to fits of changing mood and disposition. She remains to help stabilize them and bring them peace." Dara stopped with a look of confusion.

"What is wrong?" Shuran asked.

"I do not know how I knew that last part, perhaps mother spoke of it and I simply did not recall until now. In any case, the term 'mercurial' is now used anytime someone becomes moody among our people."

"I wonder that Moona isn't part Gula'Lu," Shuran laughed.

Shuran turned back to his work and completed the spell and split the silver speckled crystal he chose to use. He placed one piece of the stone upon his arm brace and used Essence to mold the metal around the gem to hold it firmly in place. He then used a sample of *gugtu* to create a ring to house the other piece. He did not have enough of the magical stone on hand to create a pendant and chain large enough for King Awilzag.

"Shall we go then? Moltar is anxiously awaiting our trip. I am surprised he did not leave ahead of us!" Dara said.

Shuran just smiled and said, "He did!"

Moltar was flying around the valley, putting on an aerial acrobatics show for the Gula'Lu when Shuran and Dara popped into the valley. King Awilzag was enjoying the performance as much as anyone. The show had gone on for many minutes before Moltar allowed himself a moment to sense the presence of his Lugaldur.

Moltar landed before Shuran and proceeded to posture. He had gained another three hundred pounds of bulk in just a short time there.

"You are going to become simply unbearable if you stay much longer!" Shuran said, trying to give a stern face.

Moltar only gave a toothy grin and took back to the air.

"I understand you wish to give me a communication stone of some kind. Your beast had already announced your intentions when he surprised us with his appearance," Awilzag said with a humored scowl. "You are, of course, always welcome, but a bit of warning might be in order next time Moltar arrives."

As Awilzag took them to see Gimagala, he explained how Moltar popped into the center of the courts and immediately launched into the air. After the initial shock wore off and the screaming of attack was settled, Moltar landed to tell them of the Shin'Ar's imminent arrival and the purpose. He then took back to the air and began his aerial dance.

Shuran gave King Awilzag the ring and explained its use. The activation was set to the touch of the Gula'Lu so a spelling word would not be required. Gula'Lu unbound to a Zidu'Si were unable to weave spells. After a long walk through the forest, they reached the banks of a silvery metal flow. The width was no more than ten paces wide, but Shuran's senses let him see how deep and how far it flowed. Shuran stopped and gasped.

"There are thousands of our kin flowing within the Nashi'Zag," Awilzag stated.

"But this flows the entire valley, and is so deep!" Shuran said with doubt.

"You forget the properties of mercury. This valley is very warm and the Gula'Lu are large and expand in the warmth even more than true mercury does."

"Some of us expand more than others," said Gimagala as she rose from the river and pointed to Awilzag's gut. "I wondered when you would be back for answers young Shin'Ar," she said turning to Shuran.

Gimagala stepped from the river and continued to reform into her natural form. She stepped up to Shuran and remained silent as she lifted her hands to him and they began to shimmer and flow into mercury. She cleared her throat and looked at his hands, indicating he should take her hands in his own.

The blending, as the Gula'Lu call it, overtook all of Shuran's senses and sent his mind spinning. As he acclimated to the sensation, he slowly began to focus. He not only saw, but also heard everything that was Gimagala. Her entire being began to become one with Shuran. As she melded mentally with him, she came against a barrier. She could merge no more.

"Where are we?" Shuran asked within the linking of minds.

"You are within the trappings of my mind, Shin'Ar. Normally this would be an equally shared experience, but something about your makeup prevents it. No matter, it is you that seeks knowledge so let us begin." Gimagala began racing through the memories that Shuran would need.

Shuran was overwhelmed with sounds and images of events from times long before the Lalli Mah. He saw the forming of the Zidu'Si bond. He experienced times of strife and those of peace. Wars waged among unknown races of man-like creatures and many more that were vile and like nothing living in the world of present. Somehow Shuran knew everything Gimagala knew.

After many normal lifetimes of memories bore into Shuran, he finally saw what he was waiting for, the task set by Gimagala's Shin'Ar.

Gimagala stood over her Shin'Ar. The golden dagger, Mi-Ib Karshi gripped in her hand, she plunged it into his heart at his command. Tears flowed down her face as the soul of her Shin'Ar flowed through the golden blade, through the hilt and into the gem-specked crystal. The tears clouded the vision and as words began to flow from her lips, Gimagala fought against the blending and forced Shuran from her. She was too late, Shuran felt the same love for her Shin'Ar that she had.

Gimagala said nothing. She turned from Shuran, kissed her husband Awilzag and retired to the Nashi'Zag. Her connection to Shuran faded, but part of her remained.

Shuran lay on the ground, trembling and covered in sweat. When he finally pulled his thoughts together, he opened his eyes to find the sky well into the dusky light of late night in the valley. Hours had passed that felt like only moments to Shuran. His first thought was of Moltar.

"Damkianna! He will have put on another thousand pounds of bulk while I was… What exactly did I just experience?" Shuran asked Awilzag.

"That my boy was a blending, the Zumru'Sa actually; a joining of body and minds. At least a partial joining. It seems that only part of you went mercurial."

"Something prevented it, but Gimagala did not elaborate, though I think she may have suspected why," Shuran said.

Dara helped Shuran up from the ground and steadied him before the three headed back toward the city. She looked at Shin'Ar differently than she previously had. She quickly regained her normally stoic expression and took the lead as they walked the paths back.

Shuran noticed the change in Dara. Perhaps her mother has never blended with her? Shuran thought to himself. She may be upset by an outsider sharing an experience with her mother that she had not. He quickly dismissed that thought. Surely she would have gone through the Zumru'Sa. Dara must have assumed what would occur. Shuran found himself with yet another mystery to think upon.

"She is a female, you are not supposed to understand them!" Moltar said, intruding upon Shuran's thoughts. "At least that is what Gregoran told Avrank when he asked why Dara did not respond to his advances."

"Great! A love struck dwarf and a 'mercurial' Gula'Lu. I am soon becoming the leader of a motley crew of misfits as Moona says," Shuran mumbled to himself as he pictured Moltar scratching his back end on the side of a Gula'Lu house. This was much to the dislike of the screaming Gula'Lu woman shouting up at the oblivious drakkon.

***

Salmetu sat before a large pit in the earth where the crack in the foundations of the Academy catacombs first appeared. She had reformed it and widened it into what would ordinarily pass as a well. There would be no water retrieved from this deep pit. However, it led into the depths of the Shadow. Salmetu leaned over the opening chanting in an ancient tongue. Her words were incomprehensible.

When she sat back, her manner changed and she spoke in her chorus of voices. "Come to me, my followers. Come to the Queen of Shadow and glory in my power!"

The murky black mists of the Shadow swirled and rippled as they carried her words across all of Ersetu. She was calling on the forces of darkness and its allies, bringing them to the Aurderian Capital.

Deep in the Mist Swamps, a kashshaptu sat before a crack in the marshy land. A mist of darkness vapored up from the depths and whispered to the ancient witch.

Chapter Nineteen

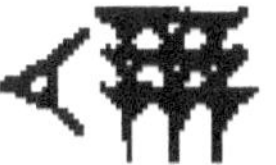

Shuran and Dara arrived back in Britengate late in the night to find nearly half the inhabitants still awake and busy at work. More refugees arrived in the day he, Dara, and Moltar were gone. The drakkon riders were patrolling the air in shifts and the Elfin Rangers kept watch in the forests surrounding the bustling city. Shuran and Dara headed for the meetinghouse. Moltar headed to the drakkon grounds that had been cleared to the east of the city.

He found the Zidu'Si awaiting his return. Although Shuran had already communicated his reasons for being later in returning than expected, his comrades wanted more explicit details of his experience. Shuran described what he felt was appropriate to the satisfaction of everyone except Dara, she knew he withheld more personal information.

"You hav' ta stop takin' that monstrous pet of yours to that valley Shuran!" Moona cried as she barged in. "Not only will he eat all the game around, his backside will be killin' anything its droppings land upon, and I ain' cleaning it up!"

Everyone laughed as Moona stood looking up to Shuran, red-faced and scolding him. When she was satisfied her complaints were satisfactorily understood, she reached up and pulled Shuran's face in for a peck on the cheek. After a light smack on the opposite check, she exited the way she entered.

Shuran left the others to rest and walked with Mallick to inspect the work that had been keeping the people busy. Shuran felt guilty for not spending more time with Mallick. He was for all intent and purpose Shuran's brother, they grew up together. With all that had been happening, the two did not have time to simply talk.

"What is on your mind sheesh?" Mallick asked.

"Am I that transparent?" Shuran asked.

"Not without a spell," Mallick joked. "You have been withdrawn and closed off. Even your usual thought sharing has waned."

"I am concerned that I am losing myself in the midst of all that is happening. These 'changes' to me are of the deepest concern."

"Your powers are growing, Shuran, this is expected," Mallick responded. "You have even gained age in the last few turns."

"I mean the memories, though I do hope this rapid aging would come to an end. I wonder if this is what being possessed feels like?" Shuran wondered. He was not truly asking Mallick, but he could feel immediately when Mallick accessed the Vault library.

Shuran felt the flow of information as Mallick scanned the archives for information on possession. Shuran had enough going through his head with his own thoughts, memories of the first Shin'Ar, as well as the residual memories of Gimagala. It was far too crowded to handle the information from the Vault, so he erected a mental conduit of sorts to direct the information past his conscious mind and directly to Mallick.

"I am afraid there is little useful information on the effects during possession. It is categorized as a dark practice. There are theories for performing removal as well as recognizing the signs, none of which match what you are experiencing." Mallick described the signs to Shuran, who agreed that they did not seem similar.

Where Shuran experienced memories and visions that were random and came without warning, a possession was a full change in personality.

A person being possessed will take on strange abilities stemming from the darker arts of Essence. They will speak with a voice entirely different from their own and will not have the full memories they should. The demon within will try to deceive by avoiding conversations that it cannot recall and will become defensive when confronted. There will often be physical changes as well. Strength will be multiplied many times and the individual's features will change, subtly at first before the demon completely takes control and burns out the body.

"There is something else, however, it is called Il'Shi Ana Dah. To carry shi for the purpose of assistance or help?" Mallick wondered at his translation.

"To carry a part or connection to another's shi for purpose of assistance," Shuran corrected Mallick and then departed, calling back to him. "I will explain when I return from the swamps!"

***

Nagutan and Penelle sat alone on the edge of the city in a secluded glade. The two of them spent a great deal of time together, so any passers-by thought nothing of seeing them talking in private. They were having a hushed yet animated conversation.

Nagutan moved in close to Penelle. "Penelle, you must not divulge that information, it is mine to share when the time comes," Nagutan implored. "Promise you will not say a word. It is imperative that this not surface yet."

Penelle loved torturing Nagutan. She owed him a great deal for his part in her being cursed. She did not blame him for what happened, but finding him still alive and having never contacted her, it stung deeply. "I will keep your little secret… But you will pay dearly," she finally answered giving him a wicked grin. "If you will excuse me, I must finish preparing for a trip to my former prison."

"Be safe my dear, and make certain he understands your true nature as I do. He is a good boy and will always do what is right."

Penelle smiled as she stood. Bending down to kiss him on the cheek, she whispered her farewell in his ear.

Nagutan watched as Penelle left. From within his robes he retrieved a small knife and used it to prick the end of his finger. Rubbing it between his thumb and the same finger, he mumbled a few ancient words. Within a few heartbeats, his odd little creature popped into existence before him.

"You know what to do my pet, see to it. They will be leaving for the swamps soon."

The Imp grinned up at his master, then nodded and changed into a cat. The creature bounded off into the dark woods.

Nagutan sat for some time, alone in his thoughts. He had been at this game for longer than he can remember at times. Now that the prophecy was reaching its most pivotal moments, he had to be extremely careful and diligent. Nothing could stand to chance a misstep. He would not be afforded another chance at fulfilling his obligations.

***

Shuran and Penelle were to leave soon for the Mist Swamps. Shuran had advised that there was no line of the Emmuku'Gu near the swamps. This was only part true, but Shuran was still not going to take a kashshaptu into the lines of power. They would be traveling on Moltar. Based on his now even larger size, Shuran estimated that the flight would take only a full day without stop.

When the time came, Penelle found Shuran and Moltar in the drakkon fields. She handed her single bag over to Shuran to secure to the new saddles finished just that morning.

"You have no other bags?" Shuran asked.

"I thought I might return here if you approve. I have no desire to stay in the swamps, and I do not think anywhere in Aurderia would be safer for me." Penelle knew Salmetu would not simply forget about her. "Your sister did not like me even before the Shadow took her completely. After my escape, she is likely even more cross with me."

"I think cross would be putting it rather lightly." Shuran looked at Penelle's expression, realizing she purposely understated the situation. "I will not turn you away, or the other kashshaptu for that matter, so long as you understand-" Shuran started.

"You have my word, I will do nothing to go against you," she assured holding up her hands. "I will take full responsibility for my coven as well." Her unspoken concern was that there was much amiss amongst her coven. Her first order of business would be to take decisive action in reprimanding her sisters that made plans without her knowledge or permission.

Moltar, along with his passengers, took to the sky with a mighty leap and flap of his massive wings.

No sooner had they left, than a lone Elfin Ranger stepped out from the trees. He watched Moltar's departure with interest. Once the drakkon was out of sight, the elf walked back into the forest and pulled out a small bowl and poured liquid into the vessel from his water skin. He wove his hand above the water and spoke his message. "They ride the drakkon for the swamps as we speak. They should arrive by setting of Utu." The elf then emptied the bowl of its contents and strode off into the woods. He did not sense the black cat following after him.

***

Moltar set a rapid pace. His increased size gave him larger wings and consequently more thrust. Additionally, Shuran cast a spell to lower his mass and adjusted their shield to reduce air drag and make breathing easier within the protective barrier.

"I have learned through Nagutan, that you used a sample of Salmetu's blood to attempt to cure your curse," Shuran finally said after over an hour of silence.

"Yes, but it was more than an attempt, it worked as you can see for yourself." Penelle gestured at her appearance with pride.

"Your symptoms appear outwardly cured, but I can see within your body. The curse is only held at bay. Sooner or later you will relapse without intervention."

Penelle held a look of horror and disbelief. "But then what are we to do?" she finally managed.

Shuran took hold of Penelle's hands and her trembling stopped abruptly. He delved into her being with his mind. He sought out the cause of her curse. He already knew where it was. He already had memories of placing the curse. The memories were different from the ones he normally had. These were not the visions of the Shin'Ar's past. Shuran put the realization out of his mind for now and focused on the task at hand.

At the base of Penelle's brain, there was a swirling red mass of viscous fluid. It was the result of Penelle's presumed cure elixir. The potion she drank only collected at the base of her brain to block the effects of the mass of tissue that did not belong. The curse set so long ago, was actually a deformation created within the kashshaptu. It was designed to attack their skin, hair, and nails from the inside out. The sulfur mixed with the humidity of the Mist Swamps, held it at bay.

Shuran pushed past the potion formed barrier and used his mind to destroy the foreign mass. He then decided it best not to leave a trace of the seven-race blood used in the potion. He had just finished eliminating the blood cells when he noticed it was too late. Penelle's body had already begun replicating the markers in Salmetu's blood. Shuran could not safely change that without the central chamber in Durangug. The only thing he could do on his own would be to destroy all abilities in her cells. He decided against doing so. The Zidu'Si and people of Ersetu could use all the magical help they could get.

Shuran needed to watch Penelle closely. She may be reformed, or not, he did not yet know for certain. With her body replicating the markers in seven race blood cells, she could develop abilities she was not meant to have. This could be good or bad, only time would tell. He withdrew from Penelle and indicated he was done.

"How is it you could do such a thing without a potion?" she asked.

Shuran explained how the body was made up of many cells and organs, each providing for particular functions necessary for the body to operate properly. He told her how he moved through her system to identify what did not belong.

"Have the kashshaptu never studied the workings of the body?" Shuran asked.

"Only so much as how different herbs and potions effect the organs. Why would that matter?" Penelle asked with curiosity.

"You could have likely learned to cure this 'curse' long ago if you knew what to look for." Shuran explained what was done to the coven to invoke the curse. Essentially, a mass was grown upon the brain in the area that effected aging. It caused the body's internal aging to slow to nearly a stop while the kashshaptu would externally age and rot. The effects of the swamp neutralized the effects as the vapors were breathed in consistently.

"To say thank you, is not enough," Penelle expressed. "I am truly indebted to you Shin'Ar. I know my past cannot be changed, but I… the Kashshaptu can change."

Many awkward moments passed before Shuran finally broke the silence. "Speaking of the past, what of the trolls, tell me about them?" Shuran was uncomfortable with the friendliness and display of gratitude Penelle beginning to show him, so he decided to change the subject.

"I suppose I should start from the beginning." Penelle began her tale of how the original clan of dwarves came into the service of the Kashshaptu.

Nine thousand years past, the Kashshaptu were widely sought after for help and guidance by the races of man. They were highly gifted in the arts of scrying, divinity, and potion making. Their gifts were based on inactive powers of Essence that came more easily to the female gender of humans. Over time covens formed and jealousies between those covens began to elevate into feuds. These enmities became hostile and eventually turned deadly.

"My coven was among the largest targets for the others. We had the largest numbers, the best talent, and favor among the Zidu'Si," Penelle explained. "Eventually the attacks upon us expanded to include those who served us."

"The dwarven clan that regularly served and traded with you?" Shuran asked.

"Yes, open threats quickly turned into abductions and eventual murder. Much of the clan abandoned us, but many hundred remained loyal, but they wanted protection. This is when we devised a potion to give them strength and vitality to help withstand the attacks from our enemies," Penelle told him.

"Initially, the potion worked as expected, but within a few cycles, the dwarves began to mutate. Once word of the effects reached the council of races, we were brought before them and the rest is well known to you now."

"What are you not telling me? I do not believe that with the talents your coven claimed to have that such a mistake in the potion was likely,"

Shuran pressed her.

"For the first several hundred years of our punishment, we believed we made a mistake. By the time we discovered the treachery, it was too late and the council would not hear our appeals." Penelle held a look of rage as she relived the memories. "We had a member of our coven who always lusted for power. She wanted to lead the coven and was always turned down when the time for selecting a Grand Kashshaptu came about. When I was placed in power, she finally left us in a fury."

"She was quite talented in twisting curses and manipulating life. My coven came to realize it was this, once sister witch, that tampered with our potions and caused the deformity to our loyal dwarven servants. The trolls have been bound to my coven since then in a pact to avenge this injustice." Penelle had a gleam in her eyes that made Shuran shiver.

"Surely the kashshaptu that wronged you is long dead?" Shuran inquired.

"She gave the curse to the Zidu'Si that was used to punish us. You can be certain that she changed herself as well to extend her life beyond normal expectancy. Her lust for power was, and likely still is, far too strong to have simply allowed aging to stop her. She will do anything, and has had many thousands of years to plan her ascension. We have had this time to plan as well." She did not elaborate.

The other clans before the change snubbed the dwarves that went into service of the Kashshaptu. Once they mutated, they were reviled and attacked by the dwarves. This started the hatred between them. Over the passing of time, neither side even remembers why they have such execration toward the other.

"Once you have healed my sisters as you have me, you will have gained a great ally, Shuran. After we help you defeat the Shadow, as I am confident you will prevail, we must be allowed to bring our banished sister to justice!" Penelle demanded.

"I will agree to this if it is justice you want. Revenge is an ugly business and does nothing to quell the shi. You must promise me that you will not give into the darkness that vengeance desires," Shuran warned.

After a long pause, Penelle nodded her acceptance of Shuran's terms.

The rest of their trip was spent in outward silence. Moltar and Shuran however shared their thoughts.

"Do you trust that she will keep to her word, Lugaldur?" Moltar asked.

"Time will tell my friend. This wrong has festered within the coven for longer than living memory of the whole of Aurderia. I am reminded of something Codger once said to Mallick and me when Moona went off on one of her tirades, 'Hells Mouth holds no fury as compared to a woman scorned'!"

"I only hope we can survive the eruption," Moltar responded in nervous jest.

Chapter Twenty

Darkness was enveloping the swamps as the massive drakkon circled the marshes, looking for a suitable place to land. His great bulk would normally cause him to sink deep into the boggy ground, but Shuran decided to leave the spell, that changed Moltar's density and lightened him, in effect until after they returned from the swamps. There was not space open enough, so Moltar chose the least overgrown area and landed, crushing a sizable section of growth beneath his prodigious body. His feet still sunk deep into the muddy ground.

Shuran and Penelle left Moltar to lick his minor wounds received from his landing. He lost more than a few scales and received a few cuts from thorny bushes. These were a small worry to him; he was most upset about the mud and mirk that splotched his gleaming red scales.

Laughing aloud, Penelle remarked about Moltar, "He is an enigma, that drakkon. How something so mountainous and fierce looking could be at the same time so… What is the word?"

"Prissy?" Shuran laughed with her. "He is rather vain I admit, but he has some right to behave so, I suppose."

Kashshaptu began to gather at the arrival of Penelle and Shuran. Most of them approached with trepidation. They were not surprised by this arrival since Penelle had already informed them of their eminent visit; very few had seen a handsome young man in longer than they could remember clearly. They were suddenly self-conscious of their appearance.

One kashshaptu was not so shy. She came to him quickly and offered her hand for the lifting of the curse.

Shuran realized that this was going to resemble a last call for spirits at a crowded inn, and he was the barkeep. He took the witch's hands in his own and began the reversal in earnest. He quickly reached the growth and destroyed it, knowing exactly what he was looking for. Different from Penelle, however, was the reversal of the effects. For this, Shuran called upon the body of the kashshaptu itself to go into hyper repair of the damaged tissues.

He realized this would cause the need for energy from the witches so he called forth a few abnu emuq from the Vault to allow them to use temporarily for the needed strength. With the first of the witches visibly healing, the others began moving forward. Shuran had to enlist Penelle's help in keeping them orderly and coming one at a time.

Shuran worked for hours, tapping into Durangug for vitality. By the time the last woman approached for healing, Shuran was exhausted beyond the point an ordinary wielder would have collapsed dead. He pressed Durangug for a final burst of power to finish this last healing. He would rest upon Moltar's back during the flight back to Britengate. He purposely avoided using Moltar's strength so the drakkon might fly back fully rested.

This last kashshaptu hesitated before Shuran. She did not eagerly extend her hands as the others had. She glared at Shuran with a look of contempt.

"If you do not wish the curse lifted, it is just the same with me. I could use the rest, but I fail to understand what I may have done to you personally to warrant such a sour look," Shuran said flatly.

With a final grunt and forced step, the last of the cursed witches moved forward and quickly pushed out her hands for Shuran. She maintained her look of disdain, but she allowed him to do his work.

Shuran delved into her form with a single intent, to locate and destroy the malignancy at the base of her brain and boost her systems self-healing. When he reached her brain, however, he discovered something different. He saw an odd difference to the growth. It appeared somehow different, but he could not identify what was different. He dismissed it and destroyed the mass. As he adjusted his thoughts to focus on healing the outward effects of the curse, the witch resisted.

The Kashshaptu pushed him out of her mind. "I will heal in time. I do not wish your Essence induced changes beyond what you have done."

"I do not understand, why would you not wish to return to the way you were?" Shuran asked.

"You misunderstand, my appearance will return in time. I will never return to the way I was." The kashshaptu glared one last time at Shuran before walking off into the marshlands.

Penelle followed after her sister kashshaptu in order to inquire what was the meaning of her poor treatment of the young asipu who has graciously cured their curse and given them their freedom.

Later, when Shuran prepared to leave, Penelle tried to make excuses for the actions of many of the kashshaptu who showed contempt for the Shin'Ar. She explained that it was his position and not him directly. Once they came to know him, she claimed their coldness would mellow. Shuran could not help but feel there was something more to their resentment.

Penelle spoke with her sister witches as they continued to rapidly heal their appearances. The majority of them would not be going to Britengate, the Shadow and Salmetu frightened them but they did not trust anyone. She discovered that it was several of her sisters that called for the trolls to march south to the Mist Swamps. They wanted what they considered their soldiers, to protect them as they found somewhere safe to settle.

In all, there were only twelve kashshaptu beside Penelle that would travel to Britengate. They promised to help in every way they could. Shuran and Penelle agreed that it might actually be easier to have only the thirteen sisters among the refugees. Some of the new citizens of Britengate were not happy about the 'witches' being released from the curse. Grumbling among the dwarves was often heard at the makeshift alehouse that was often busy each night.

The Drunkard Tavern was opened in the first days of repair in the city. Aknard was as enterprising as King Vraduun, his brother, had described. His smugglers brought in plenty of varieties of wine, ale, and distilled spirits as they sailed the magurmu around Aurderia. Aknard always provided the Zidu'Si free drinks in payment for the cloaking spells for his fleet. 'A smuggler's dream come true', Aknard frequently repeated in reference to his 'invisible flying boats'.

Shuran left Penelle to deal with her coven business, and he made his way to Moltar. Shuran was completely drained. Even with the power of Durangug funneling power to him, he still used up all his own physical strength. He also had not slept properly for days, so he was ready for a long rest strapped to Moltar's back.

Shuran found Moltar lying upon a solid bed of fire-baked mud and ash when he returned to their arrival point. It took no imagination to understand what had transpired.

Moltar told Shuran how he kept sinking in the 'vile mud' as he put it. The truth was that Moltar disliked being covered in smelly muck. He breathed fire upon the ground to bake the mud and called up rock and rubble from deep below the marshes to stabilize the earth below him.

Shuran just laughed and climbed up onto Moltar's back. Moltar was in such a hurry to get away from the stench of the swamps that Shuran had no chance to strap in. All he could do was hold on until his bonded drakkon settled and leveled out. They took off nearly vertical and angled steeply out over the great sea.

That is when the mental assault came.

***

"Who all among you decided to call upon the trolls without bothering to consult with me?" Penelle screamed. "Who among you decided they know better than I, the course the Kashshaptu should take? And do not think for a moment I believe that dribble of an excuse told me days ago when last we communicated!"

The witch that refused accelerated healing stepped forward. Many of the coven sisters stood behind her. The others either stood behind

Penelle or stood confused on the outskirts of the standoff between the two powerful kashshaptu.

"We will not stand with those who follow the establishment that cursed us to rot here for thousands of years!" the crone spat.

"Do you suppose the Shadow is the better choice?" Penelle asked.

In answer the old crone, the one that went to strike a bargain with Salmetu that first allowed Penelle to leave the swamps, lifted her hands out and threw a spell of darkness at Penelle. Penelle dodged the spell just in time, and then watched as the crone left by fire, followed by all but twelve of her sisters.

***

Shuran was too enervated to fight the mental attack. Moltar was caught off guard and could not concentrate. He did not understand what was happening. Somehow his mental link to Shuran was weakened and he could not erect a shield around Shuran's mind. As he floundered in the air, he did not realize how far out to sea he had gone. A storm began to build from nowhere. The winds whipped and buffeted the gigantic drakkon, pushing him toward the sea below.

Through his screams of agony, Shuran attempted to secure himself to Moltar in spite of the pain. Every attempt he made was thwarted by a sudden shift in direction or drop in altitude. Shuran lost his grip and began sliding along Moltar's back. He attempted to grab onto several spikes and ridges along his now slippery slide down Moltar's back. Rain was pounding, thunder was clapping, and Shuran lost his battle to gain purchase. He fell from Moltar's back and down toward the waiting waters.

The air was driven from Shuran's lungs when he hit the water. The impact took his consciousness and he soon sank beneath the waves. A glow formed around him as his body continued to sink. All around him, the waves crashed over as though folding him within their embrace.

Moltar did not sense the loss of his passenger at first. As he was circling around to head for land, he turned his head to where Shuran was seated, to find the saddle empty. The noise that erupted from his maw challenged even the thundering storm above him. He swung around and dove for the waters surface, reaching out with his thoughts, trying to find his Lugaldur. Shuran could not be found.

***

Fire streamed down over the marshes. Thirteen figures gathered in the clearing as the ground gurgled and lightning struck around them. Smoke mixed with steam adding to the smell of rot and sulfur. Moltar circled the area where he sensed the group of kashshaptu women. He continued to devastate the area with fire and lightning, and shook the earth. When he finally landed he flapped his massive wings to clear away the smoke to observe the resulting carnage of his rampage. What he found was only thirteen kashshaptu huddled below a shield.

"Moltar! What are you doing?" Penelle pleaded.

"You will pay for what you have done kashshaptu! My Lugaldur is gone because of you!" Moltar bellowed and roared as he continued to spit fire at Penelle's shield.

"What are you talking about? We have done nothing except protect ourselves from you and our traitorous sisters who abandoned us!" Penelle shouted.

Moltar stopped his attack and moved up to edge of Penelle's shield of energy. He flicked his tongue at the barrier and it wavered. Moltar grinned and moved his head closer and the shield failed as his massive head lowered at Penelle.

"Speak true and you may make it out of this vile swamp alive witch!"

Penelle explained to Moltar what happened as soon as he and Shuran left. She told him of her sister kashshaptu, betraying them and calling the trolls from the North. She was unsure what they planned or if they allied with Salmetu and the Shadow, but she knew only her and the twelve remaining sisters pledged an oath to the Shin'Ar.

Moltar told her of the mental assault. Shuran was too exhausted to put up a fight and the sudden storm caused Moltar to tumble and flail in the air. Before he knew what happened, Shuran was gone.

Penelle admitted that the kashshaptu do not have the power to assault Shuran in such a way of the mind. Although many of her sisters have talents in the weaving of weather magics, the time required to conjure up such a storm would not have allowed them such an attack without help from someone more powerful.

"We must get help!" Penelle said. "I will use the flame to travel back to Britengate and get the Zidu'Si. The rest of my sisters will stay and help you search the shore and waters."

Chapter Twenty-One

Shuran glowed like a beacon in the depths of the Great Sea. His insentient body continued to sink into the depths. As he fell deeper toward the sea floor, his presence became a curiosity to the myriad of creatures that lurked within the depths. Many odd fishes and bizarre animals approached Shuran, only to swim off at the last minute when they came within range of the odd glow that intensified more as he sank further down.

Shuran began to awake in the bitter cold of the deep waters. He was weak and his movements were sluggish. He began to vaguely recall the last few moments before he hit the raging waters of the Great Sea. As his thoughts registered, a panic came over him when realization of his surroundings, brought with it a heavy pressure upon his body. The glow around his body began to waiver and his lungs began to cry out for air.

Shuran quickly thought to propel himself toward the surface, but he was unsure which way it was. He was immersed in absolute blackness. In his panic, he could not focus on rudimentary wielding of water. He spent the next several moments trying everything he could think of but could not concentrate. He finally realized that somehow when he was not thinking about breathing, the pain in his lungs subsided. Shuran suddenly noticed the glow around his body. Then he saw the dark shadow approaching from below.

The glow surrounding Shuran added to the difficulty he was having seeing clearly. Besides the surreal feeling of being fathoms below the surface of the unknown depths in the Great Sea, Shuran was disoriented, confused, cut off from the Zidu'Si, and completely drained of energy. He felt as though he were dead. How else could he explain his still being aware after so long in the waters without breathing? But he was breathing somehow. Not breathing in an above water sort of way, but he could tell oxygen was entering his blood.

The dark shadow was getting nearer, and it was beginning to take shape. It started to appear as the shape of a human, some sort of glowing outline surrounded the body and it was riding something. As the unknown form approached, Shuran could sense it on the edges of his shi. Essence, he felt, but in someway diminished likely the effects of the salt water around him. The next thing Shuran saw was the face of a young woman with big black eyes, then his senses were blocked and everything went dark.

***

Penelle arrived back at the shores of the Great Sea, accompanied by the Zidu'Si. Penelle arrived by flame at a fire set by one of her sister's, the Zidu'Si travelled by another means they did not explain. This confirmed Penelle's suspicion of deception when Shuran had originally said there was no faster means than flight to get to the Mist Swamps. He wanted the time to speak with her and perhaps did not trust taking her into confidence on how the Zidu'Si traveled so quickly about Ersetu.

"You have returned!" Moltar said with a hint of surprise.

"I would not abandon Shuran. The Zidu'Si is here as well," Penelle answered. She could not blame Moltar for having doubts about her word. She would work that much harder to prove her loyalty to the young Shin'Ar, his bonded, and the Zidu'Si.

The Zidu'Si and Kashshaptu discussed what had occurred. Penelle spent little time in Britengate. Once telling the Zidu'Si Shuran was in trouble, they left with few details. Now as they listened to the events as told from both viewpoints of those present when Shuran disappeared, the desperation for locating him became fervent.

"Do you think your sisters who left had a hand in this?" Mallick asked Penelle.

"It is possible, but they have not the power to attack Shuran's mind as Moltar described. My sisters and I were never regular practitioners of weather wielding so they could not have caused the storms alone."

"So we have no proof of who is behind this, but we know he is still alive," Avrank said. He saw the looks of uncertainty on the faces around him, and explained. "The Zidu'Si is still connected, it stands to reason that if Shuran were dead, we would have lost that bond."

"Avrank is correct! I still feel my bond, if not the mental connection to my Lugaldur," Moltar exclaimed in excited relief.

"Salt Water," one of the kashshaptu said. "It is preventing your physical connection while the metaphysical bond remains intact."

"You are wise sister. That means he likely has been captured by the Badur'Lu!" Penelle reasoned. "They have always disliked surface dwellers, it is likely they took him prisoner if they encountered Shuran near their borders."

Penelle told the histories of the Badur'Lu and their separatist beliefs even in the days they served on the Council of Races. Even in the ancient times, the people of the sea chose to live apart from those who lived upon the land. Part of the reason the Great Sea was impassable by ship, was rumored the work of the Badur'Lu attacking vessels that sailed the waters they claimed as their domain.

"We need to work to locate their settlements at the bottom of the Great Sea; it is with the Badur'Lu that we will likely find the Shin'Ar," Gregoran said to the agreement of all those present.

***

Shuran awoke with a start, to find himself dry and laying abed in a simple room. He felt weak and dizzy, but he was certain he was awake, breathing, and disconnected from his friends. The room contained a low bed of sand covered by a silk-like material. A single table with two chairs sat on the opposite side of the room. There was a basin of water, but no linens for drying off. The most curious thing was the wall-sized window that looked out into the sea.

Shuran stood at the window gazing out at the breath-taking view of a sprawling metropolis of underwater structures connected by walkways. Through his Essence enhanced vision, Shuran could see what he assumed were the Badur'Lu, riding on the backs of some sort of creature.

The beasts had a head similar to that of a horse. There were large fins, the length of a man's leg on the upper trunk, and a long sinuous tail with a large fin on its end. A shield of some sort that contoured to their bodies surrounded the riders. The lights emanating from surrounding structures reflected off the surface of the shields, preventing Shuran from making out their features. He could see they carried a sort of a shoulder holster that held a spear.

A knock on the door of his room took his attention away from the activities outside his window. Before he could answer, the door opened to reveal a slender woman with long silky blue-green hair. Though her frame was slim, it appeared streamlined and well defined. Her face was human-like though her jaw was slightly larger and squared. Her skin was a pale silver-grey and Shuran noticed slight webbing between her fingers.

Her eyes were the most obvious feature that set her apart, they were overly large, round, and black. Then she smiled, revealing two rows of pointed teeth that looked as though they could tear through the hardened hide of a northern forest boar.

She entered the room and placed a tray of what might pass as food upon the table. She arranged the plates on the table and then turned to Shuran. With a slight nod and gesture, she indicated Shuran should sit and eat. Her smile was not reassuring. Shuran felt as though he might be getting fattened up for supping upon.

"You are different from other dirt-walkers I have… seen," she said to him in a dialect of the ancient tongue. She stood and watched Shuran look over the foodstuffs she had spread out for him. "Not accustomed to deep sea foods I would imagine. They are full of protein and will help you gain strength. The taste may be different to your palate if you are used to red meats."

Shuran looked at the food items with skepticism. He saw a spongy bright red tube-shaped creature that looked to still be moving. Next to that was a bed of green leafy plants topped with some small-clawed creatures that resembled miniature white lobsters. A glass filled with a blue liquid sat before the sea salad. He decided to taste it. He immediately regretted the decision, but rather than insult his razor-toothed host, he swallowed with some difficulty and placed the glass back down.

"It is an acquired taste, squid ink!" she laughed. "Try the prawn salad, it will be more to your liking I think. My name is Vala."

"I am Shuran Shin'Ar," he replied before realizing he used his title as leader of the Zidu'Si.

Vala did not appear to recognize the significance. She continued talking to Shuran about the food she brought him. She described how the prawns came from great smoking mounts in the sea floor. The greens were from the forest of long-stalked sea plants south of the marshy peninsula of Aurderia. As she continued, she described the various foods of the seas that her people consumed.

"How did I get here?" Shuran finally asked.

"I found you, more to the point I was called to you," she answered.

"I do not understand."

Vala explained how she had been out on regular patrols of the boundary of Hakkisuru, the Badur'Lu city. The sea floor had been riddled with cracking and separation. Great shakes of Ersetu had become regular events in recent years and patrols were setup to inspect the area and buildings for possible damage. While on one of these patrols, Vala felt a call in the back of her mind that lead her to notice an unnatural glow not far from the city.

"I had forgotten about that, the glow I mean," Shuran said.

"You really should not create such a bright breathing shield, unless you meant to attract the attention of a leviathan."

"Breathing shield, I do not recall creating it, but then I have done many things out of instinct, before understanding how to do them at will," Shuran said more to himself than Vala.

"I know you are not Badur'Lu; what are you that you can create a breathing shield on instincts only my people have?" Vala asked.

"I have Badur'Lu blood. I have all seven races flowing through my veins, that is how I became the Shin'Ar," Shuran said, expecting Vala to understand.

She did not comprehend his reference. Vala had not learned of the Shin'Ar or much of surface history, as the Badur'Lu long ago separated from the races of men that walked the dirt. They did not teach the full histories of the races of men or their former alliances.

Shuran was not surprised at Vala's ignorance of the world above the waves. He was given the impression that there would be difficulties in explaining his need for the assistance of the Badur'Lu. His conversation with Vala revealed that there was no visit from his father of which she was told.

Vala left Shuran to finish his meal and rest. She would return in several hours with more food and conversation.

Shuran slept better than he had in a long time. The salt water of the Great Sea, provided a buffer from the worries of intrusion on his mind. Though he felt a void from the disconnection of his Zidu'Si, he could still feel Moltar on the edge of his thoughts. Shuran's sleep was ended abruptly by a disturbance in the sea floor. An earthquake shook the foundations of the structure.

As he stood from the sudden shaking of his room, Shuran felt a slight jolt of awareness. The Emmuku'Gu that he could not feel near before was now just outside his range of reach. Perhaps, if the tremors continued, or he could work with the earth to shift the flow, he might reach the power. The door opening interrupted his thoughts, and two surly looking guards entered to grab hold of him.

"You will come with us pilsug!" one of the guards insisted, referring to Shuran as dirt-walker.

Shuran acquiesced, and followed between the two Badur'Lu guardsmen. He was led through many corridors and finally past a large bank of windows. As they walked by the windows, Shuran was able to get a view of what was happening outside. A fissure had opened in the seabed and magma was flowing up on the edges of the underwater city.

The guards led Shuran to a vast chamber beneath a dome of glass. Aside from the supports evenly spaced around the space, all but the floor afforded a view of the sea outside the city. He could see Badur'Lu swimming about and riding sea dragons they called Usumaba. They did not appear panicked; Shuran deduced that there was no eminent danger or damage.

His attention was brought to a large throne by a hammering noise upon the floor. A Badur'Lu man of many years sat upon the pearl encrusted seat of power. The man sat still, studying Shuran with his large black eyes. With a simple gesture of his hand, the man ordered the guards to bring Shuran forward.

"Explain to me pilsug, why I should not turn you out of our city and leave you to the depths?" the man asked in Aurderian.

"You speak the common tongue well. You are welcome to let me go, I did not ask you to bring me to your city, but it will be to your own detriment if I am forced to stay," Shuran answered flatly.

"You were brought here out of the ignorance of a young woman who thought you were something different from the dirt walker I see before me. There is nothing you can do here to threaten my people."

The Chancellor spoke loudly of the arrogance of the races above the waves. They preyed upon one another, as beasts would stalk another for food. Thieves, pirates, tyrants, and barbarians were among the many descriptions he used to illustrate his feelings of the dirt walking men of Ersetu.

"I have no intention to directly harm you, but we need each other to stand against the darkness that threatens all of Ersetu." Shuran was not certain he was getting his point across. The Chancellor sat stone-faced, contemplating Shuran's words. When at last he blinked his translucent eyelids.

The Badur'Lu leader tilted his head and softened his stare. "You speak of the Shin'Ar and perhaps the Zidu'Si? Vala has asked questions after speaking with you."

"Vala did not appear to know of the histories, but I get the impression you know more than others. Do you recognize the signs of the balance being broken?" Shuran asked while looking at the view of magma flowing up from the sea floor outside the dome. "This will continue until balance is restored."

"I suppose you believe that you can bring about balance again? It did not last the first time. I also know what resulted after the last balance. The Sikil Mah is a perfect example of how your kind turns on one another." The Chancellor seemed proud of making his point.

"Ignorance is a fault that is not exclusively held within the minds of those above the waves, Chancellor."

This challenge and insult angered the Badur'Lu Chancellor. "Then you will prove your claim upon the title Shin'Ar. Show us then, the mighty power of the Shin'Ar," the Chancellor demanded in a mocking tone.

Shuran then called forth electricity to his palms and sent it dancing across his body. He brought flames into existence before the guards who approached him in alarm. He let the flames die and just before the guards could reach him, he threw up an invisible shield that they walked directly into. He walked to the window to look over the great fissure still bleeding magma into the sea. He reached out to the earth in an attempt to seal the wound in the sea floor.

He began to link with the earth and coax it closed. As he focused on what he was attempting, his shield dropped and the Badur'Lu guards were upon him. When they pulled him away, the part of his shi that was drumming with the earth was torn free and the result was a great tremble in the earth.

"What is the meaning of this?" the Chancellor shouted. "You attempt to worsen the broken seafloor? You lie to my face and work to damage the foundations of this city! Guards, take him back to his room!"

Shuran could not resist. The effect of being ripped from the earth accompanied by not having the power of Durangug to bolster his strength caused an instantaneous drain of his energy. Shuran was limp in the arms of the guards as he was being dragged back to the room he occupied.

Vala had been watching from behind a support beam and quickly hid before the guards saw her when they exited.

Shuran was unceremoniously thrown upon the bed in his room. As the guards turned to leave, one of them spat upon Shuran. The spittle hit the back of his hand and began to smoke as the acidic saliva reacted.

Shuran was too exhausted to do more than wipe his hand upon the sheets on the bed. He only vaguely noticed the acid neutralize upon seaweed beneath the sheets it burnt through.

Chapter Twenty-Two

Shuran awoke to find Vala sitting over him with a spear to his throat.

"You attack us after I was kind to you. Why should I not kill you where you lie?" Vala asked.

Shuran calmly answered, "If you truly believed I attacked your city, you would have slit my throat already. When the guards pulled me away, they broke my connection to the earth and caused a reaction."

Vala lowered her spear, but kept her eyes locked on Shuran. "What do you mean a connection to the earth?"

"When I wield the Essence, I form a bond with the forces I choose to work with. Usually I do so with little concentration, but in my weakened state, I had to join with the earth to attempt closing the fissure."

Shuran saw his talking to her of his abilities distracted and calmed Vala. He continued to explain to Vala how he learned to wield and weave. Shuran described what it felt like to join with the earth, fire, metal, and electricity.

"It is the same with water, we learn to ride the waves at an early age,"

Vala finally spoke up. She described how she would look into the water and image herself on the waves, surfing them. This was how she first learned to work with water.

Shuran spent the next few days resting, eating, and speaking with Vala who would continue to bring him food and water. He learned quickly how to separate salt from the water she brought him. He learned to freeze, boil, and condense the water. His understanding of the three states of water began to form. Each night, Shuran focused on the Emmuku'Gu on the edge of his senses and slowly diverted it closer to Hakkisuru. On the third day, Shuran finally had his strength back.

"May I ask why they continue to let you come see me?" Shuran asked Vala.

"The guards dare not stop me, and father indulges my curiosity," she answered.

"Your father I assume is the Chancellor? Did he explain anything more to you about the balance and the history of the Zidu'Si?"

Vala nodded in the negative, so Shuran told her what she needed to know. He explained how the balancing forces of Essence were now tilted toward the darkness. The Shadow was gaining strength and threatening to destroy Ersetu. Shuran counseled Vala on the history of the Zidu'Si and their efforts over the many millennia, to restore stability to the Essence and heal the world.

"Perhaps my father should speak with you again. I do not think he treated you fairly," Vala confessed. "He does not listen to me though. I repeated to him what you had spoken of, but he feels that you attempt to deceive me."

"Tell him that I will close the fissure if the guards do not interrupt this time," Shuran suggested.

Vala quickly left the room, excited and saying she would return soon with his answer.

Vala returned within an hour of leaving Shuran. "He will see you. Father says if you do as you say, he will allow you to leave."

Shuran followed Vala out of the room. The guards quickly fell into step behind him as they headed toward the great domed chamber to meet with the Chancellor. Shuran was concerned that he may not complete his Zidu'Si.

"My daughter's incessant pestering has afforded you an opportunity to dispel the beliefs that you have come to bring us harm, pilsug. If at any time I suspect duplicity, I will have my guards strike you down," the Chancellor said.

Shuran said nothing. He slowly moved closer to the window and looked down upon the fissure that continued to expel molten rock upon the sea floor and spread the seabed apart. "It has gotten worse," he muttered before closing his eyes and reaching for the drumming beat of the earth. Simultaneously he reached for the Emmuku'Gu and pulled it the final distance he needed to gain full access.

The room began to shake, as did the entire city of Hakkisuru. The Chancellor's guards made a move for Shuran, but he was ready for their approach and made a warning motion. The guards ignored his warning and ran headlong into Shuran's shield. With access to the Emmuku'Gu, Shuran had more than enough strength to destroy the city if that were his intent, but he returned his focus on moving the seabed back together.

He called for the earth to shift and seal the crack that spread near the city borders. He shifted his shi into the molten rock and slowed the particles within to cool them down. Deeper into the ground he went until he reached the border of molten and solid rock. It was here that Shuran saw the reason for the crack. A flow of darkness, the Shadow, was pushing the earth apart. The Shadow laughed at Shuran as he crumbled under the force of darkness.

***

"Shuran!" Mallick yelled. "I feel him through the ring, something is wrong."

"I feel him as well, and he needs us now!" Moltar roared and a shield formed around him that enveloped the Zidu'Si in energy as they all disappeared in a flash of light.

***

Shuran was lying on the floor of the chamber rubbing his head. He sat up but stopped himself from standing as the tips of spears lowered to his neck. A sudden flash of light followed by the smell of ozone, alerted him to the presence of the Zidu'Si. The spears moved from Shuran to point at the new arrivals.

The silence of the chamber was deafening. A shift in the foundations of the city caused a crack to form in the glass dome. Shuran knew the cause and was quick to mentally advise his Zidu'Si of the threat. Without a word, Shuran focused on the crack in the dome and repaired it. He then joined with his Zidu'Si and as one, they collectively dove into the depths of the earth to create a barrier against the Shadow.

Molten rock swirled as minerals coalesced and were coaxed to the surface. The entire area beneath the city of Hakkisuru's foundations was being converted to gugtu. That would not be enough to hold back the Shadow, however. Shuran knew that the shadow would eventually twist the stone, so he continued the conversion along a path that took it into contact with the Emmuku'Gu. The gugtu began to glow with a light that caused the Shadow to scream and retreat. Shuran only meant to strengthen the barrier, the retreat of the Shadow was unexpected.

The tremors ended as quickly as they started. The fissure was sealed. The Shadow was chased away. The Badur'Lu were shocked into silence. The chamber was overcrowded with Moltar's bulk taking up the majority of the space.

Moltar swung his head over to Shuran and began licking him as his rumbling purr vibrated the floor.

Once Shuran was able to break free of Moltar's affectionate greeting, he made his way to the Chancellor in order to fill in the details of all that occurred. Once he finished his dissertation, the Chancellor dismissed his guards and sat back upon his pearled throne.

"A simple apology is not adequate to express my initial attitude toward you or my gratitude for what you have done for the Badur'Lu," the Chancellor began. "I had never thought it possible that the Zidu'Si actually ever existed. Everything that has been passed down from one leader to the next, I thought only tales, told to teach us the fickle nature of those who dwell above the waves."

"I would be lying if I told you that there were not these troubles with those races of man who walk the surface of Ersetu. Memories of men are blurry in the retelling of history and history is written by a biased pen. We cannot allow ignorance, fear, and pride to prevent us from uniting against the Shadow. Darkness finds its way into our lives when we choose not to shed light upon our personal shortcomings."

"You speak with wisdom beyond your years, young asipu. You are a welcome change to the fools who council my every decision, but I am still not certain what path my people should take in the matters my daughter has shared with me," the Chancellor said. "We have not dealt in the goings on above the waves in many millennia."

"It is time for that to change," Vala said as she stepped forward. "This broken balance will continue to split the world apart and Hakkisuru will be threatened again before long."

"Should that happen my dear, we will address such a matter when the time comes." Looking at Shuran, the Chancellor continued, "We wish to debate on how best to proceed. I would invite you all to stay, but I am afraid we have no accommodations for drakkon."

"My bonded will return to the surface with most of the Zidu'Si, I would ask to stay behind with my Isten, Mallick. We wish to learn more of water wielding," Shuran responded.

"It is your blood right to learn such things, I am sure Vala would be able to continue what she has already begun." The Chancellor raised the ridge above one eye that might have passed for an eyebrow.

Vala seemed excited by this proposal and soon ushered Shuran and Mallick away after the other Zidu'Si left to return to the surface.

Moltar would see them back to Britengate after checking on the kashshaptu who remained in the swamps.

Vala agreed to meet Shuran and Mallick later and left them to talk in Shuran's room. The guards were no longer posted outside since Shuran was no longer considered a threat to the Badur'Lu and now an honored guest.

"How are we to get the aid of the Badur'Lu? It feels as though they wish to remain separated from the other races," Mallick asked.

"I do not think we need them all to assist. Vala has a strong mind and opinions. I do not think it will take much persuading for her to join us." Shuran said.

"You would bring her into the Zidu'Si against the wishes of the Chancellor?" Mallick asked with surprise.

"I would give her the choice to make for herself. Vala will seek her own counsel or that of the Chancellor without my interference."

A Badur'Lu servant set a dinner for Shuran and Mallick. They ate their meal of sea salad and deep-sea white crab. The dessert was a slightly sweet spongy plant or animal, neither Shuran nor Mallick could tell. After they had finished, Vala returned to provide information on wielding water Essence.

Mallick took mental notes of everything Vala instructed Shuran to perform. He watched as they sat before a large tub of water and Shuran practiced repeating what Vala showed him. They ran through converting the water between its three states of liquid, ice, and gas. All of these Shuran mastered quickly. The difficult part came when Vala began the lessons on calling forth a breathing shield.

"I do not understand how you could do this when I found you, but are having such a time of it now?" Vala said with exasperation.

"I have said that many times I have done things without consciously knowing."

"Perhaps you are forcing it, so it will not form naturally. You need to relax and focus on what you need; a shield that allows only breathable air to enter, and keeps the pressure of the water at bay," Mallick offered.

Vala smiled at Mallick for his suggestion, while he held back a flinch at seeing her gleaming rows of sharp and pointed teeth.

After hours of practice, Shuran was finally able to create the shield while dunking his head in the tub of water. Once he gave himself time to understand the process of separating oxygen from the seawater, he could focus on wielding that into his shield.

"Mallick, are you going to try these lessons or simply sit there watching?" Vala asked.

"I do not have the blood of the Badur'Lu flowing in my veins. Until the Badur'Lu are joined to the Zidu'Si, only Shuran is capable of wielding the Essence of water."

This statement could not have been more apropos as it caused Vala to begin asking all the questions that would work toward getting her to join the Zidu'Si.

Shuran explained how once a member of each race joins the Zidu'Si,

188

their abilities are shared among the members. With little effort and practice, they would all be able to wield the same Essence to a lesser degree than a true blood Badur'Lu. Then Shuran called forth an item from the Vault. The Kibur'Zisu, it is the ancient Trident of Power, gug weapon of the Badur'Lu Zidu'Si.

"I have seen this in paintings and statues in our halls and library! What is it?" Vala asked.

"This is the Kibur'Zisu, the weapon of gug meant for the Zidu'Si member from the Badur'Lu. It represents the bond of service to the Shin'Ar and assistance to the races of men." Shuran held the trident out for Vala to hold. Without taking the oath, there was no need to worry about false bonding. He only wished her to feel the potency of the object.

Vala shuddered as she touched the weapon and both Shuran and Mallick felt the jolt of power course through them.

Chapter Twenty-Three

"But she did not take the pledge! How could this have happened?" Mallick shouted.

"I do not understand how such a thing could occur! I did not do this purposely-" Shuran was interrupted by a hand on his shoulder.

"I pled to help you the moment you sealed the fissures in the sea floor, perhaps even before then. Once I held this wondrous weapon, I knew without a doubt that I would stand beside you." Vala was the vision of an underwater warrior woman, as she stood holding the trident beside her. Power radiated off of the weapon and sizzled along her body.

"Father may be slighted a bit, but he can accept it or go scale himself!" Vala giggled.

The Chancellor was less than overjoyed at finding that his daughter was now a member of the Zidu'Si. He did not over-react, nor did he outwardly object, but Shuran could tell that Vala's father held an unspoken reservation. "Clear the room," the Chancellor said, indicating that Vala, Shuran, and Mallick were to stay.

"Chancellor, it was not my intention-" Shuran started.

"Gilean, if you are to take my only daughter off on your fools quest, then you must call me by my proper name," the Chancellor said as he pulled his daughter into a hug.

Mallick mouthed 'Gill' to Shuran, who only stifled a laughed and then scowled."

"The humor of my name does not pass me, young man," Gilean said releasing Vala. "It is not surprising that Vala would so freely commit herself to your cause, Shuran. It is a long past ancestor who once held the Kibur'Zisu long before we settled our city deep beneath the waves of the Great Sea. But as the Shin'Ar, I assume you already knew this."

"I suspected, but was not entirely certain until Vala stood before me holding the trident. The power flowing from her was breathtaking."

Gilean described his lineage and long dead grandmother fifty generations past, who once allegedly served with the Zidu'Si. The Badur'Lu soon disappeared beneath the waves, when the Zidu'Si disbanded and his ancestor returned, ashamed. It was her father, then Chancellor, that ordered their separation from the other races.

"My ancestor was shamed by the dismissal it was told, and thus my people turned away from the races above the waves, and we settled here in the depths," Gilean finished.

"There is something more to this, but I am unable to recall. I have flashes of something more, but I cannot access the memories," Shuran said. He was confused at not having access to the part the Badur'Lu Zidu'Si played in the plan the former Shin'Ar laid out.

"I am afraid I have not the knowledge to history of those times, only that which has been passed down and only for Badur'Lu leadership to know," Gilean said abruptly stopping the line of conversation. "As I have said, most of this information has been believed myths, legends, and stories told as a means of keeping our people from the ways of dirt walkers."

Breaking an uncomfortable silence, Mallick turned to Shuran. "I think it is time we joined the Zidu'Si, they have all returned to the shores anticipating our arrival, with the exception of Moltar who by the look of it, is frightening your usumaba outside the dome," Mallick pointed out.

They all turned to the sight of Moltar encased in a glowing shield, swimming and thrusting himself at great speed using his tail.

Vala said her farewells alone with Gilean, while Shuran and Mallick waited outside with Moltar. The three of them were getting accustomed to the breathing shields. Moltar was beginning to experiment with rapidly heating water behind himself to propel forward at speeds faster than his tail alone provided.

Shuran and Mallick were finally able to climb aboard Moltar's back when Vala emerged outside the dome. She carried with her, a single large travel bag and the Kibur'Zisu. They could see clearly that she was dressed in clothes normally worn by top-siders.

Shuran deduced that it was something about the shields that allowed them to see clearly beneath the water. He motioned for Vala to climb aboard Moltar and then they were off for the surface.

"Stand back! Moltar is approaching at an incredible speed," Orian said as he moved back from the sheer drop of the shoreline.

Avrank remained where he stood, choosing to ignore the elf. He soon regretted it as he was drenched with water and thrown back upon a wave of water that followed Moltar's escape from the sea.

Moltar burst forth from the waves and then sent a stream of fire out before them as he spread his wings. The fire trailed over him and his riders, immediately evaporating the water still rolling past them. The sight to those on shore was that of a massive red blur erupting from the sea in a ball of flame followed by the formation of a cloud that sprouted enormous red leathery wings.

"Show off!" Jade said as Moltar hovered and grinned down at her. "Come down here so we may properly welcome our newest member to this odd family."

Moltar performed a ground-shaking landing and let his riders climb down before he jumped back into the sea to play.

Shuran watched as the rest of the Zidu'Si got to know both Vala and the new power she brought to the fold. While the others would need to practice the ability of water wielding to become better acclimated, old memories and usage awoken in Shuran once the bond of service occurred. Rather than focusing on the water in the Great Sea as the others were. Shuran was concentrating on exploring the deeper aspects of the element. He began exhaling and centering on the water vapor that left his mouth with the air he breathed.

Shuran began alternating between breathing out ice crystals and steam. He then took deeper breaths and exhaled as much as he could, a bitter cold breeze. His limited control over air gave him a boost in the wind he pushed forth, he could only image how strong this would be once he mastered elemental air Essence wielding.

A thought occurred to Shuran as he went about his own form of exploring the wielding of water. He focused on his own body and his abilities to shift. He already knew from the books of anatomy, that the body is made of mostly water. As he focused on this thought, something odd happened. He looked down to find his clothing at what should have been his feet. What he saw was his boots with two leg shaped columns of water coming out of them. Panic brought him back to normal. It also brought the attention of the Zidu'Si.

As they all looked on in shocked silence, it was Jade that quickly came over to stand with her back to Shuran and stretched a wing to allow him privacy. "You may wish to reclothe yourself Shin'Ar, unless you plan on turning to a man shaped water sculpture again."

Shuran quickly dressed himself while blushing at the stifled laughter of his friends. He could not blame them as he began to laugh at himself. He would need to take more care with his stray thoughts. As the powers of the Zidu'Si grew, Shuran's abilities grew many times faster and stronger.

"Has there been any further information on who attacked me as I left the swamps?" Shuran asked as he stepped fully dressed, from behind Jade.

"We are unable to determine proof of who would have attacked. The kashshaptu who fled would have required help, we do not know where to begin," Gregoran answered as he looked at Orian nervously.

"What is it you are thinking Orian?" Shuran asked, noticing his agitation.

"There are those among the elves that do not agree with the work of the Zidu'Si and still distrust the Shin'Ar from wounds long ago to the pride of our kind. It would not be out of the realm of possibilities that they had a hand in this attack."

"Can you find this out for certain, discretely?" Mallick asked.

****

Orian agreed to look into the matter and then traveled the Emmuku'Gu back to Entensiama. He arrived late in the day, when most elves would be taking an afternoon respite, so he was not likely noticed. Orian quickly cloaked himself so he might remain unnoticed as he skirted the settlement and headed to the Queen's home in the hope of gaining a private audience. He did not like the feeling that he was spying on his own people, but he could not risk alerting anyone if there were elven involvement.

The great tree palace stood across the clearing from where Orian approached. There were few elves around so he would have little difficulty traversing the distance worrying about avoiding others. Elves could sense the electric pulses in others; this is how they knew when travelers wandered into their woods. Orian practiced buffering his presence with Shuran, this would be his first practical test.

Orian set his secondary shield and moved fast through the clearing. He moved without notice all the way to the palace entrance. He sensed no one on the other side of the great doors, so he opened them enough to slip through and close them behind him. Silently he worked his way toward where he sensed the Queen. She was alone. He turned the corner of the last flight of stairs to find the Queen sitting alone by the window.

"You certainly took your time getting here Orian," Florisia said as she turned and looked directly at Orian's shielded location. "Do not be over surprised child, I am the Queen for a reason. I sensed your presence the moment you arrived in Entensiama."

Orian dropped his shields and approached the Queen with his eyes downcast. He knelt before Florisia in a show of obedience and submission.

"Oh, do stand up Orian, no need for pomp and circumstance. We are alone and I know why you have come. It took the Shin'Ar long enough to send you."

"You knew of the attack?" Orian asked in surprise.

Florisia got up and indicated Orian was to follow into a private chamber where they could speak without intrusion. Once they were in a relatively secure space, the Queen told Orian about a presence she had been feeling within the woods. She was unsure what it was, but it was not elfin. She advised Orian that it did not get larger as though spreading, but she could not be certain.

Orian explained what happened to Shuran.

"I assure you that there is no way I would condone such a betrayal to the Shin'Ar, but who or whatever is sneaking about my lands may be to blame." Florisia was angry and sparks were dancing along her skin. "How do I get to the bottom of this without raising suspicion I wonder?"

"Perhaps it is wise for you to assemble a special team of elves to investigate and identify the stranger. I must get back to Shuran to inform him of what I have learned here, please be careful my Queen and do not move against this foe until we have returned to help." Orian kissed Florisia's hand and then disappeared into the power rivers of Ersetu.

Orian never noticed the old elf standing behind a column in the Chamber. After he had left, the elf walked out and approached the Queen.

Florisia looked up at him with raised brow. "You know something of this do you not Chamberlain?"

"Only whispers my Queen. It is said that the ancient wrongs are now at hand to stand corrected. But I am an old fool with poor hearing," the elf grinned at her.

"Continue to play that part my trusted friend. I wish to know everything going on within my forest. Report to me anything of interest, and you might start with checking up on the activities of Voreen and his club of miscreants!"

***

Shuran, the Zidu'Si, extended friends, and thirteen kashshaptu were meeting in the newly named Council Hall of Britengate when Orian returned. He made his way quickly to the Shin'Ar's side before being motioned to sit and wait to share his information. Shuran stood and with a slight motion sealed off the building from external sight and sound.

"Orian has just returned from Entensiama with news of a 'presence' in the elfin Capital." Shuran and the Zidu'Si already knew the basics of what Orian had learned. Through their link, they were aware the moment Orian was. Shuran explained that there was someone or something working among the elves and that the Queen would be taking care of investigating.

"Can we get back to the business o' them witches that went to the dark side?" Moona interrupted.

As exasperating and abrupt Moona could be, she always brought a smile to Shuran's face. He sat down to allow discussions to continue, when reality shifted. His vision blurred slightly and when it refocused he found himself in a dark room, seated before an assembly of people he recognized but did not know by name. He still had an overlay in his vision of his true surroundings that were similar in content to what he envisioned.

"Hebat, please proceed with your findings!" Shuran said.

Confused but not deterred, Penelle stepped forward and spoke about the kashshaptu who plotted behind her back in calling the trolls from the North. They decided that they might fair better leaving the Grand Kashshaptu, and side with Salmetu hoping for a place in the new order.

Shuran heard something entirely different. He saw Hebat standing before him accusing the young prince and princess, children of Gula, of siding with Uggae. She pleaded that Nergal punish them and bring their mother to stand accountable.

"Gula is not responsible for the actions of her children. They follow Uggae of their own free will, but I will not leave any of our children defenseless!" Shuran said the words but did not know why. As his reality came back to the present, he noticed everyone looking at him in shock. "Excuse me, I am not myself." Shuran left the hall, walking directly through the shields without dropping them.

"What the-," Moona started.

"Shut it, woman!" Codger interrupted. He began to follow Shuran when Penelle and Nagutan stopped him.

"I think this is a time where we two will be better suited to speak with the Shin'Ar," Nagutan said.

Moona snuffed at them but did not argue. She sat back down and lit her pipe while Codger stormed off in the opposite direction of Nagutan and Penelle.

"I'll be fillin' my cups at the Drunkard Inn if any o' ya is interested?" Codger shouted back.

The rest of the Zidu'Si followed in short order, leaving Moona alone with her frost moss and sour disposition.

Nagutan and Penelle followed Shuran out of the building, after Nagutan had cast a spell to remove the enchantments Shuran had placed on the hall. They did not have far to search before finding the Shin'Ar. He was sitting at the Altar of Creation. Nagutan and Penelle gathered before him and waited until he was ready to acknowledge them.

"I suppose the two of you have some words of wisdom?" Shuran finally asked.

Nagutan stood before Shuran while Penelle slid in to sit next to Shuran, forcing him to slide over. The two elder Essence users spoke at length about the names of the Gods that Shuran spoke as though having a conversation with them. Neither Penelle nor Nagutan understood the meaning of Shuran's one-sided conversation, but there was some significance.

"Do you realize that you spoke in the most ancient dialect of Sumeris?" Nagutan asked Shuran. "It is the oldest and most sacred of ancient tongues said to have been the language of the Gods themselves."

"How do you know this language?" Penelle asked Nagutan.

"I have had much free time over the long wait for Shuran's arrival; time spent researching, reading, and preparing."

"Preparing for what exactly?" Penelle asked narrow-eyed.

Ignoring her accusatory tone, Nagutan explained. "I was not certain, but I knew it would involve the balance and the most ancient of information available. I think the final fight for balance is upon us, whether we want it or not," Nagutan answered, half lying, as he gazed at the two stars growing brighter as nights passed.

"How is it that I know this language now, when I did not sooner? I mean there is a book in the Vault that is written in this language. I did not recognize it when I first saw it, but now I know how to read the strange symbols." Shuran asked.

Nagutan could not give Shuran a satisfying answer. He pondered reasons from latent memories surfacing, to only the Gods knew. What Nagutan seemed most interested in, was the book that Shuran mentioned. He asked many questions about the book and its contents, as well as where it was found and if Shuran would show it to him.

"The book stays safely where it is for now. As for where it was found, in the Vault library, buried beneath many others. I do not know the contents since I did not read it, but I will do so soon enough."

The conversation quickly returned to the old Gods. Shuran wanted as much information on them as possible, and both the elder weavers were eager to tell what they knew but they had little more information than Shuran already had. Shuran decided to take a lone trip to Durangug so he might catch up on his reading.

Chapter Twenty-Four

Shuran found the book where he left it when he first came across the tome. This time he was able to read the title and contents. The title was Sar A Nam'Mu, the Record of the Creator of Man. Shuran began to read the ancient journal. He read through the night and was awoken the next morning by the presence of Moltar outside calling to him through their bond.

"Lugaldur! What has kept you?" Moltar asked.

"I have been reading about our history, my bonded. There is much I now understand." Shuran shared a portion of what he learned while he and Moltar returned to Britengate.

Hebat, the first name Shuran remembered saying, is the Lady of the Sky. She is the matron deity of the Lil'Du, and encompasses all that is the element of air. Hebat listened to the winds and carried messages for the Gods.

Gula, the Lady Who The Dead Bring Back to Life, was the mistress of Uggae, God of Death. Gula was a benign Goddess that represented the rebirth of all. Many farmers still worshipped her to bring life back into the soil. After Uggae had seduced Gula, she was cast from the house of the Gods to give birth to her base-born children, Ninagal, the Prince of Great Waters and Kishargal, the Princess of Firm Ground.

The split among the Gods resulted in a war between two sides. Where one group of the deities wished to nurture and raise man up, the other wished to subjugate and use mankind to do their will. This war culminated in the changes to the Telukukal. They were the first and only race of man. When the Gods went to war, they created the younger seven races of man.

"The details of why are not recorded clearly. The more answers I seem to get, the more questions I have," Shuran said. "In the least I know which Gods fought against each other."

Shuran recalled the names of the two factions of the Gods that were in conflict. Among those who chose to use mankind as tools were Uggae, Gula, Ninagal, Kishargal, and led by Ereshkigal the Queen of the Netherworld.

The protectors of mankind were Hebat, Nina, Ninti, Enki, and led by Damkianna. Nina was known as the Lady of Water. Ninti was worshipped as the Lady of Life. The Lord of Earth was Enki and their leader, Damkianna, Mistress of Heaven and Earth.

These two factions were equally matched, and one side could not overtake control from the other. An overseer, Nergal, the Great Watcher, kept this balance of the warring Gods. He remained neutral yet vigilant and having the greatest power among the Gods on Ersetu, made certain neither side could ever take control of the experiment. Something happened that destroyed this balance, but Shuran could not determine what this event was from reading the journal in Durangug.

"Do you not mean the Gods 'of' Ersetu?" Penelle asked.

"No, the translation is clearly referencing the Gods 'on' Ersetu. This leads me to believe there are other Gods. Nam'Mu is named, Creator of Man, have any here ever heard of said God?" Shuran asked.

No one could recall ever hearing of this God.

"What about the reference to an experiment, what was the experiment?" Avrank asked with a look that he already knew the answer.

"Mankind, I believe they were using us for some purpose," Shuran said, confirming Avrank's summation.

Shuran left the Zidu'Si and friends in the hall to ponder his revelation. He walked about the city and greeted the people who he passed. Though the citizens of the rebuilt city seemed somewhat at ease with the safety they felt in Britengate, Shuran could sense that they were not completely at peace. The people walked past shaded areas with caution and jumped at every shadow. The very air of the city was thick with fear of attack.

Shuran worked his way to the building that served as the Zidu'Si barracks. He realized he was weary. He slept a little the night before, but not restfully. His head was aching behind his eyes and he felt the weight of his responsibilities growing. More questions of the meanings behind what he read in the journal, kept his mind grasping for answers. He soon found his cot and quickly fell into a deep vision-filled sleep.

Shuran stood atop the precipice, looking down upon the field of battle. Two opposing forces have engaged and they are decimating one another. Neither side could pass the lines of the other. If one army began to gain advantage over the other, Shuran would send down forces from the sky to disintegrate the area. He was compelled to maintain an equal playing field.

The clash of Gods had continued for several days before Shuran became weary of keeping the balance. With a final blast of force, he froze the forces of the Gods in place. Shuran moved with a thought, to the center of the field and pulled Uggae and his followers forward from their viewing pavilion. The Gods of Light emerged from a flash of light behind Shuran as he kept the dark Gods in suspension.

Shuran realized he was experiencing a vision, but instead of fighting it he continued to let it take him along. He wanted to see, no experience, part of ancient history lost to time and memory.

"This madness ends now!" Shuran commanded at Uggae. "You and your ilk have gone too far beyond the guidelines of our experiment. You have tainted the results and are no longer objective."

"We have been left here fool! There is no test any longer, the Me has forgotten us. Why should we not create a world that serves our desires?"

Uggae asked.

"Because desire is not our purpose. Desires breed selfishness. Selfishness results in any one, if not all of the reviled acts, and you have become subject to them all Uggae!" Shuran replied.

"I do not understand your piety. These are subjects of play, only meant for learning. You of all should know what it means to learn from testing the limits," Uggae pleaded.

"You go too far and have acted against the rest of us, I will suffer your darkness no longer." Shuran raised his hands and extended his spread fingers out toward all the dark Gods. He spoke the ancient words as energy spread across his body. The power shot from his hands to the dark Gods and they began to change.

Shuran felt power flow from the Gods of Light and into himself as he poured the transformation spell from his hands onto the dark Gods before him. They screamed in agony as their auras crackled and began to harden around them. Slowly at first, a dull grey stone-like surface formed over the Gods, encasing them within. Shuran felt himself burning with energy as the Essence flowed through him, but he continued to let the energy flow until the Gods were completely imprisoned in stasis containment made of gugtu.

The Telukukal that survived the battle were few and their loyalties were split. Once the Dark Gods were neutralized, a few of the Telukukal that followed Uggae willingly retreated and fled the plains while the others remained to await the will of the victorious Gods.

The vision abruptly changed, replaced with a look into the near future. Shuran watched from the Altar of Creation, as the citizens of Britengate came under attack from the Shadow. Dark misty tendrils of the Shadow stream into the city from the surrounding forest. Shadowy arms reached out in all directions to attack the fleeing Aurderians.

As each victim was touched, they were transformed into vessels of the dark Gods. Shuran attempted in vain, to reach out and save them, but he was powerless. He ran to the nearest man that was under attack and abruptly halted, stopped by a powerful shield. Momentarily stunned on the spot, he could not react to the tendrils striking toward him. The tendrils met the same wall of power from the opposite side and were

204

repelled.

Shuran gazed around him, following the line of the shield wall to its apex. It centered on the Altar of Creation, a dome formed an area of protection. Shuran stood alone in the protected area due to its inadequate power. His previous failure to properly connect the altar to the full power source of Emmuku'Gu cost the lives of all those touched by the Shadow's attack. Shuran awoke, screaming in anguish, alone in the darkness of failure.

It took all the power of the Zidu'Si and several drakkon to hold Moltar back from ripping the roof from the barracks when they all arrived, called to alarm by Shuran's jarring cries. They stopped his physical rescue of his Lugaldur, but they could not prevent him pulling Shuran from the structure. Moltar, without conscious knowledge, called upon the Essence to move Shuran from within the structure, through thought alone. His bonded master appeared in the fetal position at his feet and Moltar dropped down to lay beside him, wrapping his wings around them both and raised a shield that threw all near him back several feet.

Moltar unknowingly intensified the bond between himself and Shuran. Instead of using the Emmuku'Gu to go to Shuran, Moltar somehow managed to use the link of their shi. Shuran traveled along that link directly to Moltar, much in the way Shuran was linked to the Vault and moved things at will between himself and Durangug. Without warning, Moltar began to see the visions that Shuran experienced before awaking. The mighty drakkon suddenly understood and felt all that Shuran carried within himself. Moltar roared out in the night with helplessness and a buffeting force of Essence, knowing he is unable to protect his Lugaldur from what is to come.

In the darkness of a nearby alley, a solitary elf shrank back in horror and fear as the wave of Essence washed over him and broke his hold on the elfin form he had been wearing. The shifter was stuck in its true shape. It was a gelatinous mass of flesh with fingerless appendages at each side and two stumpy legs. Internal organs were partially visible, through the translucent membrane that held the creature together.

***

In New Draven at the Academy, Telalsu was struggling to maintain control. The body of Bastien he possessed no longer fought back mentally. Bastien found a way to fight the demon physically; he began to work at shutting down organs. His first attempt was to shut down the liver and kidneys. Bastien planned on poisoning his own body in an attempt to make Telalsu leave for a better body.

Telalsu fell to the knee under the pain of the attack. "This human is stronger than we expected, my Queen," Telalsu said as Salmetu approached him. "He poisons the body to prevent me full use of him."

"That is not my concern, demon," she replied hovering over his prone form. "Get the animal under control, we need him."

"I do not understand his resistance!"

"You should, or has it been too long? His shi is only partially present in that shell Telalsu, the other part longs for a return and is strengthening Bastien's resolve to become rid of you!"

"There were few left in Birchshire, and those who remained knew nothing of Bastien's father," Telalsu complained.

Salmetu turned from the demon possessed Bastien. "And where have all the people gone?"

"They have fled but it is unknown where they headed. Some say the dwarves while others say the elves," he answered. "Perhaps our new kashshaptu allies can do something to earn the right to remain as they are."

Chapter Twenty-Five

Shuran woke to find himself cocooned by leathery wings and bulk of scaly red skin. Moments passed as Shuran took time to realize where he was after the visions overtook him the previous night. A touch to his mind confirmed his realization that he was now sitting in the embrace of Moltar. Shuran sent a reassuring thought to his bonded drakkon that he was well and wished to be released.

Moltar reluctantly folded back his wings and rose up to a sitting position. Though he released his shields and let Shuran leave his protection, Moltar kept hold of his Lugaldur through the new and stronger link they shared. He did not understand the change but Moltar was compelled now, more than ever, to protect Shuran. The thoughts and visions that returned to him from the previous night only strengthened his resolve.

Shuran walked into the barracks to find the Zidu'Si awake and preparing for the day. They each greeted him with silent looks and nods. Though the joining of shi that made the Zidu'Si a collective of power, strength, and knowledge linked them, Shuran sensed a change in them all that morning. The silence and awkward atmosphere was broken by the arrival of Moona.

"I see your lizard guardian finally let ya' out of his grasp," Moona snarled as she walked up to Shuran. "I ain' seen nothin' like it afore, that mountainous beast actually threatened to reduce me to charcoal!"

"I apologize for Moltar's over-reaction. He did not understand what happened and acted on instinct."

"Since ya' mention it, what did happen?" Moona asked.

"Memories and visions unlike any I have experienced before. I am unclear of the reason for the memories I experienced, but the vision that followed leaves no need for explanation," Shuran began. "We must prepare for a direct assault from the Shadow."

During breakfast, Shuran explained the vision he had with what was now being called the Weavers Assembly. The mundane humans began speaking amongst themselves about those with an ability in Essence, meeting and deciding what would be done in the defense of Britengate. The name caught on, so now that is what they called themselves.

Those with wielding or weaving capabilities were all invited to the general discussions that involved the need for Essence work being done. The word assembly, however, was an exaggeration as those known to have gifts in Essence, represented less than one percent of the growing population of Britengate.

Shuran told those present that they needed to prepare for the coming assault from the Shadow. His mention of the Shadow required that he explain what the true nature of their enemy was as best he understood himself. He continued to describe how the Altar of Creation was a source of protection from the tendrils that attacked in his vision.

"The dome of protection you describe would only protect a few of the people in the city. What good does this knowledge do us?" asked one of those gathered.

"It must be strengthened and expanded, or we discover how it works and learn how to shield ourselves and those under our protection," Shuran answered. "Knowing that something about the Altar repels the Shadow is the first step in finding the means to fight back."

After the meal and meeting, the Zidu'Si stayed behind with the kashshaptu, now being called the Thirteen Sisters. Shuran enlisted them to help see to the needs of the citizenry in Britengate. The kashshaptu were gifted in healing among other abilities that would be useful. What Shuran was most interested in, was their ability to sense the gift of weaving in others. Shuran sent them out to begin looking for any citizens who could be sparked and trained.

"Penny, can you see that any found with the spark, be brought to the meeting hall for testing and briefing," Shuran said.

Completely caught off guard by the use of her nickname, Penelle stared silently at Shuran for a moment before responding. "Why did you call me that?"

"I apologize I do not know where that came from."

"I have not been called Penny by anyone for thousands of years, and even then by only one man."

"Nagutan?" Shuran asked.

Penelle did not deny the assumption nor did she answer, before turning and leaving.

Shuran knew in an instant that the knowledge and impulse to call Penelle by the pet name 'Penny' was a result of being in some way connected to Nagutan. The same faded connection existed with Gimagala and her memories and feelings became a more frequent invader of Shuran's conscious thoughts. There existed a residual link to the previous Zidu'Si. Shuran began to wonder if the same thing were true for his growing feelings of being joined to the old Gods in some way. He was assaulted by a throbbing ache behind his eyes.

Moltar's grumbling could be heard across the whole of Britengate. The moment Shuran experienced his aching head Moltar felt the same pain. The mutation in their bond joined them in new ways. Moltar felt the same impulse to speak the name Penny as Shuran did. More than the simultaneously shared thoughts, was when Moltar focused on Shuran intently enough, he felt as though he saw through his Lugaldur's eyes.

"Give me room ya' dur!" Moona complained, pushing past Codger. She waddled about the meeting hall, lining up people according to the level of abilities the Thirteen Sisters felt within each of the humans they examined.

"Don' get yur knickers twisted wench, I'm jus' tryin' to help," Codger spat back. His task was to provide spells for each of the groups to attempt. He came up with various offensive and defensive spells that would help fight when the Shadow chose to attack.

The kashshaptu, thus far, found another thirty human wielders among the population. Their abilities ranged from simple sensing of what ailed the injured, to moderate casting of spells. Those trained and already experienced, shared their knowledge in an effort to strengthen the talents of the newest weavers.

***

Salmetu stared into the scrying dish as one of her dark weavers called images of where the citizens of Aurderia were abandoning her. She watched as caravans of humans moved to the eastern borders of Aurderia. The town of Middleton was surrounded with tents and makeshift shacks to shelter the people seeking refuge. Her rage boiled when she saw more caravans heading further east toward Drakkfoth.

"I want those people stopped!" Salmetu ordered.

"What of Middleton my Queen?" Vardoran asked. "There are several thousand souls for the gathering."

"Middleton can wait, I do not want those fools entering the realm of the Drakkians."

"I do not understand, the Drakkians stand against us why have we not destroyed them yet?" Vardoran asked meekly.

"Do not question my actions, I have plans for the Baron and what remains of his people. It is not yet time to act upon them. Now take the death walkers to stop the caravan's reaching the Baron De Drakk."

Vardoran bowed as he exited the audience chamber with the other dark weavers, leaving Salmetu alone sitting upon her throne of dragon glass.

"Is this action truly necessary? Those humans simply wish to escape enslavement," Sulura said as she walked out from anti-chamber.

"They defied us Sulura, just as Shuran and his band of miscreants have. They shall pay for the crimes of their false Gods," Salmetu said with many voices.

"Salmetu this is not you talking, it is the voices of Shadow. You must fight them or be lost to me," Sulura pleaded. She repeated this same argument every day since being brought to her daughter. Little by little she was chipping away at the barrier preventing her daughter's true spirit taking control.

"You waste your energy with pleading, Sulura. Salmetu is no longer, only Shadow remains," the voices said.

With tears welling in her eyes, Sulura turned and left the chamber. She hurried back to her room. Few guards were placed in the area since she could not leave the floor. Sulura had no intention on leaving until she could get through to her daughter. She reached her room and headed directly for her bed, where she buried her head in the pillows to muffle her sobbing. It was only the standing of the hairs on her arm and a slight chill in the air that alerted her of a presence in her chambers.

"Do not cry for her mother, she is fighting in her own way," Tianna said.

"There is nothing but Shadow behind her eyes Tianna, how can she be fighting?"

"If she were lost, I would not be here."

***

Shuran walked through the crowds of people gathered in the clearing around the Altar of Creation. He had not expected so many to volunteer for what he planned. Shuran supposed that the threat of death or consumption by the Shadow broke through barriers of hate. These are people who despised Essence workers, and now they came to see if they could be transformed from mundanes into weavers.

Shuran stood before the Altar and looked out at the hundreds of humans gathered. Desperation flowed from them like fog off the Great Sea on an early fall evening. These people wanted to live and they were willing to become what they always feared and loathed in order to have a fighting chance. Shuran wondered whether it was the right thing to do, but they were here of their own choice so he would do what needed to be done.

"In a few moments I will be reaching into the depths of each of you gathered. You will feel no pain, but you may experience a tingling or slight stinging sensation; this is normal," Shuran said to them. "I have the ability to alter a part of each of you that over the centuries has mutated, preventing you from using the Essence as all men on Ersetu were once able.

"Once you have been changed, you will need testing for the strength and skill you each have gained. I do not know when the Shadow will attack, but we can assume that it will be sooner rather than later." Shuran raised his arms to shoulder level and stretched out his hands.

The power that was required to connect to so many and alter part of their genetics was astronomical, but Shuran seemed to do so now without showing signs of strain. He reached into the Altar of Creation and down into the Emmuku'Gu he connected with it previously. He was not certain why he did this, usually he would reach for his Zidu'Si and through them Durangug, but this time a deeper understanding surfaced and he went directly to the source of power.

The branch of the Emmuku'Gu changed as Shuran pulled upon it. The flow that he connected to the Altar carved a new path for itself and drove straight down into the earth toward the center of the planet. When it reached the core Shuran found the source of Essence, the pulsating life force of Ersetu.

The flow of energy rippled back along the flow of the river, through the Altar of Creation and into Shuran. His eyes shot open and glowed with a light that shone stronger than Utu at mid-day. Shuran cast power into the hundreds of gathered humans who in turn began to fall to the ground as he finished his work and released them. All of the newly kindled weavers rested upon the dirt except for those closest to Shuran.

Eight humans remained connected to Shuran as he poured more power into them and changed the flow. He left one hand stretched toward them, sparks dancing along the length of his fingers. The other arm swung back to the Altar and brought the power flow to an apex.

"GISNU SU SHI KES ANA AN-DUL A GIZZU," Shuran intoned in a voice that resonated across the entire city. A final pulse of pale blue light escaped the Altar and flowed through Shuran and out to the eight new weavers. Pulling the spell through himself had a side effect. It caused him and all of the Zidu'Si to glow suddenly then pass into unconsciousness as the light extinguished. This included Moltar and Jade.

"What in the name of Damkianna did you do Shin-for-brains?" Moona yelled after dousing Shuran with a bucket of water.

"It is fine Moona, only a protection spell-" Shuran started.

"That was more than any simple spell of protection Shuran. You spoke the ancient tongue in a voice not your own and the spell was no simple weaving. You wielded Essence into a weaving." Nagutan stood before Shuran with a look of awe, confusion, disbelief, and fear. "What are you becoming?"

"What I am becoming is what I have always been," Shuran answered. "It is you that started this after all!"

Shuran stood before the recovering eight weavers he empowered as they regained their senses. The other new weavers were already being examined by the Thirteen Sisters. Shuran indicated the eight before him would need to rest and then be sent to him at the Assembly Hall the next morning.

"You mind explainin' what you did just then, or is the rest o' us not important 'nough ta know?" Moona chided.

"I have wondered where the power of Durangug came from for some time. This question had nagged at me since I first entered the Emmuku'Gu, until it became clear when I began altering the new weavers. The moment clarity fell upon me, many of the memories and visions I have had resurfaced and I simply knew what to do."

"Spit it out boy, ol' Moony ain' gonna wait all night," Codger said.

Moona smiled at him briefly before sidling up to him and impatiently stared at Shuran, waiting for a full explanation.

Shuran told them what they needed to know. He connected to the source of Essence directly and fully repaired the Altar of Creation. After he had finished the modification of the majority of humans to kindle their Essence weaving, he chose the eight nearest himself to connect them to the Altar. They would become the protectors of the gates.

"What gates?" Mallick asked as he stepped closer.

"The gates we need to build at the four cardinal boundaries of Britengate. Now that the Altar is repaired, we can shield the city, but we need points of ingress and egress for refugees, supplies, and our own needs. The eight will guard the gates when under attack," Shuran explained.

These eight were now bound to the power of Light. They were chosen because they were already Followers of the Light and worshipped at Altar of Creation. Shuran knew this because he sensed their devotion while connected to their shi. When the battle for Britengate and the Altar of Creation came to pass, the eight zealots would be at the gates to protect those outside the main borders while they escaped to the safety within the shield. Other weavers and wielders would augment their defense.

"What else happened during your spell?" Gregoran asked. "All the Zidu'Si including Jade and Moltar were knocked senseless at the completion of your casting."

"I am not certain, perhaps a feedback of the power when I released it back to the source," Shuran answered skeptically.

"Which begs the question, what is this source you speak of?" Nagutan asked.

"Ersetu, she is alive and has her own shi. This fight, the balance that is broken, has always been about protecting the life of the planet. The Shadow is a malignancy that has been attacking Ersetu since man began walking the surface. But you already know this, so why do you ask me?"

Nagutan did not answer; he nodded then turned and left, quickly followed by Penelle.

"He has access to my memories, Penny!" Nagutan said as they walked alone into the darkening forest. "This may complicate things."

"I understand that he is connected to the living members of the previous Zidu'Si, but how will that matter? I would think it more help than hindrance."

"There are things that I have been required to do, things that I have told no one. He is not ready to know these things." Nagutan held a look of sadness. Tears welled in his eyes as Penelle took his face in her hands.

"I cannot begin to understand what all you have been through, but I know you better than any other. If you say you must not reveal things to the Shin'Ar too soon, then you should shield your thoughts. We may have ended our pairing long ago, but you are still the same man I loved then."

"I am afraid he has become far too strong for even my abilities to block. He would sense the walls, and turn them to dust with a thought. I must leave Penny. Besides I have missed some necessary visits to old friends." Nagutan kissed Penelle's hands as he stood and walked toward his hut to gather his belongings.

Penelle whispered after Nagutan, "Be careful Dalgon, and return soon."

The sound of a branch cracking called Penelle's attention away from the retreating form of her former husband. She scanned the area around the secluded glade in which she was standing alone. Her seer's sight revealed not a soul around except a few rabbits and a lone white wolf.

Chapter Twenty-Six

Work on the gugtu gates began the next morning before first light. Shuran and Dara worked to transform stones into the Essence imbued magnetic stone required for the gates to work in the shield. Dwarves worked on creating a sledge and channel system for moving the gates in and out of position. The elfin rangers went about the borders of the city to let those outside the boundary know where the entrances would be placed.

Shuran completed the transformation of all the gugtu, and left Dara to oversee the placement into the gate arches for each location. He worked his way back to the meeting hall where the eight weavers he appointed as Protectors of the Altar would be expected soon. When he arrived, the zealots were already awaiting Shuran's arrival.

They all knew what their position was by the time they left the hall. Shuran had explained why he chose them, and they all accepted the responsibility with honor. Shuran shared with them spells for casting light and their own shields powered by the Emmuku'Gu filling the Altar of

Creation. These eight men would be weaving wielders, the only full blood humans to have such ability.

By the time Shuran finished eating and left the building, news had arrived of Ogres leaving the mountains and heading toward Britengate. Shuran decided to wait where he was and instructed a page boy to bring the dwarves who carried the news back to the hall. He felt the power of the magurmu when it approached earlier that morning.

While he waited, Shuran began to think on the realizations he had while performing the casting the night before. While he knew that some information was coming from his link to Nagutan and Gimagala, he also understood that most of the memories were that of someone much older and far more powerful than simply a Shin'Ar of the past. The visions of battling Gods returned, but this time Shuran felt the pain when a bolt of energy hit him.

The vision ended and Shuran buckled at the knees in pain. His midsection felt the searing pain of an energy burn. He lifted his shirt to find a blistering wound upon his stomach. He hardly began healing it before Moltar landed and gave him a concerned nudge.

"You should warn me before you decide to daydream Lugaldur. We share thoughts, and pain now." Moltar showed Shuran his belly, where a massive blistering wound was healing at the same rate as Shuran's.

The greater bond that recently formed between Shuran and Moltar was deeper than Shuran expected. Now they were truly connected body and shi. One would not be harmed without affecting the other. Shuran saw this as a double-edged blade. Before he could put thoughts to words, the pageboy returned with the dwarves who brought news of ogres.

"Greetings Shuran Shin'Ar," Dvargan and Grafdik spoke in turn. "We come with grave news from the Orenthal Mountains. A large band of ogres march this way from their caves in the base of the Eastern Orenthal range."

"Well-met my friends, regardless of the news you carry. This message could have been sent by communication stone, what other business brings you to Britengate?" Shuran asked as he gave his friends warm embraces.

"We were without anything useful to occupy our time since the closing of the mines," they said.

"So you were bored and thought to put yourself in the middle of the upcoming battle?" Shuran knew his messages had reached the other races by communication stone the night before so the twins would already know of the vision Shuran shared.

They just grinned up at Shuran mischievously.

"Very well, go find Mallick and he will see to assigning you a place where your talents can be of use." Shuran grinned broader knowing how Mallick would react to the presence of the 'talkie twins' as he referred to them.

Just before darkness settled over Britengate, the gugtu gateways were completed and in position, ready to slide into place. Shuran visited each Cardinal gate to place an enchantment upon the structures. The purpose of the spell was simple. It would allow the gates to move freely in and out of the force shield and redirect the energy so that the arch provided a break in the field to allow passage. They worked with a command word spoken only from within the boundary of Britengate by anyone with weaving abilities.

Outside the boundary, a member of the Zidu'Si or the Protectors of the Altar could only slide the gates into position. Should they need to enter the city by themselves, they need not open the gates. The spell Shuran cast upon them, and by rebound upon the Zidu'Si, allowed them to pass unimpeded through the shields.

Shuran finished the last enchantment and tested it when he smelled something odd from beyond the border of the city. Without knowing, Shuran knew the scent belonged to a shifter. The knowledge came from Moltar, as did the sense of smell.

Shuran wasted barely a moment before activating the shield over the city.

"I did not realize you would be testing the shield as well, Shin'Ar. Perhaps we should have warned the citizens?" Dara asked.

"It was not planned. There is a shifter out there in the forest, I smell it!" Shuran said with a snarl and smoke puffed out of his nose as his eyes slit and turned red.

Moltar's massive form flew overhead and straight out through the shield.

"So much for the shield," Gregoran said.

"The shield is fine, the Zidu'Si and Protectors are not subject to the barrier. PETA BABLURDU!" Shuran said the words to move the gate before him.

Moltar hovered above the white wolf as it approached the gate. As she moved closer, Barurbe took her human appearance and continued walking through the gateway. She stepped up to Shuran before stopping and looking him directly in the eyes, expressionless.

"Explain yourself Barurbe," Shuran said flatly.

"I did not mean to spy, I felt unwelcome. Considering the information I have you may wish to destroy me, but I cannot hold my tongue," she replied without breaking eye contact.

Shuran took her to the Assembly Hall so that she might share her information before the Assembly. He sat her down in a chair that sat facing the entire room as the Weavers Assembly gathered. He was partially aware of what she might share, knowing that she was a shifter.

"My name is Barurbe, and I have spent most of my life as the adopted daughter of the Baron, Fallon de Drakk. I only recently discovered my true identity and was lured into a scheme of deception."

Barurbe revealed that a shifter who revealed to her the true nature of what she was approached her. She had been stolen away from her home in the Foresworn Territories and placed within the borders of Drakkfoth to later be found by the Baron himself. This shifter shared the true nature of what she was and how she could help further their cause by sharing information. She refused, but not before being deceived.

"Deceived how?" Shuran asked. "You had already spoken of deception when we last met in the Stone Forest."

"The shifter showed me how to take forms other than a wolf. As a test he had me change into the form of the next person I encountered, it was Sulura."

Shuran immediately understood. Though Barurbe continued to explain, Shuran played the scenario out in his mind. The shifter persuaded Barurbe to shift into the form of Sulura and then impersonated her. The shifter then created the letter stating that Sulura was leaving to visit Shuran, so that her absence would not be missed. He then delivered Shuran's mother to Vardoran, who later brought her before Salmetu.

"I did not understand what was happening at the time, but once Fallon explained what had happened. I knew I was to blame." Barurbe lowered her head shamefully.

"Do not hold yourself accountable for the actions of another. You were deceived and this creature played on your need for answers. I still call you cousin Barurbe, regardless of your heritage. You are very brave to come here with this information." Shuran walked over to Barurbe and gathered her into an embrace that caused her to begin crying.

"I do not deserve your kindness," Barurbe sobbed.

"You more than any other are most like myself, looking for answers to where we are from and what our purpose is. Come, we shall continue our talk in a less judicial atmosphere. You can tell me what you learned about the shifters and their plans." Shuran led Barurbe out of the hall and into an earthen house he instantly created from the ground before him.

Shuran sat down across form Barurbe at the stone table he called from the floor. He produced food and drink for them to replenish themselves while they spoke. Barurbe was tentative at first, but soon relaxed when Shuran began to eat and drink himself.

Finally, she spoke, "It told me that I would be serving my people. I was blinded by the need for finding my true place in this world, I could not see that I was being played for a fool," she sobbed.

"Barurbe, trust in me when I say, you were used no more than the rest of us. I have been played as the pawn my entire existence, yet I continue with the game. We all have a part to play, what matters is how we choose to make our moves," Shuran assured her.

"You mean you know what Nagutan has done?" she said without thinking.

Shuran was caught off guard but did not express it. He studied Barurbe for a moment and then reached into his scrambled memories before responding. "You mean the part he played in my birth and that of the alleged prophecies? There is little he can hide from me now that I have begun to accept my power."

"Then you know he is Dalgon," she said.

This, Shuran did not know. He was stunned silent and could not hide his shock.

Barurbe noticed, "I am sorry to have been the one to tell you. I was in the wood when I heard he and the kashshaptu speaking."

"What leads you to believe he is my father?" Shuran said in disbelief, even though the pieces were beginning to fit together. "That does not even make sense, my father is Fallon's half brother, and they grew up together."

"Nagutan spoke of your connection to the past Zidu'Si and that he could not continue to hide the things he has done. You are too powerful for him to shield his mind so he had to leave. Penelle whispered a goodbye to him and called him Dalgon."

"I will speak to Penny and Fallon about this, but I wish you to keep this to yourself," Shuran instructed. "There are many games being played here and right now, we need to focus on finishing one at a time. Are you with us or shall you pursuit your lineage?" Shuran asked.

"I am with you cousin, but there is something more you should know."

Barurbe revealed to Shuran all that the shifter had spoken. He was free with information, expecting that Barurbe would abandon her adopted family and join its cause. The Shifters were split into two factions, those who joined the guardians and those who enacted their own agenda.

The shifters were born in the Foresworn Territories, offspring of the multi-blood refugees of the Sikil Mah. Something happened during an experiment with some device built by the first settlers of the land, that poisoned their fertility. All children born in the last thousand years, were either stillborn or shifters. Most shifters born did not survive, but those that did were shunned and drove into the service of the Nabusa as Guardians.

Many of them became resentful and left the territories to form their own settlement. They wanted something, but the shifter did not share their plans.

222

"Another problem for another day," Shuran said. "Thank you for this information and as problematic as it is, we have more pressing issues. I will ask you to make a choice, however…"

"You wish me to spy for you?" she responded.

"It is your choice and I will not make it for you."

"My choice is simple, I will help my true family. You Shuran and Fallon, of course, are my family and I will do what I can to see that you are informed of the actions of the shifters who refer themselves as 'the Eighth Race'."

"Then I wish you success and will give you something to help you." Shuran took her hands and connected to her being. He imparted the knowledge of the various races, creatures, and animals of Ersetu that he had examined and learned of from the book of anatomy. This knowledge would allow Barurbe to shift into anything he shared knowledge of. He also gave her another gift, the ability to wield.

"Shifters can weave, but they cannot wield. This alone will save you if you are found out, it will also allow you to learn to travel the lines of power called the Emmuku'Gu. I want you to visit the Elves first and seek the guidance of one of the elders, Voreen. He can teach you to travel the lines. If he refuses let me know but do not protest and do not let him know your true nature. Your main purpose there is to find the shifter hiding among their people. Report to Florisia as soon as you arrive. I will let her know you are coming."

Barurbe took the form of an elf, flawless in appearance. She used the knowledge Shuran shared to alter her aura and energy signature. She was now unidentifiable among any other elves.

Chapter Twenty-Seven

Shuran awoke to the smell of ozone and the familiar presence of Tianna's spirit. He pulled on his shoes and exited the barracks wearing a cloak against the chill of the night. Tianna's ghostly form drifted closer as Shuran found a private place to speak.

"All these private meetings are beginning to wear on my nerves," Shuran said to himself.

"I am truly sorry brother but this is important."

"It is not you Tianna, I am sorry. I welcome your visits. What is it you wish to tell me?"

"Most importantly, mother sends her love," Tianna said as she settled next to Shuran on a log. "Salmetu is weakening in substance, she is being overcome by Shadow. I do not know how much more time I have."

"Tianna, can I ask you something?" Shuran asked as if not listening to her. After she had nodded he continued. "Did you know that Nagutan was actually somehow involved in our birth?"

"Yes, but before you ask, I will not share any more of what I know."

"I need not ask more of you sister, for I fear I already know more than I should. What is it you came to tell me, I feel there is more urgency to your visit?"

"Vardoran, he has been sent to attack refugees traveling toward Drakkfoth. Part of him resists but not enough that the Shadow now filling him cannot overwhelm."

"So part of the man that was, still exists?" Shuran asked.

"The Shadow is unable to control a shi-less body, it feeds on it. All meals eventually get consumed, however, so I do not know how much time there is to save them."

"Save who Tianna, Vardoran? He chose his path long ago. Salmetu, I will save, along with the others forced into the service of darkness. Vardoran, he is altogether a different situation."

"He is a damaged man, Shuran. No one is beyond redemption so long as they still have a shi that clings to right and wrong. He still longs for the love and acceptance of his parents, he went astray when he became consumed by the need to make them proud."

"One of the seven laws of mankind, pride should not overcast virtue. I will leave that decision up to Moona and Codger. He is filled by Shadow, when I destroy it, will he or any others survive?"

"I am unsure, but there is a way to save Bastien that I am certain of."

Shuran perked up immediately and gave all his attention to Tianna.

Tianna told Shuran about the daggers that were used for removing or replacing a shi within a body. They were the Mi-Ib Twin Daggers, one to take souls and another to release them. Salmetu possessed the Mi-Ib Karshi used during the sacrifice at her birth. The Mi-Ib Simshi could be used to move a shi back into a body.

"Where can I find this Mi-Ib Simsi?" Shuran asked.

"I do not know for certain, but I think you may be able to find out if you visit the Napalkua Falls. The Shadow guards the blade where first it released Uggae's shi. That is all I know. There is something more to the Shadow that you must know if you are to prevail. It is not as simple as a dark presence."

"It is a collective of shi powering the Shadow, I have already sensed this," Shuran interrupted.

"It is much more than that brother, the shi the Shadow takes are a source of power, but it is volatile. They fight for freedom, and if they find a way of being released, they will weaken the Shadow to a point that it can no longer hold sway in the corporeal realm."

Shuran paused before responding to Tianna's revelation. He began to have another memory surface to his consciousness. He looked down upon a statue, one he recognized among those of the collection in Durangug. He held a golden dagger in his hands. It is light, but heavy with power. Atop the hilt is a multi-speckled crystal. Shuran thrust the dagger into the statue and felt the power escape the hardened form, along the shaft of the blade and into the gem.

He removes the dagger and then pulled the stone from the hilt. After pocketing the crystal, he moved the statue back into place in its alcove and left durangug. The dagger is left among the collections of artifacts in an ancient library in the first school of Essence teaching.

"Tianna, how is it you are still drifting about in this realm? And why do I not see others such as Bastien?"

"I am anchored here, but not trapped within the object of my release. Bastien is both anchored and trapped, but his prison is one of his choosing. He anchored himself to a promise and a stolen object before his body was taken by the demon Telalsu. Do you understand now, Shuran?" Tianna asked as she watched Shuran palm the stone.

"I will do what I can, before you get any weaker my sister. I will see that you are returned or set free of this torturous world." Shuran looked up as he spoke to watch Tianna fade from his vision.

"Return to the Zig'Mada and do so alone," she whispered as she disappeared.

Shuran reached into his pocket to retrieve the green gemstone that he carried since his birth.

***

Shuran called the Zidu'Si to awaken and gather the leaders of the new weaver regimens in the meeting hall. He also woke Moona and Codger, much to his detriment when Moona threw a chamber pot at him. After cleaning himself, he made his way to the hall. He also awoke the captains of the magurmu still in the city.

"Why do you risk the wrath of Moona to ask us all here without the city bells ringing alarm?" Mallick asked.

"We have an external conflict of which to lend aid, sheesh. I asked Moona and Codger to awaken for another reason that I will speak to them separately about with your attendance."

Shuran waited for the last of the weavers to arrive before he addressed them. Once they all arrived and settled quietly, with the exception of Moona, who did nothing quietly, Shuran addressed the group.

"I have just become aware of a threat to a group of refugees heading toward Drakkfoth. Salmetu has sent her dark weavers and Shadow walkers to attack a group of humans heading toward Drakkfoth from Middleton. It is unclear why she has chosen to attack this group, but I can assume that it because of the Baron's defiance of the Council and thus Salmetu herself."

"Are we to prevent this attack and rescue the refugees?" Vala asked.

Shuran noticed she was looking more tired than just from lack of sleep. He would speak to her about this later. "Yes, some of you will engage in the defense while others create a distraction and yet others will shuttle the refugees to Britengate. I want only one Shadow weaver left to me. I will find and capture the mixed blood known as Vardoran." Shuran noticed Moona's shock but continued without acknowledging.

"Vardoran is currently infested by Shadow, but his shi remains, buried within him. I want to find a way to remove the Shadow."

Moona stood to speak out, but Shuran stopped her with a gesture of his hand.

"This is not a gesture of rescue, the man is still responsible for his crimes, but no man should remain subject to the Shadow. I will attempt to purge the darkness first, then judge the man afterward." Shuran looked to Moona and Codger with an expression of love and understanding.

"I have a plan that involves the Stone Forest, which I need the support of Queen Florisia to help with. Orian I need you to take a message to the Queen for me and return with a response."

Shuran saw to Orian's departure and then set the remaining Zidu'Si to prepare for the arrival of more refugees. He looked to see the shocked expressions on Moona and Codger's faces and remained to speak to them.

"Vardoran is still inside there somewhere and I know he has actions to answer for but I think there may be part of the boy you raised inside. It will be difficult, but I need your help if we are to break him free." Shuran sounded absolute in his instructions and did not present it as a question or request.

Moona and Codger only nodded before they retreated to another area of the meeting hall. Mallick remained and abruptly questioned Shuran's actions.

"What has gotten into you? You ask too much sheesh!" Mallick scolded.

"I ask too much of everyone who stands against The Shadow Mallick, why should they be exempt? I do not make these choices easily Mally, they are the hardest choices I make when it comes to them, and you."

Mallick looked at Shuran for several moments before exhaling loudly and accepting Shuran's outstretched hand. They shared a brotherly embrace before Shuran pulled free and looked Mallick in the eye with more seriousness than usual.

"What is it Shuran?" Mallick asked with worry.

"I have come to understand far more of what is happening and I fear what is to come. I need you to promise me something and not question me."

Mallick was unsure now to respond so he simply nodded.

"Look after them. Make sure they stay together and remember what it means to love, live, and laugh. This war against darkness has been brewing for far longer than we imagined. The balance has been broken since before the birth of the seven races of man and I may be the last chance to fix the damage."

"Shuran, I know you are more powerful than anyone here, perhaps more than anyone who exists in all of Ersetu, but how can you believe that you are the answer to what has plagued the world for so long?"

"Because I know now who and what I am, Mallick. I am not simply a sprat that grew uncontrollably with power and knowledge. This was all planned and my father had something to do with it."

Mallick looked at Shuran with more confusion. "What do you mean? What has Dalgon to do with this?"

"What I am about to tell you is not to be shared with anyone else, do you understand?"

***

Vala waited for Shuran outside the meeting hall as he requested earlier. She was in pain and could not hide it from Shuran. She was watering her legs when Shuran arrived.

"Why have you not told me of your condition before I had to sense it for myself?" Shuran asked a bit more tersely than required.

"I did not think it was a true malady, only a warning my people use to prevent our young from venturing onto the dirt."

"You need to rest in the water my comrade, but that will only mask the symptoms. I have a solution if you are willing to help me. I believe this will benefit us in the long run as well." Shuran called over Moona who was still sulking about.

"Moona, our friend here needs our help. She needs water to remain healthy and I need a means of allowing the Badur'Lu to come to aid us should we need them."

"You want to create an inland sea for the fish people? No offense Gilly!" Moona said.

"None took, old dirt bag," Vala responded knowing Moona was merely using sarcasm to mask her pain.

Trying not to chuckle, Shuran interrupted the banter. "Moona I would like to ask you to help me with a task I have been thinking of but am now pressed to complete."

Shuran explained to the two women what he wanted to accomplish. The three of them moved toward an empty area of the border of the city where Shuran and Moona focused on creating a trench, much like the one he created in Birchshire around the cabin. This time it was deeper and a great deal larger. The trench circled the entire border of the city and was soon hardened to a rocky surface, gugtu. Only in the area before each Cardinal Gate did the trench become a tunnel beneath the surface.

Several locations along the trench Shuran focused on creating deep holes that led to a deeper pocket in the earth where an underwater river existed. Shuran broke through to the river and allowed it to surface and fill the trenches. Shuran and Vala dove into the water and entered one of the holes. They traveled the flow until they entered the river where they moved earth by means of the Emmuku'Gu power. They checked the river for width and depth to see that it would serve Shuran's purpose.

They returned to the surface and advised Moona that all was in ready and she would work with Moltar to move forward with securing the entrances and contact the Badur'Lu.

Chapter Twenty-Eight

The Zidu'Si arrived outside the stone forest by Emmuku'Gu. Every one of them had a particular task to accomplish. Shuran traveled out to the old road where the refugees were nearing the forest. He positioned himself in the middle of the road and waited until they neared him and stopped the caravan.

"My name is Shuran Shin'Ar, and I offer you sanctuary you will not find if you venture further into Drakkfoth. The dark Queen Salmetu, she sent Shadow weavers to intercept you in the Stone Forest and destroy you for fleeing Aurderia to Drakkfoth."

"You are the Anzillu from New Draven! Why should we listen to you?" the lead driver spat at Shuran.

"I offer you a choice, where my sister Salmetu would have you consumed by the darkness of the Shadow. I would offer you refuge and a chance to survive the coming war. Salmetu would offer you eternal servitude to darkness. Pain and suffering are all that awaits you should you continue along this road toward the realm of the Drakk. My Uncle the Baron can provide shelter for only so long before his land is eventually assaulted, but you will not arrive there once the Shadow weavers from New Draven arrive here to stop you."

Shuran spoke with them for longer than he planned before the first of them stepped forward to accept his offer. Slowly, others began to accept and Shuran started sending them directly to Britengate where Moona and Codger stood ready to usher them off to safety. He worked for nearly an hour before all the refugees finally agreed, and he sent them away.

Shuran arrived back at the Forest in time to greet Orian, who had just arrived from Entensiama. He carried the answer from the Queen that Shuran had been expecting. It was favorable, so he nodded for the Zidu'Si to move ahead with the next part of the plan. Barurbe was also reported as having arrived and working secretly with the Queen's approval.

An illusion of the refugees was conjured with the spell that Shuran had already shared with his comrades. The casting was simple but the ability to maintain it required a great deal of strength and concentration. Shuran, tapping directly into the source of the Essence, lent the energy needed by the other Zidu'Si. Channeling this much power caused Shuran a great deal of pain, but he would not falter.

"I sense the weavers approaching, cloak yourselves but maintain the illusion," Shuran said.

In order for the spell to be convincing, the Zidu'Si and Shuran needed to pass an echo of their shi into it so that the human refugees would present as living people to the senses of the Shadow infested weavers. This was the most dangerous part, because it presented the Shadow a vulnerable connection to the Zidu'Si.

Shuran focused on his center and bundled an orb of energy around a portion of his shi and cast it out among the illusion of refugees. He immediately felt light-headed from the experience. After several moments of unsteadiness, Shuran regained his composure and focused on linking the orb of shi to the illusion, giving the false caravan an aura of life. The effort was proved a success when the Shadow weavers began to approach their intended victims.

The first volley of dark energy met with the refugees and hit several of them with no effect. The weavers moved in closer to investigate why their first assault yielded no results.

Vardoran moved up behind one of the humans. He was cautious, but he sensed there was something amiss. He reached out with a tendril of Shadow in order to test his summation. The tendril touched the traveler and immediately caused a small spark of light from which the tendril retreated. Vardoran did not know what to make of it, but the Shadow part of him recognized something that it felt during the brief contact.

"We are deceived!" Vardoran shouted. "There is Essence weaving at work here. Find which of these illusions is a true human, and bring it before me."

The weavers began moving around the throngs of spell created refugee humans. With each touch of Shadow, the contact produced a small burst of light, deflecting the touch of darkness.

With the weavers distracted and fully engaged, Shuran and Dara moved about the stone forest, touching petrified trees. The trees they chose, seemingly at random, were, in fact, those harboring a petrified Dryad. Once they finally made it cautiously through the area around the illusion, they began their work; reconstituting the frozen trees along with their occupants.

The effort to reanimate so many lives, both plant and creature, was beyond the normal strength of any wielder. Shuran was far from being normal. With the ease of what might be the billowing of a blacksmith's fires, Shuran turned up the flow of power coming from the core of the Essence.

Slowly at first, the stone shells of the trees began to change color. What was once grey and lifeless began to take on a rich brown. The trees, Shuran observed, were beyond help, but those hiding inside were very much intact. The Dryads were in some form of hibernation.

"There are no living humans among these apparitions, Vardoran," one of the weavers called out.

"They must be nearby, casting this illusion. Spread out and locate them!"

Vardoran was not without his own secrets. His strongest ability was always that of feeling the Essence and draining it from others, essentially stealing their gift. His Shadow tenant knew this and decided to use the tactic. The plan immediately gave Vardoran a direction to head off in.

Vala was far too distracted with maintaining the illusion to sense Vardoran's approach. She turned to late to react in time. When Vardoran's hand met with her shoulder, the pain caused her to scream out. The rest of the Zidu'Si heard the scream and revealed themselves unintentionally.

The weavers now had their targets, but at the same time Shuran and Dara completed their work. The Dryads were waking up.

Vardoran, if he were himself, would have not wasted time and simply pulled the Essence out of the girl. But Vardoran was not himself, he was filled with Shadow, and the Shadow wanted to posses the girl. Tendrils of the murky Shadow flowed out of Vardoran's eyes and toward the girl firmly within his grasp. When the Shadow trust toward Vala, it was blown back by a blast of brilliant light taking Vardoran several feet back along with it.

"Lead the weavers back to the center of the clearing, then cloak yourselves!" Shuran said. He then reached out and pulled the orb of shi back into himself.

The Zidu'Si led the weavers back to the clearing by allowing themselves pursuit. Bolts of energy flew through the air in both directions as hunter and prey volleyed at each other. Once they arrived in the clearing, the Zidu'Si waited patiently while avoiding the blasts sent to kill them. It would not be long before the Dryads fully awoke, and Shuran told them they did not want to be around when that happened.

Shuran checked on Vala and once he was certain she was unharmed, he approached Vardoran's unconscious body. He could feel the smut of Shadow within the old man laying at his feet. It took all of Shuran's inner strength, to prevent him destroying this man where he lay. For the lives he has taken, the dark arts he practiced even before the Shadow possessed him, and most of all the pain he caused Codger and Moona, Shuran wanted to end him. He did not however; Shuran reached down toward Vardoran and touched him. His body wanted to resist, and the blinding light that shone from the contact made the wielding more difficult. Shuran turned Vardoran to stone.

The only warning of the attack upon the weavers was the ear-splitting screech that echoed through the forest of petrified trees. Eons of hibernation, trapped in the petrified trees, did nothing to remove the last thoughts of anger and terror felt by the Dryads, as their beloved trees were being destroyed. The rage had time to fester until this point, when they would be released to enact vengeance upon those responsible.

The creatures said nothing. They offered no parley. The Dryads attacked every human in sight. Their long fingers extended from their hands as scraggly thorny branches of a thicket bush. The Dryads branch-like arms extended out from their trunk shaped bodies and stretched out to attack, ripping flesh from the human bodies. The Shadow did not stand a chance against this foe. As each weaver was struck down, the Shadow left its host and flowed along the ground toward the East.

The last surviving weavers cast spells to disappear into a dark void and escaped. The Dryads stood in the clearing slashing at the dead humans until their rage abated. When they finally settled, Shuran appeared in the clearing before them. The dryads stood stark still before the new human that appeared among them. The silence in the clearing was absolute. Where only moments ago the night was filled with savage screams and cries of agonizing death, not a sound could be heard.

"You have slept for thousands of years. Your beloved forest destroyed by the fires and ash of Hell's Mouth. You are now free of the prison, but the threat against Ersetu has not ended," Shuran spoke to them softly.

After several moments of silence, one of the Dryads lumbered forward. "No prison trap be it, human. We stay, we wait," it said with raspy even toned voice. "Fire Mountain not destroy forest, blackness attack at time of Great Masters War."

Somehow Shuran knew what the creature said was true. He remembered the time of the petrification as though he witnessed the event. As the memory played out, he felt the pain and fear of the trees as the light within them was extinguished. He joined the rage and horror of the Dryads, as they were helpless against the attack. A tear escaped his eye and ran down his cheek.

The Dryad moved closer and tilted its oblong, twig-topped head. An understanding passed between Shuran and the creature.

"You could have left, found new homes, why did you stay and allow yourselves bondage to the forest as it was drained of the light?" Shuran asked.

"We stay, you come. Was dreamed long past, mother tree say we stay, fight again at time of awakening. Humans new on Ersetu, the Dryad, we here before Masters come from Stars, or Telukukal walked dirt," it said to Shuran. "Now time you purge darkness Masters left behind!"

"This land is dead, there are no forests for your kind. If it please you, Florisia, Queen of the Elves, offers you sanctuary among the protected forests of Entensiama," Shuran offered.

After a few moments of counsel with its kind, the Dryad returned to Shuran. "Dryads go but bring our trees with," it said as it produced a glowing seed from within the bark-like creases of its abdomen.

The Dryads, by means of their own special magic, saved a part of their beloved forest. They knew that they would not be able to escape the destruction because it was foretold. They prepared for a long sleep after preserving a seed from each of their own trees. They would rebuild their forest, but this time they vowed that if the Dark Death as they referred to the Shadow returned, they would fight.

***

Shuran and Moltar flew back to Britengate from Entensiama where he settled the Dryads to their new home. He stayed to observe as they performed their planting rituals and breathed life into the seeds of their trees. The ground above the planted seeds glowed with a pale green light that Shuran had never before experienced. The deep memories within him stirred and found no knowledge of the strange magic the Dryads used.

The Dryads explained in their broken use of the ancient tongue that they had existed on Ersetu since long before the Masters arrived by falling stars. Along with many other sentient creatures of Ersetu, the Dryads seldom interacted with the new flesh-men that began to explore and ravage the world. Only when they were threatened did they reveal themselves. They were witness to the creation of mankind, and they shared what they observed with Shuran.

238

Shuran and Moltar landed in a clearing on the South end of Britengate. Since the shield was raised, the drakkon and their riders were relocated within the border. The South Cardinal gate was the only one constructed that would allow a walking drakkon and rider to pass, so it was there that new barracks and fields were placed within the borders.

Shuran left Moltar to his preening and over exaggerated storytelling to his drakkon friends. It was past time Shuran went to see Moona and Codger. He had yet to explain what he planned and why he returned to the city with a stone likeness of their son, imprisoning him within. Shuran arrived at a small cottage that Moona and Codger called their new home.

"She ain' in a mood to talk my boy," Codger said as he led Shuran to sit by the hearth.

"I understand. I only wanted to check on you both. This cannot be an easy situation for either of you."

"I don' pretend to understand the powers and knowledge you gain, but I admit that I don' think it wise to have brought him here. He is consumed by the Shadow and you said that power can twist gugtu. That is what you encased him in ain' it? Codger asked.

"Yes, that is what I have done, but there is a reason. In order for the Shadow to twist the gugtu and escape, it must leave his body."

Shuran explained why he had placed Vardoran in a glade outside the city, where he was under constant guard by the Zidu'si. When the gugtu began to twist, Shuran would arrive to repel the Shadow as it escaped. He would then free Vardoran so he could answer for his crimes as well as inform on the activities of Salmetu and the Shadow.

Shuran's visit with Codger was cut short by notification that a message had arrived from Queen Florisia. He made his way to the meeting hall, where Orian awaited his arrival to share the urgent news.

"It would appear that the Dryads are already lending aide," Orian started. "They have notified my Queen that, 'ugly big humans' entered the forest and were forced out of the area the Dryads claimed. It would appear that the ogres are nearing the Northern border of Britengate. They will be here by nightfall."

"Why do they come here, do they work on the orders of the

Shadow?" Avrank asked.

"I do not know. They may easily be under the command of a weaver or even Salmetu. If the Shadow felt threatened, I do not think they would respond with a few ogres. We shall find out their motivation soon enough."

As the full darkness of night settled over the city of Britengate, the Ogres began to approach the city from the North. The group was forty strong. They split into three groups, the largest cluster holding position at the North gate and the other two headed to the Eastern and Southern gates.

The gates being moved out of the shield by the Protectors on guard raised alarm. The Protectors sent bursts of Essence born light at the ogres who merely blinked hard against the light from which they shied. Having no deterring effect upon the monsters, the Protectors changed their attack to weaving spells of force and backed themselves through the shield to protection within the border.

Soon two gates were likewise closed and the Protectors choosing safety behind the shield. The ogres attempted to follow the path of the humans only to find themselves walking directly into a barely visible wall of force. Frustrated by their inability to enter the city, the ogres resorted to ransacking the evacuated camps and settlements nearest them.

"They will soon bore and move on," Gregoran commented. He stood near the shield watching the ogres outside as they vented their frustration on small huts and makeshift corrals.

"They do not leave their caves and surrounding land easily, us dwarves have attempted to drive them from the high caves in our mountain home," Avrank remarked. "They come back like a bad rash on your backside! They are here for a reason and will not likely leave until they get what they want or are killed."

"At least they only attack three of the gates," Mallick said.

"Then we must go where they are not. Why leave one unmolested?" Shuran was already heading in the direction of the Western gate where no ogres attacked. The gate would still be open to let any human's still outside a way toward safety. Shuran also realized that it would allow someone to slip out of the city as well.

Shuran arrived to see a cloaked figure hobbling out of the gate. The attention of the Protectors guarding the area was spent on seeing after people approaching the gate to enter the city's protected border. He watched as the escapee turned and looked at Shuran. The man was deformed and hobbled on disfigured limbs. The smell that came to him told him it was not a man.

"The ogres are a distraction. The true purpose is an escape of a shifter!" Shuran ran after the creature as it sped up its pace. Before Shuran could reach it, an ogre came out from the darkness and lifted the shifter into its arms and made for the cover of the forest. Shuran made to go after them when he received a thought from Dara. The gugtu prison was twisting; the Shadow was freeing itself.

Chapter Twenty-Nine

Shuran abandoned pursuit and ran for the glade where Vardoran was being kept. While Moltar and Jade saw to the departure of the ogres from the city, the rest of the Zidu'Si joined Shuran in the glade. They watched in nervous anticipation as the gugtu statue lying on the ground began to ripple and crack. Slowly at first, the thin layer of gugtu stone crumbled into chunks and then quickly fell to the ground. The Zidu'Si prepared to do what Shuran had prepared them for when this time came to pass.

With a sudden and burst, the twisted gug stone blew apart leaving an unconscious Vardoran laying on the ground and a billowing cloud of murky blackness undulating in the air above his body.

"Now!" Shuran shouted.

The Zidu'Si swiftly extended their arms with open palms. A blast of Essence born light surrounded the Shadow and ushered it away from Vardoran. The Shadow emitted a screeching sound that pierced the stillness of the night. Once the Shadow was released it dispersed into the ground.

Shuran quickly surrounded Vardoran with an Essence shield to prevent the Shadow from entering him again and allow him to transport his captive through the shield. He levitated Vardoran and headed back to within the city shield. As he passed through the border, the shield around Vardoran wavered but held. Shuran continued on until he reached the building set aside as a hospital. He lowered Vardoran onto a cot and instructed that two Zidu'Si stand guard at all times and notify Shuran when Vardoran awoke.

"Shuran! You must go now!" Tianna said as she appeared in the hospital.

"Holy yak scat! Be gone shade!" Avrank yelled.

"Ease yourself Avrank, that is my sister Tianna," Shuran said before turning to Tianna. "What is happening? I have Vardoran to deal with currently."

"Vardoran will sleep for days as his shi heals the damage of the Shadow. Bastien will not survive that long," Tianna answered. "The part of him still within his body, is no longer able to mentally challenge Telalsu. He now shuts down his organs in an attempt to force the demon warrior out."

"I will leave immediately, but how will I get to Bastien when I have found the dagger?"

"I will make certain to inform you when the opportunity presents itself," Tianna said and promptly disappeared.

"Does she always just pop in like that Shin'Ar?" Avrank asked.

"What is the problem? Is our Turd afraid of ghosts?" Orian joked.

Shuran did not stay to hear the remainder of Orian and Avrank bantering. He made his way to the barracks and gathered his travel satchel and a few tools and crystals he might need in the tunnels below the Zig'Mada. He became aware of Moltar's mind pressing against the back of his own and decided it best to include his bonded in his little quest.

"You understand that you will not be able to follow me into the tunnels. I will need you to guard the entrance at any rate," Shuran told Moltar.

"I will keep any from entering behind you Lugaldur," Moltar said just before disappearing into the Emmuku'Gu.

They arrived outside the falls near the jagged rocks. The darkness of the night lent to the eerie atmosphere of the mists that enveloped the rocks and surrounding landscape. Shuran left Moltar to keep watch as he entered the mysterious cave behind the Zig'Mada falls.

The light from Shuran's orb of energy danced off the crystals and minerals held tight within the walls. As he walked and climbed along the back of the cave, his senses were tingling to the point of burning his skin. Something dark and malicious was nearby and Shuran's shi was fighting to clear free of the area. Shuran fought past the desires to flee from danger and continued on his way deep down into the tunnels.

Shuran's climb leveled after nearly an hour. He found himself needing to reinforce the orb of light in the darkness of the deep tunnel. There were no minerals or other deposits in the walls down this far. One touch on the wall was enough to confirm his suspicions. The walls were polished smooth, indicating man-made tunnels. Every surface was made of pure gug, not the twisted form or gugtu, making this place a lodestone prison of some sort.

He had walked for several hundred paces before the tunnels opened into a chamber. Shuran could not sense the size of the chamber using Essence because the gug would not allow Shuran to wield from the Emmuku'Gu. Shuran could have used one of his crystals, but he did not wish to waste the power without knowing what he faced ahead. He placed his hand on the wall of the chamber in order to sense the size.

From his exploration of the gug walls, he could tell that the chamber was approximately fifty paces in diameter and perfectly round with a flat roof nearly fifteen feet in height. Along the walls, he could sense many large cracks that lead to the dirt beyond. Shuran felt something else while exploring the cracks, the Shadow was just beyond the wall. He broke contact immediately and waited for the attack.

After several breath-held moments, the attack did not come. Shuran was not certain what that meant, but he was not going to waste time in a futile attempt to understand. He was certain the Shadow was aware of his presence, but it must not have been concerned, or was waiting. In his brief contact with the murky black mist, he felt something odd. The Shadow here did not feel the same as what he had experienced in the past. This form had a tortured and anguished aura about it had not made his skin crawl.

His footsteps echoed around the space as he moved toward the far side of the room. The light from his orb was faltering and he found it necessary to bolster its power from a crystal. The immediate increase of illumination caused him to squint, but before he closed his eyes too tightly, he caught a glimpse of something large laying several feet to his left.

As he approached the looming object, it became clear to Shuran what it was he saw. A large statue lay on its back on the floor of the chamber. He approached it cautiously as the implications of its presence became clear. This was one of the missing statues from the Vault in Durangug. Shuran quickened his pace and was soon staring into the hardened eyes of a God's likeness.

Shuran turned and added four more glowing orbs and sent them out into the chamber in search of the statues that would represent the others belonging to the five empty alcoves of Durangug. His search was short as they were evenly dispersed around the room. Each of the statues also had a gleaming chain and colored crystal about their necks just as Damkianna in the Vault. These gems were all shattered, however, and one of the statues on the far side, had something else that reflected the light.

Shuran looked at the statue he stood next to and read the name in the remnants of the shattered crystal. 'Ninagal' it read, the Prince of Great Waters, Shuran remembered suddenly. He quickly walked toward the other statues and found their names. Kishargal, Princess of Firm Ground; Ereshkigal, Queen of the Netherworld; Gula, Lady Who the Dead Bring Back; they were all here. The fallen ones, that would mean the last one was their leader.

Shuran gathered his nerves and moved up to the last statue. Uggae, God of Death, The first to betray the edicts of the ME, Shuran thought. He was confused by the thought, but did not ponder as he then noticed the dagger jutting out of the chest of the statue. Mi-Ib Simshi, the

Dagger to Replace Shi, it has been here all this time. Shuran wondered at why the blade was here, and why it was thrust into the torso of the statue.

The memories came to him in such a torrent that he nearly lost his balance. Someone found the chamber and thrust the dagger into the statue. They tried to free someone from the gugtu prison. Uggae, this statue is not what it seems, and Shuran realized why he was compelled to turn Vardoran's aura to gugtu. These statues are not statues at all. They are, or were, vessels for the bodies of the Gods. Not Gods, Shuran realized. The Masters, as the Dryads referred to them, the creators of the Telukukal and the seven races of man.

The need to vomit overwhelmed Shuran and he buckled over and released the contents of his stomach on the floor. Several painful minutes of heaving passed before Shuran was able to properly breath and relax. The memories that crashed into his consciousness were far too strong and numerous. He now understood everything and the implications were dire.

Shuran climbed atop Uggae's gugtu aura and began to pull on the dagger. It was stuck fast within the stone. Whoever attempted to free Uggae from his prison did not know what they were doing. They needed the crystal anchor be affixed to the hilt when attempting to free the shi, but they first had to remove the gugtu spell on the aura. They also used the wrong dagger.

Shuran was so engrossed in softening the gugtu and wiggling the dagger out, he did not notice his orbs going dark. It was not until he freed the dagger and placed it in his satchel that he realized the room grew darker. When he turned to see what had occurred, the first tendril of Shadow struck out at him.

The first several strikes were met with a flash of repellent Essence from the spell Shuran used to create the Protectors in Britengate. But Shuran was no longer fully able to connect to the Emmuku'Gu and thus the source of Essence in the core of the planet. The power stored in his crystals was not adequate enough to draw upon and failed quickly.

Sorrow filled Shuran's heart as the Shadow closed around him. The tainted shi that attacked him was in a fury to avenge the deaths of their mortal bodies. The cries of revenge were deafening as they reverberated within Shuran's mind. They wanted free of their eternal suffrage and enslavement. Shuran tried to call to them and sooth their anguish, but they would not hear him.

The pain Shuran experienced became increasingly harder to withstand. He bundled his shi in a blanket of Essence, using what remained of the power from the crystals he held. He tried to focus on a single shi, he thought that if he convinced one that he was not their enemy, he might have a chance. Every disembodied presence he encountered refused his plea for understanding. They labeled him traitor and anzillu. Every captured shi was thirsty for the destruction of what they saw as an invader in their sanctuary.

Suddenly Shuran recognized a shi working its way down the flowing mass of Shadow that he now recognized as a bodiless living source of life linked to darkness. It was Vardoran, part of his shi was yet attached to the Shadow and it was coming for Shuran.

"You wretched little upstart!" Vardoran bellowed in his head. "You thought to replace me that they would take you in as their own. You were supposed to die at that altar. Why did she need be there and then secret you away to raise you as the son she should have always had!"

"She did not know I was expected be born until that night. She was told to save me!" Shuran tried to explain.

"LIAR! You are an abomination and are going to destroy everything if you remain alive!"

"I am no more an abomination than you Vardoran. And you chose your own path; your parents did not force you away. They still love you so much it kills them inside, what you have done in your life. But it is not too late."

Vardoran paused his attack momentarily giving Shuran enough mental space to think.

"You can make amends, go back to your body and rejoin that piece of yourself left behind. Change your ways and answer for the crimes you have committed against men."

Vardoran was confused and did not seem to understand. Shuran could see a mental image of Vardoran's pleading eyes. He wanted to live.

He wanted his parents.

"Go! Back to Britengate and live!" Shuran ordered as he pushed the last of his own stored Essence at Vardoran, allowing him to escape the Shadow.

The other shi hovering around Shuran's presence began to relent. They both heard what Shuran said and felt the ejection of Vardoran. They knew they no longer had bodies to return to, but they held hope for release and this began to spread within the Shadow's flowing river of darkness. As Shuran was able to regain his composure and calmed down, he stood up. He had not realized that during the mental assault, he had fallen from the top of Uggae's shelled aura.

He had just regained his footing when the Shadow surrounding him transformed. Gone were the less tortured souls that were only moments ago relaxing their grip on Shuran, the taint of the Shadow that Shuran already knew, was flooding into the chamber. They pushed against his returning strength with such force that his ribs cracked when he became trapped against the statues.

"You dare enter our chamber slave!" came the resounding voices of the most foul, ancient, and powerful presence Shuran had ever felt. "You will regret this transgression once you are absorbed into our collective."

***

Vardoran slipped back into his body and the shock woke him suddenly. He sat up in the cot and began screaming. "Shuran is in danger!"

Avrank and Orian were on watch and both stood in shocked silence at the sudden change in their captive. Avrank finally reached up and slapped the incoherent man.

Orian looked at Avrank with complete surprise and confusion.

"What? He was hysterical," Avrank said with a grin. "Ok, so I wanted to hit him. Tell me you don' feel the same, and I will call you a truth stretcher!"

"You must get to Shuran, the Gods are coming! They sensed when he set me free!" Vardoran said before passing back into a deep sleep.

"The others are preparing to leave for the Zig'Mada, go get Moona and Codger to watch their nasty spawn!" Orian ordered one of the healers. "Avrank, let us be gone."

Chapter Thirty

Shuran felt as though he were suffocating. The Shadow now had more strength and malice than he ever before experienced. Shuran could feel four ancient disembodied beings that were thought of as Gods. These fallen few were the force behind the Shadow and fed upon the strength of the shi they gathered. They were now attempting to take hold of Shuran.

"Resistance of the Shadow is futile, young wielder. You will be the boost we need to enact our vengeance." Four voices sounded in Shuran's head, calling for his shi to give in to their draw. The presence in Shuran's body swirled around his organs and into his blood. They continued through his system heading directly for his mind.

Moltar stood before the entrance of the Zig'Mada preparing to hold off the disturbance he felt in the Emmuku'Gu. When the Zidu'Si appeared, he became confused. He lowered his head to Avrank and sniffed deep.

"You are who you appear, but why have you come? Shuran said no interference would be allowed if he were to succeed."

"Shuran is in danger Moltar, he encountered Vardoran's shi and forced it free of the Shadow," Orian told him.

"A gesture of mercy, that does not explain your arrival or any danger!" Moltar was getting impatient.

"Vardoran had a moment of clarity and woke with a warning that they were coming for Shuran," Avrank said. "Who 'they' are we do not know, but why else would Vardoran have said these words?"

"To send all you fools into a trap most likely!" Moltar scowled. "All of you stay put, I will contact Shuran through our stronger bond." Moltar sat down in the water before the falls with a great splash that wet all the Zidu'Si and knocked Avrank over into the muddy bank. He closed his eyes and began to search out his Lugaldur. Moltar spasmed as he joined Shuran, and felt, saw, and heard all through his bond.

Shuran did not notice Moltar's joining. He was far too consumed with pain from fighting off the Shadow's attack. He struggled to stand but only slipped on the remains of his evening meal that he previously released. He began to stop struggling physically and focused on his barriers around his shi and mind.

The strain was becoming too great for Shuran. He was moments from losing his fight when he felt strength returning. He was not certain where it was coming from but he was not wasting time with questions. Shuran reinforced his shields around his mind and shi then focused on forcing the Shadow out of his body.

When the last of the darkness slithered from him, Shuran realized that Moltar was with him.

"Thank you my bonded, I could not have done that without your added strength," Shuran said mentally to his drakkon.

"It was not me Shuran, It is all I can do to connect with you. I can conduct no Essence to you."

As if by response, Shuran's aura began to glow and a ghostly form separated from him. It moved away and turned to face Shuran. It emitted a light that surrounded the Shadow and held it fast.

"It was I who helped you Shuran, and now that you have finally brought me here, I must leave you," the formless wrath said.

"I do not understand, what is this about?" Shuran pleaded.

"You will understand soon. I have left you with the knowledge you will need, when you need it. Now go, quickly, I cannot hold them long. You must seal the cracks and close the chamber!"

"Who are you?"

"I am the first and final watcher, I am-"

"NERGAL! BETRAYER!" the Shadow screamed.

Moltar suddenly and unceremoniously pulled Shuran free of the chamber.

With a flash and ear popping snap, Shuran appeared in the space between Moltar and the Zidu'Si.

Before anyone could reach him, Shuran was on his feet and extending his arms out toward the falls and down to the depths of the chamber. He mentally shared the need he had for the Zidu'Si to all join in the effort. They began filling the cracks in the gugtu chamber and untwisting the areas that had been altered into soured gug.

The final step was to seal the tunnel that Shuran traversed to arrive in the ancient prison. He hesitated hoping to give the spirit or shi time. Shuran was not certain what Nergal was, but he wanted time for him to escape.

"Seal the chamber Shuran Shin'Ar. Do not worry after me, I can hold them so long as they are severed from the rest!" Nergal spoke in Shuran's mind.

With a final push of force, Shuran and the Zidu'si sealed the tunnels and reinforced the chamber's walls by calling forth more elements from the surrounding land and transmuting them into pure gug. Once the Chamber was sufficiently sealed, Shuran focused his collective on pushing the chamber deeper into the earth and collapsing the caves above it.

The Zidu'Si and Shuran along with Moltar and Jade disappeared into the Emmuku'Gu just in time to miss being swept away by the rush of the Napalkua leveling out for the first time in thousands of years. The Zid'Maga was no more, replaced by a gentle slope in the river with high steep banks.

***

Salmetu gasped for air as the sudden drop in strength was felt. She lay panting on the floor for several long moments with a look of utter panic and shock. Somehow, a large portion of her power, the power of Shadow, was lost to her. The presence inside her screamed for answers that would not come.

"Has your power waned, sister?" Tianna said glowing brighter than she had in a long time.

"I am not your sister wrath!" Salmetu said.

"Oh, I know that, I was just unsure if you knew that yet!"

"What have you done with my Shadow?" Salmetu screeched. "They are failing to feed me. How have you done this?"

"It was not me, it was my brother… and yours!" Tianna disappeared before the bolt of dark energy sliced through the air to meet the empty place she had been mocking Salmetu's inner demon.

***

Shuran, back in Britengate, was a mess. "I need to clean and replace the food I now wear on the back of my breeches. Would you please see that Vardoran is prepared for my attendance within the hour?" Shuran left the pageboy to his errand and entered the bathing house to clean and dress in fresh clothes. He was exhausted, but not from the force of Essence and the fight he recently survived.

A part of his strength just left him, and he was only now beginning to understand what had happened. He always knew that something was different about him, something more than simply being born of seven bloodlines. He was a vessel for another shi, but for how long? Shuran sunk beneath the sudsy waters of his private tub.

Shuran stayed below the surface of the water. He created a shield to provide him oxygen. He wondered if all the extraordinary things he had done through his short life had been the work of Nergal or was the ancient one only guiding him the entire time. Now that he was gone, would Shuran be able to continue. He began to feel self-doubt, which was nothing new, but this time there was no inner voice to calm him.

A loud thud on the tub roused Shuran from his worries and self-pity. He sat up in the tub to find Mallick standing before him with a towel.

"You can stop thinking such scat to yourself, sheesh. You forget our thoughts share a link on some level and you were singing out to the

Zidu'Si with all your worries." Mallick tossed him a towel and turned to leave. "Vardoran is waiting your illustrious presence."

"Thank you Mally," Shuran whispered.

***

Vardoran sat in a simple, but heavy, wooden chair. His wrists were fastened to the arms with gug as were his ankles to the legs. He seemed withered and drained but wide-awake. Gone was the arrogant, and self-righteous demeanor he carried.

Moona and Codger sat off behind Vardoran and out of sight. They had yet to confront their son, and now was not the time. He was about to stand trial, publicly, for his crimes against the people of Aurderia. Moona did not want to come, but Codger insisted and for one of the few times in her life, Moona did not argue.

Crowds of citizens took every available seat. Standing observers filled every available inch of space around the edges of the meeting hall, leaving only the table before Vardoran with nine empty seats. This would be the place for the Zidu'Si to sit in judgment. Several paces to the right of Vardoran, sat a witness seat, where victims and witnesses would give their testimony.

The Zidu'Si entered the room and took seven of the empty chairs with Shuran sitting in the center. Two chairs at each end of the table remained empty, representing the as yet unfilled positions among the Zidu'Si.

The room quieted immediately after Shuran took his seat. He looked around before finally resting his eyes on Vardoran who was looking directly back at him.

"Vardoran of Britengate, son of Codge and Evalria, you have been brought before this assembly and the Zidu'Si to answer for your crimes," Shuran started. "You have been charged with no less than seventy charges of crimes against the people of Aurderia. Those crimes include the forcible taking of another's Essence, kidnapping, false imprisonment, child endangerment, murder by proxy, conspiring to commit murder, and human sacrifice.

"These are crimes of the most serious and heinous acts against humanity, and are likely not a complete list of your deeds. This court has been called to see you brought to justice." Shuran paused for a moment before he continued. "There are some, if not most, of the people assembled here that would see you put to death without trial. I am not one of them." Shuran waited until the grumbling quieted.

"In spite of the transgressions that directly involve myself, my family, and my friends, I have to become a voice of reason. The fact that you sent a warning to my Zidu'Si about my danger in recent events does not go without merit. This one good turn does not erase the past. Do you have words to share against the claims laid before you?"

Vardoran remained silent and blinked just once before lowering his head.

"Proceed with the first witness," Mallick said without waiting for Shuran's permission to continue.

One after the next, people took to the witness chair to level claims against Vardoran. The charges were testimony to the acts that Vardoran committed over the years. The testimonies continued late into the afternoon before Shuran called a recess for meals.

When the session returned Shuran stood before the assembly to address them as a witness.

"I was born during a ceremony meant to take my life. My mother and Moona were captives before that ceremony. My mother Sulura is again a captive, taken from Drakkfoth by deception. These events are well known to all, but I am not standing here to talk about these things. I wish to hear from Vardoran directly, why he has done all this. What was the ultimate goal of performing these acts against those still living to bear witness to known crimes?"

Vardoran only hesitated a moment before responding. "I am guilty of all you say here, and more. I have spent my life in pursuit of greatness that I could never achieve with the life I was graciously given." Vardoran paused and looked at Moona and Codger for the first time. "My parents were the first and deepest wounds I inflicted in my search for something I did not understand. I cannot take anything back nor can I make amends. I do not expect forgiveness and I will not ask for understanding. I do not understand it myself."

"You will receive no forgiveness!" This was shouted by several of the assembled people before Shuran quieted them down with a gesture.

Vardoran continued, "I was born with little ability, and felt I needed more to make my parents proud. My father was learned and a great weaver, my mother a wielder of earth beyond any I knew. I was lucky to be able to scatter pebbles. At some point it was not enough for me and I was lured by a man who could promise me ways of strengthening my talents. I was weak and vulnerable, and Nagutan knew this when he enlisted me."

Several gasps went up in the room before Shuran reacted. "Clear the assembly! The remainder of this trial will be held in closed session."

The Zidu'Si rose and helped to usher the people out of the hall. Despite the protests of those being ejected from the hall, Shuran did not move from his place standing before Vardoran. Once everyone but the Zidu'Si along with Moona and Codger were left with Vardoran, Shuran continued the proceedings.

"What is it that Nagutan had to do with the path you followed?" Shuran asked.

Vardoran had a moment of realization. "He has manipulated you as well I assume," he said without emotion. "I have never understood that old fool's reasons behind anything he ever did, but one thing that always remained clear was that he was up to something."

Shuran sat back against the table behind him. "Nagutan has played a great deal in the events over the past few years and now, as your words explain, he has been at this game for quite a long time. Was he, by any chance, your mentor or teacher?"

"Both actually," Vardoran replied. "He showed me how to perform most of the spells I used for taking power as well as guided me along the path to become leader of the Order of Chaos that he founded."

Vardoran described how Nagutan found him in Birchshire, playing at working earth Essence. He took an alleged liking to the young Vardoran and promised to help him grow stronger in the arts of Essence. He first gave him a spell that he could use to draw power from the trees and plants. Soon Nagutan had him try the spell on small animals and it progressed from there until one day, they tried it on an old man.

"The man was dying so why not help end his suffering, those were

Nagutan's exact words," Vardoran remembered. "I can still remember what it felt like to pull the Essence from his protesting body. I vowed never to do so again!"

"But you did anyway!" Moona whimpered.

"It was not purposely done, you had scolded me and accused me of stealing life when I told you of the plants and trees. I was angry and it just… happened." Vardoran held his composure, though his eyes began to give away his emotional state.

Chapter Thirty-One

"I have heard enough!" Shuran announced. "Reassemble the witnesses for the declaration of judgment!"

As the crowds re-entered the hall, they were confused at the short length of time they were dismissed before being allowed re-entry. Most assumed that they would enter to find a death sentence already enacted against the criminal, so there were many sighs and groans from the men and women who sat back down within the hall.

Shuran understood the discomfort and questioning noises he heard from those returning. If things had been different, perhaps he would have cast Vardoran to the fury of Hell's Mouth, or even encased him in gugtu. The issue was that Vardoran had information, he had a family, and he had a shi. Shuran could not bring himself to end a life unless out of self defense or absolute necessity. Once the room was again full to capacity, and the crowds quieted, Shuran stood and addressed the hall.

"The accused, Vardoran, has admitted to his crimes and stands ready for justice. In light of new testimony and corroboration with knowledge the Zidu'Si already has, we are ready to declare a verdict and sentence for the accused. He is guilty of his crimes without doubt. Manipulation played a part in his actions, however, and it has come to light that said manipulation becomes relevant to a greater issue.

"There is one person not yet brought to stand before this assembly. Crimes leading up to what has happened this day, as well as multiple deeds that led to unimaginable events, are the result of another man's actions. Over the thousands of years another has walked this land, many have made choices and performed actions they may have otherwise not. Once found, Nagutan will answer to the manipulation of events against the progression of natural evolution in this world."

Shuran paused as the crowds cried out for justice. He let the people have their moment of outrage, for he felt it within himself as well. Nagutan has many things to account for, least of which is taking a young boy and turning him into something he would not have been. His family torn apart and being used as tools in an unending war between the false Gods from the stars.

Though Vardoran showed regret, Shuran was not entirely certain that he was twisted much from his true nature. Shuran finally gestured for the people to quite down. He motioned for Vardoran to stand.

Shuran looked first to the crowd, then looked upon Vardoran. "I am prepared to enact judgment upon the accused at this time!" Shuran said. "He has admitted to his crimes, yet I am not prepared to put him to death." Shuran raised his hands to quiet the cries of outrage and gasps of surprise. "My reasons, in part, are my own but those that matter are a cornerstone to the justice system I wish to introduce upon the lands. Vardoran has useful knowledge and was also a pawn in a grander scheme that we as Aurderian's have all been subjected." Shuran turned back to Vardoran at the end of his speech. "Do you wish to speak before judgment is placed against you?"

Vardoran looked up at Shuran and cleared his throat. "There was a time, when I was nearly the age you appear to me. Nothing in the whole of Ersetu meant anything more to me than gaining the power of Essence. To hold the kind of power within myself that you burn through in moments, was a blinding desire that carried me through my life up until cycles ago.

"My crimes, heinous as they have been, were born of blind need for achieving something I was never destine to attain. I will not defend my actions; I am unable to voice a justifiable reason for having the desires that propelled me into the life I led. Apologies will have no meaning and I fear that I have lost my ability to feel the words at any rate." Vardoran paused before returning his eyes back to Shuran. "Do as you will, Shuran Shin'Ar. You are now the law of Ersetu."

After a stunned and silent moment, Shuran leveled his eyes upon Vardoran. "You will be stripped of your abilities indefinitely!" Shuran announced. "The Zidu'Si will decide further actions after considering the victims' wishes. You will not leave this city and must remain under house arrest."

Vardoran did not argue. He did not protest. He only spoke two words. "Thank You."

Shuran performed the wielding used to hobble Vardoran's abilities with little effort but a great deal of concentration. Now that Nergal's consciousness had left his mind, Shuran had to spend more effort in preparing spells and locating the knowledge that was left behind. Shuran Dismissed the assembly and left Vardoran in the care of his parents, who now it seemed, were ready to face their child. It was past time that he gather with his Zidu'Si and discuss what was ahead, as well as what happened in the chamber below the Zig'Mada.

Vardoran meekly accompanied Moona and Codger back to their Britengate home as a family reunited. Though the circumstances were not the best, they all made an effort. They arrived at their small earthen house without a word and Moona set the table for a meal while Codger settled Vardoran into the empty room. When they all gathered to eat, Moona was the first to break the uncomfortable silence.

"You have been a thorn in my side since the day I squatted you out boy!" Moona said with a smirk. "Don' mistake my humor as forgiveness, but we ain' all get second chances in life an' Shuran is givin' us one so I say we take it with grace!" Moona sat down after doling out portions of food she had prepared earlier in the kitchen.

"I do not know what to say mother," Vardoran said shakily. "I am sorry for what I did to you… for everything. I do not even know where to begin, but being in that mass of darkness and despair, it was beyond what I could have imagined upon the worst of my enemies and I feel shame for even surviving it. The crazed desperation of the Shadow is…"

After a long pause Codger changed the subject. "Leave it to that Shuran to find a way to bring out the best in us! You just wait, when you get to know him he will show you how to make amends."

Noticing Vardoran's discomfort at Shuran's mention, Moona interjected. "Now don' go thinkin' we replaced our only sprat with some upstart fool lookin' to save the world! He's a boy ain' had a proper family an' we was there is all. You is my one and only sprat an' Damkiana save me, I love you always! Time will heal, you jus' wait an' see Vardy!"

Vardoran watched Moona with wide eyes while she spoke and finally broke down and cried at her words. "Momma, I have missed you and Da, despite my failings and ambitions. I only wanted to make you proud of what I could be. I always felt I was less than you deserved as a son and somewhere along the way… I lost myself."

As a Family reunited, they comforted one another and commiserated on past failings and found the good in having a chance for a new beginning.

***

Shuran gathered the Zidu'Si in the barracks so that he might speak to them of what happened while he was away. The roof of the barracks had openings set into it so that Moltar and Jade could extend their heads in and join in the conversations. Although there were things that Shuran was not ready to share with all of the Zidu'Si, he would explain what was needed to the rest of his comrades.

"We have dealt our foe a weakening blow at the Zig'Mada," Shuran started. "But I need to explain the reasons why and how." Shuran started from the beginning. He explained how he already felt the shi within the Shadow and began to understand the significance. The memories and information that Nergal left in the back of Shuran's mind were becoming easier to access and made sense.

The ancients, called Sumer, came to this world to perform experiments and create beings in their own image. They originally created the Telukukal, 'the First People' as they have been called. These people were used as a labor force as well as assistants in additional experiments to further study the powerful source of Essence that Ersetu had flowing throughout the land. The work and life on Ersetu went along quietly for a few hundred years without much issue beside occasional conflict with the indigenous creatures already calling Ersetu home. When the Telukukal began worshipping their masters as Gods, the trouble began.

One of the ancient masters, Uggae, started the practice of channeling Essence through the Telukukal and into himself. He wanted to become the leader of the expedition over Nergal and started a coup among the eleven foreigners from the stars. He took his time and played out his game over many hundreds of years. He knew he needed time to build his power in order to challenge Nergal.

As the Telukukal flourished and they became more adept at wielding the Essence, the Sumer began creating another race to populate the land. Though there were already sentient life forms living on Ersetu, they did not interact with the Sumer or Telukukal and kept to themselves when left unmolested. The newest beings the Sumer created from the use of the Telukukal and power of the Essence was the Gula'Lu. They became the first race of mankind upon Ersetu.

"I do not know what the Telukukal were like, for some reason that information was not shared or left behind when Nergal vacated my mind," Shuran said. "I can only suppose they were similar to the races of man being as though we were created using a template from them." Shuran went on to explain he was unaware of how the process was performed or what else was part of the creation, but he assumed it was information stored in the Compendium. He also assumed that the central chamber in Durangug played a major part in their experiments.

While the races of man were in their infancy and the Sumer were spread across Ersetu following their own work, Uggae began to make his move. Though most of the Sumer respected Nergal, not all of them agreed with his leadership and a few of them began to follow Uggae in his dark ambitions and practices.

Again Shuran found that further information was missing from his mind, but he understood what eventually came to pass. Uggae rose up against Nergal with four other Sumer at his side. A war between sides broke out and lasted for centuries.

Shuran explained the little he knew for certain. "It only came to an end when Nergal transformed the usurpers into gugtu and then imprisoned them in the chamber we sealed below the Zig'Mada. Somehow the chamber was breached and someone attempted to release or destroy the prisoners but failed. That is when their shi was released into the world and their dark intent and desires were introduced to the Shadow thus tainting it."

"So those statues in the Vault, are they the good guys?" Avrank asked.

"I believe that is who they were. I do not think they are held within any longer. Their shi is flowing within the Emmuku'Gu," Shuran revealed. "How they came to become sealed in gugtu and why, is still a mystery to me but I believe the answers will reveal themselves."

"Where does the dagger come into all of this?" Vala asked.

"This dagger, the Mi'Ib Simshi, is meant for being used to return a shi to its body. That is why it did not work when whoever thrust it into the Sumer attempted to use it. This is how we will save Bastien."

"What of the twin dagger, the Mi'Ib Karshi?" Mallick inquired having gained the knowledge of its existence by tapping the knowledge in the Vault Library.

"Salmetu has it, as it was used in the ceremony that took Tianna from the world and allowed darkness to fill Salmetu with Shadow," said Shuran. "I assume you think we need it to pull Telalsu from Bastien before restoring his shi?"

Mallick nodded his summation being accurate.

"Telalsu is not simply a shi, it is a demon warrior and the blade will not work directly upon it. Bastien will have to fight to free himself of the demon once his shi is fully restored."

Mallick cleared his throat to get Shuran's attention. "Tell us more about the Shadow and Emmuku'Gu. They are somehow connected I am guessing?"

Shuran explained how he and Moltar could feel the shi in the Shadow as well as the Emmuku'Gu. Though the force of life was present in each, they were complete opposites. The Emmuku'Gu represents life and creation, where the Shadow carries death and destruction. They balance one another, or did until Uggae and his followers tainted the Shadow with their dark shi. As the Shadow grew stronger, it tipped the scales of that balance and the whole of Ersetu reacted with violent shakes, upheavals, and fiery mountains. The imbalance began long before the histories of man where recorded.

While man spread across Ersetu, they began worshipping the Sumer as Gods, adding to the power they possessed. Once a man died, the Shadow or the Emmuku'Gu could claim his shi. If the Emmuku'Gu claims you, your shi is cycled back into life upon Ersetu. If the Shadow claims the shi, then all the strength and knowledge of the person is carried with the shi into the darkness, adding to its power.

"My people have a long held belief that if we were to pass on and be buried in the earth, the darkness would take us into its embrace and steal our power," Dara called out. "Perhaps we were not far from the truth of the matter. The Gula'Lu always commit themselves to the mercurial state and join with the Nashi'Zag, rather than welcome true death and be buried."

"Likewise, the Drakk commit themselves to fire," Gregoran added.

"Well, bugger! We dwarves make a big deal out of being interned to the earth, it is after all our connection to the Essence," grumbled Avrank. "Suppose we have been feeding that horrid Shadow all this time!"

"Perhaps, but we cannot be certain of anything until we find more answers," Shuran tried to reassure his dwarf friend. "One thing I can say is that the Shadow is tainted and it is the darkness of the Sumer inside that want the shi to give them strength. Now that the four are trapped within the chamber, I think that we may have a reprieve."

"But I thought there were five Sumer that were among the Shadow?" Vala asked.

"Yes, but only four entered the chamber and attacked me. The fifth is still out there, and is likely weakened."

"More akin to a brain-sick boar cornered, I would imagine!" Orian observed. "I certainly am not looking forward to the backlash!"

Vala and Dara walked out of the meeting of the Zidu'Si together. Being the only two female members, they had begun staying close to one another. Another bonding element was that each of their races had long ago departed company of the other races of man, to live in isolation.

"Vala? Did you always feel that you did not belong among your own kind?" Dara asked as they walked toward the outer boundary of the city.

"It is not that I felt a lack of belonging, I felt as though I was missing some other connection to the world. I was always searching for something… More," Vala answered. "My father would scold me for going beyond our waters. He forbade me contact with dirt walkers, and I never disobeyed, technically."

Dara glanced at her friend and smiled. "What does 'technically' mean?"

"I used to travel to the edges of our domain and then beyond. I wanted to know what else was out there. Often times I would find a rocky out-cropping and sun myself and watch passing human sea vessels from a distance. Once I even saw one of these vessels lift from the waters and sail through the air to safety from a water siphon!"

"That sounds like a magurmu, one of the flying ships that are used by the pirates and their leader Aknard. It could have even been the Mellamu Nanna, Codger's vessel." Dara was excited to be having a chance for girl talk. "But what is a water siphon?" she asked.

"Normally they are a place where waters meet in such a way to cause a funnel leading to the depths, but the one I watched that day was one of my people's creation. It was placed near an ancient ruin hidden beneath the surface to keep people away long ago. The Badur'Lu do not remember why it was created, we only keep it in place."

Dara's curiosity was in full bloom. "Where is this siphon?"

"The place is on the Western coast of Aurderia in the Great Sea. We call the place, the Spires, but I believe the dirt walkers call it Serpent's Fangs."

Chapter Thirty-Two

Salmetu practically threw Bastien's demon controlled body down at the ground near the Altar of Chaos. She had travelled Shadow with him and herself to the Altar in order to attempt to locate the source of her waning strength as well as to see about purging the clinging remainder of Bastien's resistance. When she released him after they appeared from the nether of Shadow, she looked at him and tittered as he collapsed without her support. Salmetu sneered as she looked down at him. "We really need to do something about this Telalsu. You are no use to me in this state."

"Can we not simply find a new host?"

"NO!" she screamed back. "The boy Shin'Ar wants this one back."

"Then I say give him back, dead and useless," Telalsu said.

"You best of all should know that what dies does not always stay dead. Or have you forgotten your own origins?" Salmetu teased.

Bastien's demon controlled face twisted in disapproval of Salmetu's slight. Telalsu could barely remember a time before he was transformed into a demon warrior. Part of the reason demons clung so tightly to their vessels, was a tortured reminder of a time when they were not demons at all.

"Do remove that look from your borrowed face, demon. It does not suit him in the least."

Salmetu turned from her taunting and walked to the altar of dragon glass. She ran her fingers along the surface that was blacker than night and as slick as ice. She made her way from one end to the other taking small deliberate steps while chanting a low and barely audible spell. As she rounded the far side, the altar began to glow with a deep red light.

The glow peaked at a steady burning that made the altar appear as though it were burning from the inside out. A faint hum could be heard from the surrounding lintels and uprights as they began to burn with the same deep red glow.

Salmetu backed away from the altar as she waited for her casting to complete. She held a pensive look upon her face as she stared upon the sacred site. Something was wrong she realized, as the glowing faltered and suddenly went dark.

"Impossible! They cannot have left me!" she screamed. Salmetu repeated the spell, hoping she took a misstep along the way. The result was the same, the altar and surrounding lintels began to glow the same deep red, but then sputtered and faded quickly as the casting failed to produce the desired outcome. Still, Salmetu tried again and again.

***

Andra was not used to the new treatment he was receiving from not only the citizens in Britengate, but the Zidu'Si as well. The humans in the city were not hostile, but most kept their distance or avoided Andra. The Zidu'Si behaved indifferently toward Andra's presence. The shifter knew that this behavior was due to the actions of another of his race, but that did not provide any comfort. Andra could have changed his appearance, blending in with the people, but he chose to remain the image of a man that was comfortable and familiar. He wore a face that was well known to the others. A face 'he' chose as his own.

Andra approached Shuran shortly after the trial. "Shuran! May we speak privately?"

Shuran excused himself from the Zidu'Si and indicated Andra should walk with him. "I apologize for not having had time to spend with you. I hope that you have found a use for your skills among the new weavers?"

"I have been some use with instruction, but most will not work with me, and those who do, treat me with an air of suspicion," Andra shared. "I understand the reasons, but I am no more responsible for the acts of some of my kin, then you are responsible for the acts of other men."

"I can speak to the weavers and all the citizens if you wish it, but I am uncertain that doing so would help over much," Shuran empathized. "You are a new race to these people, and they are leery of everything in these unsettling times. Perhaps you might work in the hospital with Moona. She has been making healing potions and preparing the stocks of bandages for coming war."

"Moona is one of the few to treat me no differently, though that is not saying much. I was thinking more about going after the shifter that escaped. Barurbe will likely need assistance."

"How did you know of Barurbe's task?"

"You just confirmed it Shuran. You really must get better at this game if you plan on finding out so many secrets."

"And what are your secrets my friend?"

Andra did not know how to respond. After several moments of contemplation, he stopped walking. "I have never lied to you, Shuran. I have helped protect and guide you as best I could, given my other duties. The only thing that remains unsaid is the reasons and by who's instruction."

"The great Nabusa, seer of the foresworn, set me to this task. She speaks of your importance but does not explain. She is the Mother to us all and is not questioned, but now I feel I have fallen from her favor and your need of my guidance is redundant."

"I will always seek your council, but I understand your feelings on the matter. I will not stop you from seeking out your kinsman, but I would ask that you tread carefully. We do not understand the motives of this group of outcast shifters and what they are capable of doing." Shuran then turned away from Andra. "I imagine there is more to this Nabusa of yours that you are not saying?"

"You are getting better at the game. She is the oldest and wisest of the foresworn. She was there when the first shifter came into being and has acted as a mother to all, but she was a mother already. Though her daughter died while, in child birthing at a young age, her granddaughter lives. Perhaps she can one day tell you more of the Nabusa than even I."

"And who might this grand daughter be?" Shuran asked fearing he already knew the answer.

"I can see that you already know the answer. I will leave you to seek out explanations for yourself."

Andra left Shuran to prepare for a journey into the wilds of the North. He would search out the rogue shifters and find out what they were about. Supplies would be meager. Andra would provide for himself as was customary for a Guardian. The only important supply that was taken were abnu emuq that Shuran offered.

Shuran left Andra to depart quietly and without ceremony. He alerted the North gate guards that a traveler would be exiting. He was not specific since Andra was certain to wear another face as he made for the forests beyond.

Shuran was growing distracted thinking about when the time would come to rescue Bastien. Tianna was explicit in her instructions that he wait until she returned to advise him when and where to find his friend. Shuran sat near the meeting hall, fumbling with the green gemstone in his pocket. It had been his oldest and most constant companion. Now that he recognized it for what it truly was, the weight on his shoulders intensified.

"I will save you my friend," he said.

"I was unaware I needed saving!" Mallick said. "Except from the brain sharing twin dwarves you set after me!"

Shuran released an uncomfortable laugh. "I wondered how long it would be until you rebuked me for sending them to you."

"Ah ha, so you did send them! I suspected as much, but they told me they sought me out themselves. You are a devious prankster Shin'Ar, I almost feel sorry for our enemies." Mallick watched Shuran return the gem to his pocket before continuing. "Now do you wish to share what troubles you at present, sheesh?"

"Time is running short. Bastien is weakening and must be reunited with his body soon or there will be few options to save him."

"What options could possibly remain if we do not get him back in time?" Mallick was worried about the answer.

"Nothing that I would care to tamper with, my brother. I am certain there are other means to free Bastien's shi, but I am not certain how truly free he would become."

Mallick twisted the ring on his finger only a moment before looking back up at Shuran in understanding. He quickly changed the subject. "So what is this I hear about a deep trench and underground rivers?"

Welcoming the distraction from his current train of thought, Shuran perked up. "The artificial river that surrounds the city is multi-functional. First it is a larger source of fresh water, second it is a means of bringing help from the Badur'Lu."

Shuran explained how there was a massive underground reservoir of water, deep below the city. Vala and he expanded that chamber and connected the water to the river on the surface. When war came to Britengate for he was certain that it would, the Badur'Lu warriors could be called by Emmuku'Gu and wait within the Chamber. They would then become a surprise reinforcement against their enemy.

"There is something else that has been troubling me Shuran," Mallick said. "When you explained about the shi within both the Emmuku'Gu and the Shadow, it raised some questions."

"I suppose you wonder why the shi stays in the Emmuku'Gu and does not cycle back into the life cycle?" Shuran saw that this was not all Mallick wanted to know, but he would start there. "Those who choose to stay within the Emmuku'Gu seem to do so by choice to serve the Sumer. Whether they still believe them Gods, or simply agree to fight the Shadow I am uncertain, but they provide strength to the power of light and creation. Those in the Shadow are trapped by the dark power of the Sumer, who taint it."

"But how is it the Sumer taint the Shadow, I thought they were the foul thing?"

Darkness and light, creation and destruction, life and death, these are natural forces in the cycle of everything. Shuran tried to think of the simplest way in which to explain things, as he understood them. The Shadow has always been the counter force of the Light, but it never had an intent until the Sumer joined with it. Their darkness was drawn to the destructive side of the balance. Once they joined with the force behind the Shadow, they gave it something it never had, a consciousness with intent and malice.

"The balance of nature was destroyed," Shuran continued. "I believe that the benevolent Sumer somehow joined with the creation side of the forces in an effort to balance things, but it was not the best choice I imagine. They should have attempted to purge the Shadow of the malevolent Sumer."

"Why would they choose something that was destined to fail and continue tearing apart Ersetu?" Mallick wondered aloud.

"I am uncertain but I have a feeling. I fear that they were simply borrowing time," Shuran said and then looked up to the two brightest stars in the night sky.

"The stars of prophecy? What would they have to do with something that started thousands of years ago, long before man was created?"

Shuran responded. "What indeed?"

***

Shuran was dining privately with the Zidu'Si when Tianna appeared, frightening Avrank.

"DAMKIANNA! Do you have to sneak up like that?" Avrank protested.

"I do believe I smell something foul. Did you live up to your name Turd?" Orian jested.

Avrank frowned at Orian. "Oh, go shove a shoe up your backside cobbler!"

Tianna moved closer to Shuran, who stood up and greeted her with curiosity. She indicated that Salmetu and Bastien sans Telalsu headed to Drakkfoth and the Altar of Chaos. There would be no second chances at getting Bastien back. He was dying and would likely give up his body completely rather than give in to the demon possessing him.

Shuran returned to his Zidu'Si and then mentally called for Moltar to return from hunting and bring Jade along with him. "It is time to rescue Bastien! Salmetu has taken him to the Altar in Drakkfoth."

Chapter Thirty-Three

Salmetu sat angry and confused, staring at the Altar. It was unable to carry out her spell. She attempted repeating the spell for nearly a full turn before stopping to think. She could still call the Shadow out, of that she was certain, but what she was attempting was something altogether different. She finally gave up on her attempts.

"This is troubling, Telalsu. I cannot feel them and they do not return at my call," she said.

"The Shadow is gone?" Telalsu asked in shock.

"NO, you fool! The Shadow is eternal. I call for my family within, they do not respond. I am alone among the blackness."

"That must be difficult for you Ereshkigal," Shuran said as he stepped out of the light.

Shocked and caught off guard, Salmetu stood and lashed out with power. Volley after another met with the shield Shuran erected to protect himself and the Zidu'Si that followed out behind him.

Seeing the nearly complete Zidu'Si emerge to circle the Altar, Salmetu attention to Shuran. "How do you know that name?"

Shuran smiled and responded. "Nergal sends his regrets that he could not address you in person. He is otherwise engaged entertaining the rest of your Gizzu'Su friends!"

Salmetu let out a shriek that split the night before renewing her assault upon Shuran.

"Keep her distracted!" Shuran thought to the Zidu'Si. He needed to get to Bastien, who was beginning to stand up near the edge of the Altar's surrounding uprights. Shuran held the green gem in his hand and whispered to it before placing it back in his pocket. "Give the demon control and hold tight!"

The Zidu'Si moved in to circle Salmetu, allowing Shuran the opportunity to engage Bastien directly without Salmetu's interference. They deflected her attacks easily enough, but they were getting more intense and frequent. Strengthening their shields with power funneled from Shuran and the source of Essence, they pressed their defense into an offense.

Meanwhile, Shuran approached Bastien with caution. He could sense the demon gaining control and repairing the damage Bastien caused to himself in order to cripple the dark warrior possessing him. Shuran was initially uncertain if Telalsu could heal the damaged organs once Bastien relented, but his gamble paid off. Telalsu soon stood straight and tall, ready to attack Shuran.

Telalsu struck with lightening fast speed. The demon lashed out with a green glowing burst of misty force that threw Shuran back against the nearest upright. The demon churned inside Bastien, gathering his strength and knowledge. He prepared his next attack as Shuran was gaining his feet.

"You are no challenge for the power and experience of my kind child!" Telalsu howled in his own voice. "I will destroy you for my Queen, just as she planned!" Bastien's face began to mutate and take on a skeletal appearance. The demon warrior was taking complete control of his host. "I have fought stronger and more ancient forces than you can imagine!" Then he thrust his next spell at Shuran.

Shuran was ill prepared for the stream of malignant fluid that

274

knocked him back again. The viscous liquid spread across his midsection and continued along his body. Shuran felt the sickness within the attack and it threatened to make him retch. As the spell covered his body, it made its way across his face and head, entering his ears, nose, and mouth.

Telalsu laughed manically as his casting took hold of his foe. His laughter was cut short, however, when he felt the spell begin to recoil and break. He stood in stunned silence as Shuran's eyes opened and he saw the fire burning behind them.

Shuran's eyes shone red with fire as he began to burn the slimy malignancy from his body. The gooey substance fought for purchase upon his skin in vain. With a force of will and fire, Shuran cast the sickening muck from his body and smiled back at Telalsu as his latest spell turned to dust before him.

"You may have challenged more ancient foes, but I doubt they had the power of the Zidu'Si and a mountainous drakkon behind them!" Shuran spat at the demon. As Telalsu regained his composure, Shuran went on the offense. He spindled an orb of energy and sent it into the ground before the warrior and watched as it settled into the earth with no apparent effect.

"Is that the best the Shin'Ar can do with all that alleged power behind him? I had more hope of a sparing than this." Telalsu moved to send a bolt of energy at Shuran when the ground below him shuddered. To his own shock, thick spiny roots thrust from the ground at his feet and wrapped themselves around his vessel, holding him in place. As he fought off the roots, vines sprouted from them and grabbed his arms, pulling them close to his sides.

Shuran ran toward the demon pulling a blade from his belt and a green gem from his pocket. He was gaining upon his quarry when a force of energy thrust him back, knocking the blade and gem from his hands. He struggled to get to his feet but was knocked down again by an unseen assailant, the gemstone just out of his reach. He reached for the stone only to have it pulled from his grasp by the same unseen force.

***

Salmetu watched the exchanges between Telalsu and Shuran as she place were not of her liking, she planned ahead for the events that were unfolding before her. She had initially accounted for the aid of the others, but she would accomplish her plans without them. She called forth another ally to engage Shuran while Telalsu worked through the earth-binding spell attacking him.

Putting that into action, Salmetu could fully focus on the Zidu'Si assaulting her. She began to weave darkness into a ball of energy in her outstretched hand. A deep blue and black pulsing orb began to spark and hum as she built upon its potency. With a jerk of her head and raise of her free hand, she stopped an approaching burst of fire from the Drakkian Zidu'Si warrior. In return, she flicked a portion of her orb in his direction.

Blasts of fire and electricity battered Salmetu's shield from above. She looked to the skies but could not locate the source of the attack. She sent part of her spindle of energy into the air in hopes of finding a target.

Both Drakkon were cloaked as they flew around, dodging Salmetu's assault and returning fire with their own attacks. As they weaved in and around the dark power being blindly sent into the sky, they grinned toothily at one another. They were having a game of it all.

Gregoran lifted his Mi-Ib Ag in defense of the oncoming ball of power. The blade stood against the assault without resistance. As the darkness hit the blade, it reacted by splitting the orb in twain and releasing a purifying flame, nullifying the power behind Salmetu's spell.

Salmetu, angered by the impotence of her attack, poured more dark intent into her orb and sent it out in every direction. The orb split into equal sized spheres of pulsing power and sailed through the air toward different members of the Zidu'Si. Not a single assault met with success.

Each Zidu'Si retrieved their weapon and used it to repel the attack.

Gregorian again sliced through the attack with his Mi'Ib Ag and rendered it impotent.

Vala lifted her trident, the Kibur'Zisu, and a spray of energy enriched water shot from the tines and extinguished her attacker's spell.

Avrank wielded the gug war hammer and with a swing before him, molten rock sprayed from the hammer and engulfed the approaching orb. Menasutur drew the power of earth to his defense.

276

Orian drew back the string of his bow, Agal Kastu and released a pulsing arrow composed of pure electric energy. The arrow struck the on-coming sphere and destroyed it in a brilliant flash of light.

The next orb reached its target and met with the force of the A'Baddasu. The mighty gauntlet of strength was a mountain of force that held back the darkness with little effort.

The final orb headed toward the one Zidu'Si that wielded no weapon of substance. Mallick gained instant knowledge from the use of the Mudutu'Har. The twin rings of knowledge gave him a spell he could weave with a thought that destroyed the assaulting orb. Now that Shuran wore the mate ring, he could properly access the Vault Library and more. He could also feel that Shuran was in trouble.

***

Shuran was splayed out on the ground reaching for the green gemstone when it suddenly flew away from him. Confused and vulnerable, his first reaction was to restore his shield. He did so just in time. A bolt of electricity hit his shield and crackled along its surface. Shuran did not spend time thinking upon what had just occurred. He immediately sought out the gem and called it toward him.

"GIN!" Shuran commanded as he reached out to the stone when he located it. The gem resisted at first, but quickly broke free of whatever held it tight, to come sailing through the air toward Shuran's open hand. He lowered a portion of the shield only a moment to allow the stone through. The moment was long enough to allow an attack. Shuran screamed with pain as a bolt of energy followed the stone into his shield.

The searing and blinding electric force bounced throughout the interior of Shuran's shield. Trapped by his shield, the attacking force lit the area as it ricocheted around and struck Shuran repeatedly. By the time Shuran dropped his shield to release the energy, he was covered in burns and his clothing was half scorched.

As he started to heal himself, he began to look around for the dagger. He turned to look behind him when he was startled. He found the Mi-Ib Simshi, in the hand of Bastien standing only a few steps away. The demon warrior smiled wickedly at Shuran as he stood before him. Shuran

Suddenly he was on his back holding Bastien's wrists at arm's length. The Mi'Ib Simshi, slowly moved toward his heart.

Salmetu had enough of playtime. She saw Telalsu gaining the upper hand against Shuran, so it was time to call forth the power of the Shadow. She waved her hand in a flourish and then reached out to the Altar.

The Altar began to rumble and shake. Within seconds, a dark misty fog began to form around the base of the black stone. Soon the tumbling fog began to roil and billow forth, heading directly for the Zidu'Si.

The Zidu'Si struck out at the thickening fog with their weapons to no effect. The gug tools of war passed directly through the Shadow. The warriors began to converge as the Shadow corralled them together. Every so often a tendril would reach out and touch one of them, only to be repelled by the Essence spell of protection. The Shadow was not to be beaten back so easily, however.

Salmetu twisted her face in hatred and fury. With another swooping gesture, she poured Shadow out toward them from herself. The reinforcing power she added had immediate effect. Though the Shadow was being repelled at each touch of a Zidu'Si, the power was not causing as great a repellent effect, and now the Zidu'Si were surrounded.

Spell after spell, wielding after another, the Zidu'Si could not fight off the Shadow as it threatened to engulf them. They backed together in a circle and created a shield to hold back the encroaching darkness. The feeling of malice, despair, and anger that emanated from the Shadow penetrated the shield and worked upon the nerves of the warriors within. The shield began to weaken.

"Take my hand!" Dara called to Vala. "The rest grab hold of your neighbor and follow my lead."

The Zidu'Si joined hands, and Dara felt down into the rock below them looking for signs of stone that could be transmuted. All she found was obsidian. "Dragon glass will not help us. We must create our own shield." And then she sent them the thoughts. The Zidu'Si began to cover with gugtu.

Above her, Salmetu called forth flying demonic creatures to engage the cloaked drakkon that had been flying above. She watched as the deep emerald colored beast materialized then dove and swooped to avoid the jaws of her evil pets. A nasty smile spread across her face and a slight giggle erupted uncontrollably. She allowed herself a moment. Her joy did not last for long, however. She had forgotten that there were two drakkon among the followers of Shuran.

Chapter Thirty-Four

Shuran was struggling against the power Telalsu was pulling into Bastien's body. He would soon have the dagger jutting out of his own chest if he did not act quickly. As he struggled to find a way out of his current situation, he could sense the Zidu'Si all engaged in trouble of their own. They would not be coming to his aid. Shuran began to form the beginning of an idea. Slowly he reached into his pocket and retrieved the gem. He had to keep Telalsu's attention.

"Why is it you serve such an evil purpose demon? Have you no shi of your own?" Shuran asked as he looked into the demonic eyes of his friend.

Telalsu spat at Shuran. "You know nothing of the true nature of life and death man child. There is power in the darkness that would swallow the light. There will be an end to everything but the Shadow."

"Without the light, there can be no casting of shadow, but even if what you say were true, I fail to understand your motivation. If everything were to be destroyed save the Shadow then you will be no more, do you not wish to survive the end of all things?"

"I want nothing more than…" Telalsu sensed Shuran's subterfuge. He was too late to react.

With the speed of light filling a room, Shuran called out a spell. "BAL MI-IB!" he yelled out and then slammed the gemstone into the end of the dagger's hilt after it reversed in Bastien's demon controlled hands. Shuran called forth to his greatest source of power. He did not call out to the source of Essence; he called out to the bond of love he shared with Moltar. The bond of friendship he had with the Zidu'Si, and the brotherly love he held for Bastien. "KI'AGA DAB KALAG'GA!", take strength from love. Shuran pushed with the borrowed strength and thrust the dagger into Bastien's chest.

An explosion of light and dark fired from Bastien's chest. The gemstone shone with blinding emerald light that traveled the length of the hilt and blade, down into Bastien's wounded breast. The light forced its way into his body, soon followed by the darkness that previously escaped. The dagger slipped from Bastien's chest as the darkness filled him, which is when the battle of wills began.

Shuran sat up as his friend rolled over in convulsive torment. He lifted the dagger and replaced it in his belt, then moved forward to watch over his best friend's fight for dominance over the ancient demon warrior within. He did not watch for more than a few fleeting moments before he came under attack.

Bolts of electric Essence began to shower down upon him from the lintels of the Altar's ring of uprights. His shield held up against the onslaught but he needed to find out what or who was behind this attack. He could sense that it was pure Essence wielding of electricity, so he was looking for mixed blood, or elf. There was more than one and they were cloaked from his view.

The Zidu'Si were fully encased in gugtu and soon the Shadow would twist the magic stone into soured gug, trapping his comrades within or breaking it to possess those within. Jade was busily attacking and defending herself with some sort of flying creature of darkness. They were black as pitch and covered with both scale and feather. Bolts of red plasma jetted from their eyes as they dove at the emerald drakkon.

Moltar on the other hand, had just been backed into a corner and was covered in blackened vines that grew from the earth below him. Similar to those recently employed by Shuran himself, the thorns on these vines were moving as teeth gnawing at Moltar's thick, hard scales.

Salmetu stood nearby controlling the vines and warping them to her will. Suddenly she stopped her attack and stepped sideways to avoid a new assault upon her.

Tianna appeared at that moment and began taunting Salmetu. She danced in the air before the Shadow filled priestess, mocking her with the power of light and creation. Her efforts proved successful, as Moltar was free of the vines and making his way to Shuran's side.

Moltar took three short walking leaps and was upon Shuran and joining his own shield to that of his Lugaldur. "What are we to do about this Lugaldur?"

"We rise above it my friend," Shuran said with a smile.

"How very pious of you, but I think action will serve us better!" Moltar said in confusion.

Shuran leapt into the air and levitated himself to sit upon Moltar's neck. "You misunderstand, we rise above… as in fly."

Moltar understood immediately and flew up into the air. He flapped his mighty wings several times and was already high above even Jade and her attacking beasts.

Shuran began to form the spell in his mind, and allowed Moltar to join him. Together then spindled the power and might of the Essence. They were combining electricity with fire, earth, and water than would unite them with a weaving. As the power built up, Shuran noticed Tianna flinching away from Salmetu.

Salmetu waved a golden dagger at his sister's ghostly form. The Mi-Ib Karshi was in her hand as she advanced toward Tianna. The wrathe was fleeing the blade as an ogre does fire.

Shuran had no more time to wonder, the power he and Moltar gathered was ready for release. The last step was to use the energy and power of a weaving, something that would allow him to mimic the Essence of air. "Ri An-Lil!" Shuran spoke as he and Moltar released the

The resulting cast was one of pure light and energy slamming down upon the battle below. The recoil was unexpected as Shuran grabbed hold tightly to Moltar, who buffeted the backlash from him. Together they tumbled back through the sky. By the time Moltar regained his wings, they were nearly a mile away from the others.

When Moltar circled back, Shuran looked wide-eyed at the result of his wielding. His blast had been centered upon the Altar, which was now a black, shard filled crater in the earth. The surrounding uprights and lintels were toppled over and laying next to them, were several elves, one of which Shuran recognized.

Voreen woke from his momentary stunning and looked up in shocked horror. He had been discovered. Voreen immediately closed his eyes and then vanished into the Emmuku'Gu, leaving his compatriots behind. Unless they had learned the power and knowledge of traveling the lines, which Shuran doubted, they were not going anywhere so he placed a shield over them, trapping them in place.

Moltar landed near the Zidu'Si and Shuran jumped down to check them while Moltar went to Jade's side.

Shuran found the Zidu'Si free of both gugtu and Shadow. He noticed then that the Shadow had gone entirely. He was unsure whether the destruction of the Altar by the spell alone was responsible for the Shadow's retreat. The thought of Salmetu then crossed his mind and he turned to find her gone.

The place where Salmetu had been advancing upon Tianna was empty of her presence; Shuran looked for Tianna but did not find her. His calls out for her to appear went unanswered. When he turned back to return to his comrades, a glint caught the corner of his eye. There in the dust and debris of the Altar lay the Mi-Ib Karshi.

Shuran retrieved the blade. "Salmetu must have dropped and then forgotten the blade in her retreat," he thought aloud. He pulled free its twin from his belt then sent them both back to the Vault in Durangug for safekeeping. He saw Jade was well in hand with Moltar and continued back to his other friends.

"What in the name of Damkianna happened?" Avrank grumbled.

"You were all in a bit of a pinch, so I decided to shed a little light on the issue!" Shuran grinned. His grin faded however when he looked up to find Bastien still convulsing. "Gather yourselves and come with me!" Shuran ran to his childhood friend.

"Bastien you must fight the demon!" Shuran cried out as he gripped Bastien's shoulders and turned him upon his side. Shuran saw blood upon the hard earth where Bastien had been shaking uncontrollably. His head had been pounding the ground and was bleeding badly. Without thinking Shuran pushed his thoughts into Bastien's head to find and repair the damage. He was unprepared for the welcome he received.

"What have you done man child!" Telalsu screamed at Shuran.

Shuran could see the demon in his true form while inside Bastien's mind. He was less prepared for the sight than he had been for the exchange. "What are you?"

"Shuran! I am not strong enough to fight off the demon!" Bastien cried out and it echoed through Shuran's own head.

"You have to fight Bastien. I need you back, and I need you to become a member of my Zidu'Si, if that would be your wish?" Shuran said in response.

"I would gladly accept but-" Bastien's words were cut off.

Without intending a true oath ceremony, Shuran had just done so, only from within the new inductees mind. When Bastien expressed his desire to accept, Shuran felt the acceptance in his heart and the oath were sealed. Bastien was now the human weaver among the Zidu'Si and he immediately felt a rush of power inside his entire being.

Shuran was thrust out of Bastien's head and fell backward.

The rest of the Zidu'Si had arrived in time to feel the bonding to their ranks and felt a surge of knowledge and power of weaving that Bastien had gleaned from the demon while it was controlling him. They also felt the love of a brother that Shuran had for Bastien and immediately that the power flowed out through them along the bond and directly into Bastien.

Bastien sat up suddenly and screamed out. "Telal Barra!" demon, be gone, and an undulating and tortured mass of wispy energy separated from the entire surface of Bastien's body. It fought for purchase, reaching

Shuran could see the desperate look on the face of the demon as it tried in vain to hold onto life. Based on what he saw now and the image of Telalsu's true form while inside Bastien's mind, he understood why the demon wanted to cling to the host body. The demon was once a living breathing person, and it wanted that back more than anything.

"You will not have this body… whoever ever you were, you are no longer!" With a final push from his spell, Bastien freed himself from the possession.

Telalsu shrieked in agony, not from physical pain but emotional attachment to having a corporeal form.

Shuran grabbed Bastien as his body became overwhelmed from the return of all his shi. Coupled with joining the Zidu'Si and the wounds to his body yet unhealed after his convulsions, Bastien was exhausted. Shuran poured healing energy and re-energizing power into his friend while he worked on his split skull and internal bruising. Once complete, his friend sat upright on his own strength and embraced his friend.

"It is about time you got me back to my body sheesh. It has not been easy bouncing about in your pocket, trapped in a hunk of rock and resting next to your nether regions!" Bastien smirked.

Everyone laughed, Dara and Vala tried to hide their own blushing giggles.

"Now that the reunion is done, what do we do about the pointy-eared devils that attacked you?" Moltar was trying to hide his jealousy for the bond between Shuran and Bastien.

Orian looked to Shuran with confusion and horror. "What has happened?"

Shuran walked them all to the four shields that held angry and hateful elves within. "These four were cloaked and helping our enemy. One of them fled by way of Emmuku'Gu."

"Never turn your back on an elf I always say, present company excluded shoe boy!" Avrank joked uneasily.

"Voreen? But he-" Orian began.

"Fooled us all my friend. We will turn these four over to the justice of the Queen. Voreen is likely hiding somewhere, but he is not our deepest concern now."

"And what would that be then?" Gregoran asked.

"Salmetu will go in search of those we have trapped. It will not be long before she realizes where they are being held," Vala deduced.

"Can she free them?" Dara asked.

"With the full power of the Shadow trapped shi, I shudder to think what her wrath will become capable of. I am not certain she will even try to save them just the same." Shuran said.

Mallick reached over to give Bastien a hug. "Why would she not save them?"

"Because then the one that fills my sister's body would have to share all that power again."

***

Salmetu stepped away from the crack in the floor as a stream of Shadow left her. She then stormed through the catacombs of the Academy, blasting walls and cursing the Zidu'si. She was certain that when the time arrived that Shuran came for Bastien, she would be ready for him. Shuran was supposed to get overpowered by Telalsu when it regained its strength and took control of Bastien. If events had played out the way she intended, the Mi'Ib Simshi would have pierced Shuran and the Shadow would have entered him.

She stomped her way up to the private apartments, throwing a temper tantrum the entire way. When she reached her own rooms, she burst through the doors and began ransacking her bedchamber. She continued her tirade for several minutes only stopping when Sulura entered her room.

"What has happened to put you in such a state? Did things not play out as you anticipated my dear?" Sulura said with a hint of sarcasm.

Sulura sensed a change in Salmetu from the way she was behaving and carrying herself. Her daughter was acting like a normal girl, upset from not getting her own way. Her spirits were lifted; there was a piece of her daughter left inside. She could move ahead with her chosen task, the events planned out by Nergal and Nagutan might still come to pass.

"Shuran ruined everything!" Salmetu pouted. "He was supposed to join us here so we could be a family, she promised!"

promised?"

"The dark lady, she said we would all be a family again. But now she has to go look for her friends. When she returns, we will go and bring Shuran back here so we can all be together."

***

Barurbe left the Queen and set off into the forests of Entensiama. She was not sure where to begin but decided to transform into her familiar wolf shape. As a wolf, she could heighten her sense of smell and attempt to track out other shifters. Her hope was that she would find Andra first so they might find the others together.

As she traveled the woods, she did her best to avoid the Elfin Rangers that scouted the area surrounding their Capital. It would raise far too much suspicion should they spot a white wolf in this part of Aurderia. She found a scent and followed it through the dense terrain. When she eventually caught up with the quarry, she was not prepared for what she encountered.

Andra was splayed out upon the ground spread eagle with spikes through his hands and feet. She approached cautiously not only because she was frightened by the sight before her, but she also picked up the scent of other shifters in the area. One of those scents was familiar and quite nearby.

Chapter Thirty-Five

Shuran and the Zidu'Si traveled back to Britengate before taking the imprisoned elves to face their Queen. Dara fashioned wrist and ankle restraints with chains from gug to hobble their powers and prevent them escaping.

"Get them traitorous bastards out of this city afore I open the earth an' drop 'em into a bottomless pit!" Moona called as the elves were led to the Northern gate to be then transported to the capital of Entensiama. "Go after one o' my sprats an' I'll flatten 'em!"

"Ease down ol' girl, Shuran and the others got things well in hand," Codger insisted. "What is gotten into you? Now that Vardoran is back I thought you'd ease up."

"Get your mitts of o' me, ya ol' fool!" she rebelled. "They is all my responsibility ta look after, specially Vardoran. But-"

"NO BUTS now move yours! Shuran and the Zidu'Si can look after themselves. Vardoran is who you need worry 'bout now." Codger

Bastien just watched in amusement as the two just walked past him without notice.

"Come along Bastien, you look to need fattening up! That demon must'a forgot you needed feedin'," Moona said turning to him. "Don' think I didn' see ya there," she said and smiled while whacking Codger in the back of the head. He obviously overlooked Bastien's presence. "Close your mouth or you'll catch bugs ol' fool!"

***

Shuran and Orian transported their prisoners back to the courtyard of Entensiama. Florisia was already there, waiting with a grand gathering of elven elders. She was apprised of the events that took place in Drakkfoth from Shuran himself by means of the crystal he left with her. The expression she held upon her face was one of blind rage. Sparks were dancing along her fingers.

"Place them in the ring!" she ordered as several rangers came forward and dragged the chained elves to the center of the courtyard where a ring of stone had been placed. "They will stand trial immediately." She moved to her place upon a dais used for observing games and festival entertainment. There would be no festivities this evening. "Shuran Shin'Ar, if you would remove the gug shackles, they interfere with our seeking testimony."

Shuran waved a hand and did as requested, though it came across as more of an order than a request. As soon as the gug was removed, Shuran could sense the powerful field of electric charge that rose around the accused. The assault on their minds was quickly apparent when they buckled over in pain. But they did not let any sound pass their lips.

Florisia stood only moments after the trial started. "Bring in my chamberlain! He is a conspirator." Florisia closed her eyes and rolled her head back as she delved deeper into the collective of minds. She pulled every piece of relevant information from the elves on trial. "ENOUGH!"

"We have seen everything and know all there is to glean. Enact the ultimate justice!"

Orian lowered his eyes, already knowing what that justice meant to the elves. They had broken one of the laws among elves, loyalty.

Shuran watched in shocked silence as blood ran from the ears, nose, and eyes of the accused. He found it unimaginable the pain they suffered and still they did not make a sound.

***

Bastien finished eating quickly and asked for a second helping, which Moona was happy to provide. He sat across from Vardoran, who he just met but had yet to realize who he actually was. They spoke little as Bastien was busy enjoying Moona's cooking, and Vardoran was not talkative lately. Codger sat watching everyone but did not utter a sound.

"Vardy, you haven't touched your stew, are you feeling well?" Moona asked her son.

"I apologize ma, I am not feeling hungry," he answered while looking at Bastien.

Bastien dropped his spoon. "I thought that your son was-"

"Gone to us… for a time, but now he is back and we are all getting adjusted is all!" Codger interrupted.

"Do not lie on my account adda. The truth young Bastien is that I am the one behind the troubles that brought you to Birchshire and ultimately allowed your possession," Vardoran admitted. "I caused a great deal of trouble in Aurderia and beyond. I have this time with my parents until Shuran sees to my final punishment."

Bastien was contemplating how to respond to this, when flashes of the trial and what Vardoran admitted came to his mind. He shook his head briefly. "That will take some getting used to," he mumbled.

"What was that Bastien?" Codger asked.

Bastien looked at him a moment before fumbling with a response. "Well, I am certain you had your reasons. We all make mistakes." Bastien completed his meal and stood. "My own adda was prepared to turn Shuran over for coin and ends up it was me the inquisitors carried off. You did not cause that directly." Bastien excused himself and headed to the field used by weavers to practice their spell casting.

***

Florisia stepped down from the dais and motioned to Shuran and Orian. "Shuran and Orian, please accompany me to my private study, I courtyard to the massive tree that served as the royal home. After her personal guards had left them alone, Florisia sent her servant to fetch refreshments.

Looking at Shuran, Florisia sat down and bid they do the same. "You do not approve of our swift judgment?" she asked Shuran.

"It is not my place to agree or disagree with the wisdom of elfin custom. My only hope is that they would be no longer of any use," he responded.

"I assure you Shuran, every piece of information as it relates to their crimes has been extracted. I think it best I share that with you immediately so we might discuss our next course of action."

Florisia explained how Voreen had deceived them, all of them. He was never reformed, nor had he given up on old family vendettas. The feelings Voreen had toward the Zidu'Si and especially the Shin'Ar of the past drove him even further into the arms of darkness. As seen through the memories of those judged, Voreen was working with the Order of Chaos for centuries. His alliance shifted to Salmetu when she took over.

"Voreen was present the night you were born at the Altar of Chaos. It was he that held the knife, striking down your sister Tianna," Florisia said expecting a reaction of some sort. She was surprised to see Shuran's expression remain neutral. "You are not surprised by this or horrified that Voreen was the one who took your sister's life?"

"Not entirely surprised, but he did not actually take Tianna's life. In fact, he may have provided the one way to save it." Shuran indicated that there was nothing more he would say on that subject for the time being.

"His other actions may surprise you though. He has split his alliances and is also in the meadow with these shifters." This time Florisia received the astonished look she expected.

Shuran stood and retrieved a glass of wine from the servant's tray as it was brought in. "That is, as you say surprising, the shifter dissidents do not even mingle with many of their own kind let alone collaborate with solids."

"Solids?" Orian asked.

"That is what they call those without the ability to change form. They detest all who have solid form and substance, for you see they have no true solid form of their own so I am to believe. They go through life imitating all life, secretly abhorrent of their own true state."

Florisia joined Shuran in a glass of wine. "How is it you come to know this?"

"A shifter, and friend, named Andra. He protected and guided me through my early years, but he is a Guardian. The Guardians are sworn to uphold the duties set forth by their leader the Nabusa," Shuran left the explanation there. He did not wish to expound on his suspicions and further complicate matters without all the details. "Your Majes… Florisia," Shuran corrected himself as they were in private counsel and formal monikers were frowned upon in such cases. "Thank you for your detailed report, the wine, and your company especially. We must be getting back to Britengate."

Florisia extended her hand for Shuran to kiss farewell. "Of course, but I would also ask that your friend Andra, he is trustworthy then? I only ask because we know he has been about in the forest."

"He can be trusted, it is Andra that I sent word about just this morning. He will be searching, along with Barurbe for the shifters that have been hiding among us," Shuran reminded her.

"I received no such message, I gleaned this from the mind of the accused. My chamberlain, in fact, was… I see he intercepted the message. I am afraid then that this Andra creature may be in danger." Florisia looked truly apologetic but not overly concerned. "Perhaps Barurbe can find and warn him first. I am certain that there has been no leak of her presence among the elves."

Shuran turned back before exiting the room with Orian. "Andra is more than capable of taking care of himself, but I have ways of getting in touch with him also. Perhaps we leave Barurbe to her separate search, as it may complicate matters if she delays in favor of finding Andra." With a final bow, Shuran led the way out of the Royal Tree and into the courtyard.

"Are elfin trials always so, brutal when enacting justice?" Shuran asked. "An immediate death sentence seemed premature."

"Though this is the first time I have seen such a case, the methods of my Queen saw reason to end their lives, then it was by her will it be done." Orian seemed to carry doubt. "Would you not execute a member of your own Zidu'Si if they conspired to end your life, Shin'Ar? With elves, breaking a loyalty is as abhorrent to us as murder."

"Orian? Is there something you wish to tell me?" Shuran joked. Noticing Orian was serious he did his best to answer. "I suppose it would depend on the circumstances or if there were some sort of coercion or force? Was a spell involved or possession? It is all subject to interpretation, in my own opinion."

"Then I shall have to remember to claim possession should I feel the impulse to break your neck!" Orian said as he stopped on the spot where they would enter the Emmuku'Gu.

"Save your jokes for Avrank, I really do not get your sense of humor… shoemaker!" With a thought, they vanished into the river of power that would take them back to Britengate.

***

Late night in Britengate has been busier than the day as of late. When Shuran and Orian arrived back, the entire city was buzzing with activity. Orian and he parted ways near the meeting hall where Orian was to meet with the elven Rangers. Shuran headed to Moona and Codger's to check on Bastien. When he found that Bastien left earlier for the practice grounds, he went to find him there. Before he reached the yards, a man he nearly did not recognize, approached him.

"Shuran! May I have a moment of your time? Perhaps you do not remember-"

"I remember you Maldak, but perhaps it is your son you should be looking for?" Shuran said coldly and continued walking.

"That is just it, I saw him, on the practice grounds and well I just could not approach him. Especially now that… Well, since I have been awoken," Maldak explained.

Shuran stepped back and halted his pace. "You mean to tell me that you were among those I sparked the Essence of weaving into?" Shuran realized.

Maldak answered by way of creating an orb of energy and then sending it into the sky to burst apart in a glorious display of light.

Shuran wondered for a moment and then sat down. "Maldak, you may now come to understand why your prior ignorance made you frightened, but that is not going to ever excuse what happened. I can forgive you for actions against myself, but as they turned against Bastien… That is a situation I dare not interfere with."

Maldak looked away as though heartbroken.

Shuran could not help but feel pity for the man, after all his own family was not without functional difficulties. Moona and Codger have taken to mending ways with Vardoran. Perhaps Bastien may find the heart to work things out with his own father. "I will talk to him, but I can promise nothing."

Shuran accepted Maldak's words of gratitude and moved on toward the fields to find his friend. It did not take long to locate Bastien, for he was the center of attention.

Bastien may not have had practical experience directly, but he had been weaving for months by proxy of the demon warrior Telalsu. The added bonding with the Zidu'Si provided more knowledge and abilities. Bastien seemed a complete natural at weaving and casting spells. Bastien waved Shuran over when he saw his approach.

"Shuran! You have to see this!" Bastien said with excitement. "I have managed to combine a healing spell with earth Essence!" Bastien pulled Shuran over and with the help of a young weaver they demonstrated. Bastien instructed the young boy to make a cut on his hand.

The boy took a dagger from his belt and made a shallow cut on his hand. Afterward, he took the stone Bastien offered into his opposite hand and held the wounded one up for Shuran to observe. As all around watched, the cut on the boy's hand began to glow faintly and then seal up. Not even a hint of a scar remained.

Bastien's innate understanding and ingenuity impressed Shuran. Shuran took hold of the boy's hand and mentally explored the wound with Essence. There was no sign of infection causing bacteria; as a matter of fact the area around the boy's wound was hyperactive with infection-fighting cells. Shuran raised his eyebrow at Bastien with approval.

notes on the body and healing from one of your books." He began to hand the notes back.

"Keep them my friend, I have committed them to memory. If you can break away from your clutch of admirers, I would like to speak with you about a few things." Shuran was not looking forward to half of the conversation to come. Once they were away from the noise and activity on the fields, Shuran sat down with Bastien to talk.

"There are two things that need addressing. One is favorable the other… I shall leave that for you to determine." Shuran took a deep breath before continuing, but Bastien stopped him.

"I have already noticed my adda lurking about, Shuran." Bastien saw Shuran's surprise and explained how he was aware of this part of what Shuran wanted to speak with him about. "You must sometimes forget the link of the Zidu'Si of which I am just becoming introduced. Your worry about broaching the subject was bleeding into the collective thoughts of our little company of magical misfits!"

Shuran smiled at his friend. "When did you become so mature and well worded?"

"Let me recall the events of the past season shall I? There was the inquisitors, getting half of my shi trapped in that rock of yours, possession by the mutant shi of a Telukukal, nearly dying-"

Shuran interrupted. "Wait you know what the Telalsu is… or was rather?"

"He was in my head Shuran. While part of me was still in there somewhere, I was mentally connected to that tortured thing. It is really quite disheartening."

"That may be but it is beyond our help for the time. So what do you think of talking to your adda?"

Bastien looked away before answering. "I am uncertain. What he intended toward you was bad enough, that it became twisted unto me… Perhaps he has punished himself enough? I really do not know."

Shuran was unsure if Bastien was asking for advice. "It is your decision and for you to act upon in your own time. Just know that without intention, I sparked his abilities not knowing he was among the crowds of refugees."

Bastien merely cocked a single brow, but said nothing. "What of the second bit of business you wanted of me, sheesh?"

"Oh yes, we must have a formal ceremony to signify your acceptance into the Zidu'Si. That is when I can formally accept you and present you with your gug weapon," Shuran said. "Before you ask, I will be going back to retrieve it from Durangug shortly as well as check on a few other things."

"Why not just snap your fingers and make whatever you need appear here, Moona said you could use the Vault like a pocket in your breeches. Speaking of which, have I reminded you how horrid it was being stuck in your pocket next to your jibbley-bits!" Bastien tried to keep a straight face but was unable.

Shuran shared the laugh but explained why he had to go to Durangug personally. Since the weapons were made of gug, although untwisted by Shadow, it would not pass through the city's shield. He could step outside the boundary to retrieve it, but he had a need for being alone and read some from a book he would never consider needlessly removing from the Vault.

Chapter Thirty-Six

Shuran arrived in the Vault soon after leaving Bastien with Moltar. He wanted the two of them to get to know one another. He could sense Moltar's jealousy and intended not to let it fester. The thought of what Moltar might do to Bastien ran through his head, and he shuddered as he retrieved Nergal's journal the Sar A Nam'Mu, the 'Record of the Creator of Man'. He had only started reading when a noise took his attention.

Shuran stood and gathered the Essence about him in preparation for an attack when he saw Nagutan emerge from the center chamber of the Vault. "What are you doing here and how did you gain access?"

Nagutan approached with his hands raised. "All members of the Zidu'Si both present and past may enter this place. That would include me. As to why I am here? I have been waiting for you to come so we might speak."

Shuran sat down at that the table and allowed Nagutan to tell his tale. Nagutan spoke of how he was the Isten to his Shin'Ar, Nergal the Great Watcher.

Nergal had to stay behind when his supporters agreed to merge with the Essence source to stave off the growing strength of the darkness within the Shadow. He created the first official Zidu'Si from members of the races of man except the one surviving member of the Telukukal.

"I was the last of the race before man and tasked with seeing to the final instructions of my Shin'Ar." Nagutan explained. Nergal wanted his spirit released so that he might purge the Shadow of the dark influence and twisted intent of the Sumer. He would then be able to return to his own body and restore his comrades from the Emmuku'Gu.

"The Zidu'Si was not fully in agreement with his plan, but they did not know his true identity as I did. Only Gimagala and myself agreed to help him. She had her part to play, as did I. But something went wrong with the plan and it needed adjusting. The ancestor of Voreen along with a kashshaptu entered the prison chamber of the dark Sumer and destroyed their stasis encasements."

Nagutan went on to further explain that Nergal disbanded the Zidu'Si out of anger and disappointment, and then went about his planning with only his Isten and the member of the first race of man, Gimagala. They devised a plan to create suitable vessels of power, children of seven bloodlines that could restore balance and purge the darkness from Shadow. It failed and the balance shifted further toward darkness.

The influence of the tainted Shadow spread and it saw to the seed of hatred for mixed bloodlines to become spread. The Sumer within the Shadow knew that without the proper mix of bloodlines, they could not be challenged. And so the plans required adjustment again.

"Over the following five thousand years, it was left to myself to manipulate destiny and see to the creation of a new set of mixed-blood children. This time they would be created in secrecy and there would be something else to the mix," Nagutan retold.

"An eighth blood line," Shuran answered instinctively. "You introduced the blood of the Telukukal?"

"No, I introduced the blood of the Sumer."

"But there were no Sumer left, you said Nergal had gone into the Shadow. Did he come back out?"

Nagutan shook his head. "You misunderstand my boy, do not get ahead of me. The blood did not come from Nergal himself. It came from me. I am more than simply Telukukal, I am the son of Nergal. He made me from his own being and passed part of the Sumer into me."

"So it is true then, you are my father. Barurbe heard Penelle call you Dalgon."

"No, my boy I am not your father, I named my son Shinar Dalgonson. Your mother hated the name Shinar so she always called him Dalgon." Nagutan raised his hand to stop further questioning. "The irony of his name is intentional and out of respect to my own father."

Nagutan continued retelling his actions over the years. He saw to the proper development of a suitable mother and Sulura fit the purpose so Nagutan made certain that she and his son would cross paths and fall in love. Sulura went against the wishes of her mother then went off with Shinar Dalgonson and departed the lands of the Foresworn Territories. When they settled in Aurderia, she soon became heavy with child and Shuran's father went off on his quest to announce the arrival of a boy who would bring about the permanent balance.

"Why would he do this?" Shuran asked.

"Because I told him what he must do. Both he and your mother knew of what their children would mean to the world. I would not have allowed them ignorance of what would transpire. This is why your mother stays by Salmetu's side."

It was Nagutan who planted the Abnu Emuq in the ruins of Durangug for Old Codger to find. He instructed Sulura to seek the moon mother Evalria. Through all the events that led to the present time, Nagutan was there, pulling strings and pushing people to do what was required for events to unfold the way they have thus far. Visions were sent to the seers in the lands, foretelling the arrival of the children of prophecy. Nagutan used the center chamber of Durangug to send the visions out unto the lands.

The visions were meant to stir up the people and eventually lead the Order of Chaos to perform the ritual at the Altar in Drakkfoth. Nagutan provided the knowledge and the dagger required for the ceremony. He

"Vardoran, he was the apprentice? And I assume it was you who called for Coder being brought to the Academy for re-sanctioning, so that he would be in Middleton when Moona and Andra escaped with me?" Shuran realized.

"You are catching on my boy. I spent a great deal of time whispering in ears and guiding actions. Where I could not be, I sent my imp." Nagutan explained how he created the imp through blood magic and a piece of his own consciousness. "All of these actions were for one ultimate purpose, to get you in contact with the Abnu Emuq. Nergal had slept long enough and he needed to join with you in order to wake the eighth bloodline you carry. He then stayed until the time came that you delivered him to the Shadow."

"So he is joining with the Shadow? What is my part in all of what remains?" Shuran asked feeling used a game piece in Kings and Queens.

"I do not have those answers. Nergal would have left them within you to find for yourself. As I believe, you may already be starting to come to conclusions on your own."

Shuran looked at Nagutan for who he was for the first time. He got up and embraced him.

Nagutan pulled his grandson tight and shared his tears. "I am sorry for what you have been put through my boy, we all have a part to play if Ersetu is to survive. One day when this is over, we all will have time as a family to live, love, and laugh."

"What of my father? Where is he?" Shuran asked as he pulled back.

"I am uncertain where he is now, but rest assured he will return and reveal himself when the time is right. He is aware of what you have become and is prouder than you can imagine. I can say no more."

"You do not wish to effect the course of destiny I suppose," Shuran said sourly but with understanding.

"You are catching on to the game my boy. Now how about we pop on back to Britengate and celebrate Bastien's inauguration to the Zidu'Si and enjoy a slight reprise." Nagutan said as he got up and retrieved the Gidri Zisura.

Shuran looked at his grandfather crossways. "How did you know of the feast I only just planned it?"

"I was not simply sitting around here waiting for you. My imp has been following you around in secret. I would be bored senseless in this place alone for Damkianna knows how long," he said wiggling his fingers and waving at her stasis encasement.

Shuran laughed at his gesture and then remembered the guard that Nagutan had in his chambers at the Academy. "You used a similar spell on that guard in your chambers!"

Nagutan smiled and tapped Shuran on the head. "Bright boy!"

"Boy? I now look to be a man of thirty summers after all the rapid growing!" Shuran protested.

"We are all still boys at heart grandson, never let go of that."

***

It was already well past dawn in Britengate. The citizens were busy setting up tables and banners. An earthen dais of stone was created by dwarves for the Zidu'Si. The bakers and butchers were busy preparing foods for the feast. Foragers were out in the wood collecting berries, fruits, herbs, tubers, and all sorts of edibles for the delicacies planned by the chefs. Having so many refugees, now citizens of Britengate, there were no shortages of craftsmen and artisans.

Shuran and Nagutan went to the Zidu'Si barracks to catch a few hours sleep while everyone was busy preparing. Shuran slept well for the first time in a very long while in spite of the growling snore coming from his grandfather. It was early after mid-Utu when Moltar stuck his nose in through the window and snorted back at Nagutan.

He woke with a start. "What on Ersetu was that?"

Moltar snorted again. "I was trying to mimic your own snort, Shuran's Grand Sire."

"What is the time my bonded?" Shuran said as he arose.

"Past time the two slackers were up and about. Moona's words not my own," Moltar confessed.

Shuran and Nagutan got up from bed, washed and then dressed for the ceremony. Outside they were greeted by the questioning looks of the entire Zidu'Si along with Moona and Codger. After a brief explanation of the previous night's discussion, Shuran led everyone to the feast.

Bastien signaled the start of the festivities by releasing streams of power from his wand that created a dazzling display of light and sound in the sky above Britengate. Musicians and acrobats accompanied the feasting. Bastien continued entertaining small crowds with shows of light and dancing illusions.

Nagutan noticed Shuran sitting alone and walked over to join him. "What is troubling you my boy?"

"I am thinking about what will come next. I have yet to find out where the Lil'Du can be found and what trials I face in finding them. There are also the visions of future events that I now begin to wonder... are they at all changeable. Then there is Tianna's predicament."

Nagutan put his arm around Shuran in understanding. "That is quite a bit of thinking you are doing my boy. Let me just put you a bit at ease. First I can say that I can tell you where to look for the Lil'Du."

Shuran perked up a bit in response.

"They reside far to the East on the far side of the highlands, you need only look for the Pillars of Wind. As for Tianna, that is dependent upon her strength and she is strong. But I think you already know this."

"I am just uncertain how to accomplish what needs doing," Shuran confessed.

"You will when the time comes my boy," Nagutan said as he looked to the sky. It was late and the stars were already twinkling in the heavens, two brighter than all others. "My they are growing in brightness, are they not? What would make stars grow so bright?" Nagutan asked Shuran with a conspiratorial tone.

Shuran nudged his grandfather. "I think you are beginning to enjoy this. You know as well as I that they are not stars."

Nagutan turned to his grandson in surprise and raised his brows. "Do tell then mister smarty breeches. What says you of the stars called out in the prophecy."

"They are our doom or our savior. One is Chaos, the other Creation, and they come at the call of Nergal." Shuran said with complete certainty.

Nagutan simply nodded and squeezed Shuran's shoulders.

The night was calm and the mood jovial for most of Britengate. The festivities were just dying down when the alarm was raised. The protectors had retracted the cardinal gates. Shadow was on the attack.

"It would seem that your sister Salmetu has finally decided to present herself at our gates my boy," Nagutan said.

Shuran turned from his grandsire and noticed Salmetu on the edges of his senses beyond the city Shield. "That is not my sister inside her body, she is a vessel for Ereshkigal Queen of the Netherworld. Salmetu is no longer a Priestess she is now 'Queen of Shadow'!"

Maps

***

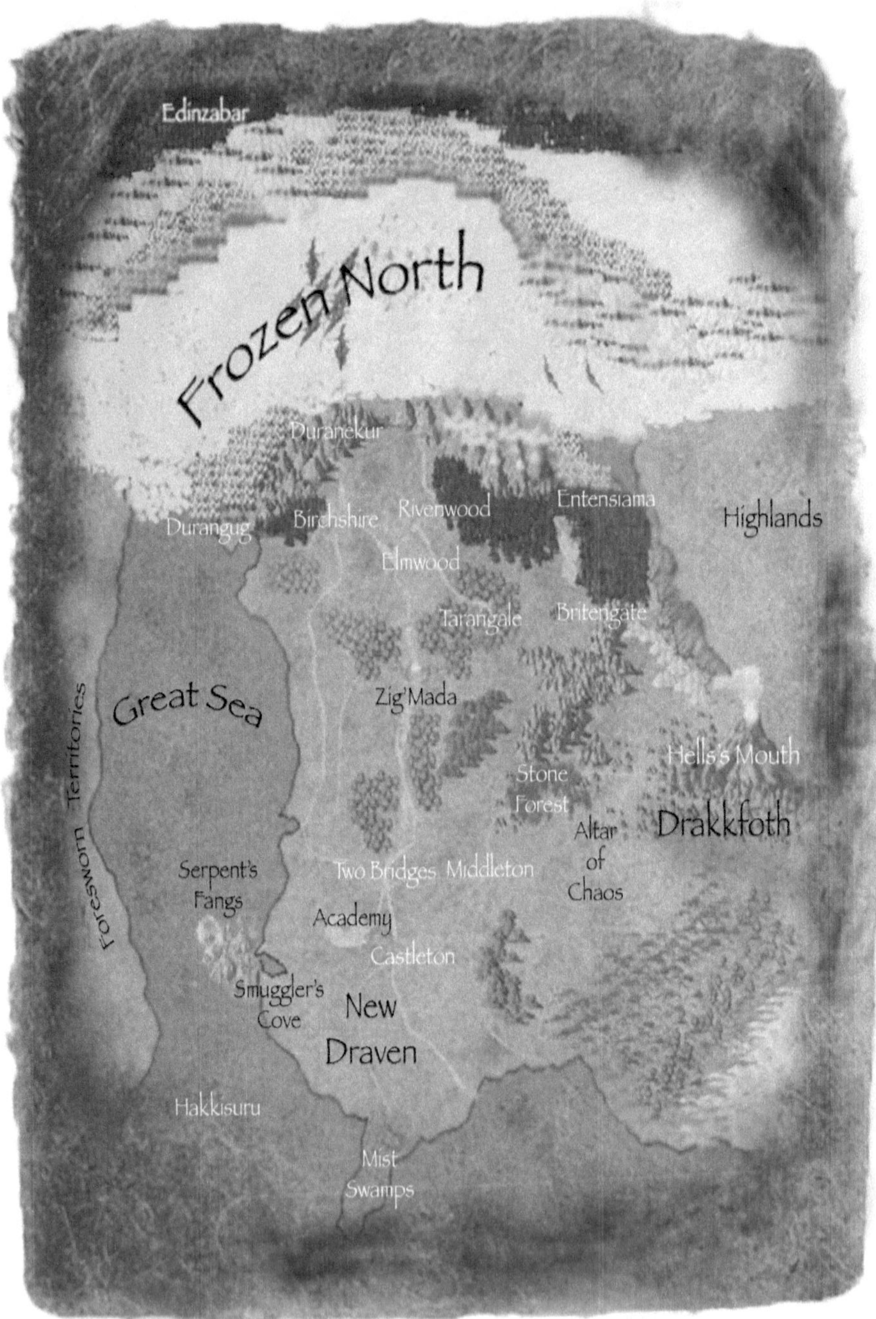

Edinzabar
Frozen North
Duranekur
Durangug
Birchshire
Rivenwood
Entensiama
Highlands
Elmwood
Tarangale
Britengate
Great Sea
Zig'Mada
Foresworn Territories
Hells's Mouth
Stone Forest
Drakkfoth
Serpent's Fangs
Two Bridges
Middleton
Altar of Chaos
Academy
Castleton
Smuggler's Cove
New Draven
Hakkisuru
Mist Swamps

Glossary of Terms

A'Baddasu - Gauntlet of Strength (gug weapon of the Gula'Lu)
Abnu Emuq - Power Stone
Abzu Mu - deep source of water
Adda - Father
Agal Kastu - Mighty Bow /Weapon of gug held by the Zidu'Si elf
Alla - Evil God
Anse - Donkey / Ass
Anzillu - Abomination
Asipu - Wizard / Mage / Magic Worker
Asakku - Earthy-watery/Dragon
Assinnu Isten - First of the Order / Cult Leader
Bad - Wall / Ground
Badgaldingir - Fortified City of the Gods
Baduruku (BA-DUR-UKU) - Water People
Bal - Transform
Bil - Burn (To)
Bitmu - Tree house
DAMKIANNA (DAM-KI-ANNA) - Mistress of Heaven and Earth
Diri - Huge
Dug - Heal
Dur - Jackass
Durani - Fortress
Ekur (E-KUR) - House that is like a Mountain
ELITUR (ELI-TUR) - Sacrilege

Emmuku'Gu (Emmuku-Gu) Ersetu - Power River (lei line) of Ersetu (World)

Emuku - Power

Entar'Lu - Caretakers (of Badgaldingir)

Ersetu (ER-SE-TU) - World

Gabara (Gaba-Ra-A) - Offering

Galla - Devil

Geshtu'Bad - Teacher / To give Wisdom

Gidri Zisura - Wand of Magical Power (Human Zidu'Si weapon)

Gug - Lodestone

Gugtu (GUG-TU) \ Zisuragug (ZI-SU)RA-GUG) - Magic Stone

Haza - Hold (used to immobilize something)

Il'Shi Ana Dah - To carry a part or a connection to another's shi for purpose of assistance

Iniminim Ma (Inim Inim Ma) - Book of Spells

Kalag-Ga - To Invigorate (Strength)

Kashshaptu (KASH-SHAP-TU) - Witch

Kes - Bind

Ki'Gal (Nether World)

Kigalba (KI-GAL-BA) - Great Fire Below / Hell

Ki'Ta (KI-TA) - Below

Kibur'Zisu - Trident of Power (gug weapon of the Badur'lu)

Kimmatu'Du (Kim-Ma-Tu'Du) - Son of the Clan/Family (adopted or honorary)

Kimmane (Kim-Ma-Ne) - Group of drakkon and riders.

Kin'Ge - Send message

Kin'Su - Accept Message

Kuliana - Mermaid

Lalli Mah (Lal-Li Mah) - Great Balance

Lam Mudutu - Abundant Knowledge

Lil - Air

Lugaldur - Bonded master of a drakkon

Maaddir (Ma-Addir) - Ferry Boat

Magurmu (Ma-Gur-Mu) - Flying Boat

Masku (Mas-Ku) - Hide

Me - The grand council of Eleven Sumer elders that govern the Laws

Mellamu Nanna - Bright Moon (Steam powered Water ship that also flies under Crystal Shard power - Codgers Ship)

Menasutur (Me-Na-Su-Tur) - Sacred War Hammer of the Dwarves / Weapon of gug held by the Dwarven Zidu'Si

Mi-Ib Ag (Mi-Ib Ag) - Fire Sword / Weapon of gug wielded by the Drakkian Zidu'Si

Mi-Ib Karshi (Mi-Ib Kar-Shi) - Golden Dagger used to take souls

Mi-Ib Simshi (Mi-Ib Sim-Shi) - Golden Dagger used to place/restore a soul

Mu - Flying Machine

Mudutu'Har - Rings of Knowledge (Zidu'Si weapon of the Isten to Shin'Ar)

Nashi - River of Souls

Nashi'Zag - River of Metal Souls

Nime'Gar (Ni-Me-Gar) - Silence

Pad - Break into Pieces

Padiri - Explode / release restrained power

Padiri'bur - Vessel of explosion / Bomb

Peta - Open (for me)

Pilsug - Dirt Walker (slang of the Badur'Lu to refer to land dwellers)

Sa'nua - Mindless / Crazy

Sar A Nam'Mu - The Record of the Creator of Man (Nergal's Journal)

Sheesh (She-Esh) - Brother

Shi'Imbi - Staff of Life's Wind (gug weapon of the Lil'Du)

Shin'Ar - Watcher of the Lands / Lands of the Watchers

Sikil Mah - great purge of abominations

Sumeris - Ancient language of the Gods

TAMU - To Swear Oath

Tartur Mamitu - Oath Breaker

Tel - Land

Telal - Warrior Demon

Tal'Ba-ad - Ice demons

Telukukal (Telu-Kuk-Al) - First Land People (First People)

Tur - Small (to be) / Derogatory term used by dwarfs naming those smaller than themselves. *Also* - Sacred

Urentel - Frost Beasts demons

Usumaba - Sea Dragon (steed of the Badur'Lu)

Xul - Devil / Evil

Zag - The shine of metals

Zidu'Si - Faithful Companions

Zisuragug (ZI-SU-RA-GUG) \ Gugtu (GUG-TU) - Magic Stone

Zumru'Sa - Joining of Body and Mind. Gula'Lu ritual of blending and sharing knowledge and souls.

<u>**Spells and Sayings**</u>

HA INA GISNU'ZI, DALLA'E ANNA TE
May the Light of Life Shine upon you

KIMA PARSI LABIRUTI
Deal her in Accordance With the Ancient Rites

PAD TEGA NERU
Explode upon the touch of Evil.

GISNU SU SHI KES ANA AN-DUL A GIZZU
Join light to flesh binding your soul to protect it from Shadow

<u>**Preview Book 3 - Queen of Shadow**</u>

Υ

Salmetu's form stood against the darkening sky outside the Western shield entrance to Britengate. Her body was not corporeal, it was gathered Shadow taking the form of Salmetu. Traces of wispy tendrils undulated around her frame, as she stood silent, waiting. She was Ereshkigal, and darkness was rising all around her.

Hundreds of Shadow Walkers emerged from the thickening blackness that rose from the ground surrounding Ereshkigal. Chaos came to life in the form of the Shadow and began to creep forward from the hordes of darkness-imbued wielders and transformed citizens of Aurderia. Slow at first, the murky cloud of Shadow billowed toward the shield boundary and spread out along its parameter. The boundary sparked and flashed with resistance to the touch of Chaos.

Salmetu's shadowy form turned toward the figure now standing just inside the shield. She floated forward, advancing on the familiar presence until she hovered inches away from the protesting energy separating her from the subject of her visit. "You should come outside to parlay young asipu. It is rude to speak to a guest from behind your door." Ereshkigal was speaking with restrained rage.

Shuran gazed at his sister's likeness unblinking, as he spoke. "You are no guest of mine or any among those seeking refuge behind this shield, Gizzu'Su!" Shuran could see the rage building behind Ereshkigal's eyes.

"You think you know who you are dealing with do you? I assure you young fool, you have not begun to know the power that you face!" The fury was building as the form of Salmetu began to drift apart. "I will have my Gizzu'Su brethren freed from whatever prison you have placed them!" As the vaporous form melted away, the Shadow expanded around the city shield and began to press upon it.

Screams of fear and horror began to fill the minds of the citizens not imbued with Essence abilities. The Shadow could not enter the city, but its influence could. The feelings of dread, despair, and helplessness filled the air so thickly that the people of Britengate appeared to move about as though in slow motion. Crippled by the emotions being spread by the Shadow, most succumbed to the struggle and collapsed where they stood.

Ereshkigal's wicked laugh echoed throughout Britengate. "You see Shuran, you have no grasp on how powerful the Shadow is, and when I find my missing Gizzu'Su comrades, we shall destroy this city and claim every citizen for the Shadow!"

Shuran remained still while he watched the effects of Ereshkigal's mental attack on the less powerful in Essence among the city's population. Something was scratching at the back of his mind. There was a familiarity to the attack that he could not focus upon, but he knew that it was a ploy of some sort. With a flick of his wrist, he sent a bolt of energy into the shield and was rewarded with a moment of silence from the emotional onslaught of the Shadow. Shuran knew what he needed to do in order to stop the attack.

Calling to his Zidu'Si, Shuran moved toward the center of the city and the location of the Altar of Creation. "The Shadow uses the influence of electric impulses to effect the people emotionally. We need to disrupt the assault with bolts of energy." Shuran instructed the Zidu'Si and any wielders with electric Essence abilities to begin periodic blasts of energy into the shield. The results were soon felt as the crippled citizens began to stir and rise to their feet in relief from the disruption in the flow of negative impulses that were previously affecting them.

"How long must we keep this up Shin'Ar?" Dara asked. "It is not currently taxing us much, but eventually we will begin to weaken."

"I believe that the Shadow will eventually give up the futile attempt to gain the shield, and as the attack wanes we can rest and resume only if and when the Shadow recommences its assault." Shuran was not certain how long the Shadow would remain outside the city. There was a reason for what was happening, but he could not yet determine what Ereshkigal hoped to gain.

The Shadow continued to undulate and spread across the city shield, attempting to influence the inhabitants with dark thoughts and intent. With every emotional charge from the murky cloud, bolts of energy flew from the hands of the Zidu'Si and the few elves in the city. The Shadow would disperse from the area and retreat for no more than an hour before renewing its assault.

The attack on the shield had continued throughout the night and well into the second before Shuran began to understand what was happening. "This is a stall tactic," he realized aloud. "Our energy bolts into the shield are not having any lasting effect on the Shadow, only gugtu would, or direct contact with the Essence."

"What do you mean Lugaldur?" Moltar asked.

Shuran explained to his bonded as well as the rest of the Zidu'Si, that Ereshkigal was directing the Shadow attack in an effort to stall while she searched for the Gizzu'Su. She was likely trying to keep the Zidu'Si busily engaged in Britengate while she searched, and doing so also kept Shuran from seeking out the Lil'Du. "We cannot all remain here while the Shadow distracts us."

"Perhaps we can enlist more elves from Entensiama to assist in the defense while you and a few of us travel to the Highlands in search of the Lil'Du?" Orian suggested.

Shuran sent Orian and Moltar to see the Queen of the Elves while he continued to bolster the strength of the energy being sent periodically gate, but it could not affect the use of the Emmuku'Gu.

***

Orian arrived in the center of the elfin Capital with Moltar close behind. Their abrupt arrival caused quite a stir as the elves were going about their evening gatherings.

Elves keep a different schedule than most other races of man on Ersetu. They are creatures of a more nocturnal nature and prefer the coolness of the night rather than the heat of mid-Utu. Several market-goers fell back in shocked surprise at the sudden electro-charged appearance of not only an elf but also a massive red drakkon on his heel.

Moltar took to the air immediately, leaving Orian to make arrangements for more elves to come aid in the defense of Britengate. He had been stuck within the city shield and unable to spread his wings to fly comfortably within the boundary. All of the other drakkon in the city were small enough to take to flight around the confines of the shield but due to Moltar's increased bulk, he could not follow suit without risk of damaging what had only recently been rebuilt.

Orian went straight to the Queen's tree to seek an audience when he was stopped in the court by a guard. He was unfamiliar to Orian, but he knew from his dress and sash that this elf served the Queen directly.

"Master Orian, you will not find the Queen within the palace tree," the elf said.

Orian turned to face the guard, then bowed slightly in greeting. "I take then that you know where I might find her majesty?" Orian asked.

"She is in conference with the tree nymphs," the guard responded with a hint of sarcasm in his voice.

The Dryads were known only from myths and legends until recently. Stories of the horrid faces frozen in time amongst the petrified trees were the greatest extent of the knowledge of their kind. The truth of the matter was that the Dryads were only one of the races of beings that lived upon Ersetu long before the Sumerians arrived to begin their experiments with the Essence. These races were mostly unknown or seldom encountered.

Orian did not appreciate the comment. "They are Dryads sir, and far older and wiser a people than even the ancients who engineered the races of man. You might be wise to show them the respect they deserve, especially after their magic kept them alive within those stone trees for thousands of years."

The guard opened his mouth to respond but thought better of it. He pointed out the direction that Orian should travel to find the Queen and hastened his exit back to his post guarding the Queen's Tree.

Orian set off in the direction the guard indicated and signaled for Moltar to stay nearby. The distance to the edge of the boundary of Entensiama was normally an hour walk or more, but with the added strength and stamina afforded the Zidu'Si, Orian ran the distance in a quarter of the time without exerting himself. When he arrived at the outer edge of the elven capital, he located Florisia, the Queen, and approached silently as not to intrude upon her conference with the Dryads.

Without turning to address him, Florisia called out to Orian. "You may approach Orian, this discussion will need sharing with the Shin'Ar."

Orian approached the Queen and greeted her with a bow and turned to silently watch the proceedings of what appeared some sort of ritual being performed by the Dryads. As he looked out at what only weeks earlier had been an empty glade, he took in the sprawling copse of new trees that filled the area. At the center, where he and the others now stood grew a much larger and extraordinary tree of a kind he never before set eyes upon.

The base of the tree was thick as houses with large leg-like roots angled up and then back down into the earth. Vast limbs stretched at opposite incline to the sky before draping back down and burrowing into the ground. The bark along the entire surface glistened with hues of green and purple and a pulsing that likened itself to the flow of blood through a man's vein. Flowers adorned the ends of branches with colors so rich and pure that Orian lost himself in the beauty that captured his very being.

Stepping up beside him and placing a hand upon his arm, Florisia drew his attention away from the splendor. "Words are few to fall from the tongue when witnessing such wonders of creation."

what I am seeing." He looked once again at the blossoms and pulsing beat of the tree before continuing. "What is this activity that I am gazing upon?"

Stepping forward to answer, the Dryad nearest guided Orian and Florisia away to an area where they could sit and speak. "It is the Gisa'Ti in your ancient tongue, our tree of life as best we can translate."

"You are born from trees?" Orian asked surprised written upon his face.

The dryad barked with laughter. "Not exactly young one, we are birthed of Coosco and it is Ersetu which gives us life." Seeing the confusion upon the elves' faces, the dryad continued. "We are part of the land as a whole being, this is why we did not die in the trees so long ago. We used the power of Coosco, the navel of the world, to contain our being until the time we would be freed by your Shin'Ar.

"Ersetu is our mother and she guides us where we are meant to best serve her and continue the cycle of life. Much of what was has gone and only now is Ersetu beginning to awaken and put things right. Your Shin'Ar is meant to free Coosco from the bonds that restrain Ersetu. It is the promise of your God Nergal."

Orian was more confused than before the dryad spoke. "Should you not be telling this to Shuran?"

"He will remember in time, the promise he made Ersetu. His mistake is his alone to undo." The dryad then turned to Florisia. "We shall do as you ask and protect the borders of your Entensiama. The tainted workings of this Shadow are no match for the true power of Ersetu, but we will not assist beyond these lands, beyond what we promised Shin'Ar in the Frozen North."

"You were in the Frozen North with Shuran?" Orian asked. "And how is it that you now speak our tongue so well compared to our first meeting in the Stone Forest?"

"So many questions," the dryad mused. "We are all of Ersetu." The dryad gestured to its tree-like form, "This form you see is but a shape we take from the trees we tend. Other places we take to different shapes as best suited for our tasks. Once we adjusted to the freedom from the Stone Forest, we rejoined the whole and learned all.

320

"Before your so-called Gods arrived upon this world from the heavens, Ersetu existed in harmony with the eternal cycle of life. When Nergal and his ilk placed their ring upon Coosco, they tainted the true magic of our world. This must be undone for Ersetu to truly heal." The dryad stood and walked away before turning back and appeared to melt into the earth then being replaced by a small fur-covered creature that hopped off into the woods.

<u>**Author**</u>

Check out the Epic and Series information from the author website:
http://jstevenyoung.com

Follow on Facebook at:
http://fb.com/Author.JStevenYoung

Follow on twitter:
@jstevenyoung

Chronicles of Aurderia
The Balance
River of Souls
Queen of Shadow

Hashtag Magic
Blue Screen of Death
Control ALT Delete
Web of Trolls (late 2015)